54332

Doubleday, c1977.

Richard
w, and again.

SINGLE COPY

54332

Llewellyn, Richard
    Tell me now, and again.   Doubleday, c1977.
    280p.

2c

TELL ME NOW,
AND AGAIN

Books by Richard Llewellyn

TELL ME NOW, AND AGAIN
AT SUNRISE, THE ROUGH MUSIC
GREEN, GREEN MY VALLEY NOW
A HILL OF MANY DREAMS
BRIDE OF ISRAEL, MY LOVE
THE NIGHT IS A CHILD
WHITE HORSE TO BANBURY CROSS
BUT WE DIDN'T GET THE FOX
THE END OF THE RUG
DOWN WHERE THE MOON IS SMALL
SWEET MORN OF JUDAS' DAY
A MAN IN A MIRROR
UP, INTO THE SINGING MOUNTAIN
CHEZ PAVAN
MR. HAMISH GLEAVE
A FLAME FOR DOUBTING THOMAS
A FEW FLOWERS FOR SHINER
NONE BUT THE LONELY HEART
HOW GREEN WAS MY VALLEY

Juveniles

WARDEN OF THE SMOKE AND BELLS
THE FLAME OF HERCULES
THE WITCH OF MERTHYN

Richard Llewellyn

TELL ME NOW, AND AGAIN

DOUBLEDAY & COMPANY, INC.
GARDEN CITY, NEW YORK   1978

c/977   280p.

94B524   ISBN: 0-385-12123-7
Library of Congress Catalog Card Number 77–80895
Copyright © 1977 by Richard Llewellyn
Printed in the United States of America
First Edition in the United States of America

Library of Congress Cataloging in Publication Data

Llewellyn, Richard.
Tell me now, and again.

I.   Title.
PZ3.L7714Te 1978   [PR6023.L47]   823'.9'12

TELL ME NOW,
AND AGAIN

Daemon Wente Waye you could see from the Whitechapel Road, going over the rise between the bombed streets never rebuilt after the war, turning down Cinnamon Alley, and along King David's Lane, toward dear pale-tea Thames, bubbling all the way across to the South Bank, sometimes with a coaster steaming west for the Pool, often with a string of barges under brown sails, east to the Estuary, and ever, thankfully, with a wonderful sense of going home.

It was the only real home I had ever known to go back to, and except that I paid rent, my own, and all in it, mine.

What a *lovely* place! You got nearer and nearer, and the nearer, the larger and longer, stretching left and right, until you were out of the lane and in Wapping High, and there it was, always a surprise, a smile, a warmth, not like an ordinary building or somewhere to stay, but a home, apart, not an hotel or bedsitter, but a real place of your own, ready with friends, shelter from weather, and comfort for the mind, the eyes, ears, meat, even for the soul, if, that is, there *is* one. Funny, you seem to yourself to know what you mean, but not in spoken words. I think I know what a soul is, and perhaps what it is supposed to do, but I never get beyond that first hurdle, the Spirit, so the whole business becomes a nuisance, and the meanings go into words of no shape, a verbal pudding, with nothing at the end except a feeling of frustration and groping, and hope for retrieval—and what is hope?—but for all that, I think I know what is meant by the soul.

I saw, I knew, the meaning and thought I felt it always, from the first moment, in Daemon Wente Waye.

1

The building had been imagined, planned, and bought piece by piece, foot by foot, and set up, day, week, month, and year after year, and was now complete, except for the yacht dock needing eight more bollards, a crane for the slipway, and lights on the buoys and along the anchorage.

Always the burthen of salt water in the air, ever the sweet of the sea, and the squeals from the open beaks of seabirds showing quills against the breeze. We loved the place, all of us, so many of us, but most of us knew little about who we were. We lived as ourselves, as people do in cities, next to each other, knowing only enough to nod, and smile, and go shopping, or out to work on the early train, through blue broken streets of rough shapes, once lived in by hearty Cockney and Hebrew bodies, now gone, and their voices calling in every brick.

A sixty-foot-long wall of granite blocks went up forty foot on the river side of Wapping High, and if you knew anything about the art of masonry you might, that first time, praise in a whistle of surprise, and a smile every time after, if only because, in the middle of it, about halfway up, the medallion of marble shards put together by Ella Broome and Dolly Wade and the other girls of the City of London School of Art, still missing a few bits here and there, smiled back at you, and for some reason you felt a joy, something nearer the blood than happiness, rising wonderfully inside you, and not only me, but all of us, and at first we talked about it almost with shame until we found we all felt it, and after a little time, hard to say when, the Daemon became part of us.

He was only the marble head, curls blowing long behind, a *bas-relievo*, almost certainly Greek, about two yards wide in a raised-circle frame, face turned to you, mouth in a smile, nostrils opened, and—I often thought—an almost viciously merry look in the eyes, though how a sculptor can make a piece of stone smile, with only a hammer and chisel, is a miracle as unbelievable in its way as walking on water, though that can be explained as an optical illusion. But the smile is there, and it never changes, and the eyes follow you, smiling whether furthest left, or right, or standing at the top of the steps, and you can only smile back

2

with that curious feeling that you have a solid friend, and he will smile for you long after you are gone.

Ken Dymmott, chief foreman at the digs, told me night after night down in the Skipper's Cabin what was going on, how they found walls, and went down, scraping with pieces of glass and wire brushes, but gently, inch by inch, while the property merchants cursed them, or tried to buy them off, a couple of cases of whisky, a big party, a car, a handful of fivers. But not Ken, and not the girls. They went on down, cheered by the team led by Ella and Dolly, and they reached floor level—with all the pieces they found, pots, urns, bits of sculpture—and they cleared it out, and there, at last, was a temple of Mithras. But all the scholars had said there could never have been a Mithraic temple in Britain. Here it was, almost perfect, in the heart of the City of London.

But the property louts gave no chance. The digs in other places went on, though the true dig, beneath the City, no. One way or another, because the digs could be taken to court and there was no money to fight, they were pushed aside or fobbed or denied, and so Ken and his lads, and Ella and Dolly, the girls with them, all of us loving what they were trying to do, no.

It ended there.

That night.

But they found the Daemon.

Big Ben sang across the river, two o'clock, and Dolly put a small pick gently in gravelly sand, and sat back on her knees, frozen. Ben McEuan, the night watchman, carried over the brazier to warm her, and Ella unpacked the tea and sandwiches, and one of the girls filled the kettle, and when the boiled water almost finished its whisper, Dolly screamed, and held a great marble piece, almost the shape of a slice of apple tart, but ten times larger, and chipped, cracked, but she held it to her lips, and kissed, eyes to the sky in a dream of raging delight, and went in with claws for all the other shards, hundreds of them, all found in the sieves, down to tiny scraps, though I saw only the harvest at the end of the week, because I had to go to Antwerp, but it was wonderful to go back and see what had been found, and

3

what the girls had done on their own, at night, when everybody else was in bed.

In that time we got five mosaic pavements, the wall paintings, and all the other items—urns, vases, tools, clay figurines—beautifully part of another time, and now, mercifully, part of ours. But the other side found where the new digs were, and put on more guards, and generally ran a cat-and-mouse game, using the police and private agencies until it became dangerous and somebody could go to prison. That's when we all had a meeting, down in the gymnasium, and by vote we decided, no more. But votes were one thing, though for those devoted, they mean nothing. Ella and Dolly and about a dozen others went on with the aid of Ben, and each morning, more beauty of a past time was spread on the swimming pool's tiled surround, or in the gymnasium, or on the library's parquet. It was there to be seen, even gloated over, and so the rest of us got dragged in, whether from shame to be left out or from pride of house, nobody cared. We were there as the Daemon team, and we had no intention of being left out, any of us, whether we were in the digs or not.

Anyway, the majority of us had our own jobs, and they had to be done. Nobody questioned it, or that students had the time to attend lectures *and* work all night at the various sites. But when Alison Dewhurst fainted with such a bump of knees and bones that Saturday, we all, suddenly, knew that martyrs were among us. Dr. Rahman came running breathless from the surgery across the road, with his nurse, Kari Bhand, and they soon had her sitting up, laughing. Apart from no sleep, she lived on sandwiches, and Dr. Rahman put down a muddy wellington in a stamp, and said the truck would not go, neither would the boat sail, unless Mrs. Jaykar, the cook, guaranteed that all of them had eaten a good solid meal, with plenty of salad, and each had a protein pack for the night.

Looking back, it was a curious place, the Daemon. We never, I think, realized our good fortune, or asked why we were there, or what kept us there. We paid the rent and took what came, and it was, truly, a great deal, though I doubt that any of us would have thought our being there in any way strange, or lucky. It was a place to stay, and we stayed there, and the rest came by

4

fortune, or the calendar, each day its own harbinger, and so it went on, for most of us, in the best of all ways.

We were in two identical buildings, separated by the wall and the sunken garden, imp-zealously looked after by Joe and Amy Briggs, a pair of pseudo-*aristo* hobgoblins, always on the hop among the beds, or shadows in the greenhouses on the other side, but there was little of the pseudo in their way of working. It was probably the finest garden I ever saw. Anything green or flowering, we had it, at its best, and I doubt the kitchen paid either for greens or fruit, and certainly the houses never paid a penny for the bowls of blossom about the place, and all we ever spent for flowers in the rooms was a twice-yearly whip-round, no more than a few pence. We never discussed it that I can remember. Everything was part of the Daemon and his smile.

Nobody had any doubt that the Germans did more to build the entire site than anyone else, because when the docks and the living areas were bombed flat over square miles with only a house or two glaring empty windows at a murk of rubble, nobody wanted to live there, and it took years, and new housing, to bring a few of the people back, but the East-Enders either moved out or died, or the memories were too much for them, and they stayed where they were, generally where their children had been evacuated, and lived a new life. They were good people. Joe and Amy were two. They lost their four girls and a boy, and that garden covered them, and that was why it blossomed, in or out of season, with love, in grief.

Both houses were built of the same granite blocks as the wall, chiselled and set by a team of masons brought in ones and twos from all over Britain, lumps dug out and gathered from the debris, piled, and then over months and years, chipped to size. At the same time, bulwarks, beams, and rafters were dragged, chained, or craned out, and piled in tall heaps, and then doors, window frames, most early Georgian, of peerless workmanship, and then furniture, in bits and pieces, and hand-rolled glass panes, tiles, crockery, and pots and pans, in fact, anything which gave us the London-that-was.

There was plenty.

Bayard Waygoes owned Daemon Wente Waye by good sense,

odd ends of fortune, and a series of raw opportunities, each beginning and going on with the bombing of London's East End, the reach of the rubble, the flight of people, the stretching of empty miles and nobodies, and the marvel of the human spirit. He bought where he could, and because land and wreckage had little value, he took and took, and nobody denied him, because nobody had his faith, or his strength of spirit, or, in fact, his vision.

In many ways he was a remarkable man. His father had owned barges and horses and taken cargoes all over the country by canal. A down-at-heels scholar-drunkard became his horse handler and so liked the life that he stayed on and during a few years, along quiet canals, he taught young Bayard the full curriculum to matriculation level, and so got him into a university for his degree.

On the death of his father he bought more barges, and property on the river, and sunken ships for scrap, ocean-going tugs, coastal freighters, and salvage equipment. In the garden, due north of the Daemon, a slab of black polished marble told the sky that here lay Valentine Harry Edwardes, bargee, scholar, and drunkard, lived a healthy life in leading willing horses, and tutoring ignorant men, and died as a hero in trying to save the lives of women and children in the bombing of London. Lord, give him enough to drink. He never wanted more. He gave enough, and with a great heart. Sweet Thames, sing softly.

Possibly that was why some of us walked in the garden, to be near Bayard's friend, and to let him know he was not forgotten. His favourite meal had been roast grouse, asparagus-and-artichoke salad, and the smallest new potatoes, with mint. Joe and Amy, when the season came near, put the cloches all round the marble slab, and we saw the artichokes and asparagus coming up, almost in prayers. The grouse were flown from Scotland, and we watched Mrs. Jaykar prepare them, and most of us wore a feather in our hats. Mrs. Rafaele, in the office, once asked Mr. Waygoes how it was that a mere drunkard could have acquired such princely whims, and he told her there was nothing mere about Valentine Edwardes, and anyway he was a scholar of King's, with splendid experience of the high table and the wine cellars, and to cap it all, game birds, asparagus, and artichokes had always been staples of the British yeoman's fare and in many parts still were, and while he lived, that menu would be served once a year, at night, in the dining room, gratis, in his honour, with wine of the diner's choice, and as much as anyone wanted, in accordance with Valentine's wish.

Mrs. Bayard Waygoes, so Mrs. Rafaele said, had "gone off" with someone after the death of a baby. Teucer, the only son, was at school or university most of the time I was at the Daemon, and on the rare times we met we nodded, smiled, and went. But then, very few had spoken to his father. Three meetings were my total, never to sit down and talk but only to raise a glass at a party to mark the opening of new space in the Daemon, the swimming pool, the gymnasium, the enlarged dining room, the Skipper's Cabin and the Bosun's Bar, the library and cinema, and the rest, though I missed most by having to travel wherever business took me, and that was often three and four months of the year.

To get back there, to peaceful days and nights in my three-room set on the west corner, high over the river, was simplest bliss—the only meaning for that word I have ever known—and deepest source of my respect and affection for Bayard Waygoes and his Daemon Wente Waye.

I never "knew" him at that time. I only knew what he did, and about him, from people I met as someone seen in an office or oftener, on his flagship, that beautiful barge, a work of art, possibly Dutch from the sixteenth-century carpentry, and then purely the best from everywhere, parquetry on the floors, brasswork on deck, masts, sails, furniture, and a galley said to have been taken, or stolen, piece by piece, from the *Victory* before she was claimed for the nation, and Lord Nelson's private kitchen, his pots and pans and his pewter plates, jugs, and ewers all shining on the original shelves.

Most of us were self-employed, and we rented cubbies down on the fourth level underground, in the vaults that went back, away from the river, probably hundreds of yards. Though I never went to the end walls, others had, and not one I ever talked to wanted to go back. They were afraid of what they felt.

7

Of the few I asked none gave me any reason I could accept, and questions were ignored or put away with a gesture of the flapping hand. Alf Straum, barman in the Skipper's Cabin, said the place was too old, and too many had been murdered and burnt, and they were all still there, biding their time, screaming in the quiet.

But it made no difference to us in the long, bright lanes nearer the stairway. The cubbies were made by taking the wine racks out, covering three sides with white formalite, fitting a door with a lock, a series of shelves, a desk and chair, and we were gratefully in business at low rent, and everything we wanted within a few steps.

My neighbour to the right was Olde Mabbs, a horn-carver, with a callus in the palm of his left hand thick as a shoe sole from scraping out the design, and I once saw him bring down that pad on the top of a thief's head and cut the scalp and crush the bone, enough for a month in hospital, and the magistrate said it was good we had self-reliant and horny-handed people in the community. Ol' Mabbs was a hero wherever he went, and the girls put a finger in his palm for luck, and tickled, and he shut his fist, but they were gone. He always gave them a good chance, and a closed-eye smile after.

At left, Mrs. Andrea Osornis made roses from cambric and buckram, and a fabric she wove herself, with her own colours for dying. The sprays, singles, and garlands hung all round her door, and sometimes over mine. I had a small printing press in my place, a jewel of machinery, and I produced the finest stationery in fonts and in styles where I had few competitors, and most said, none. My father had been a master printer and bookbinder, with a large business not far away, now weed-blown pits, holes, crags of rusting, misshapen machinery, all that told of his, and his father's, devotion to the printed word and the joy of a good book. All the tools and the stock of leather went with the bombing, and so did my mother, and after penance in hospital, he went with her, and when I came back from almost six years' evacuation and seven years at school, I had to decide. Bookbinding on my father's strict standards would have taken years. I needed the tools, the leathers, the craftsmen. But it all wanted

8

time, and I had to earn a living. I decided on printing, and by luck, bought my press from the wife of a famous printer, and went to work, and over the years had a clientele, and in later years, so many I could pick and choose, and I did very well.

Quite well, apart from being a diamond smuggler.

A few more years and I was wealthy in any currency. I had to be careful. Far beyond the everyday, I had to be more than careful. I was competing with Customs services everywhere, and they are not the least intelligent. There are always informers. I have always been charmed by what people will do for money.

I had known Penna Cately for months before I asked her to lunch, and that, I thought, was an accident of place and time. Before that, she had been a tall visitor to the Skipper's Cabin, invited by resident girls and introduced by Ella Broome as one in the dig teams, living in King David's Lane, single, a fur-grader up on Whitechapel Road. It was no surprise, that Tuesday, walking along Leman Street, to see her in front, coming from a doorway, opening an umbrella in splashing rain, smiling, and walking with me down to Bloom's, arm in arm, for a corned-beef luncheon.

We got along. She loved birdlife, and so did I. We went on weekends up the river to miles-long stretches of sand and rushes to watch the flights, and photograph, and in weekdays met at my place to develop and print, no more than that, no girl nicer, none more to be trusted. I trusted, and I told her, one night—because I was thinking of asking her to marry me and felt she should know what to expect—that the bulk of my business was not an extremely profitable printing plant, but diamond smuggling. It was the type of romantic sickness, the psychotic-pseudo-cleanbreasting—aided by a couple of bottles of wine and a few brandies—of late Victorian what-ho's just back from the far-flung wherever. Two days later, Friday, I was taken into Customs at Harwich—I had always gone by ship because I detest aircraft—and really pulled to bits, and the same thing a week later, when I went back via Boulogne. Luckily I was not carrying a package. I was picking one up in Paris.

I found it clumsy, an open signal, especially when she skipped an appointment that night without a message. I called Jayb, the go-between, and we met in Knightsbridge Underground, a space of minutes. I told him name, address, description, showed a couple of photographs, and he nodded.

"You seen the last of her," he said.

I believed him when I got back from Brussels—a rigorous Customs search both out and in—and found a note in my box, asking me to call Mrs. Rafaele. I found her in the Skipper's Cabin, and she said Mr. Waygoes had been worried about the police coming round and not being able to find me. This was a little near the bone, and I asked her to call them. They came in minutes from the station just down the road, and I had a short questioning about Penna Cately. I simply told them all I knew. But how do you "simply tell" all you know about anybody?

Going over to the bar, needing a drink after they left, I realized in those few steps that I had reached a crossroads. I could never be what I was. I was tabbed by the police. I was in shadow of the Rogues Gallery. I always would be. Until the day I died, if then, I was on file, suspected, known, open to arrest, to conviction.

Any whisper from Jayb, and I could be held as accessory.

All this, watching Alf pour a scotch.

While he pressed the siphon waiting for my nod, I knew that if "they" could get rid of Penna, then with better reason "they" could slough me. I had no notion who "they" were. Jack Firmin had introduced me to the diamond business by asking if I wanted to earn ten thousand Swiss francs paid into a Swiss bank numbered account. Of course I did. My little company at that time had growing pains. I needed money for stock, machinery, and, most important, wages for master men and apprentices. My business required them, but they work for big money. For years, they earned more than I did. I had to keep them, and the francs helped. So I went on, taking the package from Jayb, and delivering to links in Paris, Brussels, Amsterdam, sometimes Hamburg or Bonn, or Vienna or Rome, often in Berlin, and as far as Warsaw, Budapest, Prague, Sofia, Athens, and Tel Aviv. My printing business and the order books carried me. Many people all over the world prefer personal stationery, handmade, of a distinctive font. I supplied them, but only one of a kind, and that was the basis of my business. People prefer to be themselves, individual, unique where they might, and I gave them opportunity to cherish an ego.

Had I considered for a moment, in earlier years, what I wanted to do, and why I wanted to do it, I might have been better off.

"It" being what?

Follow some other trade? Or profession? What was the difference? Prestige? Nonsense.

It was something to be done to earn most money the easiest way, to live easily, to be easy in mind. All beyond was only a bother. The news, and politics, of no interest except to chat about for a moment in the bar, and forget.

I had read of the faceless man. The only one I had ever known was Jayb. Until I had his message when and where to meet him, I suppose I would never have recognised him. Thinking of him, I could bring no real memory of his face.

Yet, while Alf counted my change, I knew *I* was infinitely more faceless, if that were possible, and not merely faceless, but mindless. The original nobody, without any real reason for being alive. But which part of my mind had so suddenly turned on itself, or on me?

Curious. I had never thought like that before.

In a series of moments, perhaps not even a minute, I seemed to have come alive, horribly, starkly aware, having to pick out words to describe what I thought, and what I knew. I felt torn from a cocoon, given the birth slap, forced to cry out, emergent —red-raw—from darkness.

I was *me*. What, or who, was I before?

Before?

What *do* words mean?

Before *what?*

Well, before I was shoved into a world I had never been aware of.

That sounds silly. Of course, it *is*. But it made no difference. I woke up in another brain-world, a different type of place, not an atmosphere, nothing to do with sight, smell, taste or feel, but in another, colder, more horrible reach into—what?—living?

You wake, and you do what you must.

That's living?

So they say.

They?

Well, others. So do you. Where's the argument?

But what *is* living? Just waking up, and doing what you did before?

What else is it?

That's the doorslam.

It's as far as you get. What else is there to do?

I felt helpless, as though every movement was a waste of, well, not energy or time, but of myself. I could suddenly see myself as apart from myself. A few minutes before I might have found such a thought ridiculous, if, that is, it had thumped my mind. Now, it frightened me.

But why? I had no smallest notion.

I only knew I was frightened. As I stood there.

Frightened?

The air seemed in a prickle all round me. Small insects biting icy sweat.

Yet it was the same quiet bar, smelling of old casks and sawdust, harmless, a backwater of armchairs and leisurely drinks, no music or television or anything noisier than people enjoying a few minutes to sit down and talk about little nothings.

And I was petrified, that is, turned to stone, if what I felt was fact. I had no desire to lift the glass, no strength to move a hand.

Why?

I had no idea who I was.

No idea?

None.

I just sat there.

I had even less idea about who I *had* been.

The printing business came into mind, to the last item, with all the new ideas almost worked out in blueprints, and the technical improvements now on the lathes to bring them up to sales. Professionally, at least, I was alert. My set of rooms upstairs I could recall to the detail, even where, exactly, to put my hand on any book in my library of more than four thousand, or any file in the racks.

I seemed rational enough in terms of the job, in all aspects from buying raw pulp to maintaining accounts, and socially, or as far as schooling and education had taken me, that is, below university level. But the cipher known to some by the number of his set, A 8, and to national records as Alastair George Bessell, and always called A.G. by anyone else, stood as a trussed sheep, ready for the knife or shearing, defenceless anyway, and in fear of what lay in front, the next moment, the night, the terrifying tomorrow.

There was nobody I could ask for advice. I had no family. The people I knew were only acquaintances, certainly not to be burdened with any problem of mine, even if I respected anything they might have to say.

Alf came out of shadow into overhead light, pitting eye sockets, cheeks, and chin against the darkness, scribbling white hair in wavy lines down both sides of his face to the earlobes shining red through the tangle, a neckchain of amulets in gold and ivory jingling small glitter, and a yellow sparkle in crystal held with one hand and the thousand silver bubbles of the siphon in the other.

"Looked like you needed the reserve," he said. "What is it? Flu?"

"Could be. I feel frightened. Like an egg about to get the blade."

"Well. We've all felt like that, ain't we? Eh? One time, trawling off of Greenland we was. I was lashed to a rail, mind? She came up in front of me. The deck was flat as that there wall, there. Standing on her hinds, she was, and that exact split second, we got smashed to starboard by a forty-footer and we rolled over, taking all the water in God's seven seas, and I was crushed, and damned, and given up. But she was Belfast-built, and she waddled out of it, only the Lord Christ knows how. Since that very moment I've never been frightened. You couldn't fright me. I've looked it in the dirty teeth, and I can laugh. Know the feeling, do you?"

"Not quite. I've only been on ferries. They're safe enough. I'm no sailor. If a jug of water shakes, there's me over the side."

"Ah. All the years I was at sea, I was never sick."

This was all very well, but we all knew that Bosun Alf Straum had never been nearer Greenland than Southend, a few miles downriver by Mr. Waygoes' barge, only once, and lost his humbles in no more than a swell, and had to be sent home in the truck, and as for being a bosun, nobody would have let him cox a children's bumboat on the local lake.

"Have one yourself," I said.

"Ah, kindly took. Grog time's piped? Lovely."

How, I wondered, did Bosun Alf Straum live one life with his hands, and a quite different existence in his mind? Everybody knew that the one was mental comedy and laughable, and the other, carving model ships, an essay in hard work, perhaps artistry, and a valuable extra earning. Did one excuse the other?

Did *he* ever tremble, wondering about tomorrow?

Did Mr. Waygoes?

Did anybody I knew?

I was beginning to. And I was terrified.

I am not sure what the word means, in words. I know how it feels. I sweated cold without being able to give myself any reason. Why was I sitting there, sweating, and cold?

Idiotic.

Frightened of *what?*

Time to come?

Why hadn't I been frightened before?

I hadn't known about it. I never had reason to think about it. If I ever had, it was only tomorrow, or next week, month, year, safe enough, sun up, sun down, jobs to do, jobs done, no problems except in accounts, or supplies, or on the plant floor, or funny clients, all thought about, solved, and settled in one way or another, and all at peace.

Now, it was different. The police had me by the heels. Customs were after me. I knew I would never again leave or enter the country without a strict body search, and the same process in every other country I visited. Customs report to their own. They share knowledge.

14

But was there any need to carry diamonds?

If I refused, "they" might be offended.

I could join Penna.

Was that what frightened me?

I thought not. But I don't suppose Penna had been frightened up to moments before something had happened to her.

Something.

Kidnap?

It seemed nonsense to suppose that an intelligent and healthy latish-twenties woman could simply go. Vanish. How? Apparently, nobody knew. Except for faceless Jayb and his employers.

I could go the same way. Perhaps, obviously, in the Thames. It was near.

And when?

I could never make another run. I had to find Jayb to tell him, but I had no address or any telephone number, except for the café. That was the strength of the matter. Nobody knew anyone else, except next man up. Next man down knew nothing.

What did "they" know about me?

I had to find out.

How?

That, perhaps, frightened me most. I was up in the air. No smallest notion where attack might happen.

But still more frightened about what was to come, tonight, to morrow. The days after.

Not kidnap. Not even death. Both were only words, neither of them reducible by thought. Think of them as you like, nothing frightened or made you sweat. Then why was I frightened *and* sweating?

I had just found out I didn't know who I was, or had been. I knew I had built a business. I was successful. The years had been well used. The bank could prove evidence of initiative, service, thrift. The business would prove prosecution of new ideas, industry, sweat. But apart from those qualities, who *was* I? As I sat there, *who* was I? Who or what was I yesterday?

Tomorrow?

Bosun Alf came into light, nursing a pint mug.

15

"Nothing like a nice whet," he said, and sat. "Knives or whistles, the right sort of whet, you're quids in. Here's to your best
health, sir. Hope you're not still feeling frightened?"

"I am. I'd like to tell myself, why?"

"Like waking up in the middle of the night, thinking your
heart's going to stop? Happened to me. Many a time. I just get
up, and come down here, and have a drink, tell meself not to be
such a bloody fool, and nip back in the hammock again. Just
dreams, that's all."

"But you've never been frightened about the next five minutes,
or what happens during the night, or what might be coming tomorrow? The day after? Next week?"

Bosun Alf stared bluely over the tankard's edge, drank, sucked
the moustache.

"Don't see no sense in it," he said, and tapped out a cigarette.
"I reckon we all got our work cut out to deal with *now*. Never
mind about later. Or tomorrow. Who's bloody worried about
next week? My age? Christ, you could be dead. Eh? Any minute.
That what you're afraid of?"

"Not quite."

"Didn't you better find out? You want to get friends with yourself. While you got time. Most of us, we hate our own guts.
That's half our trouble. Or most of it. Love ye one another, that's
what they say. Christ, when you can't even love your bloody self,
where are you?"

"Thought like that for long?"

"What other way is there? Take all the people living here, or
anywhere else. They love theirselves? 'Course not. How do you
know? Look round you. Read your papers. Love? It's a spit
word. Bloke meets a piece, they live together? They have a kid
or two? Oh, lovely gossipy-columny. Somebody's living with
somebody? Big stuff. What was they doing two thousand years
ago? In a cave. Bloke and his piece. What else are they? What's
the difference? The gossip column and a lot of cheap money?
That's no difference. It's only gravy. They all end in the same
hole. Same history. Nothing."

"But they live as they want to. They're free. And they have a

16

good time. How many factory hands do? The rest? Do they have as good a time? Cars, yachts, foreign holidays, the publicity?"

"If it wasn't for the hard workers, and a lot of bloody sweat somewhere, there wouldn't be a solid backup for blokes and pieces. I mean, the pop lot. Actors, all them. They'd have nothing to live off of. 'Course, you can tell me there's just as many blokes and pieces among the hard workers. Just give me the numbers. Ever see 'em in the gossip columns, do you? 'Course not. Why? No cars, no yachts, no money. All right? I mean, Marbella for a travel tour, couple of weeks, not even as good as lodgings in Blackpool, but a lot more sun, is that gossip? Any good in a Sunday paper? I mean, bloke and piece had a set-to Saturday, and the piece shoved off to her mother's, less three teeth, plus a black eye, is that gossip? They got any money? They on the charts? Any yachts? Any anything? 'Course, if he murders her, they might get a para. Eh?"

But this was distant from what I had been thinking. I am unsure how it is that I can think quite differently from what others are saying, even while they are talking, and I catch the drift, if not the complete meaning, and yet retain exactly what was in my mind. I have no idea what my mind *is*.

I had never thought of blokes and pieces, even though, in sudden clash of memory, they were all around me. Many of the girls lived openly with men, some roomed with other girls, and at least three had a set with two men each.

Bosun Alf had gone on talking, something about abortion. One of the girls had been in hospital just up the road, and Daemon Wente Waye had passed the hat to send her on a three-week holiday.

"Nothing to do with us," he said, and sucked the moustache, a fine affront of wind on sog, and the sound of a withdrawn wave. "Girls, that is. They has to suffer, not us. Didn't ought to be anything to do with us. It's the woman's body. Not ours. In fact, we're bloody lucky. Supposing every time we had a bit, we might have a nipper? Bit different, eh? All them bleeding parsons, moaning away there. And them cows hollering about what girls ought to do, and all that. I mean, it's a right pain in the

17

bollocks. Listen, I was a girl, I'd have a bit when I felt like it, and I'd take the pill religious. Else I'd toss 'em off a couple of times first. Then it's all right. Only some blokes can't come three times. That's their bloody hard luck. Me, I'm happy. I was born *right*."

Again that twinge of fear, a small shock, as from a carelessly handled electrical gadget, but bringing back realities instead of mists. I had to move, immediately, to the Continent, where made no difference, but I had to be out of London for at least a couple of months, beyond messages or phone calls. Perhaps "they" would get tired of calling or trying to reach me, if, that is, they tried. I was far from sure. I wondered—I think for the first time —if "they" knew my clientele, or if any of *them* were part of "they." I saw no reason why "they" might want to lose me. I had always made a good run. I knew only Jayb. I could do no harm, either to him or to those behind him. Why was I frightened?

I knew, with Alf pointing at the glasses, brows up. I nodded for the refill.

I knew in that space, but it took more time to explain, because knowing and explaining are different. Knowing is in the mind, but explaining is words and they have to be found, and put together in exact shape, and given the tick as correct.

I had no words.

I knew beyond all doubt that outside business efficiency and a certain degree of general knowledge, I was nothing more than a half-grown child, caught in black night and afraid, and suddenly made aware both of what had gone and what was in being, but without any smallest hope of helping the right or preventing the wrong, only because I had no notion which was which. Most of the stuff I read in the newspapers never went deeper than the eyeballs. I never thought about what I read because there seemed so little to concern me, and with most of them I seldom more than scanned headings, skimmed the sports, looked at the back page, and turned up the radio or TV. The air world seemed so much more sure of itself, and the men and women were real as me.

But this sort of thinking, or mental fuddle, did nothing to lessen the problem.

What *was* the problem?

Perfectly simple. Who was I, what was I doing, was it enough, and where was I going?

What, so suddenly, had brought it up?

A girl's disappearance?

Partially, because of its effect, a police enquiry into my movements, and an absolute break with what had so comfortably gone on before, *plus*—and a huge plus—a feeling that I was no longer anybody, except the owner of a profitable company, several bank accounts in many countries, a special type of printing plant, and not much of an idea of anybody else except myself. I had always thought of myself as Number One. But who *was* I?

Who the devil did I pretend to be?

Apart from my name, and my company, and the people able to recognise me, *who* was I?

How could I explain myself to anyone?

Very well, but why did I have to?

What was there to tell?

Whose affair was it?

Primarily, I would have thought, mine.

But I didn't know. As I sat there, I had no notion. None.

"I think I've had too much to drink," I said. "Is Doctor Rahman still across the road?"

"Ought to be. He's on till eleven. All the day-shift wallahs see him at night."

"Be a good chap. Ring him, and say I'd like a few moments. That's all."

"*On*."

He went off in shadow, and I stood without effort, surprisingly, and whacked into the wall, which taught me, and I held onto the table, trying to manoeuvre in the haze of smoke and poor light, generally doing an unsteady best to act sober.

What *is* the difference between drunk and sober?

Drunk, the feet will never do as you wish, the eyes refuse to focus—though one, either left or right, perhaps may as a favour —and words will be difficult to find, even if the mouth may try to speak them, but too often it refuses, and the ears hear, and scorn, but the cause is hopeless.

You are drunk, and the crime is manifest.

Nobody is accused of being sober.

Bosun Alf raised an arm against the light.

"Kari's coming over," he called. "Won't be a minute or so. Doctor's just back from the hospital. You want an overcoat. It's dead cold. There's a lot of this flu about. You got to go careful. Want a bracer?"

"When I come back."

"I'll hang on."

I went out to the main gallery, where the staircases on each side went up three storeys, and stood against the main pilaster, wondering if the granite head in bearded profile from me had ever seen my granite head in profile while he waited for a nurse to take him across a road to see a physician, and which road in the Peloponnisos it might have been. I believe we all, in any age, in one way or another, double each other's experience, not exactly, perhaps, but near enough. Well, all right, what the hell, I was drunk as a fiddler's bitch, but thought was fairly clear.

The night bell rang, and security guard George Almond came out of the box and looked through the little window, switching on all the lights outside, and opened the barrier and the door, and Kari came in, wearing the small white linen cap and the short blue cape, holding her grey skirts about her legs, a simple beauty, in an amazing smile and wave.

"Come along, A.G." she sang, in echoes up the stairways, a lovely sound. "He is waiting, poor man. Five babies today and two operations, and more than sixty out-patients, and hospital seven o'clock in the morning. If not night calls before. Give me your hand. Let us run. It is freezing. A.G., I am told you are drunk? You lucky bugger."

"Any time you want to get lucky, come over to A 8. Open arms, all in fun, safety guaranteed."

"Why the hell do I want to get drunk, if safety guaranteed? What a waste."

We were running through the garden paths, among straw mounds of plants packed for the cold by Amy and Joe.

I had that warm little hand in mine. Little? It felt like a flower.

We ran over Wapping High to the other side, to the right and then left, into Pell Court, left to Coromandel Lane, and Dr. Rahman's new surgery shone a red lamp, and the end of the queue stood in the doorway to take the warmth, if only in their faces.

"I don't feel right, taking somebody's place," I said. "They've waited."

"He's just back from an operation. He's having a cup of coffee. Do you blame him? He will see you. Are you grumbling? Shall I throw you in the street? Shut up, and come in here. Take off everything, and your shirt. If you are cold, serves you right. You shouldn't be sick and giving the doctor a lot of trouble. When is he going to sleep? Does anybody care?"

"When are *you* going to sleep?"

"When I finish. Go in, and shut up."

That was Kari's way, and everybody knew it, and the queue cheered her, and I went down the rows of big eyes, wondering if anybody would take me bodily and throw me never mind where. But none did, and I went into the little changing room, and stripped to the waist, thankful for clean underwear that morning, and enough change to pay the bill. The silly things we think.

Dr. Rahman sat in shirtsleeves behind a kitchen table piled with papers, feet on another chair, a pot of coffee on a small table to the right, a black bag on the floor, and a child sleeping in a cot by the window. A woman mounded under a pink quilt in the corner.

"Come in, A.G.," Dr. Rahman said, and nodded at the chair. "Have you brought back rabies from Europe? Japanese flu? The clap? Everything curable except taxes, rates, crime, and alimony. What is the emergency?"

"There's nothing wrong with me. Physically, I'm fine."

"I'm told you are drunk."

"That was across the road, and a lot of cold air cured it. It's something more serious. Doctor, I'll put it in bald terms. I don't know who I am. I'm not sure if I'm sure. Apart from what I do, I mean, to earn a living, and where I live, which gives me an address people who know me can write to, who the hell *am* I?"

Dr. Rahman sat up and tapped ash in the saucer, frowning.

"I don't understand exactly what you mean," he said quietly, looking at me from the side. "What allows you to say something so ridiculous?"

21

"It's not ridiculous. I don't know who I am. Apart from being the proprietor of a business, and holder of a passport and a bank account and a place across the road, who *am* I?"

Dr. Rahman put his feet on the floor, and stubbed the cigarette.

"Who *are* you?" he said, and nodded at Kari. "Beyond what you have been saying, and certain other details which mean nothing, you are a piece of meat, mobile when you wish, sentient, possibly, and at all times a wonderful playground for disease. That's why I'm here. I'm the referee."

"Not a physician? You disappoint me."

"Physician heal thyself. Remember this. Pills and stuff on the shelf can pretend. I can't. You see, in most ways I'm exactly like you. A man. The same. About printing, you know. About medicine, I know. I know nothing about what is in the head. What is your opinion of yourself is secret to yourself. You can never tell me. You have not the words. I have not the understanding. And so? I check your physical condition and prescribe for what I find is wrong. Kari, take blood pressure. Do you sleep well? Are you tired in the day? Bowels, bladder, free? No trouble?"

Nods for answers, while Kari pumped the bulb and read the dial.

"Do you dream?"

"Never. Or I don't remember."

"Do you wake at night because of bladder trouble?"

"Never."

Kari fixed pads about heart and elsewhere, and something whizzed or groaned.

"How many meals do you eat in a day?"

"Two. Lunch, and supper when I finish work."

"What do you eat?"

"Anything."

"At the restaurant?"

"Generally."

"What?"

"Oh. Beef. Lamb. Stews. Fish."

"Eggs?"

"Sometimes. Not often."

"You don't eat breakfast?"

"Only before seven o'clock in the morning. After that, juice and coffee's enough."

"Till lunch?"

"Only if it's with a client. Generally, I don't eat much."

"No appetite?"

"What is appetite? Desire to fill a gut? I like what I taste. Enough."

Kari took off all the pads and looked at the long sheet from the machine.

"Waste of time," she said. "Nothing here."

"Good," Dr. Rahman said. "So far, no trouble at all. We will take specimens of blood and urine. But I shall tell you now. There is nothing the matter with you. Except."

I looked at him. He rustled the heart sheet through his fingers.

"*Except*," he said. "A perfect example of the British malaise. You are sick in small mental areas. No physician can do anything. You have not any longer an Empire. Because of past history, and promises, you must accept the detritus. That's *us*. You care nothing that *we* must accept *you*. We were thrown out of our houses. Far better than anything here. We had a far better life. Better schools for our children. Here, we have nothing, except what we make ourselves. There, we had money. Here, we have none except what we earn. It is little. There we had much. And bank credit. We are a people displaced. Many of us could be millionaires. Here, we are all nearly mendicants. Except that we can earn to pay our way. Do you blame us?"

"But what is this to do with me?"

"So much. You, and everybody like you. How do you think *our* people feel? *My* people? *Me*. How do you think *I* feel? I had an entire hospital. It was mine. My father's. As you take a toy from a child, it was taken from me. I was pushed on a plane. Goodbye. How do you think *I* am sure? *I* should like to ask *you*. Who am *I*?"

"Doctor Rahman, of course?"

"And you are A.G.? You work at printing? I work at doctoring.

23

Both are jobs. Both give us pay. We both pay our bills. We employ people. Where is the difference? Have you become childish? Do you wish to run to your father?"

"I came here for advice."

"You have got it. You are a healthy man. Nothing is wrong with you. Go to the nearest church, fall on your knees, and thank God. You don't believe? Look up at the stars. Thank them. Thank anything. Now, go away. This woman behind me has cancer. This baby has glaucoma. Or something worse. She will never see. Please go away. I can do nothing for either of them, and nothing for you. They are rejects of our human system. What are *you?*"

I took the black stare and crushed cheek under the fist as memory, and put my clothes on in the changing room, and Kari came in to help me on with my overcoat and took me between the waiting lines, and big eyes, out to the street.

"You can find your way?" she said.

I nodded.

She patted my shoulder.

"He is not in the best thinking," she said. "He lost three patients today. Always he is angry to lose. He knows he will lose at least three more tomorrow. So he was angry with you. One balances the other. Be kind to think of him?"

"Very much. When you feel like a drink, come over."

"I can bring somebody?"

"Any number. If, but only *if*, they are girls. Understood?"

"Of course. You don't like boys?"

"Girls are more beautiful. Better games. Who wants a boy if I can have you? Or any of your friends? Bring them over."

"Something to eat, as well?"

"I'll have a buffet. Never fear. How many?"

"At least twelve. Counting me."

"Very well. Saturday?"

"The weekend? Lovely. We will be there."

She touched my face, and turned back into the lines of eyes, and I trotted down, out to Wapping High, and across to the steps, through the darkness of the garden, to the bell, and the

24

lights coming on and the door opening, and a nod for George Almond's smile, and a run up the first stair, a little steadier on the second, and a plod up the third, to my set, A 8.

Nothing is better than opening a door and knowing by smell and warmth that you are home, in your own place, where you may be yourself and do as you please. I was surprised to find the lights on, because I make a habit of turning them off. I looked about, among the books and pictures, and all the old friends of years. I took off my overcoat and threw it over the armchair. I rubbed my hands. I was cold. I went over to the drinks tray, a beautiful wide silver Georgian, and then remembered Bosun Alf's promise to stay.

I saw a movement to the left. I turned, cold, seeing a hump in shadow. I switched on all the lights. Something sat in the odd chair. Odd, because it was unlike any chair I had ever seen. I bought it because it had three legs.

Light shone on Jayb's face looking at my feet.

"How did you get in here?" I said.

"Usual way."

"How?"

"Don't be soppy. We go where we're told. What, you think you're boss of creation, do you? You got a run, day after tomorrow."

"I can't. I'm searched in, and out. Look, they'll start using X rays."

"No worry. While they search you, the other bloke goes through. So you'll do the run, see? The money's in your bank. Everything fixed. Day after tomorrow. Eleven o'clock out of Victoria. Your tickets are here, this envelope. Everything else, settled. As usual. Any questions?"

"Did you come in through the front door?"

"'Course not."

"Then how?"

"Way I'm going out. That's it. G'night. Nice place, here."

He got up and went to my right, out of the kitchen door. I waited, hearing no sound. I sat there thinking, I'm not sure what, for minutes after. I'm not alive to what clutters our heads at a time. In that frozen space I only remember I was frightened. That somebody could get into my place was not the happiest thought. That they could face me and go away was rather worse. I went through into the kitchen. The door was locked, and so was the window.

How did he get out?

Cold and worried, I went downstairs. Bosun Alf had a bar of a dozen or more, sitting in peach glow from wall lights. It made the girls look even better. I called for a double. The two waving at me from the corner were a delightful pair, by some sublime element in time, meant for each other and making the wonderful best of it. They had no use for men, and made no secret. We got along because I never made any attempt to find out how deep the anti-male business went, and, of course, there was never any suggestion of bed, or if there had been—and there had—as a joke, it went open-ended, without answer or any comment, even the coy or evasive. Simply a passing to something else. I believe we all knew exactly how far to go. It was healthy, because there were no quarrels. They gave no room. We were too well aware that we would be held responsible. Bosun Alf was a harsh master. His orders came direct from Mr. Waygoes. It was well known that touch his girls, Christ help you. We all knew it. I went across, and pulled up a chair to sit between them. They always sat with their feet up to take the weight off long legs. They were tall girls, a honey blonde and a black, with magnificent manes below their waists, and natural, as other vital evidence proved, and both had a good head, a fair opinion, and, on any occasion, a sharp reply.

"Hi, A.G.," Celli called. "I hear Kari's got a party at your place Saturday. She just phoned. We'll be there. You going to have that smoked salmon pâté?"

"Of course. And charcoal-grilled hamburgers. The nut of grilled cutlets. And a Madras curry by Kari's mother. And I'm making the zabaglione."

"I can't wait," Botti, the honey blonde, exulted. "I'm having nothing to eat the next three days. Last time I was sick for a week. Worth it. That was the oysters."

"Wasn't," Celli said. "It was that crap you had that lunchtime.

26

Nothing to do with his party. What was it? Shepherd's pie? They sling everything in that, 'cluding the cat's guts. And they're not so tasty. What made you choose it? Didn't you take your glasses?"

"Haven't I done telling you I never had shepherd's pie? I had toad in the hole, if you must know for the umptieth time."

"Toad in the hole? A toad's a lovely job, isn't it? I mean, gobble it quick. In whose hole? If I mentioned a few?"

"Go on, chum. It's all been said before. It was the oysters on top of it. That's all. Shepherd's pie's lovely when it's right."

"You had shepherd's pooh, and you blamed him."

"Way I felt, I'd have blamed the Government. Not A.G. Never A.G. He's my own boy."

"Tell me when the banns are called. I'll be there to shout a few times."

"No banns, dear. Just a spiritual get-together."

"What sort of scotch? As if it mattered. Listen, A.G. We've found a lovely girl for you. We took one look, and we both said A.G. Right for him. Shame to waste it."

"Where is she?"

"We'll bring her to the party."

"Well, now, look. Tomorrow I've got to be in Paris. I might be late getting back on Saturday. If I am, I'm leaving the keys with Mrs. Rafaele, and you two take charge. I'll order the food and drink. The butler and his wife know what to do. No slipups. Worst comes to the worst, I shouldn't be later than something after midnight."

"Wonderful," Celli said. "You'll be in Paris? Listen. We've got a marvellous friend there. Get in touch. Give me a pencil."

I gave her a Cross and a note pad, and she wrote.

"There," she said. "Made for you. I hope she hasn't got off with somebody else. You know, if you take it by and large, who *is* lucky in this world?"

"I think I must be," I said. "I've got through, so far. I know a few beautiful people, like you, and all the people here. I've got a business. A good place to live. I can travel. Go where I like. Pretty nearly do as I please. Looking about, I think I'm lucky, yes."

"I think you are," Botti said. "Always thought so. Always

smart. Even in the towel sarong. Nice, any time. I wonder somebody hasn't stuck her tabby claws in you long before this."

"I lost my wife eight years ago."

"Sorry," Botti said. "My big mouth again. You had somebody nice a few weeks ago, though?"

"God knows what happened. The police have been enquiring. I know that."

"So do we," Celli said. "They asked us. What do we know?"

"How does a girl disappear? A perfectly healthy, intelligent girl?"

"Didn't she have any family?"

"What difference?" Celli said. "What's a family know? What does *my* family know about me? They don't even know where I am."

"Me, too," Botti said. "Funny how we treat families. I couldn't bear any of mine. I'm better off without them. The *lot*."

"Talking for me," Celli said, signing to Alf for a round. "This is mine. No argument. Listen. Last time I went home, my mother's funeral, my eldest brother started laying down the law to my youngest sister. My opinion, she's the best of the lot. Got through all her exams. Paid me back. Did a lot for my youngest brother. Which I didn't know about. Anyway, he lays down the law about her living with a man at the lab she's working with. He's never met him. He starts spouting on a throne. The high moral stuff. Look. He'd been to bed with my mother and two of my sisters, and he tried it with me. I was too young to know. And I left home too soon. And he's the moral judge? I slung the teapot at him. Last time I'll ever see him, I can tell you."

"I wasn't that unlucky," Botti said. "Not far off, though. Anyway, what's it all about? Either you want to, or you don't. What's all the fuss? Your father, or somebody else? Never happened to me, but I can't see much wrong with it. I can't remember my father."

"Listen," Celli said, rattling coins to pay the Bosun. "What was that place in Paris we went to? Where they had that marvellous Hungarian band?"

"Closed last year," Botti said. "I told you."

"Why does everything marvellous have to close up? Why can't enough people find out, and go?"

"Well, I suppose they don't like it Hungarian," Botti said. "They were all trying to feel me, I know that. So a man wouldn't want to take a girl there again. I certainly wouldn't. I loved the music. Why can't we have the music without the rest? Something I've always wondered. Any place you ever knew where girls felt the men? Music and lovely food, all in?"

"I think the men might like it," I said. "But I've never known a place like it. Saunas, and all that, yes. I suppose. But the only saunas I've ever been to were in Finland. No nonsense there. You get your sauna. That's it. I haven't been to one in London. Except at the gym here. No nonsense either."

"What do you call nonsense?" Botti asked.

"Sex. Or any small fraction. If you want a hot bath, if you want to sweat, all right, go to a sauna. If it's a whoreshop, get on with it. It's the same old nonsense with another more fashionable title. It's the same orgasm."

"Lovely word," Celli said. "Nothing to touch it. All right. It's a do-it-yourself kit. But it's not the same. We ought to've been born with a longer tongue."

"But we weren't," Botti said. "We make do. Any complaints?"

"Not here. Here's to it. Listen, A.G. Mind me asking a question? That girl, what's her name, Penna something? What did you find attractive about her? I mean, treat me like a man. What was it? Prospect of bed? Her legs? Umm?"

"No. I can honestly say, none of those things. Or all of them, behind something else. I think that was loneliness. Hers and mine. We shared something. The river, the rain, fishing, fine days with a picnic basket. The camera. Ourselves, what we thought."

"You never knew she was always nosey about you?" Celli said, lighting a cigarette for Botti. "She was after everything about you. Look, she said she had a job up the road, here? At the dress-wear place? Aronfelt's? They never heard of her. After all, that's part of our business. We run a model agency. We never had her name. Cately. That's it. So we started asking questions. Because we happen to like you. Her landlady up there, Mrs.

Tukes, thought she was a secretary somewhere. Always brought home lots of paper. Worked long hours. Well, Mrs. T. had worked in an office till she went on the Old Age. The papers she was supposed to be working at were all in a foreign language. When she left, all that paper had gone before the police came in. Wasn't a scrap. Why?"

"Don't know," I said. "Not interested. I can tell you, now, I might have married her. She was sympathetic. She followed a lot of what I did. Good brain. Knew her way about. I don't understand the paper business. Don't understand any of the rest of it."

"That's it, for me," Botti said, and drank dregs. "Listen, A.G. Ever you need a couple of pals, no need to look further than us. Anything, anytime, just call."

"Anything, that is, except *that*," Celli said, standing. "We can do without it."

They leaned over to kiss me on the cheek, one and one, and I sniffed the scent of their womanliness, and mourned again that we were so far apart. Nothing is quite so desirable as the impossible.

I went upstairs and looked in the kitchen again and found, I thought, where Jayb, the tich, had got in. Under the sink, in a cupboard, opening out at a touch, a chute went down taking the garbage bags to the destructor. Remembering the chimney-sweep boys from Victorian times, I saw he would have it easy, both coming up and sliding down. A thick wire filter with a heavy catch from my side would prevent any more. A note to Mrs. Hine about rats would do it. I could almost see her face at mention.

My bag was almost always ready, and nearly packed itself. My order case was satisfactorily fat, and the morning's mail gave two more good excuses to go to Rome and Athens. Just before lunch I went along to King David's Lane, marvelling that so long after the war, East London was so empty, so moon-cratered, so unused, in what had once been a marvel of human ebullience. The time of the magnificent Hebrew trader. When the sisters worked the shoe machines to keep a brother at university. I thought of them, most ghosts under rubble, and kissed them in their rough tombs, of far greater majesty than those of many a king or any filthy dictator—so-called—a bastard politician carried on a swell of ignorance and importance to find power, and disaster replete.

The little house in King David's Lane had survived with aid of boards, corrugated iron, and concrete block walls. The bell brought Mrs. Tukes, still in overcoat and hat. The shopping cart almost filled the hallway. The place smelled of soap. She was tall, lined, grey, sharp.

"No, I've heard no news," she said. "The police have been here, on and off. There's been no post for her. Couple of callers. Nothing much. Most girls from down the road. She was taking part in this business about archi-wasname, and digging, and whatnot. Always made a mess. Y'know. Muddy boots. But she was a nice girl. I'm sorry to have lost her. Funny thing. There's a lot going on, but her family's never come nigh. Not even a postcard. What's happened to people? I mean, if that was my girl, I'd be screaming in the streets. Not a word? Not a sound? What is it? Don't we *care* about anybody any more?"

"I understand she brought home a lot of paper?"

"That's right. But when the police came here to look round, it'd all gone. The lot. I never saw her taking anything out. Proper ol' mystery, you ask me. You was a friend of hers, wasn't you? Yes. Thought I remembered you. Couple of Saturday mornings, wasn't it? Taking a boat down the river? Yes. Well. If I hear anything, I'll let you know. Still at the Daemon?"

The door shut, and in that quiet street, so grey, with only a black front door and a low red brick wall for colour, in small rain, I seemed somebody in a bare Utrillo painting, with not even a cat, a sparrow, for company.

I wished I had asked Jayb what had happened to Penna, but there had been no time, and, in fact, I wanted him out of the place. I think I was frightened of him, or the people behind him. I had evidence of what "they" could do. I was far from being proud of that fear. It was simply that I preferred the quiet life, the days of work without worry, and nights of sleep. A notion of that rat creeping up the rubbish chute, and having to wake up to somebody in the odd chair, really made me shrivel.

31

The six staircases were good exercise, and I reached the top just as Ol' Mabbs came out of his set, putting his lower teeth in.

"Morning," he called. "Lot of funny noises in your place last night. I was going to ring you, but it quietened off."

"I think there was somebody in there. They heard me come in, and shoved off."

Ol' Mabbs showed the callused palms, and put them together. They rasped.

"My Christ, it's coming to something, ain't it? Eh? Not even safe in your own place? Listen, I catch anybody in here, they can order their own tomb. Just save time, that's all."

"I'm off for a couple of days. I'd be grateful if you'd report anything."

"Will that. Keep a special eye. You're safe enough. Now I got to go down the 'ployment Exchange. Try to find a 'prentice. Been at it over six months. They don't want to take the money. And the time. Lazy bastards. Signing on the dole gives them nearly three times what I can pay. Why should they sign with me? Years of hard work? No. They won't. So I keep on trying. I might find a lad worth taking trouble over. No harm in that, is there?"

"Why don't you try the girls? After all, they buy most of your stuff, don't they?"

Ol' Mabbs took his lower teeth out and put them in his top right-hand waistcoat pocket, smacked his lips.

"Damn if I ever thought of that," he said, looking wide across the top landing, at the big copper bowl of flowers. "I believe you might just be right. I learned off of a woman. Why not one of them learn off of me? Tit for tat? Marvellous. Thanks, A.G. Your place is safe as the Bank. Anybody farting about, I'd bloody murder 'em. Get back safe."

I called a cab and puffed down the stairs, put the bags in, and went to the London Terminal for a bus to Heathrow.

All along I looked at the mess the brainy, greedy louts had made of London. All shapes, any size, no harmony, less imagination, with the shadow of the money-grub like an ugly fist over all of it. Poor old London. Nearly fifty thousand women and children killed in the war of bombs, and not a memorial, not a garden to mark them. What a bloody lot we are without making the effort. The lords of make-do, and fuck it.

Heathrow got worse in the crowd and the smell every time I used the place. People, me among them, shoving trolleys or trying to find one, all knowing where we were going, and everybody in the way or blocking someone else, and the counter clerks, poor girls, getting terse, and buffets a rude mess, pouring drinks only as favours, and well-slopped, and sandwiches a triangle of cheap dough with a hint of pig or cow if you asked for ham or cheese. A cheapjack parcel, asking for rubbish and paying for it, and never a word against.

What a lot.

But I got a real going over by Customs, a strip-down in a little room, everything felt, looked at. I expected a doctor and a finger in the canal, but not.

"What *is* all this?" I asked the officer.

"Routine check," he said, routinely checking without looking up. "You come in and out a lot, don't you?"

"Certainly?"

"We like to make sure who we're dealing with."

"I'm a taxpayer. You all know what you can go and do."

"Rudeness get you nowhere."

"I'm not rude. I'm right."

He chalked on the bags, part of himself, mark of nonentity, hallmark of the gold-banded pricks above him.

"Right," he said, and turned away. "You can go."

"How kind. The Nazis, those bastards you might have heard of? That's how *they* treated people."

"Way out's behind you."

I was unlucky, because I knew that he and his kind were right to suspect. I had no front. I was, in truth, rotten. I had no complaint, in justice or in luck. If, without Penna—and I was sure she had been the informer—I had been arrested, with the pack, there would have been nothing to say, no defence.

At this moment, I could use words, bawl, kick up a row.

He, and his kind, had their duty.

Pity.

33

But had I been "clean," I might have shouted much louder, and—who knows?—got into a lot of talk-trouble—it's always easy—especially with the police outside the door.

What defence have you?

I had none. And so what was the use?

Yes, but there was something else.

I was still a citizen. They might suspect, but there was no proof.

Should every suspect, every citizen, be treated in the same way?

As in a hospital?

Were we all patients? Nothing more? Not ourselves? Each a self?

But what *was* a self?

Each capable of cheating?

In some way, each dishonest?

Who judged?

Which *was* the judge? The self, knowing, or someone else, judging?

I made up my mind—and what is that?—how does a mind make itself up?—what *is* a mind?—a collection of cogs to be pushed together at any moment?—to what? Say something? What? More agreeable? Less? How *does* a mind decide? I decided that never again would I make a run. In rage—what is rage?—I decided that I was not to be treated as a carrier of items making me a violator of Customs regulations.

But what a lot of nonsense.

Somebody—who?—ran a Bill through the House of Commons to put a tax on diamonds, among other things, and somebody else had used—had been using—me, among perhaps others, to escape the tax.

That's all I was. An evader. And the saintly ones could put a finger on me.

But what a disgusting notion. Any small accident, and a little carelessness, and I was a convict?

I was sure, then, that I would never again make a run.

We *are* so stupid. We pretend, but we don't know.

I had a fair lunch aboard, and I got the same welcome from

34

the French Customs. The little room, the strip, the search, and just enough time to catch the bus.

I have a warm fondness for Paris at any time.

It's a different world, another language, and a quite changed human being. I don't say better. Just changed by those few miles across the Channel. How? As selfish, or worse, yes. There is no bigger thief than the Parisian cabman. He was born a thief, and he lives as a thief, and he will never be anything else. So? I was careful, and he got a tip strictly on the clock, and he spat. Why not? As I was a foreigner, he was entitled to cheat me. It didn't come off? Spit.

My spit matched his. He looked up at me, might have spoken, thought better, moved his arms, and went to the other side of the cab, shouting something at the porter picking up my bags. The cigarette never left the corner of his mouth.

The hotel I had always stayed at, and it was like going home. I got the same broad-smile welcome from Jean-Jacques Brodier, the concierge-receptionist, my friend of so many years, and he gave me my usual room, on the third floor, with a wonderful view over the rooftops of grey, mulberry, and lilac tiles, and the same sounds from the open window, of dogs, pigeons, radios, talk and yells in background, and traffic. I could never pick them out, but they were the voice of Paris, a sound I always remember, that could never be mistaken for anywhere else.

Only one other city has a voice all its own, and that's my beautiful Venice, and I intended to go there soonest.

I dealt with two clients in less than two hours, and picked up two prospectives, and just after five o'clock I was at my favourite café on the Champs, drinking Pernod, the only drink in Paris before six o'clock. I like coffee and brandy any time before, and scotch after, but why, I'm not sure. It's a love of Paris. But in reaching for money, I found the telephone number of the girl given to me by Botti. I went back to the booth, bought a metal disc from the cashier, and waited. I got a smelly telephone—how often are they cleaned?—and called, and after a few rings somebody said *Allo?* and I said I was a friend of Botti and Celli in London, and blah-blah-blah. I realized I had no notion of their real names.

"Oh-h-h-h, of course, I had a telegram. Where are you?"

I told her, and she said twenty minutes, half an hour, she would be there. I still didn't know what to expect, and I went back to the table, bought a *Herald Trib*, ordered another Pernod, and wondered again what I had to look for, or get rid of.

A taxi stopped and a girl got out, in a red cape and a little black hat, high-heeled black satin shoes, black stockings, and long black gloves. When she turned, looking about, she seemed late twenties, beautiful grey eyes, lovely, and from the way she moved, a dancer, graceful.

She looked over the tables, and I stood, dragging out a chair to make a noise.

Smiling at me, she took a telegram from her purse, and came toward me, and I went to meet her.

"Mr. Bessell?" she said, and held out the form.

"I'm sorry I don't know your name," I said. "They didn't tell me."

"Doesn't matter. What's a name?"

"A rose is a rose?"

"That's Gertrude. I'll follow you with a Pernod, please. Where are you staying?"

"Up the hill on the Rue Balzac. Been going there for years."

"I'm not far away. How long will you be here?"

"Two, three days. Would you care for dinner with me?"

"But yes. I'm not dressed."

"La Coupole?"

"Ah, very well. My favourite. With some exceptions. Lipp, Maxim, Le Relais. And little places here and there. And our own kitchen. We have a wonderful girl. Born in Port-au-Prince. She cooks small things, but as an angel. We are six. A big apartment. We all have a room for ourselves. An enormous reception. You must have dinner with me. That was their order. Please tell me. I have always wondered. Why Botti and Celli?"

I laughed, and people looked at me.

"Very simple," I said. "Come to London, and see for yourself. We have a place built on one end of where we live, like a Greek temple. Round, with pillars. A central mosaic floor. Everything was dug out of London subsoil. You understand me?"

"Of course."

"Good. Well, it's always warm. It's just off the men's and women's sauna. We go there to get cool, sleep, anything we like. Sometimes, often, possibly, we don't wear anything. A towel, or not. Nothing. Men, women, we really don't take any notice. That's a fact. I haven't thought of it, but it's correct. There's no attempt to interfere, you understand? Women, men, total nudity, accepted. A fact."

"Unusual?"

"Possibly. But natural. Anybody breaking the rules would be thrown out. We can always invite anyone upstairs to our place. But there, the rule holds."

"Interesting."

"It is, indeed. Well. Botti and Celli are both extremely beautiful girls. One day, some time ago, they came out of the sauna, and they leaned over one of the marble benches to talk to somebody, and one of the regulars said the pair of them reminded him of a painting by Botticelli, though the girl on the left had a prettier botti. So she became Botti, and the other, Celli. And I still don't know their proper names."

"They are two darlings. They are strange to me. They are not men's women. Very well. It is their affair. But to me, they are completely friends. Three years ago they were broke. They slept on the floor of my apartment. Now they are established, and I am happy for them. You have seen them in love?"

"Never."

"It is so wonderful. The two personalities, lost in each other. I have never felt so. They have more from life, I think. And they are good. *Good.* They have big hearts. You don't find it like this?"

"From what I know of them, yes. I don't know an awful lot. To me, they're a couple of girls staying at the same place. Helping at the digs, sorting out the pieces."

"What is digs?"

"A lot of us at the Daemon help dig up bits of London to see what we can find. We've found a lot. Statuary. Pillars. Pots. Mosaics. Wall paintings. After all, the Romans were in Britain for more than four hundred years. A lot of their places got buried. Nobody knows why."

"Perhaps the same here? Paris was completely Roman. Gaul.

37

More than four hundred years. *Far* more. But what happened to the Romans? Where did they go? Did they all die suddenly?"

I found it funny to be sitting at a café on the Champs and drinking Pernod, with what the French call an *exquise,* and talking about the Romans. Fortunately I knew a bit about them because I had some books, and we chattered on until the air got chilly, and I suggested La Coupole, and off we went, but I was wondering what the Romans would think, as if it mattered. I had often thought about them. What sort of men *were* they? We carried it on, all the way up the Raspail, and when we were passing the Champ de Mars I started about the house of Bébe Bérard and how he died, and she said, yes, but then again, what happened to the Normans? One day they're up, and next day, gone. I almost said, Christ, we'll have to lose this, and nobody's ever been happier to get out of a cab.

La Coupole was just as it always was, crowded, warm, good smells of food and black cigarettes, back wall almost out of sight, shellfish in neat patterns at the fish stall, waiters doing conjuring tricks with loaded trays, and the pride of Paris—they liked to think—sitting along the rows of red velvet banquettes.

We got a table about halfway down, and I ordered champagne cocktails, the only before-dinner apéritif, and we each chose a plate of shellfish of about eight varieties and could have gone on, but eyes are not always bigger, and enough is enough. The champagne came in time for the first oyster, and all that had gone before, up to that moment—her long fingernails in glisten of pink, the Arab girl across the way in a little hat and veil using her fingers in a bowl of rice, each a different coloured sequin, the course of the day—all seemed hit, hammered, *crushed* in place by Jayb's face looking at me, in the doorway beyond the glass.

There was no mistake.

He nodded to a table, and moved away for people to come in.

I said whatever I said in pardon, and, still chewing whelk, went to the door, out, and over to the table.

"You done it very nice," he said. "You took their eye off. The packet and your tickets are at your hotel. Geneva, by train, seven o'clock. Be there ten minutes before. G'night. Watch the bit with you. She ain't been looked over. Cop?"

I went back, cold, into the warmth, to the table, and she looked at me.

"Not a happy visit," she said. "You are very pale."

"Freezing wind," I said. "How are the *fruits de mer?*"

"So good. *So* good. Instead of a second choice, I would like more. Oysters, shellfish, I can eat and eat and *eat*. Then, please, a lobster Rockefeller?"

"Let's try it."

I simply could not think. How had Jayb found me? Had I been followed? What a ridiculous question. Of course. And he was outside? And I would be followed to my hotel? And the girl with me? Not, please God, another Penna? Why not? If one could go, why not two? For what reason? The same that brought Jayb to La Coupole, of course. But I simply could not tolerate the thought of sitting next to a beauty enjoying herself, knowing what I did. How was I *not* to tolerate it? What could I *do?* Only sit there, and munch, and pretend to listen to what she was saying? We do manage to get into some strange situations. How do we excuse ourselves? How was *I* to excuse myself? To anybody. Far less me—I—the fool I had become. By being greedy and thinking little of it. Travel here, go there, drop the pack, go away, money in the bank, so easy. But there was a Penna. And now, another, as beautiful, probably even more innocent.

Cop?

The netherworld term froze me. Cop? You understand? Got it? How was I to take care of her?

I was certain I would, if I had to kill Jayb.

At that moment, I knew I could not go home with her, not even to see her to her door.

We could be followed.

She talked, I had no notion what about, and it was unfair, and rude, but I had something else in mind. Something horribly else.

"I had news from the office, here," I said, interrupting I-don't-know-what. "I've got a call coming through in thirty minutes. Would you mind very much if we cut this short? D'you object to going home by yourself? I'll come part of the way, if you don't mind?"

"Not a bit," she said, pretty as that. "Business is business, isn't it? I knew there was something wrong. You haven't got your proper colour back yet. I hope it's not too terribly serious? That's what's awful about today. You don't want to open a paper. The terrible things in it. It was a lovely dinner, though. When you come through, going back, give me a ring. Come and have dinner with us. Won't be as good as this."

"I won't bet."

She smiled, putting on a glove. She was nice.

"Better not," she said. "I'll be in London in three weeks, please tell the girls."

"Stay with me. I've got an extra room. They haven't. You're on your own. No nonse'."

Turning to me, an elbow on the banquette, a hand on the table, I was sorry not to be going back with her.

"Very well," she said. "I'll stay with you. But next time you are here, you will stay with me?"

We went down the Raspail in the same cab. I saw nothing outside or anything behind, and I got out at the bridge, and kissed her cheek, and while I stood waiting for a taxi, I realised I had no idea of her name.

There were asses and asses, and of them all, I was the prize.

I got back to the hotel, and called her number, and got the *Allo?*

"You're back?"

"I am here."

"All well? Just wanted to make sure."

"Everything very well. Thanks for that lovely dinner. We shall go there again? I love La Coupole. It has everything of Paris. You feel better?"

"I shall, after a couple of calls. I'll be back in London tomorrow. Any time you want to be in touch, call the Daemon. Sleep well."

A half of a conversation. I felt a rag, a nothing.

I called Jayb's number in London. Generally a man or woman answered. I had a notion, because of background noise, it was a café. Not a pub. They have hours of opening and closing. This place seemed open night and day, anytime.

"'Lo? Say it?"

"Jayb there?"

"No. Any message?"

"Say, urgent, there's a message for him, and a package, at A.G.'s place in Paris. That's A.G.'s place. Urgent. Got it?"

"A.G. Paris. Package. Got. That all?"

"No more."

"Where's he get in touch?"

"Anywhere."

"Ah. Good luck. You'll want it."

I had never known it before, but I knew it then, as a red blotch, that I had to find that place. I had, if necessary, to kill Jayb. But what good would it do? For what reason? I was sure that the girl I was with had not been followed. I stood on the corner for a good half minute before anything passed because of the traffic lights just up the road. The cab I took was part of the jam. Perhaps I was getting into a panic for nothing.

But I was in no panic.

I had to be cold.

As I had expected, the bumpy brown envelope lay on the desk in my room, with the room number in the porter's writing. I addressed it to Jayb, confidential, to be called for, and took it downstairs with my bags, and told the nightman that someone would collect it, and asked for my account. It was not ready, poor man, and I left enough to cover, and he phoned for a cab.

My guess was correct. I had just time to catch the train for the night ferry, and—as I had expected—I was searched viciously on the French side, and on the English, but I put up with it, and got into London sleepless but wholly myself, and even more ready for a fight. I had been used for far too long as a greedy courier. I was that no longer. I was almost surprised to know in myself no fear of death or, for that matter, of anything "they" might do.

But how ridiculous.

A man with two bags, waiting in the taxi-queue outside Victoria, thinking in such a way, and shivering, whether with the cold or anything else.

41

Yes, all very well.

I knew I would be foolish to go back to the Daemon. Even as bait.

It was shivering, then, that I got the idea, in a shudder, a cold spasm, and I knew I was right. I could go anywhere, except to the Daemon.

Even if I knew where to find Jayb, and if I killed him or not—and that was a foreign idea—"they," whoever "they" were, knew me and where to find me. Going back to the Daemon made things easier for "them." But then, where the devil *was* I going? What about the business? I knew the plant had work for at least two months, and Jo Hibbs was quite capable of paying out wages and dealing with day-to-day, and she could find other contracts as she had so many times before.

Where should I go?

Waiting for the cabs to come up, I remembered the Lomax, near the East India Dock, a place for ship chandlers and pilots, and the captains and chief engineers, that the Bosun had once said was the best place anywhere for food and drink, or kip.

The cabbie turned out, and again I was surprised at the strict knowledge of London's cabmen. I never found one at loss. He went direct to the Lomax, and the sleep-eyed girl told me I had twenty-two, and breakfast was in five minutes on the first floor. A porter took up my bags, and I followed up the stairs to a fine big room, a double bed, and a shower and lav to the side, and a small icebox full of soda and whatnot. I had a wash, and went downstairs. There was no card, and I said to the tall girl, breakfast, please.

She brought me a soup plate of real porridge, brown sugar, and cream. I hadn't seen it for years. I tucked in. I went out and got a paper and I was reading it when she came back.

A steak, and three eggs. I could hardly believe it. And hot rolls. And salt butter. And thick marmalade. And honey.

I thought, well, Christ, might as well stay here.

Upstairs, I had a hot shower and got into a very good bed, and had the best sleep for a long time, and woke up to the telephone ringing.

"That A.G.? What are you doing down there? You got a place at the Daemon, ain't you? What's your lark?"

Jayb's voice.

Worse than any nightmare, or was it?

"I've got some work to do. Any interest?"

"Listen. You turn left out your front door, cross the road, you got the Doll's House Caff on the corner. One hour from now? Got it? Better *be* there. All right?"

The phone clicked.

Red rage, yes, I knew about it, but I felt the truth, and the hurt and burn, then, looking at the lump of white plastic in my fist, I cracked it down as if to expel a fiend, and sat back on the pillows, trying to decide what to do. Even the wallpaper looked red. I could hardly kill him in a public place. I had no wish to face a judge. In any event, "they" would know, and without effort, I would go the same way as Penna. Odd, how she constantly came back, her voice, her walk, the feel of her hand. No day passed that I never thought of her. She was always near, and I wondered in horror if she would haunt me for the rest of my life. It was a new way of thinking, but I knew there was no hope of feeling in any other way. Nothing excused me. I was responsible. Jayb was merely a channel. Because of my gab, she had disappeared. Died?

How to live with the ghost? Ghost, ah Christ, she most certainly was, and she was never far from my thinking day. But what is thinking? We go through the hours, and what are we doing? Thinking? Thinking what? Strange how the brain uses us. Do we use the brain? Who is "we"? Or does the brain direct "us"? Who uses the meat and bone, ligaments, nerves, everything known as us?

Me.

Who am I?

I am somebody summoned to the Doll's House Caff by a man I have such a hate for, I want to kill. But I never wanted to kill anybody before. I never thought of it. Thinking of Penna, I was ready.

I went through the bathroom ritual, shook out a shirt, put on

43

clean underwear, a blue suit, shining black shoes, found a hand-
kerchief, changed money from yesterday's jacket, some of the little fatheaded things that get you ready for the street, all, only to
present myself to Jayb, the faceless one, waiting for me at the
Doll's House Caff—as he called it—the worm I hoped to tread
on.

I went out, to the left, seeing the Doll's House across the road,
on the corner, and waited for the trucks to pass and turn into the
dock gates, tall black grilles keeping the unwanted out of miles
of warehouses, all red brick, run down, almost out of shipping
use, and condemned, but because of apathy, lack of money, or
plain neglect, left to rot.

Poor old London.

Over thirty years after the nights of terror, nothing done except a few high-rise blocks prodding the skyline, monstrous aliens, piling slum on slum, swept streets, cookshops, curry dives,
chopstick joints, two-storey-knocked-together houses, bricked,
boarded, homes of Asians, Africans, Chinese, and the few whites
staying on for a roof and low rental.

The Doll's House said it all, in broken, taped windows, with a
few chipped enamel letters still stuck, enough left beyond the
gaps to tell a sad story of a more generous day, and Roast Beef
and Two Veg Treacle Roll and a Cup of Tea one shilling. Best in
London.

Today's 12p might buy the cup of tea, though not of the qual-
ity in that time, and I knew it, walking in, seeing Jayb at a
corner table, holding a tea bag in a cup of hot water. He nodded
at a chair, dangled a few times, and put a slop in the saucer. The
place had a faint stench of long-stewed cabbage, onions perhaps,
and nests of mice.

"What you doing down here?" he asked, signing to the waitress, an African in a blobby blue overall. "You got a place up the
road, ain't you?"

"Do I have to ask you?"

He bent forward, nodding, and his eyes squeezed threat.

"They like to know where you are," he said, looking up at the
waitress. "Another tea, please. What about bacon and eggs?"

"Not in this place."

44

"Don't blame you. I used to live round here. This was the best carman's pull-up outside the old Covent Garden. That's gone now, too. This was Ol' Mrs. Wheelhouse and her girls. Cooking was marvellous. Why you here?"

"Business."

"What sort?"

"Mine."

He leaned back, waiting till the girl put down the cup and stuck a tea bag in the saucer.

"I don't want to fall out with you," he said, taking a cigarette from a pack and feeling for matches. "You done a lovely job for us. Long time, no slips. 'Cept when that bride came along. She nigh done you, didn't she? You was dead lucky to tell us. Else you be doing ten to fifteen, now. Wouldn't you? 'Stead of that, you'll do your usual run. As, and when. You'll find your tickets and out-of-pockets waiting for you. At the Daemon. And don't make too many moves. And watch the girls. Don't forget, there's *us*. We like to know where you are. See? Here's a sweetener for you. I'll be in touch. The run's Tuesday."

"But what's the reason for keeping me on?"

"Because while they're scragging you, the real bloke's gone through. They'll scrag you in and out the next three months or so. But you'll be clean, see? Then they'll let you go a month or so and scrag you again. Clean. Then they'll leave you alone. You got a good business? Legit? *That's* why you're useful. All weighed, all paid? 'Joy your money. S'long."

All in barest whispers, a clink of coin near the waitress, and the door shut behind me, and the yowl of a rock group went on, background to a bad dream. The package, looked at from a lifted flap, showed twenty-pound notes, possibly from thickness and weight, one thousand pounds. Not to be sniffed at. Yet from his appearance Jayb seemed little more than a street yob, dressed from a slopshop, unshaven, broken boots. But I was learning. If "they" trusted him, then obviously he was not what he seemed. A someone else? And the more dangerous for that.

I realized I had quite forgotten about Penna Cately. The package had taken my mind off her.

A male whore? A snitch?

45

Neither term suited me, or what I liked to think of as my pride. Whatever that was.

But did I take him by the throat?

For possibly a thousand pounds or more, no.

What was I?

A disgust.

Penna cried.

I could almost hear what she said.

But a thousand pounds is no fairy tale, and the days of chivalry went under with Excalibur.

Outside on the step, the door's long creak seemed fanfare to misery. I stood, breathing truck fumes, and a reek of sulphur from factory chimneys sticking up along the road, London's body odour, poor old girl, and none to defend her, or her people, from stink, landhogs, usurers. And bastards.

Such as myself.

And what are we to do? Watch points, and do it right. "Their" way?

Get on with it, or join the dole queue?

But I had a business.

Knowing what I did of Jayb, and "them," how long would I be in charge?

How little time would I enjoy peaceful control of my samples bag? My order book? My special papers. My fonts. My shop. My machinery. My sixteen lads, all specialists. My twelve girls, as good as the men. Jo Hibbs, my accountant, and her three assistants, and Bijrath Shankar, editor-in-charge, flower of the greatest days of *The Times of India*, and constant reminder that mastery is a nice mixture of practice, intelligence, sweat, and courage.

I was responsible for each one of them, and their families.

Without me, they were in the wilderness of East London, an empty, paper-blown desert, with only the crying of hungry gulls to give them courage, not more than drumthump and Bible-punching bellow for hope, and when that was past, a horrid silence of the unburied for company, or solace, or abiding threat.

A space between the trucks got me across the road, and I went down to the bar, fairly crowded with dockers and seamen, in a curious reek of beer casks, crude oil, cigar smoke, and sawdust, and stood at the bar, waiting for the sleep-eyed girl of that morning, now a barmaid, and expert, and not less than a sonsy piece of all right, and that she was, tall, everything in the right place, and nicely rationed, nothing too much or too little, but just an eyeful, dead on, and lovely.

"A whiplash, please," I said, into her smile.

"Whiplash? Never heard of it. Tell me what."

"Pernod and Slivovitz, dash of lemon juice, and soda."

"Hold tight. I'll get the bottles. You can show me."

"I'll show you without the bottles."

She pulled in her mouth, smiled deeper, and let go in a *phwatch!*

"I'd go for that," she said. "I'll get the bottles first, though, eh?"

She brought them back, and while I poured a measure of each, she squeezed a lemon, put the glass on the bar, and rested her elbows, chin on fists.

"Where'd you learn that?" she asked. "It's proper foreign. First time here?"

"I hope it won't be the last. Want one?"

"No fear. I don't drink. Not even beer. But I do. I fancy you."

"And I've got to shove off in half an hour?"

"You what?"

"Fact. I was just coming up for the bill."

She leaned forward.

"Listen," she said. "Won't do you no harm to stay over the weekend. I don't often fancy a bloke. When I do, I want it. Do any harm to put it back a day or two?"

Clean, fresh, no lipstick, no eye-stuff, only crystal blood in her eyes, how often does it come your turn? Never, with me. A real Cockney, giving me the Jolly Roger? I could hardly believe it.

"All right," I said. "Till Sunday morning."

"Tonight, and tomorrow? Suit me lovely. Have your dinner here. I'll have something cooked special. Come down here afterwards till I close up. Then we'll go to my place. Stay there till Sunday morning. Let me taste that."

I slid the glass across, and she sipped, lapped, widened her mouth, shook her head.

47

"A drink's one thing," she said, and pushed the glass to me. "A lavatory cleaner's another. That's what it ought to be called. Come to think of it, be a smashing nightcap for a bloke making a nuisance of hisself. Eh? Chucking his weight about? I'll have to remember it."

"Have many of them?"

"Not so many now. Ten years ago, when I was a kid, yes. Then my old manager, he either worked them a mickey—a little pellet in a glass of beer—or else he belted 'em. He never stood no nonsense. A man had to hold his drink, else stick to ice cream. I still think the same. You're not going to get soppy on me, are you?"

"I never got soppy on anybody else. Why on you?"

"Don't quite know. This little bloke came in while you was out. Asking a lot of questions. I told him to have done, and clear off. You the boss here? he says. Yes, I says. All right, he says. Give him this. And he gives me this little brown envelope. Careful how you go, he says. If he don't get it, I'll come back. Won't be too nice. All right? And off he goes. So I put it in your room. What's the lark?"

"You know how it is," I said, playing it well down. "People get in a firm. They think they're important. They're given a job. They do it. Their way. Is it upstairs?"

"It's where I put it."

"I'll go up. Make sure."

"Stay there till I come for you. We'll go to my place. Other side of the house. Champagne suit you?"

"Lovely. I'll be waiting."

"On. You ain't finished your drink."

"Taking it with me. Don't be long."

I took her wave, and went upstairs to my fine, big room, shadowy in drawn curtains, and found the package, in the same brown envelope, a wad of notes, and a book of tickets, London to Venice. I thought I knew why. A lot of stuff was coming out of Yugoslavia, Greece, Cyprus, and Turkey.

A lot of items were coming into the big auctioneers, Sotheby's and Christie's, but more to the smaller dealers, and I had a quick idea, going up the stairs of the Lomax. On the first-floor window ledge, a lovely alabaster Andromeda, only about a foot high,

48

shone white in the sun. I knew, because my uncle, a ship's broker, often bought items from seamen, and over years collected a fine room of exhibits, and then went to two and three, and built another room on the house, and made a name, and he taught me little enough, and yet, quite enough, and left me his collection, and by reading and going to museums, I knew Andromeda, and wondered how she got there, and I asked where she came from.

"I've got shelves of them, downstairs, from my father," she said, surprised. "What are they except dust catchers? Why make work?"

"They might be valuable?"

"Dust, and insurance. What for? Who's interested? Let them stay in the dark."

"Why not sell them?"

"My father thought a lot of them."

"In the dark?"

"They were always on show in his time here. Couple of years."

"Not now?"

"Labour's too expensive. All that takes days to dust. Why?"

A frowning defence in the eyes—but suddenly—and a tremor in the voice, rising.

"Well, I don't know," I said. "Buy something useful? If it's only an insurance policy. They might be worth a bit."

"Are you in insurance?"

"No. Printing."

"Stick to it."

"Let me see them. I might buy."

"Might. What are you? A tout, or something?"

"Hold on. I'm no tout."

"No? Well, shove off. I don't want you here. Sorry I ever talked to you. You've got half an hour. Else you pay for another day. And be careful. There's a few lads here'd think it a right lark to put a boot in. Twig?"

Funny how a few seconds can alter everything. Whatever strange ideas I had about her were wrong. Anything I imagined was ridiculous.

She went out, showing a small waist, fat calves, leaving the door open. I packed, especially puzzled, and disappointed about

49

the jaunt, and just as I shut the catches, the porter came in, looked about, took the bag, and I went after him downstairs. I paid him at the desk, and waited outside for the taxi, looking at the red brick ruin of the dock buildings beyond the railings, and sniffing flume from trucks going to the container depot. I wanted to scream laughing, because I had been in line to weekend with a girl I had never heard called by her name, and now where was I? She was as much a mystery as anyone I could see passing in the street.

A prime piece.

With something to hide?

All right.

What?

Standing there, I thought of the statuary downstairs, in the dark.

How could I get in there?

That would be silly enough. The police had opened a file. All I needed was another entry. Breaking in was not for me. I needed a pro team. Who would know? Jayb, of course.

The cabman came, and I stopped him along the Whitechapel Road to call Jayb's number. Again the clatter and rattle, and music, and the same man's voice.

"Would you tell Jayb I want to see him?"

"Hold tight. He's here. You the bloke called before?"

"Yes. Anything wrong?"

"Nothink's ever wrong here. Hold tight."

But in the ear-bungle of the put-down phone I heard a warning. I was throwing myself to the Jayb lions. Any favour he did would require payment, besides guaranteeing another entry in the police file if a burglary job were traced to me.

I hung up, and went out to the cab. London seemed to have become pale blue, a cloudy shadow making the reddest buildings greyish, and all the others barely seen, marvellously proper in a city of the people of the tombs.

Most of them were still there, sporting their bones, calling. No wonder nobody wanted to build. Who would pay good money to live over shrieks? And the way things were going, it could happen again. But quicker, and no time for shrieks. They could become a luxury.

We turned down at the Daemon garage, and the flowers and shrubs were like a kiss, and all the window boxes seemed to wave. Botti and Celli, in wellies, jeans, and T-shirts were hosing their orange Mini, and dropped tools to run, arms wide.

"A.G.," Botti shouted, "we missed you. Where've you been?"

I put an arm round both of them, feeling lovely breasts pressed against me, knowing again the mourn of beauty denied.

"Paris and points east," I said. "Next time, why don't you come with?"

"Couldn't afford it," Celli said, while I paid the cabman. "We just got the phone bill, the electricity, the rent, and the bloody rates. How they expect you to live, Christ knows."

"And he won't tell," Botti said. "Listen, we'll finish washing down, and you come up and have a cup of tea. Mmh?"

"Or a drink in my place?"

"You're on. Be there in twenty minutes? We missed you."

"Nice to know. Who else does?"

Botti looked the truly-blue eyes.

"Be surprised," she said. "Not many live decent. Or talk decent. Be surprised how many missed you. We'll be there."

Munn, of Security, came from the back door and helped me with the bags up to my set, and Mrs. Rapajan had been in to give the place a splendid shine and put flowers in all the vases, and I felt at home, where I most wanted to be, and never wanted to go away, and that's exactly what a good woman's touch will do for a man.

When he had gone, I took Andromeda from under my overcoat, and put her on the right-hand corner of the desk.

She shone all her two thousand years or more of magnificent Grecian summers, through the Spartans and Athenians, beyond Ulysses and Agamemnon, even to the green fire of Helen's eyes, and I almost felt the caress of vestal hands, and heard the tinkle of those years-ago timbrels in barefoot bacchante drum-dance and the skirl of shepherds' pipes.

How does a sculptor bring that marvel of thought from a piece

51

of stone? For *me. I* marvelled. Did anyone else? Or was I imagining something not there? But how do you imagine something not there? How *do* you imagine, anyway? It seemed ridiculous to waste time on it. All very well, but there must be an answer. There had to be. Who could give it?

I looked up at the rows and tiers of books. I had most of the philosophers and over the years I had read them, without any proper light or real understanding. They all talked words. The words got them into trouble, created verbal sandbanks, bogs, labyrinths, and they still went on, leading themselves—and us—into silly troubles of Yes-it-is-No-it's-not, and nobody had an answer of any weight, or any solid reason for what they said, or what we were, or where we might be going, though *we* knew we were going into a hole, or a flame, and nobody could tell us what it was all for, or for whose benefit, or why any of it had to *be*. It seemed ridiculous that the children we loved must one day cry for us, as we had cried for our own mothers and fathers, or not, if families died as they had in the desert of East London, and South, in all Thamesland, the womb of Lady London, poor old girl, and not a bastard to stand up to defend what was left of her.

Bastards.

Beyond the law. Nothing to do with marriage. *Bâtard.* Rotten Norman. French. Lack of Saxon. Nothing to do with out-of-wedlock. Simply beyond the law of that disastrous day. But well into ours. Bastards. Landgrabbers. Pimps. And the rest, of raging stench. Living off the dead. Carrion-eaters.

But what made me think so? Years of reading, seeing, listening, thinking? Perhaps. But most of all being with the survivors, or their children, the few, the forlorn, the defenceless. I was so often mired in savagery thinking about them, and poor old Lady London. I had no notion that others agreed until I had drinks that afternoon with Botti and Celli, and their friends of the Boudicaa Club. They came up to my set in ones and twos, and it was only when I finished pouring drinks, and poured one for myself, that I saw I was one man among more than a dozen girls, and more coming in. It was like looking at a flower show.

"Just a moment," I said. "What's this?"

"You told us we could bring a couple of friends," Celli said, smiling into her glass. "So we did. The others sort of joined in. What do we do? Boot them down the stairs?"

"They all live here?"

"Certainly."

"I never saw many of them before."

"How often are you here? Besides, most of them live on the other side of the garden."

"Why did you invite them? Listen. I invited you and Botti. A couple more or less, all right. But not a bloody circus?"

"Anything wrong with them?"

"Not that I can see."

"So? Let's have a drink. Eh?"

"All right."

I sat in the Queen Anne chair. Most of them lay on the floor, all hipbones and haloes of hair from late sun through the western window. Why should I complain about beauty?

Botti stood, and clapped to stop the talk.

"Hold tight," she said. "Look. This is a marvellous time for us to meet and try to get something done. It's all the kindness of A.G. here, so I won't waste time. I wish to Christ I could put it to you right. Be impossible. Listen. I'll tell you what I really think? I'd love to get houses built out there for people like us to live in. Get married. Settle down. Have a decent home life. Any idea what chance we got?"

They were so gentle. So beautiful. All of them. Quiet. Not a move. But they seemed electric. Waiting?

Botti put the glass down.

"None," she said. "That's what. *No* chance."

"Wait a bit," I said. "I thought you didn't want anything to do with men *or* marriage?"

"That's right. Why not? Some girls want to marry and have a house. Get a man. Have a baby. How? In a couple of rooms? Me and Celli want to marry. We never want to see anybody else. But we want a house of our own. A garden. Not like this. It's only lodgings. It's not *ours*. Never will be. And all that wreckage of streets outside there's never going to be built on. Can't get planning permission. No money. Who says so? Who's the dead

53

hand at the top? What's his name? Can you find out? We've tried, and we can't. Who *is* it?"

Nobody moved far enough to lift a drink.

"A moment," I said. "How would you two get married?"

"Easy. There's ways round it when you know."

"And babies?"

"Well, we thought about a sperm bank. But we'd rather know the father. Still, that's not the question. How do we get this housing mess put right? That's what we're here for."

"Mr. Waygoes owns a lot of land," I said.

"He told us to forget it. There's no money. And if there was, there's no permission. We're stuck."

"What's the next move? Write to our Member of Parliament?"

They all rolled, laughing. Botti clapped her hands.

"Listen, A.G.," she said, almost as a joke, "we've *been* writing. Members, Minister of Housing, Prime Minister, the lot. We always get a reply. Matter's being studied. That's *it*. Now, how do we get moving? We want homes, out *there. How?*"

"Newspapers?"

"It's been done. There's too much money on the other side. Nothing."

"If there's too much money on the other side, what's it waiting for?"

"High rents. That's what Mr. Waygoes says. Till they can see a big return on capital, they'll turn any town-planning down. They don't want the working class back here. They want to build a—well—sort-of-a—far better job than Paris. Or anywhere else. In the world. They can do it. No hurry. They can wait. The money's there."

"What's the answer?"

"That's what we're here to try finding out, isn't it?"

I looked round at them, all beautiful of their many types, all, I supposed, capable at their various jobs. And absolutely helpless. Not an idea, or any notion, far less any thought of action that might get them somewhere beyond where they were. Toward the end of a dream. And reality, where they might come alive.

"We're going to go on like this," Celli said. "While that lot's waiting to make some money."

"That's all that counts," Botti said. "You've got no money? You've got no *nothing*. That's *us*. And all that land out there, what is it? Hitler's garden. Who owns it? Do *we? Do* we? Then why are we waiting?"

"For what?" I asked. "If there's no money, what's the use?"

Celli turned to me, a real Cockney girl in a white Cockney rage, and that's right, she was white in the face, and seemed white in the eyes, and I caught the heat of her breath, that to me smelled white.

"Who *are* we?" she whispered, fierce as a snarling cat. "Just a load of *cunts?* Is that *all* we are? That's all they *think* we are."

"What about the men?"

"What about the *what?*" Botti screamed, bending down. "Men? Listen, give 'em their beer and their bloody football, what else they want? TV? Continental matches? Everything stops. I cheer every time England dies. What a dead rotten lot. It's a blind for the other dead pricks to do nothing."

"Who?"

"The politicians, the local lads, the shits in the chairs, on the Boards? Who else got charge in this country? Y'know? Take their eye off TV, football, and beer. Sport. What more they want? What about the wives and kids? Anybody interested? 'Course not. They want more money? Why not? It'll go on motorbikes, cars, beer, foreign holidays, and birds, hi-fi sets, anything you can think of. Put them up there where they want to think they'd like to be. Wife and kids? Nowhere. Wife? Who's she? You can always get another. Always some wet-arse waiting. Eat cheap. No-cost pad. Why not?"

The hip-bones were getting up in lovely colours from the western window's darkening light. They made a rumbling whisper.

"It's dead right," a girl called at the back. "We've got no chance. No say."

"One reason we're here," Celli said. "We've got to make up our minds. What to do. Processions? No good. Lot of people walking about? No. Writing to the lads in office? No. Nothing happens. What's the next move?"

Everybody quiet, in shadow of the dying sun, all beautiful, lovely light and colour in their hair, all silent.

"How about talking to Mr. Waygoes?" I said, in the quiet, except for a tugboat's saucy hoot. "He'll know a lot more."

"Won't tell," Celli said. "He's got the land. He wants the permits. Why don't he get them?"

"He's in with the rest," somebody said, from the darkness.

"I don't want to think that," Botti said quietly. "I've talked to him. I think he's a real man. But he can't do what they don't want him to. There's the law."

"Who says what the law is?" a girl's voice called.

"Now you're asking questions," Celli said. "I reckon we gone far enough. Come on. Clean up. Glasses washed. Everything put away. I wish to Christ we could do everything as neat. I wish we could say, please build those houses. For us. Why can't we?"

"Nobody listening," Botti said, collecting glasses from hands in half-light. "Who wants to listen when there's hundreds of millions on the other side?"

"What gives you the idea?" I asked.

"Have a look at the map," she said. "Didn't you ever see it? My darling daddy was a local surveyor. Till he got killed. Listen. I was born just long enough ago to see this as it is now. Nothing more. They built those bloody horrible high rises, and stopped. Why? No profit? Why didn't they build a few more? People didn't like them? Why not? Upended shit-holes? What else were they? Half a dozen streets upended in one high rise? Who wants to live there? People wanting a roof? They soon find out. *We* want a *house*."

"And a bit of garden," the same voice called. "'S a use of a house, and no garden? We'd like to grow something."

"House *and* garden," Botti said, clattering glasses. "How?"

"How many women do you deal with," I asked. "Women, let's say, thinking the same as you?"

"Lots. We're all in touch."

"All right. Why not fill the mailbags?"

"Who to?"

"Your M.P.'s."

"What good's that do?"

"Day after day? Packed mailbags? Every letter to be answered? How many? How many thousands of women are there?

56

Put out the word. Tell them to write. Write what they think. What they *want*. Keep on. Week after week. Month after month. What have you got those people in Westminster *for?* To do what you *put* them there to do? Why aren't they doing it? Write to them. You want to know. You were good enough to give them your vote. Now you want to know. Simple?"

"A.G., listen, we love you," Celli said, whisking a dry glass from the cloth to a hand putting it into the rack. "What good's it going to do *us?*"

"Doll-darl," I said. "There would be the god-damnedest snarl of mailbags. That's the first thing. Then there's the business of replying. But in the meantime, there's the second week's mailbags. Then the third. Fourth. Fifth. And on. Get the idea?"

In the dark evening, no light, only quiet, and shadows, clink of glasses and plates.

"Wish I thought it'd get us somewhere," Botti said. "We could do it."

"Why don't you? Anything to lose? Not a couple of dozen. Not a mouldy hundred. Get the other gals going. A couple of thousand? Ten thousand? Twenty? You've *got* them. They're *here*. They can write. They can lick stamps. Fill up the mailbags. Drive them daft. Don't give them a moment's peace. You know the Commons has always been a beer club? Make it something else. You didn't elect a beer club or a lot of boozers. Make them earn their money. That's what they're there for. And, of course, a bit over a hundred and forty quid a week, plus perks. Not a bad job?"

The murmur grew to loud talk, and Botti clapped her hands.

"Come on," she said. "Glasses up. Out. Make up your minds. Let me know. It's the best idea we've had. If it works or not, least it's something. Better than nothing."

"Why can't we get what we want?" that voice asked, from the dark.

"You haven't got the money," I said. "If you *had* the money, you still wouldn't get the permits."

"Why not?" the pretty voice said. "Money's money."

"Depends *whose*," I said.

"Come on," Celli said, flashing a dish towel. "Everybody out.

Out. Finish. A.G., we love you. You've done a lot. All right. Everybody out."

I watched them all go, in waves of hands and thank-you's, in half-light, most unknown, and felt a sadness I found it hard to define. I felt sad for them. Why? I had no answer. But I felt sad, almost as a stone in the gut, watching them walking into darkness, until Almond, downstairs, switched on the lights.

I didn't know what to think, or how.

After all, men were just as helpless. It was a city of men and women. And children.

But it seemed to me to be a bloody shame that a lot of good girls, with a splendid idea, were stopped, blinded, baffled by the pot-bellies on councils, committees, or in Parliament, all throwing weight against what should be done, what ought to be done, what shouted to be done.

Why was it denied?

The telephone's ring seemed to strip skin off the evening.

Celli picked it up with a towel-hand, holding a glass to the light.

"Yes," she said. "He's here."

I seemed to know.

"Jayb here. Listening?"

"Yes?"

"Got a run tomorrow. Packet'll be there next five, ten minutes. Different job. Have a nice time. That bride at the Lomax. Any trouble?"

"No."

"Ah. She's a bit of a lush piece. Just old enough to know what she don't want. I could take me teeth out for her. She was left that place by her dad. She's the boss. And she bosses. Give you any trouble?"

"She threw me out. I wanted to buy a collection of statuary. She's got it all downstairs, somewhere. It was her father's. She didn't like me wanting to buy. Why not?"

"I see. We don't like that, do we?"

"I didn't. It was unreasonable. Unless she's got something to hide?"

"Well. You go off tomorrow. No trouble. All right?"

"Yes."

"She'll be put to rights. So long."

I knew by her eyes that Celli heard, and knew.

"Sounds like a dead rough boy," she said. "You in with them?"

"No," I said. "He's got his way. I've got mine."

"I wouldn't mind getting in *your* way. I wouldn't like getting in his."

"You might be right."

"You wouldn't let it happen, would you?"

"What?"

""Well. Way he said it, some poor cow's going to get it."

"Not if I can help it."

"You didn't say much?"

"What *could* I say?"

"You could have said *no*."

"Look. What's the use? Face facts."

She nodded, polishing glasses, holding them up, putting them in the cupboard.

"I've been telling Botti all this time, don't get any big ideas about what you're going to do, or not going to. It's all mapped out somewhere else. You haven't got a chance. Know why? No money. And in this world? No money? That's a sin. Going to argue?"

"*No*."

"That's what I say about this lot out here," she said, folding the towel in half darkness. "Nothing's going to happen. We'll never make it. We can talk. We can dream. But the *only* one's going to be the one with the money. Know who he is?"

"No?"

"You find out. I'm off. Thank you, A.G. You're all right. Now. Where's this silly cow, Bottsi-wotts?"

"Why don't you both have dinner with me?"

"I'll tell you. I've got a stew on. You come and have dinner with us. Like stew?"

"I'm on."

"Half an hour? Lovely."

Stew?

In that first year of evacuation I remember Mrs. Parran, a

skimp, white, frilly apron always floppy at the shoulders, bony arms and legs, cutting up the scrags of meat, and knocking the frost off bones, and then filling the big aluminium pot with blue enamel bowls of water, and giving Mrs. Treece a hand to lift it on the fire, and the grind of knives through cabbage stalks, and the rip of the leaves, and us washing potatoes and carrots—the long, dried, and woody—and sometimes turnips and swedes, and the peel-talk of onions, soft enough to sink a thumb, and us four- and five-year-olds going out to gather firewood, twigs, branches, saving money for the sailors and soldiers and airmen, and then at the bell, sitting down to eat the ladleful of gobs and salty water.

Stew. For years.

Or fish. Boiled. There was no fat. Boiled fish, with onions and potatoes.

It was going on while that London, outside there, was being flattened, night after night.

Stew and boiled fish, on one side, wreckage and murder on the other.

Lovely balance.

It stopped, for me, when Uncle Lionel came in one day, and pointed to me, and took my hand, and we went to London in the train, and then the Tube, and out in ruined streets to a tearoom, and I had tea with sugar, and two sponge cakes. I had never tasted such a feast, till the next morning, when I shared half an egg with Uncle Lionel's girl, same age, Christina. The family were killed in a car crash. I hated cars ever since. I went back to the solicitor, Mr. Grosvenor, and stayed with his family, though I have no real memory of them, and then school. If I think of it, it's stew, and fish, and boiled puddings, and quiet times in the library. Thinking of childhood, I have a blank. Of early boyhood, a blank. I put everybody away. I think children defend themselves like that. They refuse to remember. I have a clear memory of Mrs. Parran, God bless her bones, and the salty taste of her stews, because I heard her say, Poor little bastards, how are they going to live on this? She had nothing else to give us.

But we lived. I did. London was being flattened every night, but I was getting Mrs. Parran's stew, or the fish, and I lived. So many of us did.

To hate stew, and fish.

God love the Mrs. Parrans.

At least, they kept us alive.

When she dropped something—and she was a bit shaky—and said, Sod it, she always turned to see if we were there, and pointed a finger under her nose, and said, Now, you never heard me say that, did you? and we always said, No, Mrs. Parran, and she always said, That's right. Never hear what you didn't ought to. It's somebody's own private business. It happened so many times, and I still hear myself saying, Sod it. It doesn't seem so bad. It *doesn't* seem so bad. But in those days it was supposed to be awful.

What happened to words?

When did I learn to speak?

I have no memory of any lesson. Of teachers, only a shape, and not a real shape, but the sort seen in opaque bathroom glass. The only one I remember was Miss Langdon, that afternoon, pulling up her stockings behind the desk, and she knew I was there, and went on pulling, all the way up, and smiling, the bitch. I know it now. Poor girl. To tempt a small boy was poultice to her starvation.

Celli's stew was different, a rich mix of fine beef and fresh vegetables, with three other girls, and myself the only man among five women, not that I minded. But in the middle of talk about the digs, and finding pre-Roman remains in the latest, the telephone rasped, and Botti got up to answer in the next room. I was saying something about who might be digging for us in two thousand years' time, and she stood in the doorway, crooking a finger at me.

"Mr. Waygoes," she whispered, and danced her thighs, as if God was out there, and God knows why, but I went out as to the Last Trump.

"Mr. Waygoes?"

"Yes. Mr. Bessell? Could you make it convenient to meet me at ten-thirty?"

"Certainly."

"Right. My set, A One, ten-thirty? Thank you."

That *clack* seemed an integral part of the conversation.

61

I went back to the table, and Celli brought the covered plate from the oven.

"Ten minutes," I said. "Then I have an audience with God."

"God?" one of the girls said. "Why?"

"Look round you. Except for personal possessions, everything you see, in or out of the windows, and what you tread on, belongs to him."

"Not right," the same girl said. "That's why I'm a Marxist."

"Give over," Botti said. "You're not in Trafalgar Square."

"And I've got to get going," I said. "Mustn't be late."

"Bootlicker," the girl said.

"All right, Thel', that's your *lot*," Celli said, and stood. "Nobody's insulted at this table. Waltz your arse out of here, and don't come back."

"Boojwah shit," Thel' said, walking to the door. "You'll find out."

"Not from you," Celli said. "Anybody else want to follow? You, Dah'?"

Dah' looked at her plate, shook her dark head.

"Always knew it, you dirty wart," Thel' shouted, from the corridor. "Don't ever come near me again. Nothing but a bloody wart. Living off what's there."

Botti slammed the door.

"You can stay with us," she said. "We'll have the van round there in the morning for your stuff. She's no good. Never was."

"Never mind, darl'," Celli said, with a hand on Dah's crying shoulder. "Better off without her. I've watched her. She's no real Commie. She's in with the bombers. You'd get thirty years. You're well out of it."

I stood.

"That's the best stew of the century," I said. "Or let's see them come up with better. Wait for me. I'll bring the coffee and brandy."

Botti gave me the driest whiff of a kiss on the cheek, and I ran for the stairs, and down, to A 1, and rapped, at one minute from ten-thirty.

The door swung in a *thud* and I walked into the foyer, and the door shut *thud* and I stood in silence, listening, feeling it as a garment, a little frightened though I have no notion why, and wanting to shout.

"Mr. Bessell," a voice said, loud, over a speaker, and turned down. "Please do come in. I *love* punctual people. The door in front, please. My man's off. I'm reduced to electronics. Handle to the left."

I lifted the twist of bronze, and walked into a room at least four times the size of my largest, walled in books and oils, carpeted on shining parquet, and Mr. Waygoes sat at a desk in front of windows at the far end, holding up an arm in greeting.

"Can't get up," he called. "Gout. Awful, isn't it? Supposed to be port. Never touched the stuff. Do come in. Make yourself comfortable. Drinks over there. Please help yourself. I can't move, damn it. Ever had gout?"

"No."

"Lucky. Bloody painful. Hurts even to think. I wonder what the poor old lads in past centuries had to put up with? Shakespeare was crippled with it? I don't blame him for dying youngish. Agonies of the damned. And supposing he had a bladder complaint into the bargain? Or, let's say, piles? That's a pretty one. Fashionable word's haemorrhoids. Well, they used those black things—leeches—didn't they? Poor Doctor Johnson. How he must have groaned. In vain, of course. A mighty brain eaten by worms of one sort or another. Evils that flesh is heir to? Really is too awful to think about. The suffering of people down the centuries. What? We've got biotics. What did they have? Leeches? Possets? Alchemies? Think about it long enough, it blights the mind, doesn't it? And what about teeth? They go rotten. Then you haven't any. What do you *do*? Chew with your gums? Poor Shakespeare. Poor Johnson. Poor anybody. Except today. We've got all sorts of wonderful stoppers. Surgeons, physicians, and whatnot. Are we any the better for it? Have we poetry to match Shakespeare's? The wisdom of Doctor Johnson? Where's it gone? I think we're breeding a different lot. I listened to what they called a pop concert just now. A bestial howl of maniacs. Have you a drink? Do bring it here, there's a good chap. I get a twinge now and again. Quite shattering. I hear you're off again, tomorrow?"

63

The room seemed to clutch me. I was looking at the crystal in my hand without seeing it. A burning hole appeared in the middle of grey space. I listened to the high-pitched chatter and then sudden—deadly—change in voice. That question could only mean that somebody had told.

Told what?

I knew I had said no word. But the notice had come over the switchboard downstairs. Somebody listened in, and informed? What interest would anybody else have?

"I'm not sure I understand," I said.

"Oh, now, come along, Mr. Bessell, there's no time for this sort of thing, is there? You know perfectly well what I'm talking about."

"I don't."

"I like your defensive armour," he said, almost playfully. "But there's really no time for niceties, d'you see? Among other things, I'm in diamonds. That's one of the reasons you're living here. Jayb is an employee of mine. Tomorrow you go to Lausanne. You have a drop there. You'll find your tickets in your set. You'll go on to Venice. You will meet the six o'clock train from Belgrade. There are two girls in third class. Two in second class. Two in first class. You will take them to three hotels. They'll have two days' rest. They're booked by air to San Francisco, via Paris, London, and New York over a period of eight days. It will be your business to see that they are properly taken care of."

"I'm going to tie myself up, getting them here to there?"

"Use your intelligence. They're all ticketed. Those tickets are in your set. None of them's under suspicion. What's so difficult?"

"And after that?"

"You return here for the next run. To Bucharest."

"Diamonds?"

"No more. The finger's on you."

"Then why bother?"

"You have a good business. An excellent cover. Why not?"

"Aren't you making yourself a little too obvious?"

As if everything had rolled into a huge smoking ball, I saw his eyes, blue, pale, misty, baggy in a pink face, long white hair drooping over his ears, mouth no more than an opening for a cigar butt, hands as claws trying to take something back, and a curious little twitch of the nose, here and gone, twitch and gone, just at the tip.

"If I am obvious to you, very well," he said, and took out the cigar. "I speak to you in this manner because you are known to the police. You're too near. That's why I'm talking to you. You may say what the devil you like. There's no torture here."

"But what the devil *are* you talking about?"

He looked at the cigar, and tapped the ash, almost as a treaty signed and sealed.

"Look," he said. "For the first time, you're in a police file. Don't you understand what that means? It's countrywide. It's available to every other police force. You're damned."

"Then why am I given runs?"

"You've got the cover. Private business. What's better?"

"But the girls?"

"Deal with them. They know where they're going. Let them go. They get plenty at the other end."

"Miserable business."

"All right. Miserable. But it's business. It goes on. Want to say something?"

"Ha. *Shit.*"

"I'll step round it. It's so much easier. *Out.* Now, what have you got?"

"I wish to God I knew."

A tune, a thread of sound over distance, came from a passing barge, and faded. Again I was in wonder that two humans could talk drivel for minutes on end and say nothing of any value to each other, far less to a listener. But I was determined that I would have an understanding.

"Are you using this police file business as blackmail?" I asked him.

"Nothing so stupid. I could very easily put you away with an anonymous message, here, France, or anywhere else. You're useful to me. I'm useful to you. You have a healthy bank account because of me. In a few years you'll be free. Of anybody. Live where you please. Anywhere on earth. Who else could do that for you? One human being, completely free?"

"But aren't *you?*"

"I wish I were. *No.* I'm *not.*"

"Why not?"

"I have this ridiculous scheme. I want to re*build* East London. This area. It's enormous. I own a lot of it. In lots. Here and there. But I want to build towns. *Not* a city. I don't want cathedrals. I want to bring people back here to *live*. Decently."

"I'm with you."

"Good. Then you won't get in my way when I want to take your share of Green Pepper Street and shift you over to Brittle Candy Lane. It's no further away than where you are now. Simply cross the road. There are ten houses in good condition. Cost you nothing. My people will shift you. No charge. Overnight. Well?"

I knew the street, of larger houses, bombed in cracks, empty-windowed, possibly without light or sewage.

"What utilities have they?" I asked.

"Everything. Rather better than you have where you are at the moment. And far more space. Yes or no?"

"I'll look at it."

"My men are in there at this moment. Tomorrow you'll be in Brittle Candy Lane. Your present stationery will be a loss. But now you have an even more picturesque address. I'll pay for the new. Anything else? Your staff and neighbours are informed."

"In other words, I don't matter?"

"Of course not."

"Is that what you think of me?"

"Why not?"

Feudal baron and serf?

Any difference, except in time?

Another peasant upstart to be cracked on the head? Why stop there? A nobody? A Jack Straw? Nothing between now, and when? Eleven hundred, 1200, 1300 A.D.?

A. G. Bessell. A messenger boy. Go here, go there. Do this, do that. Jayb will let you know.

A. G. Bessell.

Who?

I got up, without looking at those bluish washout eyes, and

grasped the furniture toward the door—my legs were trembly—
and raised the handle, and got out on the landing, and leaned
against the wall outside.

I asked myself who I was.

Who *was* I?

Beyond a number in the National Census, the voting register,
the local rates, water, electricity, gas, a bank account number,
credit cards, rental of a set, who *was* I? A voter? User of utilities? Client of a bank? Owner of a prosperous printing press?
Employer of thirty-odd people? What else? A fair knowledge of
the country, and most of Europe?

All that.

What did it amount to?

A hunk of mobile meat inside a tailored bag of linen and
tweed, ready to jump at any order from one presumed to be superior, wealthier, owning more.

Superior in what? Owning more what?

Obviously, money.

I had plenty, but I was still at beck of Jayb, and that beck was
shadow of Mr. Waygoes, and every time I obeyed there was
more money for him, rather less for me, and Jayb made what he
could.

A pretty pattern.

For those few moments, all I knew hung. I could go this way
or that. I wanted to walk out, leave everything, and start again.
In the same moments I knew the crass impossibility. There was
too much to lose, all I had built, saved. But more, that desire to
rebuild East London touched a dream. I had always wanted to,
or help those bent on helping London, poor old girl. I had the
notion of digging out my father's place, and perhaps of finding
some of the little things he and my mother had enjoyed together.
But the chief of the fire brigade had warned there might be
unexploded bombs. The salvage squad, the engineers, sappers,
and all their equipment would be needed at high cost, even if
permits were granted. That was the biggest if. The boys in
charge, and those behind them, had no intention of permitting or
granting permits. They wanted the lot. The days, weeks, months,
and then the years of waiting, hoping, faded to a throb in the

back of the mind that one day, perhaps, a permit would arrive, work could begin, and riches, of value only to me, would come from the city. The permit never came. That office changed to another, a different authority, but the same reply. Hope is like the cry of gulls on breeze, here now, and gone.

After the years I stopped wishing, though hope stayed. I clung to the plans of Bayard Waygoes. He had the property, the rights, and the money. But not the permits, and not so much land or as much money as the competition, or any of the political power.

It surprised me that he had so little influence, but the Bosun had once given me a pointer.

"It's all Labour round here," he said, as if that were be-all and end-all. "He's dead straight-fight'em-and-blind'em Conservative. Don't stand a chance. 'Part from that, everything's gone up. It was millions before. It's hundreds of millions now. They can wait their time. We can't. The lot coming after them'll do the job. We won't be here. We'll be dead. That's what they're waiting for. Plus the racial business."

"What's that?"

"Don't you never use your eyes? The bloody place is crawling with 'em. Afros, Indos, anythink you like"o"s, it's all there. All them thousands, they've popped into any hole they could find. Now try chasing 'em to rebuild. Where they going? Who'll take 'em? Waygoes wants to build a city. Low rents. The big boys'll never let him. He'll destroy rental values. Everywhere. They can't have that, can they? Profit bashing? Oh no. Keep him out."

"But aren't they Conservatives? Landlords?"

"You better talk to Mr. Waygoes. Then think about trades unions' weekly dues. Fastest-growing capital anywhere. *They* can afford to build houses. *And* sell them at a nice profit. I don't know a lot about it, except from him. Have a word with him. You'll come out straightened up. Like I was. Ask Mrs. Rafaele."

But talking to Mr. Waygoes was talking to God. Curious the airs we give ourselves. Threescore and ten, plus or minus a few, and the years seem to go in a series of birthday cakes, sweet-toothed fiats, orders, dicta, all part of pretended omnipotence, fed, of course, by servitors, grovellers, and I was one.

68

"You can't see him for at least a month," Mrs. Rafaele said. "His book's full. Anything I can do?"

"Question of building permits," I said. "And a few other items."

"Oh, I wouldn't dare get into that. Have to wait for him. Sorry. Didn't you just see him?"

"I forgot a few things."

She raised eyes and hands in saintly despair.

"One thing you don't do," she said, on a long breath. "Always take a note. He doesn't like careless people. The sort forgets things."

The booted pup knows how I felt.

I took my favourite train to Paris, left the drop in Lausanne, and read my way on to Venice. Customs nowhere made me a mark. That was a pleasant surprise. A night in the sleeper, and an excellent breakfast and lunch got me outside the station in the wonderful gold of a Venetian sunset, and I took a gondola over to one of the world's best small hotels, kept by Emilio and Paolina Agrandarelli and had a homecoming reception with a bottle of spumante, and a kiss from all the five girls, and a smacker from Mamma. I was assured the Belgrade train was on time, and although I hate them, I hired a motor launch, and I was at the station when the train grumble-clanked in, and I could smell trouble from the squad of plainclothes police, and the carabinieri officer just behind me.

I was right. They all walked among the passengers, people met and kissed, and the porters pushed trolleys of luggage, and the platform cleared, and the squad came by with six young women, and went round to the carabinieri office on the other platform. Two of the girls were smiling, one talked to the policeman beside her, and they all looked as if bath-and-bed would be the right mixture.

Telephoning the Daemon or Jayb would have been stupid, linking me with them, and us to the six. I walked over to the bookstall, bought some papers and magazines, and went to the café, taking a table where I could see the office. The first woman came out sixteen minutes later. The second after twelve minutes, and the others followed in a group. They all seemed in good humour, and from the way they walked, with heavy suitcases, only wanted to get out in the air. I waited a few moments, and followed.

Three sat on the steps above the Grand Canal. Three had gone.

I pretended to read a magazine, and made certain of falling over a suitcase, scrambling up, apologising in English, and they smiled.

"It's nothing," one of them said, a tall, fair girl. "You English? Any idea where our consul is?"

"Just down the canal," I said. "It's too late tonight, though."

"They shoved us in third class," another, dark-haired girl, said. "I spent most of what I had going up to first. It was terrible."

"Stuck for some cash?"

"Stuck's right."

"Are you by yourselves?"

"No. There's three more. They're in that café, down there. They offered to pay for us. But we said no. Can't start scrounging this early."

"You go down and join them, and let me worry about the bill. Question of an hotel tonight? No worry. I'll get a porter to carry your bags. You're home and dry."

"Somebody was going to meet us," the fair girl said.

"If it looked as if all six of you were pinched, that somebody'd keep his head down. Doesn't take too much to get pinched here, you know. What did they want?"

"Oh, where we'd come from, where we were going, what for, all that. They wanted to search us, but we said we wanted to phone the consul first."

"That cooked it," the other girl said, probably from Yorkshire. "We were having none of it. We could have had a go at 'em, any road."

A porter brought a truck, and I nodded to the launch, and walked to the café. The other three were finishing omelettes and glasses of beer at an outside table. Nobody offered an introduction. They talked in whispers, and I sat away from them. As well, because the carabinieri officer strolled by, smiled at them, looked at me, but I was reading the *Herald Trib*, and he went on, and the girls ignored him. He seemed a little huffy.

The porter came for the other suitcases, I paid the bill, and led the way to the launch. The girls seemed to accept me as a leader and followed, oh-ing and ah-ing at the late sunset beauty of the green canal, and gondolas dancing a flash of blades, and giant peaches heaped on stalls. I got them aboard, paid the porter, gave the pilot a list of hotels, and went to the forepeak, away from the cabin, and sat on the roof for a smoke.

The use of the launch is a saving of time. What would take a gondola a couple of hours is a matter of minutes, and I was surprised to find the Bauer Grunwald coming from a different direction. The two girls named on the list went ashore with their baggage, and I went on to check their reservations—in order—and gave each ten sterling in lire, and a red luggage disc.

"I'll be here at ten to seven, sharp, in the morning," I said. "Have a good night's rest. Tie this in your buttonholes. You'll be met at the airport in Paris by somebody wearing the same disc. All your troubles are over. Any questions, ask the hall porter. Come with me."

I took them to the concierge's desk, and showed him the Agrandarelli hotel card.

"These are guests 387 and 389," I said. "If they require anything, they'll come to you. I shall be at this hotel. You know it?"

He raised his hands, looking at the card.

"Agrandarelli? We are friends forty years. Since boys. Everything in order."

"You're safe," I told them. "Go up and rest. The restaurant here is first class. You could meet me in the Piazza San Marco at nine-thirty for a coffee at Florian's. Go out of the door, turn right, straight on a couple of hundred yards, under the archway, and it's in front of you."

The same with the two at the Monaco, and at the Royal Danieli, but they were both two departure days apart. I had picked the tall fair-hair as the brain of the lot, and we made a date for Florian's. At nine-thirty, she was there with a girl from the Monaco, equally nice, and if I fail to explain to myself what "nice" means, at least I know what I feel.

"The others went to bed," she said, turning to the chair I pulled out for her. "We've all had a blistering rotten time. It's been nearly three weeks."

"Why?"

"We came from Beirut."

"What were you carrying?"

"Everything. Anything."

"Where is it?"

"People came aboard here and there."

"How about Customs?"

She rubbed thumb and index.

"When we had to. That's why we ran short."

I looked at her pale-blue eyes, and the Venetian city silver band played Dvořák's dances, a marvellous sound in the Piazza, and all the people strolled as if nothing mattered.

"Need any help?"

"Only money, through Customs. They are the worst bastards."

I listened to the music, and the waiter brought coffee and cognac.

The language seemed to me beyond her station.

(What *is* a station? Accent, school, what?)

"You find them corrupt?"

They both laughed, sliding down in their chairs, fair-hair and dark-hair, mouths open, lovely.

"You don't know the meaning of the word," dark-hair said, leaning forward. "The stuff we got through was millions. We all knew that. But we had to pay plenty we could have kept for ourselves. *Bastards* is the word."

"What stuff was it?"

"Oh, stuff in deposit boxes, banknotes, all that," fair-hair said. "Diamonds, emeralds, rubies, all of it. Gold bars. Everybody getting out. Poor sods. Poor little kids. It was unbelievable. The stuff was dropping everywhere. And snipers. We were lucky to get here. Only because we were girls. They let us past."

"How did you get it out?"

"Under our dresses," fair-hair said. "You can carry a lot of light stuff under that sort of job. Besides, we had a nun with us. Christ, what a nun. It was Georgie, here. She saved us."

She smiled at dark-hair, and they raised glasses.

"But what made you do it?" I asked.

Fair-hair looked at me in the band-platform lights.

72

"Money," she said, and dark-hair nodded. "I'll have enough to start my own business after this. I'll have my own boutique. Won't have to worry about anybody. I'll never go through this again."

"Right," Georgie said. "Fourth time for me. Must have brought out millions. All right. But that's the lot. I'll never go back. Poor, poor people. Nobody interested. A lot of bloody men banging away. Guns and rifles. Did they care? Your children? Mine? Any difference? They're killed. They're wounded. The hospitals are not just full. They can't deal with what they've got. They're bursting through the doors. No water. No electric light. No anaesthetics. Look. I don't want to spoil your coffee."

"Don't worry. All right. What's to be done?"

"By us?" fair-hair said. "Nothing. You can't *do* anything with a lot of vicious bastards like that. If you could see that lovely place, you'd do what we did."

"What?"

"Cry."

I listened to the silver horns, smelling coffee, thinking of Beirut as I had known it. The café on the corner, not far from the Embassy, and the beauty behind the cash register with the red notebook fat with the names and phone numbers of sumptuous girls of all nations, none of them over twenty, but for the business drunks only, the pot bellies, unable to attract on their own except with money. The rest of us had to think of visiting the V.D. clinic, and there were plenty, and not the happiest horror to think about. A lay is lovely, but a lay plus penicillin or something more radical, the hell with it.

"Did you travel the crystals?" I asked fair-hair.

"Of course," she said, sliding her eyes at me, catching light. "Any interest?"

"You clean?"

"Clean as a lovely wash, dear. You worried?"

"Airport Customs are rough. You're going through to London. Rougher. You sure?"

"Certain. Else I wouldn't be here. I know enough about it. What *are* you? Did I ought to be talking to you?"

"I've got your tickets and your money. Why not?"

"This game, you never know. I don't like to think we got this far to get pinched. This is my last run. I want it to be the best."

"So far as I'm concerned, it is. But you've got a run. How do you get rid of it?"

She looked at her watch, and the band flourished into Schubert.

"All right," she said, almost laughing, and looking at dark-hair. "I'll tell you. First you take an anti-dysentery dose. A strong one. Then you swallow the run. One by one. You don't drink anything. Then you eat a big plate of porridge and honey. Then eggs and bacon, kippers, the lot. No fruit. No coffee. On the plane you drink champagne. When you get there, you spread a square of plastic, with lots of newspapers on top. You drink lots of coffee. You wait. When it's ready, you drop it, make sure everything's out, and go through it for what you want. Scoop it all in the john, fold the newspapers small, tear them up, and let them go. Have a bath, and you're ready for the drop. Simple?"

Dark-hair laughed.

"I bet it's no news to you," she said, and got up. "Thanks for the drink. Ten to seven in the morning?"

"I'll be there."

Fair-hair raised a hand, and they walked under the arcade, away, two lush rumps in tight denim, and gone.

I had another cognac, and walked slowly, in and out of the crowd, around the Campanile and down to the Schiavoni, over the bridge, almost to the Biennale, and turned back for the steamer to the Redentore, thinking of a drink at Harry's Bar, but it was too far, and I had to be up at six.

Leaning on the rail of the steamer, watching water purling from the prow as it had down the generations from every sort of ship, seen by men and women of the day, exactly as I saw, I wondered about fair-hair and dark-hair.

They could be called the female mercenary *plus ultra*, except that they risked years in prison instead of execution. Why did they do it?

Money. They could never hope to make as much at anything else.

I asked myself, staring at light in the spray, was money really

74

what mattered? I had to answer, in my case, certainly, yes, without doubt or any excuse.

Money.

For years I had accepted money for what I knew to be unlawful. Without conscience. Or any regard for what I understood to be decent dealing, fair play, or proper conduct. In fact, I had never given a damn that I was an unconvicted criminal. I never thought of it. I liked the travel, I had a perfect excuse in the exercise of my trade, and my Swiss bank account filled up against old age, or whatever.

Why did I think of it in this quiet reach of water, built about by poignant beauty? Why poignant? It called. It called out. In so many voices. Over such a long time.

Venice.

The great bell of the Campanile crawled out across the water, reminding of so many thieves, murderers, or political idiots, chained in cells, living in darkness among the ordure of years, or the months they managed to live, taken from their chains to die, less alive than the lice infesting them.

If I went to prison, at least I would be kept physically clean.

A curious thought. Bottled up, but clean. Hell, with a smell of soap.

I wondered why, recently, I seemed to be thinking of punishment.

I threw it off, remembering six o'clock in the morning.

The bell at the Agrandarelli was one of the old-fashioned chain affairs at the side of the gate that had to be given a couple of tugs to be heard in the house. I heard it, but poor old Gerhard had probably been cleaning the top staircase, and it took him a little time to get down, and he cursed a whisperous pad up the garden, unlocked the gates, and let me in.

"There is a package for the Herr Doktor," he said, in his excellent German-English. "Also two messages. And a nice bedtime drink?"

We had known each other for years, and we always had a cold bottle of beer before I went to bed.

I wondered about the package until I opened the first message, from the concierge of the Bauer Grunwald. The two ladies had paid for their tickets, and the hotel, and left for Geneva on the night train, and he hoped everything was in order.

The second message, from the Monaco's concierge, begged to inform me that the two guests in 257 and 253 had left on the night train to Cannes, but had not paid for the launch to the station, and he hoped he had been correct in assuming that I would repay him, with all respects.

Four birds flown.

One heavy package in hand.

A bomb?

I asked Gerhard to call the Danieli, and had a drink while he prodded the board, but our third bottle of beer was opened before we got the ringle-ringle, and I spoke to the night man. Yes, the two signorine had caught the connection to Frankfurt-am-Main. All the accounts were paid, except the launch to the station.

Six birds flown, here, there, everywhere.

Hopeless to chase them.

To the devil with them.

But why?

With air tickets booked, why take trains before time?

The most sensible job I ever did was take that bulk of air tickets, rip them in bits, and put them down the pipe. I made sure there were no floaters.

Why leave a package for me?

I took it up to my room, weighing it in my right hand. I judged five pounds or a little more.

The knot in the middle I kept a finger on, and slit the string and paper, getting at the cardboard ends, cutting them, seeing the cotton wool and tissue. Keeping a finger on the central knot, gently I pulled at the tissue, and then at the cotton wool padding, opening a small space, and tipped the package.

Stones fell in soft stream, diamonds, sapphires, rubies, emeralds, pearls, a fortune, heaping on the desk top.

But something about a large diamond made me look.

I am not a gemologist, but after so many years I think I know a diamond, or any other stone, for what it is with a fair idea of its worth on the market.

The huge "diamond" I looked at was trash. So were the rest. The pearls were merely costume jewellery. For pennies.

What was this nonsense? Why was I saddled with a package of rubbish? I dropped the lot out of the window into the canal.

"Who brought this?" I asked Gerhard.

"It was a woman. Young. French."

"How do you know?"

"Accent. Manners. *Chic.*"

"She simply left it?"

"Simply.

I took my finger off the knot, and threw the box at the wastebasket through the archway into the next room. I turned to take the fourth bottle from the tray, and the bomb blew scarlet, throwing me on Gerhard, and both of us fell with spurting bottles and shattering glass.

We put out the fire by beating with carpets, and among flame and burning bits, opened the window, letting out the smoke and stench. Gerhard ran to phone the police and fire brigade, and when they hooted alongside the quay, we had the entire Agrandarelli family with us, and hot coffee from Mamma, cognac from Papa, and soft pretty coos from the girls.

I was lucky to have Agrandarelli as translator. The police asked umpteen questions, few anything to do with what had gone on. Police are all the same, and they set questions to trap, but it all centred on the package, and why I had kept a finger on the knot—as I had told them—and why I had accepted the package if I suspected a bomb, and why should anyone wish to kill me? I told them that radio bulletins and news reports had made me suspicious since I had no friends in Venice and no expectation of any parcel.

They went on. Who was the Frenchwoman? How did she know my address? Had I met anyone that evening?

I had to be careful.

I told them of meeting two girls in the Piazza, staying at the Bauer Grunwald, and of two more at the Monaco, and two at the Royal Danieli.

"You are well supplied," the inspector said.

I explained that they had all gone by train that night to other places.

"The Frenchwoman was not among them?" the inspector asked.

"I'm sure not," I said. "Her appearance here was long after the trains had gone."

A sergeant came in to whisper, head away from me.

"How did you meet these women?" the inspector asked.

"At the station," I said. "They were in some sort of trouble, they told me. As a compatriot of two of them, I did what I could. I took them to their hotels. I told the concierge to help them. I gave this address."

"What was in the package?"

"Nothing. Cotton wool. Paper."

"You are not in any terrorist movement?"

Agrandarelli became advocate for the defence in a loud voice and restless hands, and when the sergeant had gone through my briefcase, opening files, accounts, diary appointments in various places, the inspector turned to me.

"How long do you intend to stay here?" he asked, through Agrandarelli.

"My next appointment is in Milan in three days."

"While you are here, what will you do?"

"Enjoy Venice, and the Lido. Eat peaches and look at bikinis. Have you any better idea?"

"We are in accord," he said. "If I want you in the next three days, you are here?"

"With Mr. Agrandarelli's permission, yes."

"The signor is a regular patron, an honoured guest and a friend of this family," Agrandarelli said, bless him. "If there is doubt, come to me."

I called for a bottle of spumante, and we drank after the police had gone, and I had a bath, and fell into bed, and woke while the bells charmed noon, and looked at the smoke stains, and opened the windows, feeling breeze on me, and went to the bellpull to call for coffee and newspapers.

But all the time, in sleep or out, I was thinking of the bomb, meant—obviously—to destroy me, and the six girls—decoys?—

78

equally, got together to put me out of business? One way or another, somebody meant to throw me on the ashpile.

Why?

All the time, whether in the sunny silence of my room, alight with water ripples over the ceiling, and the vases of flowers from the girls, or walking through the *calles,* or in the Piazza, or over on the Lido, gnawing munificent peaches, or looking at bikinis—and there were thousands and all beautiful—the question was there, between my eyes.

Who wanted me out?

It seemed to me it must be Waygoes.

He was top of the heap, and I knew a good deal about him.

I could talk.

That I had no intention was neither here nor there.

I made a snap decision to do nothing except enjoy Venice for the next three days and I started by taking a deck chair and towels and an ice box up on the roof in marvellous sunshine among all the plants in flower, and a breeze off the water.

Lying there I thought back, and realized I was having the first real holiday for a lifetime. Three days doing nothing seemed a dream, but there I was, looking down at the waterway on both sides of the point, watching wine barges pushed by sweeps, and crowded steamers, and gondolas ferrying standees to the other side, and sometimes a little one, muscled by two oars on the cross, bumping in wash from traffic, and the smell of green water, bells wafting, and the Campanile tolling the hours.

That first afternoon, the girls and their friends in bikinis came up and stayed until they had to help to prepare dinner. Agrandarelli's was a family hotel, and everybody worked, even fifteen-year-old Amalfi, a sylph, studying English and mathematics, queen of the books and enthroned behind the cash register. Mamma cooked, and threatened my waistband, but her pasta and the sauce, and the veal escalope and creamed spinach were small experiences, and the lobster and shrimp pie at night with a flaky pastry sent me to bed but dreaming before I got there.

The next day I walked through the calles, and found a café a little way down from the station, with the most excellent espresso and the best croissant I ever tasted anywhere, and wandered on, to the Schiavoni, and the steamer to the Lido, among the crowd of all sorts from everywhere, in every kind of dress, from denims and cheesecloth to blazers and grey flannels, and bikinis and cotton singlets to kaftans and nightshirts. What surprised me, among the cheapjacks, was that any normally intelligent creature would wear an advertisement on breast or rump to promote a name not their own. A crocodile over the left teat was supposedly fashionable. It put idiots in the swim. They could afford it? The rest wore every other type of animal, or a label on their heads, or their backsides, proclaiming they were at least in part of the swim, a pathetic reach to be somebody in a mulch of nobodies and nothing, in a general mart of commercialised squalor.

What the hell kind of a world was it becoming, I wondered, if even the Italians—those individualists—were poisoned? What weakness of personality allowed them to wear the imprimatur of some oaf as an advertisement, as much a tribute to his business acumen as to the snob wearer's desire to impress the even more ignorant?

I lunched at the Excelsior among hundreds of beautiful women, and hundreds not so beautiful—I never saw so many bellies, the bulging saggy greedy guts—but Mamma Agrandarelli had restored my taste buds, and although the kitchen staff did wonders with ice and decoration, the food was not to Mamma's standards, her pasta was streets ahead, the sauce was not to be compared, and the salmon mayonnaise was a slimy failure. But all the others seemed to clatter through, and I went out with that clatter stinging my ears.

What made me into such a curmudgeon? The prospect of a thousand people enjoying themselves—apparently—offended me. Why? Their taste buds were not so responsive as mine? But mine had been nurtured on Mrs. Parran's stews and boiled fish. Where was I the judge? How? But perhaps, starting over long years of scratch, my taste buds—whatever that may mean—had been sharpened to accept something better. Taste had become more important than bulk. Certainly I ate very little, and once taste was satisfied, I stopped eating. Watching somebody carve through a steak made me feel sick.

All these were questions, sailing over the lagoon toward the lights, and I wished that Canaletto had seen Venice by gaslight or electrics, though in his time candles and oil lamps could never have carried far enough, and there would have been no Lido. We are far luckier. We can lean on the rail and enjoy what was built those years ago, that the builders and artists never saw, and we can even go to the bar for a drink.

Mamma Agrandarelli outdid herself with a turkey breast, a slice of ham and a cut of veal, with a chopped anchovy and black olives, in a pastry envelope toasted to a gold crisp, with a mash of potatoes, swedes, turnips, carrots and broccoli heads whipped soft, and after that, her jelly of peaches, white cherries, and greengages, each giving a tartness and sweetness, cooked in dry Orvieto, wine of her birthplace. Agrandarelli came with a bottle of Greek brandy, and an espresso, and I remember speaking in a maze of food and wine, and I pulled myself up the banister to my room, though I never remember reaching the bed.

I awoke in the white tiles of the hospital, with a nun leaning over me.

I was dull in the left arm, in the head, and my breathing was spitty. I felt I had run a fast 440.

A man's head topped the nun's coif.

"You hear me?" he said, and I blinked a nod. "Very well. It's of no importance. You probably got a pill in your drink. Hard luck. You should be fit to leave tomorrow."

I rolled over to sleep, and came alive to hear Agrandarelli arguing in whispers, and I turned, opening my eyes, sharply awake.

"What is it?" I asked him.

He pulled in a deep breath and clasped hands almost in supplication.

"Your room has been robbed," he said. "Everything, everywhere. What is missing I don't know. Who are these people?"

"Don't know and don't care," I said, and sat up. "Be the best of friends. Ask Mamma to pack my stuff. What's the time?"

"Two minutes past seven."

"Get me a sleeper on the Paris train tonight, first class. Include the cost in your bill. Give the girls a kiss for me. I'll go from here. I shall be downstairs to wait for the launch. They can go to hell."

Agrandarelli had friends—not least at Thomas Cook's—and at a few minutes to the hour I was in my compartment, with both suitcases, and my accounts case, door locked, and two bottles of scotch flanked by half a dozen Perrier in solid support. I looked through the accounts case, but it was in order. The suitcase had been beautifully packed—dear Mamma!—all ironed and folded, and again I found nothing missing.

Then what was the reason for knocking me out, or trying to bomb me?

I had a curious feeling. Something was going on I knew nothing about. It sounded stupid. But it was like waiting for the morning mail. You never knew what was in any envelope.

I made up my mind with that first drink I was going straight back to the Daemon to look Waygoes in the eye and ask him what the devil the game was.

A second drink put me to sleep, and all I had to do later was change stations, and it was damnably cold, and get back into bed, and then turn out at Victoria, more or less human, half a bottle of scotch gone, but at least vital, thoughtful, and surer than ever of getting a proper reply.

What I thought I meant by "proper" I shall never know.

A taxi brought me to the Daemon's smile, and a feeling of new life, of being home and embraced by a friend, with Thameside breeze to help and all the flowers bobbing their own kinds of curtsey.

Almond's shy welcome helped, and his big arms made nothing of the suitcases, and I tottered behind, with my accounts case, into familiar warmth, and bowls of blossom and faint smells of beeswax and turpentine, and hanging in the air, a fragrance of years of flowers, all mixed in a scent I knew was only of the Daemon, and his smile, and the love of home.

I fell into the big chair, and sat there, eyes shut for moments, savouring the wonder of my own place, where I could be myself, not a guest, not a visitor, not anybody except myself, where I could walk naked or not at will, among the items chosen by me, treasured by me, loved by me, and that I felt as a certainty loved me and knew I would protect, and utterly, to any extent.

But looking up, from a doze or reverie, suddenly in bright sunlight, I was blinded or amazed, whichever, to find nearly every space filled by statuettes in bronze, alabaster, marble, carnelian, everywhere, a dream of treasure and beauty never imagined. I got up, certain I dreamt, and picked them up, one after another, making certain they were solid, that I was sane.

They were the joys of a museum, the glory of any lover of Greece.

Stolen?

By my friend Jayb? From the Lomax?

I was in commission of a crime.

Should I warn the police? Tell the girl at the Lomax?

Or keep them? Let others find out?

Who was to prove anything?

Andromeda was still there, on the corner of my desk, pale gold, beautiful.

Tell? Report? To the police? Saying what? To the Lomax? Would anybody know?

I changed clothes, had a wash, and called a cab. On the way I called in at Mrs. Rafaele's office and asked to see Mr. Waygoes, but urgently, and without any delay.

She seemed a mite confused.

"Well, I don't know if you can see him any day this week," she said, and looked at a diary.

"Tonight, or I'll invite myself."

"I'll see what I can do, but I'm not promising anything, mind?"

"Tell him it's about Venice. That should be enough."

"I said, I'll *see*."

The cab took me to the Lomax, and I went down to the long bar, busy as I remembered it, and the same girl served further on, in the saloon bar, and I went in.

She saw me, and smiled, and twiddled her hips coming down.

"'Lo, dear," she said. "What you drinking?"

"Bloody Mary, please. Plenty of soy."

"I believe you done me a favour," she said. "You know, about that junk downstairs? I got a bloke along here to find me a buyer. He give me fifty pounds, the lot. That's two weeks' extra sunshine for me. And I got you to thank. I reckon I ought to offer you the weekend, but I'm booked. There's more of that junk downstairs, if you want to see it?"

"Certainly."

"Hold on, I'll get the cellarman."

He limped in ragged carpet slippers and outsize overalls, a little grey-faced ruin of a fellow, and I followed down four flights into a sour of beer drippings and rotted mash. He felt for a switch and opened the door of a small room filled, floor and tables, with another museum full, most larger than mine, of busts, figurines, frescoes, black and amber vases, a joy, and I counted and recounted, to the sneezy impatience of grey-face, 183 items, correct. But how they came to be down there in charge of a mindless slut really did stop my clock. I went back to the bar to finish my drink and grey-face threw the keys on the counter.

"All right?" she said, wide-eyed, big smile of teeth. "What's the offer?"

"Another two weeks in the sun?"

She put a hand out.

"Done with you, lovely," she said. "Get your own blokes to move 'em and your own van."

"All right. This afternoon? With any luck. Pay you then, cash?"

She blew a kiss.

"Knew I was right, minute I saw you," she said. "Give us a call in a couple of weeks. After me curse. We'll have a right bash. Promise? Nothink like it, is there?"

She winked, I drank, waved, and went out, turning left for a removal company I had seen near the Doll's House Caff. A Sikh in a dark-blue turban behind the table nodded and wrote my order to pack 183 pieces in the cellar of the Lomax, and deliver them to the Daemon Wente Waye.

"We had this order some ten days ago," he said, flipping through a file. "Mr. A. G. Bessell?"

"The same. Who gave the order?"

"Only delivery name and address. One half of charge now, one half on delivery?"

"How much?"

He scribbled, totalled, and looked up.

"Well packed against damage, six men, return journey of van, one hundred and eighty-three items, in round figures, one hundred and twenty pounds."

I wrote a cheque for sixty pounds, and he smiled, nodding.

"I hope they are ready for us," he said. "We shall deliver before ten o'clock tonight. I hope you will give the men a little per cent for overtime?"

"Of course."

I went back to the Daemon, looking at broken-down London, hating the brutes responsible, and feeling drear—I suppose that's the word—or flatulently helpless. There was nothing I could do. Nothing any hundreds of thousands of us could do. We were the new type of slave, not out of Egypt, but out of London, dearest of cities, and God damn it, we were helpless. What can you do, looking at miles of ruin?

I sat down on the banks of the Jordan, and wept. Read, not Jordan, but Thames, and cry your bloody eyes out.

What else *can* you do?

I believe a man's generation can be told by the hat he wears, or does not. Some have always gone bareheaded, but they were never of any value. In the Royal Household where all go hatless in presence of the Sovereign, except those of the Armed Services, the business is different, though I have never known why. Why should a civilian not wear a hat when those of the Armed Services may? I don't know but I knew, when the cab stopped at the Daemon, that the young man going down the steps was Teucer Waygoes, and from his hat, a flop-brimmed brown fedora, one of the present generation. I have never been able to wear other than a felt in blue or brown. I could never wear a bowler. Only rarely a black homburg to a funeral, perhaps, or a top hat. But a fedora, of that floppy extent, no.

Teucer slipped down the steps, and in, before I got there.

I went to Mrs. Rafaele's office. At a touch of the bell, she came out smiling.

"Oh, Mr. Bessell, Mr. Waygoes will see you at six o'clock," she said comfortably. "Is that all right?"

I told Almond to warn the night man of a vanload of packages, and went up to my set, and two messages under the door. One from Celli. "Like to see you when you can." Another from Ella Broome. "We are in trouble. Could you please help us?"

I liked Ella. I'm not sure I didn't love her. What is love? She was a big girl, quiet, with a fire inside you saw only when she was doing something she wanted to do, and then try to stop her. She steam-rollered anything, quietly, and got her way because we were always with her, and we knew she was right. After all, we had the proof in the mosaics, the everything else she and her team had unearthed. There was so much more to come, and we knew she would find it, and we wanted her to. She loved London, and that was enough for us.

I went up to the set, almost like going in a church, a silly feeling if you merely unlock a door to go home, and yet good for the inner man, and how many times is he consulted? Do we ever give a damn about ourselves—or anyone else—as feeling, sensitive, even spiritual creatures? When? Do we ever take a day off to think about what we are, or what we were, or what we are going to be, or intend to become? We know, and attempt to deny, we are going into the box, and the hole, or taking the slide into the iron doors of the oven to be ash, moments before Hell's wrath. Or do we burn again? What a bloody lot Christians—or anybody—are, of any sect, or feeling, or belief. And what *is* belief?

I called Celli.

"Oh. A.G.? Lovely to hear you. Had a good time?"

"Fair. What's wrong?"

"Rather not on the phone. Come down for a drink?"

"I'm seeing Mr. Waygoes. In about an hour? To do with what?"

"Penna. See you?"

It was a shock. The haunt was still on.

I had a splash of cologne, and a scotch and soda, and at a minute to six I rang the bell of A 1.

Teucer opened the door. He was about my height, a flux of

dark brown hair to the collar blown anyhow, brown eyes—
though his father's were blue—but sharp, a straight nose, wide
mouth, thickish underlip—but his father's mouth was thin—and
not much of a chin with a bristle of beard, either morning carelessness, razor-shy, or start of a bush.

He gestured, and I went in, and Mr. Waygoes, foot on stool,
held up an arm in greeting.

"Well, young man," he called, from the end of the room.
"What's urgent? And what *about* Venice? Teucer, a scotch and
soda for our guest, please."

He nodded to a chair, and I sat, and began the saga of the six,
the bomb, the hospital, the purported robbery, and the journey
home. I hoisted the drink in a toast, he lifted a finger in return,
and I drank in silence.

"This worries me," he said, and looked it. "The girls did well to
take other routes. That's standing orders. Any doubt, clear out.
But the bomb. That's a new one. Frenchwoman? No possible
idea. You don't think I was behind this, do you?"

"Yes," I said. "That's why I'm here."

"Then let me tell you, you're quite, quite wrong," he said, leaning forward. "I find it very disturbing, in fact. I've always
worked quietly. So far as I know I never had a rival. Certainly
not an enemy. Any ideas, Teucer?"

He shook his head.

"Everybody's reported in except the two for San Francisco,
and all receipts are correct, in order," he said, pulling a lock
behind his ear. "I don't understand it. A bomb in this operation
could have caused, all right, God knows what. And why?"

A grandfather clock ticked.

"Where did they get the money to pay their bills and buy rail
tickets?" I asked. "They told me they were broke."

"We have agents, of course," Waygoes said.

"But you gave me the wet-nurse job?"

"I knew you would carry out what you were asked to do."

"Ever strike you that your agents might be ready to take over?
It's a profitable business, evidently?"

"It had certainly occurred to me," Waygoes said. "There are
always militant limpets. Thing is, place them. Name them."

"Might be European," Teucer said. "French, Italian, so forth. We've used them as agents. They might feel they can ladle the gravy themselves. We've used the older people. Perhaps the youngsters feel they could handle it better. More profitable?"

"Possibly," Waygoes said, looking at the cigar. "We've had it all, in our own small way, until now. We don't want to start what might be a tong war. We haven't got the people. They evidently have a nucleus of operatives. After all, youngsters are always coming along. You have the Palestinians. They've almost finished in the Lebanon. Why not start with something new and rather more profitable outside? At least there's comfort, and a lot more reward. Don't you think?"

"Reasonable," Teucer said. "I'll make a suggestion. Let's get out while we're clean."

Waygoes looked down at the cigar, nodding, white hair covering his ears.

"I don't think we can do better than that," he said, and raised lids to stare at me. "What does Mr. Bessell think?"

"I'm quite sure I want nothing more to do with it," I said. "With anything. From now on I'm simply a printer's journeyman. I've got a very good business, and with as much energy as I've given to you, I could have been far better off."

"But you wouldn't have made tax-free profits for anywhere near the figures appearing annually in your Swiss bank account," Waygoes said. "Be at least grateful. I'd like you to do at least one more run for us."

"Absolutely not," I said. "Get somebody else."

"That's a pity. You *are* our oldest operative. You've earned more than any two. You won't do a final job?"

"What is it?"

"Go back to Venice. Find out who that Frenchwoman was."

"How?"

"How did she know where to find you? Who told her? Have you thought about it? Even such a simple business as a letter bomb requires organisation. Skill. Planning. How else are we to find out? You're the only bait."

"Nice feeling."

"Ten times the usual fee only for a pointer. Not even a name.

Simply a pointer in the general direction. Our people can take over from there. I think you owe it to us?"

"Have you asked yourselves? How *could* they have got on to me? Were any of those half-dozen girls informers? Were they working for you, *and* somebody else? And would I be walking into trouble? Should I mention the word? A trap?"

Waygoes puffed lippily at the cigar. It was dead. He reached for the matchbox.

"I find it unfortunate that word should be used," he said, looking at Teucer. "We've always been essentially a 'clean' operation. I've never known competition. This is something new."

"There was the matter of Penna Cately," I said. "It's never been cleared, so far as I know?"

"Coincidence, possibly," Teucer said. "From what I've seen, she lived a curious sort of life."

"That's no business of ours, is it?"

"Well, let's say, on the periphery, she had other business we knew nothing about."

"Customs informer, perhaps?"

Waygoes sat back, eyes shut, apparently too tired to light the cigar.

"Never heard such rot," he said, and sat up, eyes in small shine, hard. "Look here, are you going or not? If *not*, I'm giving you two weeks' notice according to the terms of your lease. Understood?"

"I could appeal to the rental tribunal about that. I've been here since the house opened."

"And you've taken every advantage. You've had covens of women in your set. I direct your attention to clause eight of your lease. No lessee is to permit more than four guests. Furthermore, you have a number of stone and other statues. Their combined weight is a hazard to the flooring. Get them out before you kill someone downstairs. Clear?"

I had to think.

Any notion of leaving the Daemon tore at the entrails. Where could I go?

The grandfather clock struck seven.

I looked at my watch.

"I could probably get the night train to Paris," I said, easily as I might. "Venice tomorrow evening."

"Call the agent and book a sleeper," Waygoes said, to Teucer. "Or get a place on the night plane. I know our friend doesn't like flying, but the Devil drives. Your set is safe, and a place will be found for your statues. You have a beautiful collection. Extremely valuable. May I ask? Where did you find them?"

"A few moments' idle talk."

"With the girl at the Lomax? Of course. I've been sitting on them for years, and I never knew. So much for stock-taking. That's my place. I should have been more thorough. Do you wish to sell?"

"I'd have to ask Sotheby's or Christie's to send a valuer."

"Shouldn't if I were you. That's a pirate lot. You'd have the Greek and Cypriot and Turkish governments on your neck in short order. We'll discuss it when you get back. Well, Teucer?"

"Night plane to Milan, and a connection's the best he could do. First class. You'll be in Venice about midnight, or before. All right? Gritti Palace is booked, a night, one week, or more as required. Tickets at the Alitalia desk, Heathrow."

No use arguing. I wanted to keep the set. I had to.

I nodded, paused a moment, wondering if I should ask again about Penna, thought not, and went out, leaving them silent except for the grandfather clock marking time for the three of us. One of those tocks would name the time when my toes turned up and the daisies began to blow.

I never liked clocks, or daisies.

Celli opened the door in a pretty dressing gown, autumn-leaf shade, wonderful against her hair.

"Hey," she said, and put her arms round me and kissed my chin. "Been trying for days to get you. Guess what happened? Mrs. Tukes—Penna's landlady?—she came here last Monday. She said a couple of men went round there for Penna's things. They gave her twelve months' rent, cash."

"No names? Details?"

"None. Twelve months, cash. What could she say?"

"And now there's no further hope? Of finding out where she went? She didn't ask their names?"

"Nothing. She took the cash, and they took everything out."

"A girl disappears. Is that it? Could be you. Anybody else. What for?"

She turned away, starting to cry, and smudged tears with her fingers.

"Don't know," she said. "Poor kid. Wish we'd taken more notice. But you know how some girls are. They just go off. Like this Bottsi lot. She's gone off with Thelma. 'Member her, do you? Darling Thel'? Packed up. Left the job. I'm on my own. Why? Ah, Christ."

She screamed, hands up, fingers apart, and fell on her knees and rolled over, sounding as if she was being strangled. I put a hand on her thigh to comfort, but she threw me off, and turned to the floor coughing tears into her arms, and I went up to get my bag, sorry more than I could say.

Ol' Mabbs came out and saw me, feeling in the top right-hand waistcoat pocket for his lower teeth.

"A.G.," he called. "Gotcher at last. Listen, four nights ago, half a dozen Indian blokes, least I think they was Indian. They was all wearing rag hats. They came up and dumped dozens of statues in your place. All right?"

"Right enough. There'll be more coming in tonight. Do me a big favour?"

"Anything you like."

"Ask them to carry them all downstairs to the cubbies, further along than where we are, in the unoccupied niches where they won't be fallen over. Then come up here and carry all these down, same place. A tenner each, and a tenner for Almond. Could I buy you a drink?"

"When you come back. Don't worry about nothing. It'll all get done. *And* right. Here. And I took your tip. I found a girl 'prentice. She's top. Real feeling for the job. We're on coral. Get back *soon.*"

All the way in the taxi to Heathrow I began thinking of myself in some strange way as I had as a child, sent out of London to a place I had to accept because there was no other, and left in a Dorset village to be looked after by people speaking a language I had never heard before, kindly, but strict, always ready with a push or a smack, or stern words if we were slow, either from homesickness, or fear, or simply the obstinacy in our characters. I remembered so clearly the medieval plays in the little church—I had no idea what they were called—we had to sit through for endless hours, with Mr. Seaford, the grocer, dressed up as Saint George in a long sheet with a red cross, and Mr. Darkin as Gramercy in a green shirt to his ankles, and Mrs. Dollance as the Virgin Mary, in cloth stuck with white goose feathers, and all talking strange, none of it less than terrors, and going to bed crying. We were in a foreign land, and foreigners had their own way of thinking, and we were not part of them. Curious how Londoners regard bucolics. But even as children, yes, we did think of them as lesser beings, and those plays put them further apart from us. To see Mr. Torrance, the butcher, pretending to be the Holy Ghost, and Mrs. Crathy lifting up a baby we all knew was a doll and singing so croaky the Magnificat, made us laugh, and there were smacks here and there, and I got a couple, and Mrs. Parran sent me to bed with bread and water. Those moments of hate I remembered, burned in as a horse's hoof.

That was the feeling I had never forgotten.

Of being back, there, defenceless. I was still there. I had always been there.

In a world I hated, detested, among people I despised for pretending to be what they plainly were not.

But *I* was not.

That hurt.

I was not what I pretended.

Bayard and Teucer Waygoes were not.

Where were we different? That was what hurt.

What could I do?

I simplified the equation by having a bottle of champagne and a couple of crunches of caviar toast on the aircraft, and we were skimming down at Venice before I finished the book.

Lovely the Venetian night, no moon, ten thousand lights on the water, the smell of coffee, a mandolin somewhere, beyond the warm wind a voice, only Italian, singing a bouncy pastoral song across the little waves, and the launch pilot humming counterpoint, a fair tenor, lovely. I could have gone to sleep.

But it stabbed home.

I was a mark.

Somebody was—might be?—looking for me.

Why?

Beyond being a courier—a what?—for Waygoes, what had I done?

What crime?

Penna Cately? Once again, that haunt. And it was.

Certainly I took all responsibility. Without my stupid mouthings she might still have been living. I could almost see her over the dark water, touched in lights, with a greenish glow showing faces in a strip-lit bar as we went closer to go down the canal beside the hospital, and the giant bulk of the Sforza monument seeming ready to fly off. Taking a suite at the Gritti Palace placed me square in the bull's eye as a mark. I could go somewhere else. But why? A matter of hours or a couple of days till I was found? What was I to do in the meantime?

Find the French girl? Be an open target? Take part in a new mystery play as Jack-a-Bun?

The more I thought, the more inane I found it, and in a moment, without thought, I said to hell with them, and crossed my ankles, leaning back against green leather cushions, ready for anything, including slaps in the ear and bed with bread and water.

The Gritti Palace was the last place to think of it. I was escorted to my suite on the top floor, overlooking the Grand Canal, all the way up there, the night manager told me, because I would not be bothered by chatter and clatter from the terrace restaurant. A bottle of champagne, with best wishes and warmest welcome from the management—and why not?—and the floor waiter poured a tulip for me, and the valet unpacked me, and the housekeeper came in to look at towels and the turned-down bed, and then I was alone.

I walked out on the terrace, with the sumptuous teat of Santa Maria Della Salute opposite, to my left, over the silver and black water churned white by passenger boats taking people where? A lit gondola led a pontoon staging amateur singers—or the passé —with a thin string backing, an entertainment for strangers,

93

doing tour-style a Venice unknown by Venetians. I wondered, then, what might happen if a pop group sailed the same fleet one night.

The noise passed. The night grew quiet. I could hear the water splashing over on the other side. That gentle sound had been heard by Canaletto and Guardi, and the Doges those hundreds of years ago, and certainly by the original owner of the palace where I had a suite. His background and mine? Had he ever thought of himself as a Jack-a-Bun? Or had a clout for laughing at some other fat Mrs. Crathy of his time, pretending to be someone she could never be?

I finished off the bottle and went to bed via the bathroom and pyjamas, ready to believe that the Gritti Palace would not be the worst place to die, and awoke, marvellously, to sunlight on vases of roses, and the voice of bells. No other city is so blessed by a civic voice given free by the Church, and I lay, listening, almost in a dream, until the Campanile bell raised his mighty voice, male, basso, and reminded me I was above the world's loveliest highway.

Now find that Frenchwoman.

Gerhard, the night porter, and only he, could tell me. He went on duty at the Agrandarelli at seven o'clock to eat his evening meal in the kitchen till eight, when his tour started till six next morning. I knew he went to Silvestrino's café about halfway down the Redentore for a couple of grappas before going in by the back door, and he always, man of habit, had a couple of strong espressos when he finished in the morning, at the same table, within minutes of the bells tolling a quarter past.

I sent out for papers and weeklies, and sat on the terrace in glorious sunshine, daylong, savouring the delights of the kitchen and the best on the wine list, because if I was to die, I would be dined and wined with the best, and no complaints. In all the years since I had begun to read newspapers and magazines, I had never taken any real notice of what went on or what others were doing or why. It seemed to me that everybody had their own business, as I had mine, and any outside interference only made matters worse, though after reading through that pile of pulp I started to think, but without getting much further, or, certainly, doing much to stop the rot. It seemed to me that only the

Second Coming would do any good, and even then the Muslims and Buddhists and a few others would refuse to listen, and if our own Roman Catholics, Anglicans, and Nonconformists, all using the same Bible, could not agree, I wondered what might be said Upstairs, if, that is, there *was* an Upstairs, with Anybody at home, and what the rest of us, unbelievers, might expect.

The sheer stupidity of existence seemed without explanation. Some, with money, lived as I did, on the cream, and some of the rest put up with milk. But the majority got skim, or little more than water, if that. But why? Which discipline kept hundreds of millions in bounds? In bounds of what?

The waiter brought in coffee at five o'clock that morning, and I was down in the gondola at five-thirty, in foggy canals, looking at all the window boxes in bloom, and Venetians hurrying to work across the bridges, wondering what they knew of the pile of news pulp I had read and left behind in the wastebasket. What *did* they know? What did *anybody* know? And knowing, what could they *do*?

But seeing Gerhard coming round the corner swept all the argument out of mind, and I wondered what we really called thinking, if it must be mathematics, or science, or something on paper, or plotted on graphs, or the university treatises, or this, that, or the other, but what happens in between? Anything like the welter of nonsense in my mind that all seemed to sum up to a query? Of nothing?

Gerhard's heavy sandals, tyre-soled, slapped along the stones, and his white shirt shone, and the kneed trousers showed the worn patches of years, brownish, shiny, and a braided skipper's cap told in crumpled fray that days for wear were few.

He saw me and stopped in disbelief, and held out his arms in a big smile, and came on, and I pushed out a chair. We talked over each other, and around, but I got in that I had just arrived, and I had no reason to go to the Agrandarelli, but I only wanted to talk to him about the Frenchwoman. On the instant he became wary, turning away until the waiter put down the coffee-pot, milk, hot rolls, butter, and jam, and he looked at me.

His eyes showed a vacuous fear, empty, startled, and his lips were dry, and his tongue flicked.

I poured coffee, and turned the milk jug. He helped himself.

His hands shook a little and twice he missed the pour and scraped the chair back to brush off milk splashes.

"I shall leave Venice at the end of the month," he said, over the cup rim. "Finish here. Too much trouble. I retire. I go to Austria."

"There could be a fair reward for useful information."

"I have no information."

"It could bring some thousands of Austrian schillings."

"Thousands?"

"That's right. Depending on the information."

"Who is to judge?"

"Myself. I was the target. I want to know who. Why? That's all. With your help? I have always thought of you as a friend. Isn't it true?"

"It is certainly true. When shall I have the money?"

"When I have the information."

"Guarantee?"

"My word."

Bells clashed flat across the water. A long-funnelled Greek merchantman's siren whooped along the quay.

"Very well," Gerhard said. "I think I know what is a man. I was four years in Gelsenkirchen. It is sociological education. I look at your eyes. It is enough. I trust."

He took a cigaret, and a light.

"Well," he said, pulling hard on the cigaret. "That girl had come to the hotel three or four times, always at night, and once in the early morning, to ask if you were there. The girls told me she went there sometimes in the day. Always asking about you. Agrandarelli never allowed your address in the register to be given. He, also, is your friend. This woman is late twenties, early thirties. Thirty-two, most. I think younger from the face. She is always nervous. The hands, the face, the neck, the feet. *Nervous*. She is not ordinary. Well educated. French, of course. Very good Italian. Good German. I tried Russian. She answered correctly. But she was afraid. Always nervous."

He drank the cup dry, and I raised a finger for more coffee.

"How about a brandy?" I asked.

"Grappa," he said. "Better for the liver."

"Questionable," I said, and ordered a brandy and a grappa.

(Why do we ignore waiters? After all, they live, too. And what a rotten, disjointed world it would be without them. I hate self-service. What is being saved? Jobs? But we need them.)

"Well, I've seen her twice, coming to work," he said. "She was at the Caffe Quadri, one morning. I live behind San Marco. I walk through the Piazza to take the ferry to the Redentore. I like the walk. She was there with a professor of languages at the school, here."

"How did you know him?"

"I was a professor of English at the University of Reval, now Tallinn. I was a survivor. I am still a survivor. I am a night porter. I have a place. I am myself. Nobody has a whip."

"This woman?" I said, but gently.

"He told me she studies English."

"His name?"

"Guglielmo Artisoni. I spell it?"

"I have it. Any more?"

"She works in an insurance office. The number I am not sure. Calle Frollo. Not far from the Piazza. I have been there. I never saw her. The second time I saw her was at the Fenice. When the opera season is on, I treat myself to dinner and the opera. I take advantage of my savings once or twice in the season. I work hard? I earn? Why not?"

"Agree."

"She was with a man I know. Well, not *know*. I know who he *is*. He is Emilio Frazzoni, and he works in the office of the podestà. The office of the mayor. I think in the library. It is very big. Important."

"You know nothing about her, apart from this?"

"Nothing. She is a smart girl, ordinary, well dressed. How does she deliver a packet bomb? God knows, and there is *no* God. I *know*."

The three-quarter chime belled across green water.

"I think you have done exceptionally well," I said. "You have certainly earned your reward. No small details you may have forgotten?"

He raised brows, looking at a fat wine barge piled with casks fut-a-fut-futting somewhere south.

"Yes," he said, sucking lips about his tongue. "She had a li-

97

brary book. The library I belong to. Number one-nine-nine-eight-five B. Second, she was trying shoes at Tricionni, the handmade workshop behind the Piazza. If she was trying on shoes, she must have lasts. And her name and address. What else?"

"All right," I said. "Write down your name and address, and the bank where you wish the money sent."

"I am an old soldier, and an older citizen, and I survived Gelsenkirchen. I also expect to survive you, if you are dishonest."

"How do I know *you* are honest? Was Gelsenkirchen some sort of gold standard?"

"Gold melts. The human spirit does not. Mine did not. It was tried. You wish to argue?"

"Never. We agree. Write."

"How much do I expect?"

"One hundred thousand lire. Five thousand Austrian schillings. The bank of your choice. Here, or in Vienna."

"It is generous. I am grateful. If I find more, where shall I send?"

Perhaps I had been in a state of warning for some time, but the buzzer sounded somewhere at the back of my mind. The seeming innocence, the quiet voice? But he had been my partner in the bomb job? Careful? Of course. As usual.

I wrote the address of Waygoes' travel agent in Moorgate, London, and put his slip in my pocket.

"But still, supposing today I have more?" he said, playing with the grappa glass.

"I shall be sunning on the Lido. Or be at the station at a quarter to six."

"You leave?"

"Today."

He got up, putting out a hand.

"If I have any more, I will be at the station. If not, dear friend, I shall think of you in the winters left to me. You have made them more comfortable. But it's something? The defeat of Mr. Frost?"

We shook, and I turned into the calle, away from his tyre-soled slap-slap along the quay.

I was warned.

A curious feeling.

I found a post office in the square and sent off a message to Moorgate with all details, and others from a couple of piazza offices later. I crossed by gondola ferry, and sent a fourth telegram from the main post office behind the Piazza San Marco. I strolled down the Calle Frollo, and found the Assicuranze Yugo-Adriatico with a polished brass plaque, and walked into a small foyer with a door ahead and one left and right, but on the right, a sign read ENTRE, and I knocked, and entered. A young man with an Afro haircut looked up, and I asked him, in English, if this was the Yugo-Adriatico Assurance Company.

"We are not in business," he said, standing. "We are now part of Providente, at this address."

He gave me a card.

"Thank you," I said. "You have no women on your staff?"

"Women?" He turned away, frowning. "We have no women here. What information do you require?"

"I'd heard I might have a relative here. She's dark, small, and she speaks four languages."

He laughed.

"*Four* languages?" he said. "She would never be here. She would be stupid to work for chicken bones. No. She is not here. Nobody is here. Only me. For only one week more. Thank God."

I walked out, down to the Piazza, along to the Schiavoni, and the steamer to the Lido, and all the time I was thinking of Gerhard and that girl. It was ridiculous to suppose that Gerhard, after so many years as a night porter, would have anything in common with a little somebody chosen to deliver a fire bomb. The entire business defeated me. I went into the corner café, and got a half loaf of crisp bread with the dough torn out, filled with salami slices, ham, cheese, and olives, and a half-flask of chianti, and went down to the beach, and paid to go in the Bagno, and sat in the sand, in the sun, and chewed, and drank, and watched the hundreds of beauties in their biks, no man happier or more replete. At five o'clock I took a launch to Venice and through the canals to the station. I had no luggage, and I got a ticket to Mestre, first stop across the bridge to the mainland, only to board the international train and look at the platform.

99

I leaned out of the window, making myself plain to anyone watching, but the guard held his whistle, looking at the clock for those few seconds, and I got off, and the whistle blew behind me, and the train moved. I walked down to the gate and out, toward the café, and Gerhard, in suit, collar, tie, and patent-leather boots with buttons, walked out of the ticket bureau swinging a stick, and saw me, perhaps not so comfortably, and waved, smiling, but no attempt to speak, and walked on, stick under arm, a bastion of propriety. That was enough.

Gerhard, or the people behind him, were a little too smart. At least, for me.

I went down the steps, and signed for a launch, and told him the Gritti Palace *subito*. He went down a couple of side canals and in surprisingly short time, I was on the Gritti pontoon, trotting through the lobby, calling for my account. I knew there were a couple of aircraft out to Paris or London that night, and I asked the girl in the travel bureau to get me a seat on one, or any.

I was packed, paid, and out, with a ticket on the aircraft I could easily get just before eight o'clock, and the launch took me through the canals and on to the broad water, direct to the airport.

We made straight approach between the black guide stakes marking the channel, and looking back for a memory of my favourite city, I saw the heavy ship, sounding like a tug, coming up to us. Almost then, we swung around in a wide arc, barely missing a stake, and I knew my pilot wanted to go alongside.

For some reason I ran down to the cabin and grabbed him, and hit a left and right, putting him down, and took his legs and threw him overboard, reached for the wheel, righting our course, and on full power, steered for the blue lights of the airport. Without looking round I came alongside the stairs, threw my bags up, jumped ashore, letting the launch go, and the shouts were as nuisance, and I joined the small queue checking tickets.

Once inside the airport I felt better. I went through passport control and Customs, and had a double brandy in the bar, but seat-belted and cowering in a warm chair on board, I began to feel as if I might have been a little too fatheaded. And yet not.

But what could somebody want with me? I felt little boy among grownups.

I made no nonsense at Heathrow. I took a cab direct to the Daemon, lit in pale orange, and nobody was ever happier to see that smile in marble of thousands of years ago. Perhaps some of us have always smiled, and so many of us have forgotten there is any need. But of course there is. And the Daemon made me aware, and I laughed back at his face in bright light and deep shadow, making his smile seem the wider, the merrier.

Soult came out to help me with the bags, and I telephoned Mrs. Rafaele's office, but of course she had gone, and Soult said he would leave a message downstairs, and I was having a wash when the telephone rang.

"Hullo? A.G.? Just heard you were back. This is Teucer. Care to come down? My father'd like to have a drink with you. I'll be waiting."

He was, and he nodded at a smaller room, from the large desk piled with paper and a teak filing system, an office. Mr. Waygoes, in a heavy black satin half-kimono and black suede slippers with his initials in gold on the toes, waved me in with a cigar.

"Well done," he said. "Got your telegrams. Everything's in order. Two questions. Do you trust this man Agrandarelli? His hotel?"

"Implicitly. Or I wouldn't be here. Why?"

"It's used almost exclusively by East Europeans, Russians, so forth. On leave, or passing through. You never noticed it?"

"No. I mind my own business."

"You never felt you were followed in Venice?"

"Never."

"At all times, in fact. You went to the Yugo-Adriatico Assurance to enquire about a woman speaking four languages?"

"I did."

"You see? Every moment since you left here, you were followed. That was protection. Why did you board the express for Milan this afternoon?"

"To see if Gerhard would be there."

"And he was? Of course."

He turned away to tap ash, and looked across at the green

shade of a lamp, and pulled in a surprisingly deep breath, and let it go in a *pah!*

"My son and I have agreed to stop the runs and end all agreements, both in Europe and elsewhere. Others are taking over. Copying our methods. They send in a dozen. If they get two going through, it's a success. Not for us. We were always one hundred per cent. With you and the others we could rely on. We can't any more. There's the Mafia. We know there are others. Not worth the risk. A little bad luck and we could be pulled in, here. That was never the idea. In a word, finish. I say it sadly."

"Why?"

He looked round at me without surprise.

"I lose an extremely profitable enterprise for the worst of reasons," he said. "I'm bludgeoned into it. I've lost eight top-class operatives in the past couple of months. I could have lost you. But you used your common sense. Instinct for self-preservation. The others were informed on. Hadn't a chance. Too many people have become aware of the profit in what we do. And the rest."

"What 'rest'?"

"Well. Four of our people were stopped in Moscow en route from Thailand. An informer, obviously. We paid twenty thousand dollars for that cargo. What they carried was worth between three and four million pounds here. More in the United States. That's when I called it off. It went on for a long time. But word gets about. Operatives don't always keep their mouths shut. It's why you were a favourite until that Penna Cately business."

Again that horrid thought. The haunt.

"What happened to her?"

"She was put where she deserved," Waygoes said, and relit the cigar.

"Killed?"

He put both fists on the desk, staring at Teucer.

"Did you ever hear anything so obtuse?" he whispered, and turned angrily to me. "She was put in a private nursing home until a little time ago. She is perfectly well now. She's been through a course of memory diminishment. Medically supervised. She hasn't suffered. She has more in her savings bank than she had. Doesn't that satisfy? Ask one of the girls? Botti, or the other."

"I don't like it."

"Who could *possibly* be interested in what you like or dislike?"

"The police, possibly?"

Waygoes sat down, or more properly, enthroned himself in the high-backed red leather chair, pushing white hair from his eyes, sitting back, throwing away the dead cigar, reaching to take another.

"Look here, Bessell. I must warn you that I still have an extremely active and muscular organisation," he said. "Any word in the wrong place would be most unwise. You would be obliterated. In the moment. You do understand, don't you?"

Pity in the voice?

"Yes."

"Then we shall go on to something else. Teucer, call Mr. Arnward."

Teucer opened the door, and nodded.

Mr. Arnward, tall, in blue, showed bowed-bald-head deference to Waygoes, looked at me and held out a hand with stubby fingers, polished nails.

"Mr. Arnward is agent for a new party," Waygoes said. "Political party, that is. Mr. Bessell is a printer. But far from the usual one. Do, please, put your proposal before him."

"All right, Mr. Bessell," he said, in a voice I thought hoarse with public speaking. "I have a series of pamphlets here I'd like printed, with leaflets and posters to follow. After that, a book. Part of a campaign. Interested?"

"All business interests me. But what sort of campaign? Liberal?"

"Not quite. It's a different approach."

"Nothing to do with Communism?"

"The reverse. I'm glad to hear you're biased. So am I."

He gave me a thick folio of typescript.

"Those are the pamphlets. Five thousand of each. Those are the posters. Three thousand. You'll note I want them in fonts as close as possible to Bank of England notes. That applies throughout."

"Money no object," Waygoes said. "We want posters, pamphlets, book or books, the lot, instantly recognizable by the print. Understood?"

"Proofs, when?"

"As soon as possible," Arnward said.

"One thousand pounds immediately for preliminary work," I said. "Pulls on the pamphlets, two days' time, in the evening. The rest, except the book, within the week. Proofs, only."

"Why a thousand pounds?" Teucer asked.

"Design of a font," I said. "D'you think it's done by waving a wand? This is a matter for craftsmen. They have to be paid."

"All right," Waygoes said. "The cheque will be delivered over the road tomorrow. Anything else?"

I went out, both arms loaded with paper, wondering whether to go to the plant and start, or take it up to my set and read, and I did that. But then I remembered poor Celli, and ran over the landing and downstairs. She opened the door in a pale pink dressing gown, hair in braids, a warm hand and a thumping scotch and soda in a tall glass full of ice.

"That's better," she said, and lay down on the chaise, pulling the robe about her legs, and punching a pillow. "Place isn't the same without you."

"Good to know. Anything new with Bottsi?"

"She said she wants to come back. I'm thinking about it."

"Why?"

"She's a funny lot. Could happen again. 'Sides. I don't want Thel's cast-off."

"Isn't she supposed to be your friend?"

"Supposed, yes. Friends don't go off with snakes like that if they haven't got a bit of snake in them. I can do without it. She found out a bit late that the Daemon's better place to live. And I don't think Mr. Waygoes'll have her back. He thought she was a bad influence. So Mrs. Hine said. I believe it's because young Teucer tried a feel, and got smacked in the chops. She's a big girl, y'know. She *can* be dead nasty. I don't think they'll *let* her back. Else *I'd* have to leave. I can't even *think* about it. There *isn't* anywhere else, far's I'm concerned."

"I agree. Funny what you'll do to stay here."

"You had a bit of trouble, too?"

"A bit. Mr. Waygoes said you know something about Penna Cately?"

She sat up, eyes wide, hands together, hair gilt in lamplight.

"*That's* what I wanted to tell you," she said, and clapped. "Of course. Look. I got this phone call just after you left. The man sounded a real roughie. It was at the office, so I scribbled it. Anyhow, he said Penna's somewhere near Didcot, and she's working with a doll company. It's only an hour or so from Paddington. I thought of popping down there. Want to come?"

"A doll company? At Didcot?"

"The Exhibition complex. It's the toy fair. Yes?"

"Wednesday or Thursday, yes. How did she get *there?*"

"No idea. Why didn't she write to you? Or Mrs. Tukes? You'd think she ought to, didn't she?"

"We'll find out. Well, now. I've got a pile of work upstairs, and it's late."

I drank till the ice rattled, and put the glass down.

"Why don't you sleep here?" she said, smiling, pouting. "I haven't had a man for years. First one I thought of when she left. That was you."

"Something effeminate about me?"

"Opposite. I've seen you look at us, 'specially what's-name. Ella Broome. She's a smasher. Wouldn't mind her myself. But it's been tried. She's strictly boy, and nice with it. Doesn't sling herself about. Well? Sleep here? I can promise *almost* the original virgin. Any case, it's no *period* piece. And that's no lie."

I thought of the pile of work upstairs. But the alarm set for seven would give me time to sort the copy out before the staff got in.

"I'd enjoy it," I said. "Always wanted to's a matter of fact. But you made it plain it was teats only. So gradually the swelling went down."

She got up, stretching.

"Hope you won't need a poultice," she said, and reached for my glass. "One for the job? You know where everything is? I'll go first. A pee and some perfume, that's all. Don't hurry. Have a quiet drink. Or perhaps you'd like another night?"

"No fear. Always drink it while it's hot. My Sunday school teacher taught us that."

"Much hotter, I'd blow up. Haven't been in this state for years. It's lovely. And healthy. Are you a one-comer or a two?"

"I've been known to go two. With the right treatment."

"I'll see what I can do. Second one's always the longest. That's what I like. Taking my time. You go three, I'll go straight round the bend. *Promise*."

I have never, trying to remember, been able to decide what I think about in those, as it were, stolen times. I believe it to be more a matter of feeling than thinking, and for that reason memory for the most part is absent, but the glow stays, with a feeling of gratitude for time almost impossible to describe, although sights, sounds, stay and make a next meeting imperative.

So I felt about Celli, crossing the road in London's beautiful blue dawn just before five o'clock. Celli had fallen asleep surprisingly early, and I waited until I was sure, and kissed her, and quietly let myself out, going upstairs, shoes off, and letting myself in, wide awake, ready for coffee. So much for the dream. The jar was empty. No sugar. Bachelor's harvest.

I felt no desire to sleep. The paper made an armload, and I went downstairs, let out by the night security guard, and crossed Wapping High, not a sound or move anywhere, and up Pell Court to Brittle Candy Lane. I had to juggle the keys and try a few, and then I was in the reception area, far larger and more flattering, and the general office had been partitioned in glass, and my office surprised me by size and furnishing. But I ached for a cup of coffee. I looked for the kitchen, white, brand new dishwasher—something I'd never thought of—but all the cupboards were locked—smart girl, Jo—but remembered an all-night bar up in Green Tea Alley, not far, and a nice walk.

I could hear the buses in Whitechapel Road, but nothing else moved. I had never before noticed that silence. It came over the ears, like a cup. But then, just as I got to the café, the little miracle happened.

The sparrows woke up.

London's oldest citizens let everybody know they were ready for the day, a marvellous sound, a noble chatter, an ancient chorus, plainsong challenge to any, and truest voice of the city, that lovely old girl.

I went down the stairs to the café, surprised to find the place almost full of Asians, Africans, and a few whites. The barmen were black and so was the waitress. They simply looked at me, and I took a stool at the bar.

"Morning," I said, to the waitress, a big girl in an apricot overall. "How's the coffee?"

"Best in the whole country," she said, and nodded at the man behind a battery of coffee pots. "He's a Brazilian. Makes it the Brazilian way. With Brazilian coffee."

"I'll have an entire pot to myself," I said. "What's to eat?"

"Hot rolls or croissants, butter and three sorts of jam, or marmalade. Cooper's. Oxford. Know it?"

"Give me two croissants, butter, and Cooper's. And the coffee. The pot."

"Coming up."

I looked about, not a little surprised at the number of people, possibly a couple of hundred, or more because of the big room at the back. The waitress put down the plates and the portion of marmalade in thick rinds, and the croissants—fluffy, crisp, hot—cup, saucer, spoon, sugar.

"Who *are* all these?" I asked her. "It's pretty early."

"You should be here before," she said. "They are office cleaners, train cleaners. Early shift, hotels. Late shifts, coming off. No-goods, up-all-nights, no-place-to-stays, drunks-getting-over-it, drugheads, pimps, kitchen hands going in the little places round here. People don't want to go home. All sorts. They like the warm. Company. They're awful lonely. Got nothing. *Nobody*. 'Specially the girls. Not the whores. They got a room. They can go home. Girl got no money, can't."

"What do they do?"

"Stay here on a cup of coffee. Sleep in a doorway. Some warehouse. Any place."

"Don't they get welfare?"

She smiled beautiful white teeth, clicked her tongue.

"And get sent back? They don't have permits. They 'fraid."

"You give all of those you know more hot coffee, and if you've got a big sandwich, that, too. Here's the money. If it's more, it'll be here."

I munched wonderful croissants—made around the corner, I found, by Maritte St. Jal, from Guadaloupe, though how she got there was anybody's business—and I put in an order for our elevenses, with two pots of coffee from João, and I was brushing off the crumbs to go, and the waitress put down a slip of paper.

"Money wasn't enough," she said. "Sorry. There's lots of them. Another three pounds and sixty. Can't stop them. They give the sandwiches to the boy friends. And most the coffee. They' all mamas. Silly hearts. Empty guts."

"What's your name?"

"Edwina Somerset."

"All right. We'll have a bargain. You've got my address for coffee and croissants. You give any girl you know's down on her luck plenty of coffee and a sandwich. *Nothing* for any man. Bargain?"

She looked up at me, eyes closed, smiling.

"Bargain," she said. "I bet Christ like to talk to you."

I took her hand, and kissed.

"As long as *you* do, I can manage," I said. "Good night. Don't forget. This morning. Ten to eleven, we break for elevenses. Thirty-four of us."

"Wish I was one," she said. "I could make all the coffee. Clean the place. Scrub. Anything except the croissants. That's taking it away from Mama Maritte. But I wished I got steady day work. This here's money. But not the way I like."

"Come and work for me today," I said. "It's a five-and-a-half-day week. Ask for Jo Hibbs. That's all. I'll tell her. She's the accountant."

"I'll see God Almighty get your name. Sleep like any honest-got baby. You' looking tired."

I felt it, and I went back in daylight, people walking about, and left notes for Jo, and for Davie of the foundry about the font, and Farquhar of the paper factory, and about Edwina, and went back to the Daemon's smile, and climbed the stairs, and bathed, and got into bed, and woke at something after four o'clock.

Hardly believable.

The clock looked at me. It told me what it had to say.

Four-ten.

It was Saturday. We closed at one.

I got up, deliberately, and bathed, shaved, taking all the time, and I was ready at about ten to five. By the time I got to the plant, the clock somewhere struck the quarter.

Jo Hibbs met me, sitting in reception, with Roy Afflin, second foreman, Bob Crowe, and Stan Greaves. Edwina smoothed her apron and went toward the kitchen.

"Sorry," I said. "I slept a slide of the clock."

"We thought that was it," Jo said, short, pudgy, anything-you-like, a rock of Gibraltar. "All this copy. We got most of it off. But there's a lot needs looking into."

"I'll do that tonight."

"There's a lot there I don't agree with," Roy said, and his eyes slipped away from mine. "It's dead political."

"It's work. It's what brings your wages. Bread. I'm not prepared to talk about it."

"I think I'll have to call a strike."

"You don't have to. You no longer work here. Get out."

"I'll take the rest with me."

"Do that. I don't need you."

Roy—I had always thought him a fair example of the decent and solid craftsman—waved several sheets of paper.

"You won't do this to us," he shouted.

"This being *what?*"

"Taking over trade-union funds."

"Oh. I know nothing about it. But I'll read it and treat it as a job. A job that pays your wages."

"We won't put it up."

"We?"

"The members of this chapel."

"I never heard of it. *What* chapel?"

"You never mind. We've had enough of your people putting out the slush. Now it's our turn. You won't print this. We say you won't."

Jo had turned away. Dollimore, the works accountant, took off his glasses and rubbed his eyes.

"You're caught in the closed shop, sir," he said. "Not much we can do."

"*Nothing* he can do," Roy said, and laughed. "That's *it*. We won't set it. That settles *that*."

"You no longer work for me," I said. "You've been paid your week's money. Get off these premises. That applies to anyone with you."

"Me arse. The lads are all in there waiting to take over. We'll squat it out. Think we're a lot of mugs, do you?"

"Get out and don't come back. Jo, get the police, and give this fellow or anybody else their cards, stamped to date. They're not entitled to extra pay. They gave no notice. They're nothings."

"I don't want your money, and we don't take threats. Let the police come here. See what we care. Listen, we'll wreck this place. You won't have nothing left."

He walked to the red fire door and tried to close it, but the key was in its box, and he went in and we heard him shouting. But there were other shouts, and Dennis, Whitmore, Charles, Verrit, Mathey, George, Bilsby, Cannon, Lizzy, MacElhone, Bartron, Price, and Cape came in a crowd, with others behind, and Wilkinson elbowing at the back.

"Mr. Bessell," Whitmore said. "All of us don't want anything to do with this take-over stuff. We hope you'll stand by us if the blokes upstairs try anything?"

"You rely on me," I said. "You come in Monday morning, as usual. Thank you for your support."

They all seemed glad to get out, and I thought quickly that possibly more than half were loyal to me, incidentally, the best men I had.

Edwina came with coffee in wonderful aroma, and thin unsalted ham, chipped olives, Cheshire cheese, sliced chipolata sausage, fried banana, black-currant and peanut butter sandwiches, little ones, each a triangle of different taste, going back to other, far better days, and her smile an extra taste, a blessing.

"What are we to do, sir?" Jo asked me in mid-chew. "They might make it awkward."

"I was always taught it's rude to speak through a mouthful," I said. "Let me tell you, now. However awkward these bastards are, the more awkward I'll be."

A police car clanged up Pell Court and stopped outside, and we waited.

Jo went to the door. A uniformed inspector came in, taking his time, and Jo told what was happening, and he nodded, listening, and stopped by the licenses framed on the wall, looking up.

"Who's the proprietor here?" he asked.

"I am," I said, and went into the main office. "I've discharged these men inside. I want them off the premises."

"You what?" Afflin shouted, inside the fire door. "You try getting me out."

"Just a minute," the inspector said. "Had a look up here, have you?"

"No," Afflin said. "What?"

"These are licensed premises. You're in trespass. You want to go out quietly, and clear off home? Or come with me?"

Afflin looked round the open door at the few with him, and turned.

"You haven't got a warrant," he said. "You can't arrest me."

"I don't need a warrant. This is a breach of the peace and trespass on licensed premises. That's enough to take you in. It's Saturday, so you'd go in the cells till Monday. Then you could apply for bail."

"Listen," Afflin said—spacing it to l-i-i-i-s-s-u-un!—"you know you can't do that? I'll have our people round there—"

"You do that," the inspector said, slapping his gloves, and turned to another police officer. "Sar'nt Porter, either they shift themselves in the next couple of minutes or take the lot in for trespass."

"Sir," the sergeant said, and walked toward Afflin. "Come on. Get yourselves moving. Out of it."

"You got no right," Afflin began in bubbly soprano.

"Talk to the magistrate. Going out, or taking the weekend off?"

Afflin looked about and at me, but his eyes slid away, to his friends almost running outside.

"This one you win," he said to nobody. "But you'll pay. By Christ, you will."

"Another lovely Christian," the inspector said. "Go on. Out of it."

Afflin and the others with him crowded out of the door, and the inspector looked about.

"You've had a look round in there?" he said, nodding toward the plant. "They could have left some trouble?"

"Being done now," I said. "They didn't have much opportunity."

Bill Garrold came in from the fire door, and waved against shining red paint.

"It's all safe, guv," he called. "We tested everything. We can work anytime you like. Any chance of overtime?"

"Certainly. Any of you want to stay, copy or not, welcome, today and tomorrow. I think we need somebody to take care of our jobs. That bastard may try to set fire to us."

"All right," Bill said. "It's up to him. I catch him or any other fucker, I'll tell you what I do. His own mother wouldn't want him."

"That's the ticket," the inspector said, turning for the door. "Always down there if you want us."

He went out, Edwina brought in another tray and coffeepot, and we all went into separate corners to eat, drink, and talk; but before there was any real buzz, thumps on the door brought silence.

"Who the hell's *that?*" Wilkinson said. "Coppers again?"

But when Jo trotted to open the door, Ella Broome leaned an arm against each jamb and seemed as though she might fall in. Several ran to hold her and she was brought in to sit down just inside the main room, but I signed for her to be helped into my office and put on the couch.

"Your best coffee," I told Edwina, and I loved her wink, one eye completely closed, no move in the other.

Ella leaned against the leather, rather pale.

"All right," I said. "What's wrong?"

"We have something on a lower level," she said. "It might be a tomb. We're not down deep enough. It could be Celtic. If it is, it'll be the first. You understand the importance of that?"

"Yes."

112

"We need enough money to bring in men. Real navvies. To clear the ground. And a van. When we get it out, whatever it is, to bring it back here."

She looked at me. She must have come straight from the dig. Dust lay over her sweat. She was a dull, muddy colour. Only her eyes were alive. I had never found out where she lived, though I thought somewhere in the Daemon.

"I'd like a bath, and go to sleep," she said, shaky, looking away.

"Why can't you?"

"The public bath and the swimming pool's turned off."

"Why do you need the *public* bath, for Christ's sake?"

She pulled in a deep breath, that creased her forehead in black lines.

"I stay with Mr. and Mrs. Briggs," she said. "I sleep in the main greenhouse in the summer, and in their kitchen in the winter. They haven't got a real bathroom."

She put down her head.

"I'd love a bath," she whispered, in tears. "I'd so *love* a bath. And somewhere clean to sleep."

I swung an arm about her.

"You've got it," I said. "Come with me. Edwina, take care of everybody here."

I had no trouble helping her across the road and up to my set. She seemed dead on her feet. The set looked even better than I remembered, and I took her into the bedroom and sat her down on the bed and opened the bathroom door, and started the hot and cold pour.

"Everything's here," I said, and brought pyjamas from the drawer. "Have a lovely bath and go to sleep. Nobody's going to wake you."

She stood and threw off the sleeves of the overcoat, and pulled the jersey over her head, and undid the button of the skirt and shook it down, and felt for the catch at the back of the bra, but I thought it unfair to enjoy a strip when she was out on her feet.

"I'll be back," I said, and turned for the door.

"No, no," she whispered. "I could drown in that bath. Take me in. Wait for me to come out. *Please.*"

Any girl of her age is beautiful, but I had no idea what to

think about *her*. She was my height, barefoot, small Grecian breasts that would fit a champagne goblet, and the rest was purest, loveliest, herself. I turned off the pour, and felt the water, less hot than warm, and she stepped in, hand on my shoulder, and sat, sighing deeply, and looked up at me.

"I should have washed my hair," she said. "I'll dirty the pillows."

"Dirty them. You'll have a fine time tomorrow. There's the sponge. Takes care of your face."

"Don't leave me. I'm afraid I'll fall asleep. It's so lovely and warm. Don't leave me."

"I won't. I'll just go out and get us a drink."

"All right. Mine's tea. Not too strong."

But she seemed to have known, because when the kettle was on, I went back, and she slept, with her chin barely above the water, breathing deep, and with every breath sinking a little more. I took a lax hand and pulled her up, putting a towel round her waist and another about her shoulders, leaning her against me to sponge her face, and she was heavy. I got one leg out of the bath, and pulled her, and saved the other leg from a scraping, and half-carried her to the bed, sitting her down, patting her more or less dry, threading arms into the pyjama jacket, letting her fall flat, taking her legs in the crook of an arm to swing them under the sheets, and tucking the blanket in, no girl dearer or more beautiful, and I was my own truthful witness.

I let the bath water out and poured another, and soaked, thinking of Afflin in the most disagreeable surprise for a long time because I had thought him loyal to me, and dried on damp towels, no suffering, and let out the water, went quietly through the bedroom—slow breaths, not quite snores—to the living room, threw cushions on the floor, pulled a rug over me, and slept.

Dragged out of dreams is pain only remotely remembered, but the telephone racked me, it seemed, for hours, and I heard Soult's voice from downstairs.

"Your place over there's on fire, sir. They want you across there, quick."

I pulled on trousers, a sweater, and shoes, and ran through

London's blue early morning silence, up to Brittle Candy Lane, two fire engines, and a small crowd.

No real fire. Three partly scorched doors, and that was all.

"You were dead lucky, sir," the fire chief said. "They put a can of petrol and a Molotov cocktail in three of these here doorways. The Molotov would ha' blew up, and set the cans afire. Wouldn't've been nothink left. But some of them coming out of that all-night coffee dump down there, they see the blaze start and a car drive off, and they sent the alarm. No more'n a paint job, seems like."

"Somebody loves you," the police sergeant said. "Anybody in mind?"

"A few I sacked today, perhaps."

"Could I have their names and addresses? We'd be round there in a few minutes. If they've been out and just got back, they'd have to explain it."

I opened a red-hot door and went in. Nothing was even smoked. The files gave Afflin and the others' addresses, and the sergeant ran.

"Dead lucky," the fire chief said. "You can lock up, but leave the keys with me. Never know if a spark's waiting about somewhere. Two of my lads'll be here till the morning. Just in case."

"Ask that bar to send them coffee and sandwiches. I'll pay."

I went back to the Daemon with an armful of Waygoes' copy. The plaque still smiled in rising morning light, and I stood there, looking at him, thinking of all the centuries of wickedness and evil. Evidently they were not yet done, and more would follow, and none could stop it, and no use asking why not, because nobody had an answer, or if they had, some of us had yet to hear it.

I went up to the set, put the armful on the desk, and went to the bedroom door, listening to deep breathing, and out to the kitchen to put the kettle on, and back to the desk, emptying the pile, and started at page one of the copy.

Afflin had been right to worry.

Trade unions were prime meat for Mr. Waygoes' cleaver, with the banking fraternity, property developers and county councils in close order. I flipped through it all, looking at it as an editor, and knew I had the devil of a job, if only in law.

The risk of libel grinned sharp teeth in most paragraphs.

For all that, I called Jon Davie at Marget's Print, and Leslie Farquhar at the paper mills, and asked them to send a man over.

It was obvious to me that win, lose, or draw, I was sitting on the publishing bomb of the century, whether as printer or publisher, though the more I read, the more content I was to be where I was, to do what I had to do.

For the main poster, I knew I must bring in Henny Loomis, the finest copperplate craftsman in the business, the highest priced, with the longest order book and the shortest temper, but an easy one to deal with because he named a price and you paid or not, and you got the job or not. Simple as that. His wife said he was still asleep, but he would call in the afternoon.

The smaller posters and handbills all had a note in Waygoes' scrawl stapled in the corner.

"Print these in big letters. People don't take the trouble to read a lot of print. Put all verbs in RED. Underline opening and final sentences. I would like plain Roman. As soon as poss, pls."

Jim Murdoch, the new master printer, took the copy for setting, and I went on to the rest of the daily stuff piled in the tray, and there was plenty, but only correspondence about headings, alteration in addresses and telephone numbers, all small stuff, part of the ordinary do. But one letter touched the hackles. I hardly read it and put it face down to the left of the blotting pad to be read after Jo had brought in the accounts, and that took a couple of hours.

Edwina came in with coffee, croissants, and hot rolls with shrimp paste, anchovy paste, and little sausages.

"How's everything?" I asked her.

"Anybody think they never taste coffee," she said, and closed that eye. "The rolls and filling I make myself. Any complain?"

"Keep right on. Do the girls and boys like it?"

"Just love it."

"So do I. Any chance of putting fruit in this pastry?"

"No troub'."

"Let's see it. Taste it. You might have a business."

"I'll work my ass off."

"It's a nice ass. Let me know. I'll set you up."

She turned her back.

"Mean that?"

"I don't say what I don't mean."

She walked out—I thought tiredly—and Ben Grimes came in with paint samples for the doors. I chose a good blue, with white jambs, and the same for the windows.

"Make a nice job," he said. "Round the back as well?"

"Everywhere you can splash paint."

"Good enough. It's non-flam, you might like to know. Be a smashing job, finished."

In that pause I reached for the letter from Paul Letivier. I had met him at Les Deux Magots, a professor of English, and regularly gave him my *Herald Trib* when I was in Paris, often ten days at a time, and we talked about politics, the social scene, and the European Community, which I know little or nothing about, and Sartre, even less, and Marchais, Mitterand, and President Giscard d'Estaing. He was small, thin, with black frizzy hair, falling out, and large pale-grey eyes, sad, I thought. He admired nobody. They were all traitors, except himself, and he was a dedicated follower of Robespierre, though he said nothing to convince me of what he thought, exactly. I considered him a Frenchman, with all that must mean, and as such, an argument against himself and most of what he said.

Dear Friend,

By logical coincidence I was in the office of a mutual acquaintance, I must say with some surprise, Jeanine-Françoise Thon, to deliver a thesis for typing, and having our coffee, she mentioned that she had a most interesting dinner at La Coupole with this Englishman who completely enchanted her and seemed to know the entire world. By judicious questioning, who should this Englishman be except yourself. It sweetened our coffee, I must say, and I arranged to take her to dinner three nights later but not at La Coupole, of course, because professorial emolument, having no elastic, does not stretch so far.

Jeanine-Françoise has a travel and secretarial agency, and one also for models, and she has an arrangement with two women in London, staying—imagine!—at your address, though they have an office, also for secretaries and models, at Full Moon Lane, near Throgmorton Street. They are often here, and they exchange secretaries and models with each other. But though Jeanine-Françoise is certainly not, her London colleagues are wreathed with the flowers of Lesbos, which adds a certain piquance, if, for my part, as a blundering male, I have never solved to my satisfaction how fingers and tongue yield a full horn of pleasure. However, my doubts in this matter are not the object of this letter.

To my great disappointment, Jeanine-Françoise did not meet me as she had promised, and I telephoned many times to her office, and also to her apartment shared by other girls, but no reply from one, and only that she had not arrived from the other.

Have you any information? Because now we are desperate. So many days go by. Her business suffers. But she is so nice. A good family. The best education. Serious. How does she permit herself to disappear? Who is responsible?

We looked at all possibilities. If we have no substantial news by this coming Friday, we shall go to Interpol. We have no intention of permitting our beautiful Jeanine-Françoise to be drowned in the sea of anonyme.

I am so sorry to bring you such news.

Please reply immediately.

I am always your friend.

Paul L.

P.S. A telegram will be appreciated.

I sat back in a state of almost maudlin shock.

Interpol enquiries must reach the police station down the road. They had a file on me for almost the same reason. A girl, missing.

What was I to say?

I telephoned Celli, but she was not in her set, or at the office.

That inner freeze, as if I were on a peak in snow cloud, seeing nothing, feeling only that horrid squeeze of the gut, was all I could think about.

I sent Paul a long telegram of regrets that I had no news after the dinner at La Coupole, and to let me know any development immediately.

But I was remembering Jayb and cursing, in black night, that I had let him bludgeon me into letting her go, instead of taking her home and having the pleasure of seeing her shut the door.

To protect her, or because I was a shrinking craven and afraid of him?

A wonderful discovery to find I was afraid of Jayb.

But I was, and I had to make sure I realised it, without excuses.

Afraid of Jayb?

Yes. I was, and had been for too long.

I was sickened.

That ape-faced neophron, a stinking vulture, of eye, beak and talons, but nothing of heart, less of spirit, none in all the realms of human decency.

I had to take the bull by the horns.

Celli called from her set, sounding bad-tempered.

"Come up here and look at a letter. Instead of going to Didcot, let's go to the police down the road."

"Are you stupid?"

"Possibly. We could save ourselves some trouble. Why *must* we go to Didcot?"

"I see. All right. Meet you downstairs?"

Inspector Wheatman knew more than we did. He opened a file—2293 AD—and read Penna Cately's background, and opened another—2293 ADX1—and a different sequence of facts. He held up three photographs of Penna I had taken from the boat, and two of someone else taken somewhere else.

"Which is Penna Cately?" he asked, and we both agreed my photographs were of her.

The other girl I had never seen before.

"Oh," he said, and put his chin on his fists. "We were making enquiries. Penna Cately's not a common name, neither is Penna, nor Cately. Two together's *far* from common. This lot in Didcot we knew about a few days ago, but she doesn't fit in with Mrs. Tukes down the road here. She doesn't recognise her. You don't. So she's not the one? All right. Why does somebody take the trouble to phone up and tell us she *is?*"

"They phoned us up, too," Celli said. "Why? Hoping we'd give over?"

"Give over what?"

"Well. Looking for her. Didcot's a fair distance. Who wants to go out there? Just to see a face, and say yoo-hoo?"

Inspector Wheatman took Paul's letter, and looked at me. He had white hair, and eyes, I thought, to match, arctic grey and bright.

"Here's the same thing, different country," he said. "Two girls go out with you. Then they've gone. Why?"

"That's why we're here," I said. "We want—or I want—to know—why?"

"No crystal balls here. We'll have to work on it."

"Talk to Mrs. Tukes," I said. "Penna lived with her. Two men took her stuff away. Gave her twelve months' rent. Cash. It's a lot of money. Why? Who *was* it? *Why?* Leaked? By phone call? Why? It's not the Penna we knew."

"Take an oath on it?"

"Anytime. I saw her—how many times?—in a bikini. That girl you've got couldn't wear one."

"Why not?"

"The shape. Nothing like it. Any more?"

"Thanks for coming. We've still got some work to do. I'll be in touch."

We walked along Wapping High in the bare, drab part, brickwork here and there, gates, walls, the desert.

"Christ," Celli said. "It could have been me."

"It could *still* be you."

She nodded, walking slowly, a pace at a time.

"Been thinking about it," she said. "Did either of them know something? I mean, something they shouldn't've?"

"Come on, Celli. What *something?*"

She stopped, looking at me, and her eyes seemed the same colour as the rain, but they were aware with fear and oddly lit, almost with the glint of a seagull's.

"Look, A.G.," she said. "You're no bee-eff. I've been doing your travel tickets for the past few years. I know where you've been. And what for. Why do you think we had those offices? Where do you think Waygoes got his runners?"

A landscape seemed to be coming out of fog.

"All right," I said. "Explain Penna Cately."

"Easy. She wasn't part of the job. Interfering. With what? A run. *Your* run. You refused three jobs just to go with her, didn't you? You put them off over the weekends. Oh yes. You did the runs. But not when they said so, the last three times. What happened? Tickets changed. Reservations changed. Pickups changed. Everything upside down. A lot of people keep an eye on that sort of thing. You'd be surprised. A couple of our people were locked up in Moscow. Why? They'd had telegrams changing dates and places. No more than that. So they were made a mark. Taken out of the air queue. Questioned. Searched. A couple of students? But they were found to be carrying about a couple of million pounds worth of heroin. All very innocent? And who gave the word?"

I looked down quiet, drab Wapping High, of crumbling bricks and sad concrete. The Daemon was just around the curve.

"All right," I said. "Who?"

Celli started walking.

"Ah, come on, A.G., for Christ's sake," she said. "Who? Penna. Who else? She was a plant. Cambridge? M.A.? London School of Economics? Think we didn't know? She wanted to join us. As a model. She filled in the form. A fur-grader? At Aronfelt's. They never heard of her. It's all the same with that sort. They think anything they say's Gospel. You? Who are you? Take it or leave it. We were after her the minute she left the office. We got her to the Daemon. Bottsi introduced her to you. And you know what happened."

"What?"

"You went bloody mad, of course."

"She was a lovely girl."

"A bloody snake, that's what you mean. She nigh shopped the lot of us. If you'd done the run she thought you were making, you'd have been inside, this moment. Not walking down here with me."

Her voice broke and she coughed into her hands, turning away, threw off my arm.

"Biggest mistake I ever made," she said, into a tissue. "Got the police in. That got you in. So? Poor old Waygoes had to get in, both feet."

"*Poor* old Waygoes?"

"Why not?" She looked at me, tears dried, a real cat, claws out. "Who lets me stay at the Daemon for this rent? Where else could I get it? Who else pays me my money? Where else could I get it? Where could I get the life I've got now? Where could *you?* Except here. At the Daemon. Where?"

It was fact. I had nothing to say.

"Come on up and have a drink."

She ran to cross the road.

"No," she said, over her shoulder. "I've got to find Botts'."

"Where is she?"

"With that bastard, Thelma. I get my hands on her, I swear to Christ I'll do her. I will, I'll rip her guts."

"Wouldn't be too sensible."

"Christ's sake, give over. What do you know? Ever been in love, have you?"

Not in that manner, and I suppose I had missed a lot, and in many ways regretted that loss of experience, but then, less-than-the-horn-of-pleasure seemed overflowing with pain of a certain sort that, again, I could never know, or even so much as imagine.

I let her go on ahead, and walked through the garden, pruned and cleaned for winter, beautiful anyway, and picked up mail, a couple of tradesmen's bills and a newspaper, and walked slowly upstairs, asking myself how it was to live at the Daemon.

In a word, delicious.

I could almost "taste" the atmosphere. The polish, the cleanliness, the flowers and plants, the quiet, all, everything meant by the Daemon, and the big rooms of my set, and the shining, heavy front door that whispered open, and breathed shut, in warm, known welcome.

Yes. Celli was right.

Where else could I live at that rental, absurd at any time? Or where else, at any rental, live at all?

Who else paid me that amount of money? To a Swiss bank?

I had to remember when it was necessary to be grateful. Sometimes we are not always aware. We pretend, but the facts poke fun and, savagely in mid-laugh, put a boot in the face.

I went over to the telephone, and in the comfortable leather armchair, asked for Enquiries and got the Didcot number, and Personnel, and waited, looking at walls of books, statuary, bronzes, wondering what I might do without them, or with them, elsewhere. I simply could not see them, or me, anywhere else.

Personnel came on, a woman's voice, Yes, may I help you? I said I was looking for Penna Cately, and wanted her address. Cately—Cately, the voice said. Yes, I know the name. Wait, please. A couple of moments. Yes, I knew I'd seen it. She left the day before yesterday. Well, from what I've heard, to go up to Leicester for a better job. We can't give further particulars. No. Absolutely against the rules. You could apply to the director. If you can't prove you're a near relative, we can't give an address. Sorry. You aren't the police, are you? No? Sorry. Nothing we can do.

Half a dozen notions jostled. She could have been planted. The moment she served her time, leave, tell any story, and where do you look? But someone called Penna Cately had been there. Therefore? She was alive. Where was she at the moment? Find out.

I put the phone down.

Find out? How?

All right. How about Jeanine-Françoise?

I still heard her voice.

Was she, too, to be "planted," and then sent somewhere else? To confuse, to be a red herring? How long could a search for missing persons go on? The police never closed a file until evidence of death or the identity of a body. Where to find the body?

And what the hell—all right, the *hell*—could I do about it?

I?

Who the hell was *I*?

Or any of us?

Was it, really, that anybody could do what they liked if they had the cunning, *and* the money?

Was it true?

Of course.

It had been done, it was being done, and apparently it could be done again, always with impunity if, that is, somebody made no mistake to give a lead to the police.

There had been no mistake, and that meant skilful planning, because no healthy girl can be spirited away without somebody's complaining, though what amazed me was that nobody had. Even her landlady, Mrs. Tukes, had let more than a week go by, and then only because her tenant was a week behind in rent.

Nobody gave a damn about anybody any more.

Money was all.

Got it? Right. *Not* got? Too bad.

But what a *rotten* way to be. *Rotten*.

Who was behind it?

Waygoes? His servant, Jayb?

I had to get rid of Jayb. But there could be others. The two, at least, taking Penna's clothes from Mrs. Tukes's place. How were men employed like that? But, then, how were men got to place a bomb? Or to shoot innocents, unaware?

How was a human being to be suborned to a level where any human being became a victim? A spiritual vacuum? How was it to be filled?

What nonsense. There *was* a Jayb. Explain *him*. Explain any bastard planting a bomb or pulling a trigger on any man, whoever he might be. Explain it. Give it words.

No.

It was nothing more than a high lark of vicious, unregenerate brutes, twisted infants.

But then, Jayb and the people with him were no infants. Whether in London or anywhere else. In France, obviously, Jayb had his opposites. He could depend on them. They would depend on hm. Or in any other country.

The very devil of a conclusion.

But correct.

They could send the rest of us to the devil, and go free.

A bloody fine conclusion, but correct.

What to do?

Nothing.

I looked about at my library of hundreds of years—who knew how many?—of human thought confined to print and bindings, and certainly thousands of years of artistry in statuary, and the craft of the potter, and through it all, the same thought had flourished. Kill, or banish. Those left to live were merely harmless, as with lice on the body.

As our coffee goddess said, no troub'.

But what had all of us been doing all that time? Not enough to get together to promote something of a better life? Evidently not. But the churches had been busy torturing people, not that it did much good. The politicians tortured people, and the churches had the bare-face to point a finger. Very few were any better off.

Suddenly, I was sick of arguing with myself.

I had no answers.

What a stupid way of evading responsibility.

All right. To hell with it. Stupider, but clean-cut.

Jo knocked, and Jim Murdoch came in with the first pulls, clammy with printer's ink.

"I don't know what people are going to say about this, sir," he said.

"All right. What do *you* say? You're people, too, aren't you?"

"I don't know what to say about it."

"Why not?"

"It's a way of thinking. I'm not sure I've the ability."

"If you've got the ability to set it, and run the press, what's stopping you?"

"Well, sir. I don't know. I've never thought about it."

"About what?"

"Banking, and that. Money. It's all strange. I'm not sure many people'll like it. Or understand it."

"It's part of their lives."

"Not the part they want to think about."

"When do they *do* any thinking?"

Jim put his hands flat on the desk.

"Have you read all this, sir?" he asked, almost as a small boy. "Christ, if it's all true, we've devils in charge of us."

"Wouldn't surprise me. Leave it for the moment. I'll edit."

Devils in charge of us?

From Jim, the best of the plainest best?

After all, what *are* people? They only do what they *can* do. Pay the rent, pay off a mortgage. Get by in the week. Do better if they can. What else are they *supposed* to do? Who supposes they are going to do it? Politicians? Who gives *them* the right to think so? When did they ever help *people?*

Arguing with myself again.

Like arguing with the telly, fatheaded.

"Have you read any of this, Jo?" I asked her.

"All of it, sir. I think it's marvellous. 'Specially the part about giving everybody a thousand pounds, and any child born five thousand pounds, and women to draw fifty a week, from birth, to make them economically free. I'd certainly vote for that."

"Something for nothing? It never worked."

"It's not what *he* says. He says it's ours, but we're too ignorant to see it. Cattle, he calls us. Way he puts it, I reckon he's dead right. I'd like to know a lot more about it."

"It would finish off the pound. Put the banks out of business."

"That's part of the idea. It's not Parliament or the trade unions governing the country. It's the banks. Every idiot dances to their tune. But nobody dares say so. That's what he says. Way he says it, I believe him."

"I didn't know you were interested in politics?"

"I'm not. But I'm interested in the state of the people, me in-cluded. My mum's been a widow since I was born. How she's got along, I don't know. She's scraped to send me to school. But if I wasn't earning decent money now, I don't know what'd become of her. Why don't people think of the old? After all, the country was *built* on them. Without them, where'd we be?"

"Fair enough. I'll read this stuff and see. Anything else?"

"Trouble. Jon Davie called. The printers are picketing. Afflin and that lot. We won't get the font. Leslie Farquhar called. Pickets. You won't get your paper."

"Get them on the phone, will you? Tell them to go out to a call box. There could be pairs of ears in the office."

"Not worried about them here?"

"No."

She shut her eyes and wrinkled her nose in a smile, a real, rock-solid Cockney, and went out, and I got on with the editing.

I saw what Jo and Jim had meant. While I ran over it with the pencil, Jon called. I had to persuade him to go in on Sunday evening, and I would take the van there, and run the font out. I did the same with Leslie Farquhar, with the same argument. I simply could not afford to lose the order, and neither could they.

"But listen," Leslie said, "you make sure you have a dry run, first. If you see pickets, you shove off. Come back later. I'll wait till, let's say, ten."

"I'll be there at seven-thirty Sunday night. I don't know of a more desolate hole on this earth than your place on a Sunday night. I don't think you'll have many pickets there."

"Listen, chum. You'd be surprised what a lovely coke brazier, a big teapot, and a pile of sandwiches and sausage rolls and pork pies'll do for desolation. Ever tried a bacon sandwich and a cup of hot, sweet tea round a nice red-hot brazier, have you?"

"No."

"You better go back to living."

I put all the paper together and told Jo I was going across to Mr. Ram Das Motilal's office, and strolled down a quiet street, and left, into Love and Vinegar Lane, and the Motilal office in two houses knocked together, and the clack of typewriters. He had several people waiting to see him, and he unclipped his pince-nez, took the bundle in his usual gentle way, and said he would telephone.

"I know about it," he said, holding a hand flat to a brown, bald head. "I am a little worried. He is *very* hard on the banks and the Stock Exchange. That is one thing. The law is another. Leave it with me, if you please."

I went downstairs through a queue of brown clients, all of them with the same air of reaching for God through the fogs of hopelessness. I could feel despair. Feel it, as if feeling material. They seemed to sweat a fear of living.

"What's wrong?" I asked Miss Holkar, a big woman in a pale blue sari with pink roses, at the reception counter, punching a rubber stamp at paper.

"We are all having hell," she called, staring big, beautiful eyes, blacked with kohl. "It is Emigration. They have found a lot of them coming in, and no papers. Or forged, no good. A lot will have to go back. But where to? Pakistan, Bangladesh, they are big. Where does a family go? India is much bigger. Can a man see his family starve? Here, he has a job. He can pay rent and buy things and send his children to school. Be respectable. *How* can they go back? To *what?*

"Don't you have committees to deal with it?"

"Talk. Air. But an official can put a stamp—like this—and you have finished in this country. Everything you have saved or bought has all gone. Where is justice, here?"

"But they shouldn't have come in, should they?"

She slammed down the stamp and shuffled the pile of forms.

"Don't get in bad temper, Khunti," a man said, on the side. "It is always worse for us. We are at the mercy. Even in the temple we are not safe. Prayers are no good. What is? Let us try to be calm. Even if we would like to cry."

I walked down Love and Vinegar Lane, wondering, in that barren of broken brick and boarded doors and windows, exactly what I would do if I were Asian, with or without a family, threatened with deportation for any reason, and I had no reply. But I knew that in a position of authority I would let them all stay, and let time wipe away the bruises. They were all good people. Those I knew worked hard. What more was expected? We had stayed in their country for a couple of hundred years, and in great comfort. It was time to return the kindness.

Almond told me at the Daemon that Mr. Waygoes was lunching at the Skipper's Cabin and would like me to join him.

I went downstairs and found him sitting opposite Teucer at the captain's table, eating from a silver tureen of wonderful stew.

"Sit down and tuck in," he said. "I hear you're having trouble with pickets. Not on any account must you cross that line, wherever, however. The working people of this country are just beginning to get on their feet. I have no intention in the smallest way of preventing their getting what they want. Justice is in question."

"You're spitting in your own face," I said. "And in mine. They didn't want to print your copy. *They* made up *their* minds. Never mind about you or me. I object. Justice *is* in question. I've employed them at top wages. And they tell me—and you—what they will or will not print? There's justice for me as well, y'know?"

"That's your business. I don't want that job to cross picket lines. That's final. You have some other sort of print, haven't you? And paper?"

"Of course. I object to throwing money away on a font I'm not allowed to accept because of a lot of blackguards misusing a privilege."

Waygoes put down the fork.

"They aren't blackguards," he said quietly. "They're using the pathetically little power they have to protect themselves from what they see as an attack on the unions. They've misread what's been written. It's that ignorance I want to expunge. Their schooling doesn't teach them to use their heads. They're examined on their ability to absorb what's been taught. That's precious damn little. I'll defray any loss, depend on it. When may I expect the copy?"

He cut the pieces of lamb and spread potatoes on the fork, and looked at me. The pale eyes half smiled, half threatened, though how I thought that, God only knows, and I was last to know.

"I feel like slinging the job back at you," I said, equally steady in choosing a forkful. "I'm the boss. I pay their wages. I have the say. They're not going to tell me what to do."

"Who's going to do it without them?" Teucer asked quietly.

"The people loyal to me. We can put that job out with what we've got."

"You *had* people loyal to you. You haven't now. They've gone home."

Instantly I thought I knew what had happened.

Afflin and his friends had cut the powerlines.

"Very well," I said. "No sense going on with it. Get another printer."

"That's already been decided," Teucer said. "The printing will be done in Paris. You will be there to supervise."

"I have no intention of going to Paris."

Teucer helped himself to another ladle of stew.

"If that's final, then you must consider the possibility of

finding your personal effects on the pavement outside within the next couple of hours," Waygoes said, stripping a bone with a goat's long teeth. "Either people work with or against. If they are against, they have no place here. Understood?"

I leaned back and laughed.

"I believe you're behind Afflin," I said. "You could have put him up to it."

"But of course, and why not? We need publicity. A story about loyalty to a union is front page. Did you see the papers this morning?"

"No. I don't read them."

"You see? I've often thought you were far more Continental than British. You don't know what's going on. Well, Mr. Afflin is a hero. He stands as a champion of the unions. Now, I can reply. I can ram at least the main idea home."

"I've edited the copy. What *is* the main idea?"

"Teucer, tell him."

I had never before looked so closely at Teucer. He had a likeness to his father, slender, a bit of a pot in the trousers, hands of short fingers, almost bamboo stems, long fingernails, short straight nose, wide nostrils—it seemed that he might have the profile of the Daemon—jowls of good living and appetite, that fat lower lip, good teeth, and an uprising stook of hair, now glossy with cream, combed up from the forehead, with long sideburns to the jaw, and a carefully razored moustache across the upper lip, curving down almost to the chin. He had a notion about his appearance. He was vain. Evidently he looked in the glass. He pretended to himself. But on what assumption? Instantly I thought of the copy.

"Is there any need?" he asked gently, almost affectedly. "He's read it, hasn't he?"

"Read it, in that sense, no," I said. "Edited for setting, yes."

"What's the difference?"

"Read, for interest. Edit, for the job. The format."

"But do you mean to tell me you can read something without its meaning becoming clear?"

"Of course. I'm not a reader as such. I'm a printer. I put words into print. Type size. Font. The 'meaning'—whatever it is—means nothing to me. I just want a good job. That answer you?"

"To some extent," Waygoes said, clanging the ladle on the tureen for service. "I never understood professional blindness. Either you read what you're looking at and it has a meaning, or you're simply classifying arcana. In your men, Afflin and company, there seems a higher intelligence at work. They recognised what they were reading. It seemed to attack them and their fellow union members, and they refused to work. That is their right. Never mind that they were wrong-headed, and didn't understand what was in front of them. That's a fault of their lack of education. Our fault. That's those of us pretending *to* know."

"Paying their wages, I have nothing to say?"

"Of course not. They have only one life. They use it as they wish. They defend themselves as they may, and must. *You* pay them for their work. If they refuse to work, you *don't* pay. Simple?"

"But they call in pickets."

"Why not? They protect themselves."

"But there's no protection for us?"

"Of course there is. But you don't use it. You've never even thought of it."

"What is it?"

Sylvia reached for the plates, and Dhara lifted the tureen.

"The destruction of the banking monopoly," he said, shifting his head between Dhara's bottom and the tureen. "That's the underlying cause of our trouble world-wide. I'd like apricot tart, please."

"I'd like the apple pudding with cream," Teucer said.

"I'd like a cup of espresso," I said. "Underlying cause?"

Bosun came in striding in a hurry, lifting Sylvia out of the way.

"Par'me," he said. "Guvnor, here's a ripe bit. Ol' Mabbs got hisself in dead trouble. He's down at Hammersmith, there. Some bloke was mucking about with his daughter. She's a teacher. She never wanted to have nothing to do with him. So last night he had a dead go at her. She called her dad. He done no more, he went acrost there, and—you remember that horny mitt?—he bashed his head in. Clobbered him soft, he did."

"Very well done," Waygoes said. "What more?"

"They're holding him, charge of murder."

Waygoes pointed at Teucer.

"Go to Motilal," he said. "Take him down there. Get the best legal defence. See that he has all the amenities possible. Food. Drink. Books, etcetera. If it had been *my* daughter, same thing. Women *must* be protected. For the most part they're defenceless. I'd certainly have killed the bastard. Need some money?"

"I can do with a little more."

"Here."

Waygoes took out a wallet and slid notes, and Teucer followed the Bosun.

"That's the end of luncheon," Waygoes said, clapping hands. "You'll be on the night train to Paris?"

"I suppose so."

"Good. Sad to see such a lovely collection of books and statuary lining the pavement outside here. Bring back a good job, there's a good chap."

Aftermath of ultimatum? Residue of open threat? Patronage at its most mephitic? Whatever. I writhed, but without the guts to say or do anything. I felt myself despicable, without respect or any present grace. But to assert myself meant leaving the Daemon, and in all conscience, I asked myself, was mere self-righteousness worth it?

And what *was* self-righteousness? I did not give, in those moments, one small damn. To hell with it. Everybody has to pay a rent or tax of some sort to be able to live, and I was paying mine.

I went downstairs to the work cubicle and looked at the tidy way Jo had left it, and then along, through the lights to the steps, and down to the lower level, and cool river air, walking a fair way to an open space of old heavy wine racks, and there was the collection, in rows, by torchlight a real wonder of beauty from other time. But somebody had named and classified them, by period, which I could never have done, and each wore a cardboard collar with details printed in excellent script. That lovely parade of wonder from so long ago seemed to bring other hope. So many generations had suffered, but work had survived to assure that minds and spirits and concepts of beauty had existed even among the earliest of us, and they all seemed to ask the same question.

Why had beauty gone to the Devil?

Were we all insane? A little on the loose? Victims of advertising? Photographs of lumescent mediocrity? Were we blinded by the act of reading? Because we could read, were we coddled? Because we could write, were we stupefied with our cleverness?

I put a hand on cool marble, and tried to imagine myself in place of the artist, but the marble only warmed under my caress, nothing more. There was link only of sympathy, and that was all, except for admiration, even love, whatever that is, in thinking of skill, or mastery in stone, even though the flame of the artist denied me any warmth.

Up in the set, I called Celli and asked for Jeanine-Françoise's address, and she told me to hold on, and came back to spell it out.

"Listen," she said, suddenly loud, "we haven't been able to get in touch. She told us she was coming here and she was going to stay with you. Not a peep since."

"That's funny."

"She's got friends she's sharing an apartment with. They're all very worried."

"Anything I can do?"

"Not much, from here."

"And Botti?"

"Nothing. I'm going bloody barmy."

"About?"

"Her. That's all. 'bye."

I called Ella, but she was out and I left a message. My tickets were on the desk, held down by Andromeda's plinth. I stroked her, and saw I had to be at Heathrow at five-thirty. I swallowed hate of flying, and swore I would return by train and ferry. But getting to Paris that night I thought a good idea, saving a night's sleep and more than half a day.

But.

I had a thought, thoroughly nasty. Celli had said nothing about those tickets.

I crossed the landing and went down two flights to her set, and rapped a quiet tattoo of fingernails.

She opened the door open-mouthed to ask, and I held up a warning index, and she let me in. She had a Hungarian dance on, and so I whispered. Her stare was answer enough.

"You didn't know?"

"What tickets?"

"For Paris. British Airways. Seven o'clock."

She shook her head.

"This set might be bugged. And mine. Go across the road. There's a café not far down. I'll meet you there, fifteen minutes. Try to get hold of somebody. Book me on the night train to Paris. Sleeper. I'll pay when I get there."

She nodded, and reached for a sheepskin coat from the stand, and I went upstairs, saw to my luggage, and went down, seeing Amy and Joe Briggs in the garden cutting blossom, waving, crossing Wapping High, going down Cinnamon Lane toward the café, seeing Celli about three hundred yards in front. I crossed the road and ran into Edwina coming out of a small, boarded house, carrying a covered wooden tray and the billycan she made the coffee in.

"Oh, sir," she called, and the echo reached the gulls. "Just taking the tea break up to your place. This is where I want to open. Like to see it? Take a see."

I went in the small passage, a room opening off to the right, a mattress on the floor, blankets folded neatly, a pillow, a table, chair, candlestick, and out to a kitchen, gas stove, cupboard, all in a faint stink of sewage, rats, and long disuse.

"Make the coffee or tea and anything else in the shop in future," I said. "Not here. I'll get the workmen in and do the place over. Don't sleep here. You're asking for trouble. Sleep in the shop. There's a room and bath. You'll be safe. And healthy. Understood?"

She nodded, out to the rubble of a back garden and a flourish of dandelion and thistles.

"Thought I was getting a place of my own," she said, but her lips barely moved. "Mean I can't have it?"

"You've got it. I'll have the workmen in tomorrow. But you move out *now*."

"'Kay."

I almost ran along to the café on the corner, empty upstairs, and down below. I looked about, but no Celli, not in the lower arm of the L, or in the telephone niche. I thought of the girls' room, and sat down. The waitress had seen nobody like Celli—I told her of the sheepskin coat—and I ordered a cup of tea, listening to rattle-bang noise and slum howling, watching the stairway. But no Celli.

It was the longest thirty minutes, and I kept it by my watch, deliberately. Celli did not meet me. Did *not*.

Then?

She was in with the boys and girls. On the other side. Poor Waygoes. I went to the telephone and rang British Airways, and asked which agency had booked my tickets. Delay and buzzing and pips, but anyway the agency was in Sloane Street, and the nice girl there said it was closed, but I could call this number. I had no intention. I thought I saw what could have happened if I had gone by train. Obviously, I was a mark. For what? I was anxious to find out, but I could guess with the best.

I went back to the Daemon and ordered a taxi, and left in plenty of time for the airport bus to Heathrow from the Kensington Terminal, all the while in a cold lather, wondering if the teeth were going to snap on me, and why? It was the fact that I could give certain information to the police. But where was the proof? I could list addresses of drops all over Europe, but those "drops" were cafés or bistros or travel offices, none of them with the name of any person.

Over the years I had no proof. The only real proof was in my bank account at Credit Swiss. On the dates of those payments I had made runs. For whom? Where was the proof? What other evidence? My word against whose?

I thought I saw a pattern, but thought is a fragile monster, running all ways, ending never, except in doubt.

I sent Paul Letivier a telegram from Heathrow to say I would meet him at the Relais Plaza at ten o'clock, and I checked in for the eight o'clock flight and changed my ticket from economy to first class, if only to put a further, smaller spanner in the works, whatever they were.

We were in Paris on time, and I took a cab to the Plaza-Athénée, and luckily a room was vacant, and after a spruce, went downstairs, through the passage to the Relais, and there was Paul on a high stool at the bar. We had a few moments' chit-chat, and ordered a champagne cocktail—it never tastes the same elsewhere—and had a look at the menu, and the maître advised a small steak, cream of spinach, and sauté potatoes, and the sommelier chose a Cheval Blanc.

"It is impossible," Paul said. "Here is a girl, so intelligent, so really smart, she conducts her own travel and currency exchange business, and without a word, she disappears? Extremely successful, most profitable, everything a dream, really, of success, employing eleven people, but they cannot enter the offices? It defies rational explanation. Unless we consider death. Kidnapping. Why? She stays with other girls. They had a habit of discussing each other's problems. But they remember not a word that would lead to this. Hmh? Then?"

Eyes up, hands up, a shrug, and the maître came to show us a table, though we ate without appetite. Paul put the napkin down, looking at his watch.

"Iva said she would be back at this time. I'll telephone."

While he was away I had time to compare the business of Penna Cately with Jeanine-Françoise Thon. They came out at about the same. Both seemed to have walked out of a life they enjoyed, without a word or any sign, even to their friends.

Overall I seemed to see Jayb's leer, and I had to put the knife and fork down.

I wanted to kill him more than I wanted to eat.

Paul came back smiling.

"Three of her friends are in," he said. "They will see us. Shall we go? They are business girls, so they must be up with the pigeons. Thank you for my dinner. But I refuse to leave the wine."

"Good. Here's to hope."

Paul put down the glass.

"With such a bouquet, who could refuse us?"

The apartment was only a few streets farther on from my old hotel in the Rue Balzac, and I got out with a feeling of being home. The lift took us to the fourth floor, and Biffi opened the door, a beauty in a red woollen dressing gown, and Iva, in a black kimono and face cream, and Lakshmi, from somewhere in the East, in red pyjamas, three beauties out of the book. We had a babble of talk, and then I asked if "Niné"—as they called Jeanine-Françoise—had got back from her dinner with me that night.

"No," Iva said. "We thought she slept with you, of course?"

"She didn't. We had a cab from La Coupole, and because I had a business engagement, I left her at the bridge, and took another cab. There's no news at all?"

"None," Lakshmi said, small teats exquisitely shadowed in red. "I was there this morning. Her staff are frantic. Many have left. Mail is piled on the floor. What is to happen?"

"But don't the police or the fire brigade have a key for emergency?" I asked.

"From their point of view, there is no emergency," Paul said. "She might have gone off for ten days or so—"

"We know that's nonsense," Iva said. "Ten days, two weeks, three weeks, where does it end?"

"Pity there isn't a spare key," I said.

Iva turned in a flurry, and ran to the door.

"There is," she called. "Give me time to dress."

Paul called a cab, and we found the place just off the Rivoli. There was no concierge, and Iva let us in, and Paul sent the lift creaking to the fourth floor. There were notes stuck in the door cracks and others half under the mat. Iva used the key, and we went in to a surprising pile of mail on the floor, a tidy front office, a tidy larger office behind, and a smaller, well-furnished office on the side. But despite air-conditioning hum, a smell became an affliction.

Iva put hands to her face and stared away, and turned, running out screaming, echoing in the corridor, gut screams, horror.

"The smell of death," Paul said, a sleepwalker. "But, Christ."

"Call the police," I said. "They'll need the firemen."

There are times when clocks mean nothing, and time beats in

the brain with voices. We were taken to a station near the Champs, and the forms were filled in, and an English Interpol sergeant asked me questions. Fortunately, I was staying at the Plaza-Athénée, which gave me a further measure of respectability, and I had an appointment at Edouard Riannes, the printer in the Faubourg St. Honoré, at eleven o'clock.

"Won't get much sleep," the sergeant said, pressing the stud on his ball pen. "Right. You carry on your business, and you can expect to hear from us tomorrow sometime. But don't leave Paris."

"No intention. Any idea what happened to her?"

"Strangled. With her pantyhose. Some nice blokes about. Ought to bring back the death penalty everywhere. They've got the guillotine here. We could do with it."

Sergeant Wren was right. Even a wonderfully comfortable bed was no help, and I went puff-eyed down the Matignon, and turned past our embassy to the office of Edouard Riannes, an old-fashioned place, with the beat of machines thumping under the feet. The copy took no time to read through, and Riannes put it all together in a folder, sent a boy out with it, and brought a bottle of cognac from a cupboard, and two tulip glasses.

"It should take no more than today, tonight, and perhaps a couple of hours tomorrow," he said, pushing the spectacles up the bridge of his nose with a little finger. "I am always interested in new ideas, of course. That poster, for example. The Charter of the Bank of England. But is it true? A fact? This bank was formed to create money out of nothing?"

"It's in the charter. In so many words."

"But out of nothing?"

"That's what they did. You probably had the same with the Bank of France."

"Surely impossible?"

"The records must be available. Find out when the first paper money was issued. On what authority."

"What does Mr. Waygoes intend to do?"

"Form a new political party, I understand. To take power away from the banks. Give it back where it belongs. To the people."

He shook his head, raised the tulip.

"Truly an impossible idea," he said, and laughed. "Elementary economics forbids such a ridiculous move. Currency would be worth nothing. After all, we have memories of Weimar. Worthless money. A wheelbarrow full of marks for a loaf of bread?"

I raised my glass to his toast.

"I'm an economic moron," I said. "I believe most of us are in the same trough. We don't know enough. Others take advantage? People like Waygoes would like to put it right. We're in a bondage of our own making."

"A bondage of bankers? I agree. But which genius will set us free? Where is the promised land? Where are the answers?"

"Read the posters and the pamphlets. They'll probably give you some sort of understanding. I shall come for them tomorrow? At noon?"

"Make it three, and be certain."

I strolled along I suppose my favourite stretch on earth, past Hermès and Lanvin, down to the Madeleine and over to Fouquet's, to sit at a table and drink more coffee and a cognac and buy the *Herald Trib*, and sit, happily enjoying life, but remembering Jeanine-Françoise, that perfectly beautiful girl, reduced to horror, and the indignity of foreign hands, and a plastic bag, and the print evaded me, and the coffee held the taste of ash. I paid, and walked by Maxim's and the Crillon, down to the Rond-Point-that-was, and along the Matignon again, left, to the Plaza. The concierge gave me the key, and a page presented a note on a salver and said someone waited. I expected the sergeant, but the man coming toward me was taller, with another man beside him.

"Mr. Bessell? I'm Inspector Coningsby, of Interpol. Could I have a word?"

I led into the salon, filled with flowers and silken furniture, perfect for a wake.

"About this case of Jeanine-Françoise Thon," he said, putting a folder on his knee. "I shan't take your time. Go back to La Coupole. You say, when you left her you took a cab to your hotel in the Rue Balzac, and you phoned her, and she said she was all right?"

"That is correct."

"Her friends, living there with her, say she never came home."

"Sorry. I telephoned her, and she answered. Just a moment."

I undid my case and went through the file of accounts I kept for tax, and brought out the hotel bill at the Anvers. The telephone call, and its number, was there, and I blessed the bookkeeper.

"Whoever it was mistook the night," I said. "Often happens."

He took a note.

"Right," he said. "You were introduced to her by a Miss Lois Brownlow?"

It was a shock to hear Celli's correct name.

"Yes."

"They ran the same sort of business. Travel, foreign currency exchange, models, and that sort of thing. You knew a Miss Penna Cately?"

"Yes."

"She disappeared?"

"Yes."

He looked at me with a smiling, though icy, eye and settled back in a Louis XV chair, pale green, suiting his complexion.

"You know you have a card with our Customs, and here? You're thoroughly searched, both sides?"

"It's happened."

"Why?"

"I don't know."

He nodded.

"I'd like to look at that case and its contents," he said. "If you object, I can get a warrant."

"Don't bother. Go ahead."

At his look, it seemed, two men came in, and with small tools took the case to pieces, measuring, pressing, prising, squeezing, and he took the diary, order book, journal and files, going through them all, detail by detail.

"You see," he said, same smile, "the French police have doubts about you, and we don't want a British subject pinched if we can help it. So we're doing the donkey work. Unpleasant, but there it is. A girl's dead. Somebody's responsible. Who? That's what we all want to know. Follow?"

I nodded, miserable, thinking of Jeanine-Françoise and Penna, sniffing that disgust, and wondering if Penna, too, had gone into a plastic bag. I had to live with my own filth.

"Well, that's it," the inspector said, more cheerful, and giving me the briefcase, and pushing the books across. "There's nothing here to interest us. I don't think the police here want to talk to you. But you won't be surprised if you have an enquiry on the other side, will you?"

I went out with them and got my key, and upstairs I lay on the bed and slept in my clothes, dead, till early morning, and I took off everything, and had a hot bath, and got back into bed, feeling I had never deserved it, and I woke up, cold, calm, just in time to hear the BBC one o'clock news. I turned it over to the music of Brahms and lay there, wondering what I could do. Well, all right. What *could* I do? Put the scent on Waygoes? He deserved it. But what about the Daemon? Risk having to move away? Everything shifted out, lined up on the pavement, going where?

No.

Never. I needed that set. Nothing else mattered, blackmail or not. In any event, if I informed on Waygoes, the police job must come back to me, and Swiss bank accounts over the years, and probably a visit from Jayb and another plastic bag.

Not worth it.

Only to be free, to come and go as I wished, in a normal day, was worth a little nonsense from Waygoes. He, in fact, over the years had never bothered me. Everything I had done, everywhere I had gone, was of my own free will.

What was my complaint?

None.

Except Penna and Jeanine-Françoise.

There, I felt, I owed a debt, though I was unsure how to pay, or in what coin, or if to Waygoes or Jayb, or both.

It was a grey journey back to London, without any trouble from Customs on either side, and it was grey because rain brought mist and spray, and calls to Paul and Iva had been buzzes and clicks without answers, and I was unsure what to do, the greyest area, where conscience screamed one thing and common sense whispered another.

Coming back to the Daemon was a joy. Hotels, however luxurious, are nothing compared with a set looked after by Mrs. Rapajan and Bhula. I came back to an over-all shine, a faint buoyant smell of wax polish, a gloss of parquet, the old wonder of a fragrance of flowers and welcome from my friends on the shelves, and Andromeda, on the corner of the desk, giving her breasts for my respect, and a kiss for each.

The phone rang. I wondered if to answer.

"Hullo? I've called so often. A.G.? This is Ella Broome."

"Ella. I just got back. Come on up."

"You sure? Not busy or anything?"

"*Come on up.*"

"Be there."

I had never seen Ella in a dress. She had always worn working clothes for the dig, an army surplus jacket of sorts, trousers, and boots, and her hair in a mop and her face a testimony to soap, the whole endeared by her smile and the grace of her movements, all hinting at a hidden beauty.

Herself in the open doorway, hinted nothing.

She was beautiful, simply, plainly, lovely in some sort of a blue dress, silk perhaps, that showed her bony thighs, teatsy up top, small waist, long legs, ankles like wrists, calves of a ballet dancer, fairish hair piled, little make-up, well, yes, and all that, and I was shoved over, not pushed but shoved, and flat.

"Please come in," I said, the original idiot.

"Thank you," she said. "I wondered if you'd recognise me."

"The eyes have it. Incidentally, the rest isn't exactly tiring."

"I'm glad. After all, we had a night in bed, and nothing happened. I can't think why not."

"Sit down and have a drink, and I'll tell you why. What would you like?"

"Fruit juice. But I'd prefer tea. China tea?"

"The kitchen's there. Make it yourself. I've got a couple of calls to make."

"I came at the wrong time."

"At the right time. You're beautiful. A beauty. I wish I had words. Make your tea."

I called Paul in Paris. No reply.

The girls' flat, many a buzz but no reply.

I called Mrs. Rafaele, and she said that Ol' Mabbs was doing fine, well fed, well read, and looking forward to his trial, because Mr. Motilal had got him a good barrister, and he believed the Law was on his side.

That seemed to me to be cockeyed, but after all, it is said that the Law is an ass, and if a "good" barrister could twist it, so that the horny palm of Ol' Mabbs crushing somebody's skull could be explained away in terms of innocence, so be it. I thought of a plastic bag and a smell or two.

"Well," Ella said, tray, teapot, cups, and biscuits in order, "shall we sit down?"

"Let's, and enjoy a bit of peace. It's rare."

"It is. Sugar?"

"Honey."

"Same caloric value."

"Better taste."

"All right. Now. The reason I'm here."

"You want some money."

She nodded, pouring her cup, staring as if she saw something else.

"I think we have a special relationship," she said, as if forcing herself. "You're the only man I've ever slept with. And nothing happened. That's not a compliment. But I know the reason. Next time, better."

"You want a next time?"

"I woke up for a couple of moments. I saw your body. I can't get it out of my mind. I've never been the sort. Well, playing funny with men. Never. But you're different. Let's settle the money. We've found either a Roman or Celtic tomb. We can't tell. Either of them, it's a marvellous find. We want to take it out whole. There's a lot of other, smaller stuff, all important. Apart from that, there's a mosaic pavement. Mosaic's supposed to be Roman. This one's Celtic. We know it is from the lettering we've found. So far. We're beginning to find out about London. This poor old city. We're starting to find out what she was. What she meant. Before the brutes took her. Smashed her. Blasted her

143

beauty. God damn them. Generations of them. Romans. Saxons. Normans. The lot. And the swine are at it today. Look at the place. Who wants to save her?"

She bent her head. I watched little crystals splashing on her clasped hands.

"How much do you need?"

"About three hundred pounds. The van, and ten men."

"Nothing for your people?"

"We never worked for money."

"What kept you going?"

"London."

"Right. You've got it."

I went to the desk and wrote a cheque.

"Where are you going to put the stuff?" I asked.

"Where your collection is. Down under the cubicles."

"Sensible. But is it wise? You put the lot in the hands of Waygoes."

"I've thought of that. But where else?"

"Next door to my place across the road. It's empty, dry. It's mine. I have leasehold. Here's a good van hire firm. They're Asians, but they'll do a good job."

I gave her the card, and she poured more tea.

"If I get worried, could I come up here?" she asked, in a high voice, sharply, unlike her. "Late, say. Middle of the night?"

"Any time. What would you be worried about?"

"Waygoes' son. He's got a master key to all the sets. He comes in when he feels like it. If the girls don't feel like it, he tells them he'll throw them out. He's tried it twice with me. In the main greenhouse. But I can fight. I sleep with a big kitchen knife. He knows it. But if you're fast asleep and a man comes on top of you, what can you do?"

"Are you the only one?"

"Of course not. Anybody he fancies. I believe that's why poor old Botti left. He was after the pair of them. Celli's a real toughie. She said she'd dig his eyes out. That poor Mrs. Osornis, I mean, she's forties. She calls it her rent. Lots of girls here are starting to sleep three and four in a room when he's about the

144

place. Pity we haven't got a few men to go in and smash him up."

"First I've heard of it."

"Nobody wants to get put out on the street. That's the fear."

Immediately I thought of the barmaid at the Lomax and her threat of a team to take care of me, but I also remembered that Waygoes had said he owned the place. She might tell him. Might. But needs must, and the devil was in me. Any thought that girls could be forced against their will, only for the sake of a roof they preferred, that was it.

"Stay here for an hour or so till I get back," I said. "There's the telly, radio, the stereo, books, magazines. Enjoy yourself. I'm going to see if I can fix Mr. Teucer."

She threw a cushion on the floor and sat down, drawing up her knees, smiling.

"I knew you would," she said. "I'll stay."

A cab took me to the Lomax, and I went in, to the beery, kitcheny smells, and the sounds of glasses grasped together, and the tills dinging, people talking, and the pop yelp and twang and, even if early, the place was fairly full.

I saw her about the same time she saw me, and she came along the bar, big smile, a really dangerous piece in black satin, no bra, and something to look at.

"Oh, hullo there," she called. "Thought you'd gone ashore in China. What's it going to be?"

"One for you, and a scotch and soda for me. Look. You once told me you could get a few of the lads to give me a bashing. Remember?"

"I was only pulling your leg."

"I'm at the Daemon. A lot of girls there are in singles. Doubles. They're getting a nasty time from Waygoes' son. He's got a master key. Get the idea?"

Her smile went, her eyes darkened, and she leaned on her elbows, looking along the bar.

"He's tried it here," she said, too quietly. "I told his dad, I says, there's a lot of likely lads here, and the river's not far away. He's never tried it since. I'll tear the bollocks out of him, and chance it. What' you want me to do?"

145

"Find me a few likely lads. I'll pay a pony each. Do him right."

"Twenty-five nicker? Each? Sounds dead on. Half a mo'."

She went along the bar, I drank a little, and she came back on her side, and a few men came along toward me.

"All right, lads," she said to them. "Make your own arrangements. Best of luck."

They were all big, shoulders and height, and cold-eyed, no smiles, silent, sizing me.

"I want a job done right," I said. "This bastard's been worrying girls. If they were whores, all right. They've got people to protect them. These girls haven't. They're decent girls. Got the picture?"

One of them nodded.

"It's a couple of miles away. You might know the place?"

"She's told us," the nodder said. "It's Teucer Waygoes. He's been asking for it. When do you want it done?"

"As soon as."

"A pony apiece?"

"That's it. How do you want paying?"

"A tenner now. Rest after the job?"

"Done. But you'll have the excuse. Anybody wants to know, you shifted little statues from the Daemon to my place across the road. Here's the address. Couple of hundred yards across Wapping High."

I took out the notes, and gave them one each.

"Where do we meet?" I asked.

"When you hear the doctor's got him, and he's nice and comfortable, come down here and pay us off."

"On."

I went back to Daemon Wente Waye, down the steps to the garden, every plant and flower in usual order, wondering at the thought of devoted Amy and Joe Briggs, and the dirty minds of the rest of us.

Ella had gone. For some reason I was first empty, and then enraged. I phoned Victoria and got a place on the night train, took my bag, called a cab, went to the station, bought an armful of readables from the bookstall, and got aboard, booking a place in the dining car. I have never been more at home than on the night train to Paris, a drink or two before a good dinner, a bottle, a cognac, and bed, and waking an hour outside Paris to coffee-and-milk and croissants, shave, dress, ready for anything on arrival.

I was at Riannes' at a little before eleven o'clock, and to my surprise, went in to his office there and then, and he unrolled the copy, a lot of it, spreading it over the desk.

"This is a strange piece of business," he said over the hornrims. "Do you have any idea what it means?"

"I can tell you in terms of profit," I said. "What other idea? Does it concern us?"

He nodded, and looked at the girl coming in with coffee.

"It means the end of the banking system," he said, and opened his hands above his head. "Where are we to go?"

"Are you talking about France?"

"Of course not. I speak for all of us, naturally?"

"Us? Europe?"

"Everybody. World-wide. Haven't you read what is in this material?"

"Beyond editing, no."

He looked at me, in surprise or pity, I was unsure.

"But surely England is in terrible economic difficulties," he said, back of the throat, sounding scandalized. "You have no interest?"

"No. I can *do* nothing. I have nothing *to* do. What *should* I do?"

"But at least you can complain?"

"To whom. Who listens? What, in all this, do *you* complain about?"

"It has never been put to me. But here, in this, I have a legitimate reason, politic, let us say, all of us, in every country. The entire body is being put to ransom by the banking fraternity. That is, if these statements are correct. Don't you see?"

"That's all very well. But what do I—what do *we*—do? How do we act? I wish to God I spoke French as you speak English. What do you call the *entire* body?"

He held out his arms.

"In a word, Europe and the United States," he said. "What else

147

matters? Where else is banking principle important? Only where people work. Produce. Sell. Have a market. *There* is worth, and *that's* profit or loss."

"Well?"

"*Well?*"

He slammed his hands on the copy piled across the desk.

"What does *this* say? Everything we are taught is a lie. Don't you see? *Everything* we are taught is a *lie*. Most things we are *not* taught. For example. We borrow so many millions. Are we taught to see that many millions—ten to fifteen per cent—is interest? Where does it go? Into interested pockets, naturally. Not into children's mouths. How does this happen? Because we are disgustingly ignorant in the matter of money. Isn't it so?"

"I'm surprised you feel like this. Isn't it a bit late?"

He looked out of the window at a whitewashed wall, nodding.

"It is always late," he said. "But I have never seen facts presented in such a manner. Crude as raw vegetables. The Bank of England was formed to create money out of nothing? Who could believe it? And the Bank of France, the same? Who can believe any longer in economists? Their 'science' is founded on a myth? Most of what I was taught in school, even at university, is simply lies? Don't you know why I am angry? My sons are being taught the same nonsense. What can *I* do?"

"Talk to the headmaster?"

"They would immediately be sent home. Priests and scholars do not like their lessons to be called nonsense. But of course. That is what they are. Who will teach them? Is this to be a book?"

"As I understand it, a new political party's being formed and this is the basis of their appeal. I don't think they'll get far. I don't think they'll get anywhere."

"Why?"

I felt a little dull. Economics was not a strong point.

"Well, first of all, I don't think many people give much of a damn," I said. "They like sport, and pub crawling, and strippers, and they're earning the money, so why think about something they're not used to? Banks are banks. That's where the money is. If you want to borrow or get a loan, you pay interest. It's always been. Always will be. How do you get a car or anything else on the never-never? That's the way it is. Who says so? Who's interested? If you want your money, sign there and get on with it. Isn't it the same here?"

"Exactly."

"Well?"

He took copies from each pile and put them aside.

"Your order is packed and ready," he said. "Would you like them to go by air?"

"I'll take them by rail. Is the poster ready?"

"Not today. It will be ready tomorrow. Our presses were engaged until four o'clock this morning. It's a considerable job. Four colours. We had jobs like that in London, but in those days we had more time. We haven't yet got our new machinery installed. When it is, please come again. It is always a pleasure to speak to a Londoner. I had sixteen years there. Both my sons were born in Kensington."

He tapped the copy he set aside.

"With this I hope to start a new train of thought in their minds. Thought for the future. Obviously we are not yet out of the era of cowrie shells. But *their* future requires something more. Of intelligence, certainly. May I offer you luncheon?"

"Unfortunately, my day isn't finished," I said. "If the order's put in a cab, I'll take it to the station, and it'll come with me tonight. The posters by air, tomorrow?"

"As you wish."

On the way, in the cab, I read a few of the handbills again, and I thought I saw what he meant, but I was not at all sure what they might mean to the voters, those, at any rate, bothering to read them. I was unsure what I meant by voters, except, I supposed, those appearing as numbers in a poll, to give Conservatives or Liberals or Labour a majority to take a seat in Parliament. I had never voted. I had always been out of the country. What went on was always without me. I lived with what was there, and spent what I wanted, because I earned what I could, and everything went on the same, never mind who was in or out. What was the use of taking any notice? The handbills were evidence enough, at any rate, for me.

When will you stop being stupid? the first read, in classic Roman type. *You are told that the presses are printing money, and that this will lead to an even worse inflation. Have you ever stopped to think how much money is written by cheque? Why, then, does the Government permit the writing of cheques? Who is the Government? Who takes profit from the writing of cheques? You? Me? Any of us? Of course not. Who, then? The banks, naturally. Did you see their profits last year? The year before? On what? Did you ever ask yourself how a bank makes a profit? On you, you bloody fool.*

That was a bit rough, I thought. But there seemed something in it. It was all well over my head, and truly I felt not all that interested. It was for somebody else to argue about, somebody, let us say, knowing more about it. If they could get something done, all right.

Why do you squat in your own stink? another asked in red and black print. *Don't you know the Civil Service and the Banks work hand-in-glove? How else does a Chancellor appointed by a political party consistently make a fool of himself, his Party, and you? Isn't he advised by the self-indulgent-in-power? Do they ever lose anything? Have you looked at their salaries? Do you suppose any of them ever looked at yours?*

But my favourites came from the end of the roll.

You women, what's the matter with you? the larger handbill read, in calmest Roman, red and black, an exemplary font. *You have a "liberation" movement, and Equal Rights, and all the rest of it. Where has it got you? Where are you? If you let a man in, you can always have a baby. Just about where you let him in is a little beauty of a puzzle. One of lifetime's wonders. Just rub it, and like Aladdin's lamp, it flows, in orgasm, and God love us all. Why don't you start using the other end? The one that counts? All the way through history you have been used as unpaid servants. When will you start putting yourselves out of economic misery? Demand your own money. Why not? Use your heads, for a change. The other end is wonderful for the seeking prick. But what about you, and the babies? If there isn't a man who provides? You want your own money. Issued for women, to be used only by women, never by men, never to be lent, for your own*

wants, without yea or nay from any except yourselves. Now
begin to liberate yourselves. The rest is nonsense. Put men in
their proper place. As partners. Nothing more. Love will make
things better. But it doesn't pay the rent. Only your own money
will make you free. And living will be so much better. Don't you
think?

Daemon Wente Waye was its own delightful self, as ever,
when I got back that morning, after dropping the packages at
my plant for breaking into packets of one hundreds. Gulls flew in
a chilling breeze, and plastic covers were over all the roses and
shrubs, ready for winter. I called Ella and Celli, but they were
out, and Almond gave me a message to call Mrs. Rafaele. I went
up to the set, all shining in perfect order, and went out to the
kitchen to make a pot of coffee. My buzzer called, and I
switched on.

"Mrs. Rafaele here. Mr. Waygoes wants to see you soon as possible."

"Tell him all the handbills are here. They're being wrapped in
small packets. I'm going out to Heathrow this afternoon for the
posters, tell him."

"He wants to see you before that. Soon as you can."

"All right. I'm just in. Wash and brush up. Half an hour?"

I read the mail, drank the coffee, ordered a cab for the air terminal, and went down to A 1 without a care in the world. Mrs.
Hine opened the door without looking at me, and I went in to the
big room, with Waygoes at the desk, a spread of glossy green
leather with a blotting pad, pen rack, and a couple of files.

"Good morning," he said, down at the cigar. "Please pull up a
chair. Riannes' been on to me. He's very pleased, and interested.
The posters will be on the four o'clock plane to Heathrow."

"I'll be there."

"Yes. I wanted to see you about my son. He's been badly in-
jured. He's in the London clinic. What do you know of the
Lomax?"

"I've stayed there."

"Do you know the manageress?"

"I've met her."

"Yes. Did you ask her to find four men?"

151

"Yes. To shift some statuary from below the cubicles over to my place across the road."

"And did they?"

"So far as I know."

"So far as you know? You paid them twenty-five pounds each before you had ascertained the job was done?"

"Not at all. I paid them ten pounds each to begin. Another fifteen when I was satisfied the job was properly done."

"That 'job' was not to waylay my son and kick him to a pulp?"

"I don't know what you're talking about."

He blew cigar smoke, looking washy eyes out of the window.

"You can spare twenty-five pounds a man to do a certain job? I can afford a hundred pounds to find out what the job *was*. All right, Mrs. Hine. Let the men in."

The door opened, and the four men I had paid strolled without hurry, and stood a pace or so away from me.

"Do you identify anybody here?" Waygoes asked.

"No," the man I recognised said, and pointed his middle finger at me. "This wasn't the bloke. Eh?"

The others nodded.

"You're quite sure?" Waygoes said, licking a leaf on the cigar.

"I'm bloody certain," the man said. "The other bloke was older. Listen. We don't know nothing about this job. Like we told you. But you said hundred nicker to come here and point the finger. There's nobody here we know. Right, lads?"

The other three moved, nodded, made noises.

"All we want now's the nicker," the man said. "Let's have it."

Waygoes drew deep on the cigar, and suddenly reached for the bellpull.

"Very well," he said. "You'll be paid outside. Good day to you."

I thought I caught the flick of a wink from the spokesman, but I made no sign, and the door shut.

"Apparently, that's that," Waygoes said. "You can never tell. Cockneys can't be got to grass. They never talk. But my son's in the hospital, and I intend to find out why."

"I'm sorry for it. I know nothing except what you've told me."

"I'll do what I may. That's all."

I went out as a boy from the head's study, under sentence of a flogging, and glad to be free. But it was far more serious than that. Waygoes could also pay the lads to do a job on me. What defence could I count on? I felt zeroed by a marksman's rifle, no cover, and flight no answer. But I had no intention of running. I made up my mind, listening to myself going up the stairs. I had to go to the Lomax to pay the lads off, and from there to Heathrow to pick up the posters. A better idea seemed to do Heathrow first and the Lomax on the way back. The testimony of those four men stood between me, and what? A bashing? A dip in the Thames? I saw the mask of Jayb. I wondered where I might see him again. On the three-legged chair? I could hear the sirens howling as I had as a small boy. In my ears. I had never forgotten.

Warning. Go for the shelter. Or die.

Lady London stretched outside there, broken witness, a million times, and a million accusers, in one.

What could I do? That sense of helplessness seemed to drip inside me in a spiritual sludge, clogging thought, stifling movement.

I could do nothing. That was all. Thinking, wishing, was waste of time. The property boys and the banks had got together—with who?—and nothing would be done until they said so. It was the answer in the beginning, and it was the answer now, years later. All in between had been a waste of time. London was in the hands of crooks, so far as I was concerned, and Waygoes was one.

I was another.

What could I do about it?

Nothing.

I wanted my set, my books, and statuary, and the comfort of all I had wished for.

I thought it all over on the way out to Heathrow, passing factories and high-rise flats, and the fields and gardens, but it all worked out the same. I liked my life as it was, and to hell with the rest.

153

The same dreary runaround from Customs, and the rubber stamps, and go here, go there, but at last I had the posters, almost filling the cab, and I went back to the Lomax.

The bar was busy, and she was down at the end, in a scarlet dress, and she saw me and came along, truly an eyeful of juice, and smiled, taking my favourite scotch from the shelf.

"Waiting for you," she said, easing side to side in the braless bodice. "The lads told me about this morning. Don't worry. They'll never split. I'll call them down."

"Don't bother," I said. "Here's the pay. I wanted you to know they got it."

She took the notes, and counted, laughing.

"Dead funny," she said. "Look, I've got forty lads here. They call themselves Cecilia's Own. Cecilia. That's me. They'll do *any-thing* for me. I'm the bastard of Waygoes. Did you know? That's why I've got this place. Teucer, he's my half brother, he came to stay here after he left Oxford. The big bloke. Y'know? Degree, all that. He thought he was going to lord it. I've got a lot of girls, here. Indians, Pakis, Jamaicans, so forth. He thought he could have the lot. Else, he told them, he'd get them slung out. Well, those girls *need* their jobs. They're keeping their families. Well, when one of them came crying to me, and the others told me what was going on, I went up there, and I had him out of kip, and I says, pack up and get out, *now*, I says, else I'll have the lads up here, and you'll go through the window. Straight in the drink. Now, piss off. Well, he's never liked me. So when you told me he was trying the same lark up there, I had a word with Cecilia's Own. Now he's in dock, and everybody's happy. I told 'em, I says, when you put the boot in, make sure it's *in*, I says. It's for me. And a lot of poor kids, can't help themselves. Anything else you want done, let me know. How about a refill?"

I looked at what I thought to be perfect breasts, and she moved, and her eyes crinkled, and she turned to pour.

"Don't worry," she said, opening a soda water bottle. "It'll be your turn one day. All the better for the wait. Eh?"

A curious girl. Entirely herself.

"Listen," I said. "Who told Waygoes about me? That I'd been

here? Is it that little grey rat of a cellarman of yours? I just saw him looking in."

"You mean Crippen," she said, and laughed. "Oh yes. There's plenty. They'll talk. But don't get worried. Pa don't take too much notice. 'Cept of me. I know all about him. About the runs. *And* you."

"What *do* you know?"

She laughed, head up, eyes up, pretty.

"Listen," she said. "'Fore I took this place over, like, I mean, the boss, I was in the office. Down there nigh Moorgate. That's where everything starts and finishes. I had a couple of years there. So I know all about it. *And* you. *And* what goes on. That's enough, isn't it? Listen. Don't worry. There's nothing you could call nice between the old bloke and me. This is my bit of the family estate. To keep m' mouth shut. Easy enough, isn't it? Listen. Let me give you a tip. Take care what goes on, see? You can get done. Don't go out at night. Else have a couple of blokes with you. I know this game. Listening?"

"Listening. And thank you."

"Nothing of it. You'd be just one of the lot. Know it? Listen. I've got to look after the business. But I'll call you. One lovely weekend soon. Not here. I'll pick it. All right with you?"

"Lovely."

"'S what I think. S'long, ducks."

She mouthed a kiss, walking away, and a barman took her place, and I left the rest of the drink and went out to the cab, for the first time feeling really worried, not about anyone else, but strictly for myself. Too many people beyond my knowledge knew too much, and suddenly the full extent of my position seemed to be clear, almost as if a load had fallen on both shoulders and I could feel it. I had no defence anywhere, or at any rate, that I could trust. So far, I had been of use in doing regular runs and earning my keep. But now I was a liability, both as a non-runner and as a potential deadly witness. It would take Jayb and his lot very little time to put me in the knacker's yard, that dump of the unwanted. I almost felt my teeth chatter. Certainly I felt cold, even if the sun shone, with not even enough breeze to raise a wisp of hair. That warning yelped in my head, and she knew exactly what she was talking about, and I had to take notice. The joking voice and big smile were all very well, but she was not the sort for stage whispers and hints behind the hand. Everybody took their chances, and that was all. What she said, it seemed to me, was stay alive and our weekend might be on, or if not, too bad.

A hell of a prospect.

And nowhere to look for help, except run for it.

Run for it?

Where?

That was a cold moment.

Cold.

I had no friends.

Not one.

Nobody I could trust. None I could go to.

In all the years I had been in and out of the country, doing the runs, dropping the stuff, and coming back to the printing business, I never had time to make real friends. Girl friends, here and there, yes. They were different. You met, you liked each other, yes. That was different from a man. I knew of no man I could turn to for help. I knew of a few girls across Europe, but why —what excuse could I offer?—should I ask them for help? What sort of help? Rescue? Hide me? It sounded ridiculous. What would they do with me? A lump, to be buried or thrown from here to there? Put in a cellar? An attic? How do you hide a man? From what?

I had plenty of money. Where could I go? Anywhere in the world? Where?

I was standing in the road, thinking, and the cab driver tooted to bring me back to where I was in the middle of truck traffic, no safe place to be, and in a gap I ran, grabbed for the door handle and got in.

"Lucky man, guv," the cabbie said. "I thought you was a goner, there. Straight up. You was dead lucky. What, was you betting your luck, was you?"

"I wish I *had* a little luck," I said. "Two, Brittle Candy Lane."

"Know it," he said, starting up. "Just off Wapping High. What, they rebuilt, have they?"

"Not exactly. Just got the slates on, and the water running. Lights, so forth."

"Ah. Won't do though, will it? When they going to get the rest done? I mean, build it proper."

"Better ask who owns it."

"Always that, ain't it? Who owns it. Not who *lives* in it. How they come to own it?"

"Have to go back in time."

"How far?"

"Ask your Member of Parliament."

"My *who?* What use is *he?*"

"What's his name?"

"What's it matter? What *use* is he?"

"He's there to represent *you*. He earns the money for it."

"*Don't* make me laugh, will you? Them bastards? They're hand in glove. Look at this bloody place. It's miles and miles. Nothing done. Since I was a kid. What d'you mean, represent *me?*"

"Why did you vote for him?"

"I never. But I never liked the other bloke."

"That's it. The other bloke might have had something to say."

"I never liked him. The Mrs. didn't. So we never voted, see?"

"Hard luck. What about next time?"

"All right. What? Listen. Here, it's all Indians and Pakis, and them. What's the use? Whose bloody country *is* it?"

I sat back. What *was* the use? A human being is a human being. It has its own ideas. Who is to say what is right or wrong? A Prime Minister? A priest? Too many have been wrong. But I was bound to think of Waygoes. The wrapping on the roll of posters near me had been torn, and I could see some of the wording in old-fashioned lettering, written in 1694, and still in being, beautifully printed in the script of the time, and I wondered who the original penman was, or who wrote his paragraphs, or how many decided the final draft. Certainly nobody from the House of Commons.

157

Those men had bonded the rest of us, through the centuries, into a specific form of slavery.

We all became, from that moment, servants to those men, and their successors, down to the day, and worse, tomorrow, and into the future.

The Bank of England was lord of all.

It issued the money. It called the tune. The Mint was its partner.

Why?

Who said so?

For what reason?

To keep a few in power?

Who were they?

The same throughout Europe, the United States, Japan, India, Africa? Everywhere the lordlings ruled. For what reason? Certainly not by popular vote, or any democratic move anywhere in the body politic. The Bank seemed to have gone unnoticed by the ignorant, slyly nurtured by the knowing, and in the course of time, over generations, was accepted for what it pretended to be, a guardian of the national currency, a repository of financial wisdom, and a bottomless treasure chest for the rest of the world to dip in, at, of course, a rate of interest, until, that is, until we lost the Empire. That was a nasty period. Exactly how was the Bank of India funded? Or any other bank in the Commonwealth? Who issued the figures? On what assumption? I could read bits of paragraphs without being able to read all of it, but it was enough to inform, to bring questions, and I got out of the cab asking a few.

What were we all living for?

To be merest servitors of the banks?

They use the national currency, and us, to impose their will because we all need money to live to spend in exchange for what we want.

I tore a little more from the poster.

The world is starved for money. There has never been too much. There has always been too little. The bankers or usurers or loan sharks—whatever—keep tight hold on supply from the Mint, because too much money in the hands of the general pub-

lic means a fall in bank rate, or interest, and that fall is a loss of profit to the money-grubbers, the leeches sucking the anus of a benighted public, without defence because uneducated, illiterate, stupid.

Untaught. Blighted by a custom of not thinking. About anything. Worse, about anybody or anything.

The telephone rang.

"Mrs. Hine, here, sir. Mr. Waygoes would like all the posters immediately, please. And would you come over? He's free now."

"All right."

To heel, Fido. Your master whistles. Some call it coals in the belly, and it's right enough. The blaze almost burns blisters, but you have to grill in your shame because a set on the third floor, looking out on the Thames, depends upon it, and you want it, you need it, and there is nothing to be done except submit.

Submit.

What the hell had I done all my life?

Apart from that, who the hell *was* I?

Me?

Did I have any friends? In trouble, could I depend on anybody? How many would lend me money? Who would give me a welcome?

How many more were in the same place?

All of us?

Most of us?

What had become of the brotherhood of man?

Another saying of no meaning? The kiss of the Christians? The Masonic handshake? All the other nonsense? Where was, and *what* was, brotherhood?

We were a dead lot, doing what we had to, day after day, earning a living, eating, going home to sleep, and what else? A nonsense? Rocks, gravel? No human flesh? But what *was* it? What *were* we all, running around every day? Where was the soul? *What* was the soul? What was the spirit? Who put it in us? Whom should we thank? What *was* the spirit? Who could tell us? Who tried?

Not the priests or preachers or ministers. They were as poisoned as the rest of us, and worse.

159

At least, those of us outside had an excuse.

Religion, if it was Roman Catholic, or Protestant, or Methodist, or Presbyterian—O, listen to the bell-ringing—not forgetting the dead clappers of all the others ringing the changes—had no reason.

None.

No excuse. None of them could wriggle out.

They, all of them, had to confront one repeated precept, the essence of Christianity, beginning at Genesis, on, through Psalms, to Luke, Old to New, Aramaic through Hebrew to pseudo-Greek, and so to English.

I went over and got the Bible my mother had given to me, long before I was able to remember, and kept by my Auntie Helen, the best cake-maker, the finest tart-maker of any time, with French crispy pastry she had learned to bake in Paris, and French bread. God knows, I had never thought of her in all these years, and yet, now I did, looking through the Bible she had kept for me. I remembered the cinnamon-and-green-apple smell in her shoulder while she wrapped me when the sirens howled in those nights before I was evacuated, though she was killed in the bombing and I never saw her again. But she left me a few hundred pounds and what came out of the rubble, and the Bible was one of the books. It still had a palm cross in Corinthians, and a big tear in the leather.

Is it an accident that tear, and tear, are spelt the same way?

But it's there. It's plain enough. For those who run, believing.

Exodus. Leviticus. Deuteronomy. Nehemiah. Psalms. Isaiah. Jeremiah. Ezekiel. Matthew. Luke. Throughout the Book.

Thou shalt not lend on usury.

An eleventh Commandment, never part of the Ten Commandments, but conveniently hidden by the Jamesian translators of the English Bible? And why not? They were bishops, in the line of the original usurers, and the Church went on lending at interest down to the day, landlords, rentiers, unChristian because unBelieving, unFaithful, unHeeding, renegade cheats, in flagrant disregard of Holy Writ, hiding behind the ignorance of the multitude, taking refuge in the criminal inertia of the knowing, passive, content, craven because peccant, the original uncrucified thieves, nameless, but known.

I went downstairs in a seethe of words, not quite sure what they meant but feeling them in a strange way, though I could never have talked about them or given anyone else a reasonable account of what I was thinking. That, possibly, is the strangest part of living, or thinking, whichever it may be. So much of what can be thought cannot be put in words. Impatience with groping comes to banish the rough idea and consign it to Hell. So much of good is lost in those raging moments.

Jim Ross, my storeman at the plant, and his helper were coming through the door with the poster cylinders, and I added mine of the badly torn wrapper, and went on to A 1. I pressed the bell, and the same old nonsense of automatic doors, slams, and whacks went on, and I walked down the long room to Waygoes' desk, and his face, pale, pleading. I felt quite sorry for him.

"Pour yourself a drink," he said. "I've had a bloody awful night and another damnable day of it. The saddest part is, I can't drink. Simply makes it worse. So? What is there to do? Take pills? That's what I do. A chemist's dummy. The doctor says I can last another twenty years. Like this? Christ. I've had a feeling for a long time that Hell's really where we live. I never had any time for that bosh of Dante's. It's no inferno. Simply a vast cookshop. Sort of thing he'd see in the dungeons and kitchens of the castles of his time. Never saw or heard any poetry in it. Barren's the word. The posters are very well done. Surprisingly so. You must have spent a lot of supervisory time. You won't suffer."

I pressed the siphon, and took the drink to the chair facing him on the left, and raised the tumbler.

"Health," I said, and he nodded. "Riannes knows the job. So did his men. He talked to me about the copy. What it meant. Of course, I knew as much as he did. Not much use."

"You agree with the general idea?"

"I do, yes. It sounds right. But I don't know enough about it. Seems to me it'd put everything in the very devil of a mess."

"That's what it's in now. My ideas would put us on the right road."

"Could you get the politicians and bankers to follow you?"

"In a word, no."

"Then?"

"We'd have to wait for the opportunity."

"When?"

"When it was generally agreed that we were, in present-day terms, bankrupt. Nothing left. Nothing to pay anybody with."

"Could that happen?"

"It's happening."

"Anything to stop it?"

"No. As we go at the moment. The entire system has to be changed. That's going to be agony for some. Insolvency for many. The gutter for others. But a very good life for the rest of us."

"I'd like to know a lot more about it. But I'm not sure what's being said."

"You're printing the pamphlet. Read it. Then ask me questions. Fair?"

"But I'm not an economist."

"Neither am I. But I was taught to use my brain. By a great man. He became an alcoholic because his ideas were disregarded. The banking system pertaining then was too strong. It's why I've withheld Harry Edwardes' project until now. It wasn't on the cards before. He said this would happen—oh—twenty-five or more years ago. Conservatives? No brains. Liberals? No ideas. Labour? No proper concept of themselves. Marx? He never even looked at the start of the banking system. He wrote his *Das Kapital* in the British Museum Library. What was he, any more than a journeyman? Nothing to offer anyone, except a lot of words. No target. An idiot followed by a couple of generations of idiots. The human race is infinitely the poorer because of Marx. Where did he see profit?"

"Profit's important?"

"Don't be a bloody fool. Of course. Keep a hen. She lays an egg. That's profit. Dig a garden. Plant. Gather. That's profit. A man and woman make love. They have a baby. That's profit. Isn't it? Profit is what we live for. Or if not, then what the devil *are* we living for?"

162

A door opened to my right, and closed clumsily, because it thumped a couple of times and stayed off-latch. There were quiet paces, and Teucer passed me to sit in the chair in front, to the right.

He turned to look at me, but slowly, almost regally, and nodded, chin up, the vacuous, gently knowing, palest, slyest blue-shining smile of the gone, long-gone, forever-gone alcoholic.

"At this time of day," Waygoes said, nodding at his son. "That's him. A dirty drunken bastard. He thought I'd leave him a multimillionaire. Be damned if I will. He's not worth spit."

"Ah, for Christ's sake," Teucer said. "Why don't you bundle off? Then we'll get on with it."

"You see?" Waygoes said, looking at me. "That's what I have to put up with, twenty-four hours in the day. As if physical pain wasn't enough."

"Ah, go on," Teucer said, looking through the windows. "Shove off. Bloody old fool. I'll develop this property. You have no idea. Where did you make any money?"

"I've made quite a bit. Without your help."

"You could have made more. With it."

"Doubt it."

"What about the Whitechapel lot?"

Waygoes breathed out at the ceiling, but horribly not laughing.

"I shall never have the smallest intention of helping squatters," he said. "No property of mine will become available to them while I can prevent it."

"You've got streets up there," Teucer said. "Streets and streets. Hundreds of rooms. You could open them to people. Your own kind. They need a place to *live*. To sleep. Why can't you see their—what?—despair? If you had a wife and a couple of kids, wouldn't you like a bit of help if the luck wasn't with you?"

"Luck, my arse," Waygoes said. "Workshy shysters. That's what they are. Yes, I'd give them room. *If.* If they paid rent. I'd get the water and light turned on. Of course. I'd be landlord. *If.* *If* they paid rent. But they don't want to. They want to live free. Free? I can't. You *can.* Because you're my son. And you're no bloody good. Hear me? Listening? You're no *good.* A dirty, drunken minus. It's no use calling you names. You *aren't* anything. You are the perfect minus."

Teucer twisted his head to look all the way round at me.

"Hark at him," he said, pretending fright. "You'd think he'd been to Hell and back. In fact, he's never been farther than a couple of penn'orth on the Tube this past ten years. Here to Moorgate, and that's it. Too bloody mean to buy a car. I can't have a car. I could use one. Earn some money. *No.*"

Waygoes nodded.

"*No* is right," he said. "There's no need for a car. Of course, he'd like one to take a girl out. All right. Nothing against it. Take a hire car. Use it. Do what you like. Take it back. That's it. But buying a car? All the costs? Garage? Maintenance? Insurance? The whole stupid nonsense? No. I can have a lovely walk up the road here, get aboard the train, and I'm comfortable in my office twenty minutes later, coffee brewing, everything lovely, cost me what? Fifteen pence? No garage. No petrol. No oil. No *nothing*. And it doesn't cost me how-many-thousands to buy the bloody thing. All I do is pop up the road, get on the Tube, and twenty minutes, 'pending on the weather, I'm drinking a lovely cup of coffee in my office, with hot rolls and what's on from Garaglio's, a couple of doors down. Who wants a car? For what? They're the furthest filthy nuisance. Shouldn't be allowed."

"Christ, the way you talk," Teucer said, chin down. "I wish I had some money. I'd build East London. The entire place. All the miles. I wouldn't let it go to rot. That's all it's doing. Look at it. Since I was born. Hasn't changed. Can't you see it? Don't you *feel* it?"

"Everything's seen and felt," Waygoes said. "You're not the only one alive. But I want those permits first. I don't build till I've got them. They won't arrest me again."

"Listen to that rubbermouth, will you?" Teucer said, pretending a laugh, a rattle in the lungs, ending in a cough. "Great God, he'll have a devil's own job getting through the Gate. I think he's had a curse put on him. Some of the witch doctors living here. Plenty of *them*. All they need is to hit the time right. Witches only fail when the time's wrong. A seed opens at a certain time. It's marked. That's not conjuring or legerdemain. It's the work of

164

witches. That green sprout isn't accidental. It's ordained. Natural order. Same as the witch's job. Natural. When you know how. If you don't, you have the right to snigger at it. While you may. But you *can* get caught. Then the laugh's brutally the other way."

"Why don't you for Christ's sake stop boozing, drugging, pill-popping, whatever you do?" Waygoes shouted suddenly. "I'm sick of seeing you about the place. Let me tell you now. It's no use you hanging on till I curl up. I've seen to it. My will's made. You're not in it. You won't break it. You've never done a decent stroke of work in your life. You went to Oxford? What for? To get sent down? Waste of good money."

"Where did you do so much better?"

Waygoes laughed two rows of bluish teeth, with gaps up and down.

"I got my degree," he said, at the ceiling. "That's what you never did. See? You can pretend for so long. But then you've got to put it on the table. You couldn't. You had to come here and pretend you were a millionaire. My son? That you never were. Like your sister. Nothing more than a bastard."

"Why are you saying this in front of *him*?" Teucer screamed, pointing to me, sounding dry.

"That's what he's here for," Waygoes said. "I asked him here to tell him in front of you. Or anybody else. He's been a lot more use to me than you have. Always done a good job. Years, no mistakes. Never a word wrong. It's worth a reward."

He took an envelope stuck in the pipe-rack, and gave it to me.

"Take that on Monday morning to those people," he said. "Bream, Mackesson, Bailey and Somerford. If not, that's that. Now. Another matter. Where's Ella?"

I looked at him.

"Ella?" I said, dull as that.

"Ella Broome," he said nodding. "That dear girl looking after the digs. She can't be found. It's been a few days."

"I haven't the faintest. I saw her for a drink the night I went to Paris. I left after she'd gone."

Teucer kicked a chair aside, and went to the door.

"You can change the subject," he shouted, suddenly. "You al-

165

ways pretend to take control, don't you? Well, don't try it with me. I'll have my proper rights. I'm warning you. You gave Cec' a pub, and pretended that was all she was entitled to. She was fool enough to sign? But I won't. I'll have everything I can legally lay hands on. And I've got the right solicitors. They like money, too."

"A passing nuisance," Waygoes said to me. "Have another drink."

Teucer slammed the door.

"I'd better go and see the police," I said. "I'm worried."

"I think you should be. They've been here again. Asking for you."

"But *why* me?"

Waygoes put a little finger in his ear, and rattled it.

"Well, there've been three or four others, haven't there?" he said. "One curiosity after another. Here, and on the Continent. All a coincidence, perhaps? Ask for Sergeant Kemp. C.I.D. He's in charge. He's young, and smart. And really *mean*."

"Meaning?"

"If he's got you on a hook, he'll keep you there. Be careful."

"Careful of *what*?"

"Sergeant Kemp, and the C.I.D."

I trotted down the length of the room, and across the foyer, out to the garden, up the steps to Wapping High, shining pale-blue tarmac in the cold sou'easter, curving left, and the Thames's pale-tea brown on the right, and crossed over, coat collar up, hands in trousers pockets, down, through the Saturday afternoon quiet, to the police station.

The man at the desk knew me by the instant light in his eyes, and he got off the chair, and opened the door, walking in, talking at a level not to be heard. Another constable got up and stood, hands behind, between me and the street door.

I got a mild attack of the shakes.

The first constable came out, and a man in an orangey tweed jacket and grey flannels came behind, and put a dark green file on the desk.

Whatever he said, I nodded. He had my name and address right, and then came Penna Cately, and what seemed to me to

166

be a dozen others, and then Ella, at an address in Doncaster I never heard of, and I told him so.

He said I often went to the Continent, and I nodded. To France. Germany, Belgium, Holland, Switzerland, Italy and other places, and I nodded.

"Why?"

"Work. Come along to my office. I'll show you."

"Look. These girls are missing. One, we know for a fact, is a corpse. Nothing to say?"

"No."

"You were the last one seen with them. Your name's in every one of these statements."

"Find out a bit more about the people making the statements. I've got travel documents and stamps in my passport. Anything else?"

He shook his head.

"My name's Kemp," he said. "You'll see more of me."

"That's fine. But just remember who you're dealing with. I can always sue you. Just give me an excuse. That's all."

"All right, Billings. He can go."

The constable in front of the door stepped aside, still with hands behind his back, and I went out to that blast of cold wind, and suffered all the way up the street, and down the steps, seeing the beauty of the Daemon's smile, wondering where Ella was, and the others, and getting into the warmth of the foyer with a groan of relief. I went down to the Bosun's Bar and ordered a double brandy, drank in a gulp, and ran up two flights, slowed on the others, and had a little trouble with the key getting into the set, and kneed the door shut, walked through to the bedroom, and fell across the bed.

Waking up is a damnable business. Everything comes falling in on you. I awoke with Bhula leaning over me, wiping my face. The sweat glazed cold across my forehead. I was still dressed. My feet hurt from the shoes. Christ, is there anything more painful than waking? You know immediately what is, and what is not, the truth. What is the truth, Pontius Pilate said. Of course he knew. He had it in front of him. It's what you know when you wake up. There's no argument. It is so plain. You know, and you have to live with it. What you live with is the truth. The words, the arguments, are anything else. The truth is what you *know*. Nobody can tell you different.

You *know*. Now try to explain it. Even to yourself.

Bhula brought in a Chemex of coffee, and poured a cup for me, and undressed, and got into bed in her usual beautifully calm way, that I loved. She had been married as a little girl in Travancore, and she had come to Britain at about ten years of age, though she had no real notion but she thought she might be nineteen or twenty-two—and she wanted nothing to do with her own men. They wanted to do as they wanted. She did not. When she came to clean for me for the first time, I was packed and ready for Bonn. She wore a dull red sari. She showed the lines of her body, bending to dust the wainscot. She saw me looking. She smiled with her eyes. I put a hand on the small of her back, and felt down. She stayed there, no move, no sound, and I undressed, and so did she, and I missed trains and ferries, everything except her, and I was never happier, but I was a day late on the drop, and my vis-à-vis was delighted because the police had turned up on the day before, had found nothing, and he thought that it was a prime example of staff work. But it was not. It was Bhula, and her lovely Indian womanliness. Her body. Or the way she used it. And my stupidity. Or is it stupid to love a woman so much that you blow an important job? Love?

Love. All right.

What is it?

I loved Bhula. Very well.

What did I mean?

I had no words. What *did* I mean?

If you think of it, what the hell *is* love?

Hands? Why did I think of her hands? Lips? Why did I think of her lips on me? Everywhere. Why did I think of her moaning, marvellous? What *is* marvellous? Why did she moan? What is moan? What *is* that extraordinary sound a woman squeezes from her throat? But if you can hear it, why bother? It has its own beauty, and I'm grateful to listen.

168

"Has anybody permission to come in this set while you are away?" she asked, making a lovely ballet of putting on the sari. "Twice I have found this horrible little man. He said he had permission."

"Nobody except Mrs. Hine or Mrs. Rafaele on inspection duty, or you or Mrs. Rapajan, when you're on the work roster, are permitted here. Next time ask the guard to throw him out."

"I told Mr. Almond. He said nothing."

"Bhula, let me do the worrying. I doubt he'll come here again."

But I had no doubt he would, and no doubt he was Jayb, and I had a sense of fright. Why was he waiting for me? It was during the time I was away. He must have known it. Then why wait? Was somebody meeting him here? It was pretty well a perfect place. Then why would he let Bhula find him, see him, with further possibility of identifying him?

I was getting raw at the edges. I went over to pour drinks, and gave Bhula hers, and sat down. I felt love-weary, knee-wobbly, and at peace with everyone except Jayb.

"We don't like to kill snakes," Bhula said. "They are gods. For some. I have never had that belief. I have always detested them. They frightened me so much. The little man has the same wicked head. I would put my heel on him, and chop with the axe."

"You'd be silly to put your heel on a snake."

"I would make sure it was dead. The axe is to cut up, so that it will not grow another head."

"You believe it?"

"It's what they say. They remove the poison sacs for medicinal purposes, and the teeth to make necklaces, the eyes for aphrodisiacs, the skin for shoes and bags, and they cook the meat as a delicacy, and save the bones to make ornaments. It is not pleasant. But I would like to kill that little man in such a way. His bones would make splendid ornaments. I would keep his skull in a clear glass jar of vinegar. In such a way he could not escape."

"I'm glad you're not after *me*."

"Oh no. How could I? Except with kisses, and everything else. But him? If he touched you, my people would chop him."

169

"*Your* people?"

"We are many in this area, and in Southall. You know it? They would all help. They know you are a good friend. Have we so many?"

"Must you go home?"

"I have two more sets to clean. Yes. I must go home to take my mother to the temple. She believes. I, no. All religion is mumbo. They have got African temples here. Umbanda, they call it. And Quimbanda. Worse. If you go out at night on Fridays and Saturdays, or when the moon is full, you will hear the drums from the cellars. In the ruins they have dug. How many cats and dogs do you see on the streets? They are the sacrifice. They worship Satanas. Mumbo. And Jumbo. Very well. But strange matters happen. I go to our temple to defend my mother. I hope it defends me. I will see you tomorrow. I have had a horrible life. You make it worthwhile. Now I take my bucket and soaps and polish. While I clean, I think of you. I clean away any threat. I shall ring the bells in the temple many times. They will guard you. Isn't it so silly?"

She shut the door in a whisper.

I listened to a tug piping on the river, sad sound, dead water, miles of docks, empty, tens of thousands of men looking for work, many more dead, and who mentioned women? Or children?

What a lot of brutes we all were.

Nobody gave a damn about anybody.

Churches shut, chapels shut. Even the Salvation Army had taken the flags and drums away.

Onward, into battle.

Against what?

Jo Hibbs telephoned from the office to say there were letters to sign, and a call from Malcolm George that he had a large contract to offer, and if I would like to spend a working weekend at Little Burley to settle details. Little Burley I had been to once, a lovely place, and I said yes, and she said he called from Paris, and she would find out train times and the rest.

Malcolm George I had found remarkable in many ways. He had been first to snap at TV rentals, made a fortune, began a printing works for paperbacks in the French style without pictures on the cover, started a sex magazine, *Genit*, got into cut-price domestic goods, bought into this, that and whatnot, and now wanted to buy land and build in the Waygoes manner all across East London. He was stumped for the same reason. No permits. A political or other chasm existed. It could not be crossed. Apparently nobody knew why. But it was being said it depended on the pay-off.

By?

Who knew?

To?

Who knew?

I walked in chilly breeze over to the office, looked in at the plant, waving to Arnie Daye, one of the master printers, went in the transport bay, along to the packing tables, a little surprised there was that amount of work. I signed the letters, and Malcolm George's office called to tell me that the eleven-forty-five from Paddington would be met to take me to Little Burley.

"Mr. Waygoes doubled the first order for posters, and he wants another fifty thousand pamphlets," Jo said. "Shall I cable Paris for the posters, and have the pamphlets done here? I don't see much sense letting them have what we can do. Come to that, we could have done the posters."

"Except that we had the other job. We'll do the pamphlets. Paris can do a repeat on the posters. They might have a job for me. Doesn't do to be greedy. What did you think of the posters?"

"Lovely job. They know their business. Colour was marvellous."

"I'm talking about the copy. What they said."

"Oh. The copy?"

She stood on one foot, looking over my head.

"Yes. What it said. It was meant to say something to *you*. And people *like* you."

She half-turned away.

"We're fed up with people talking," she said. "We've heard it all. Labour. Conservatives. Trade unions, the lot. What have they done? Where *are* we? Shit street. That's what my uncle says. He's worked hard all his life. So's my mum. He left it all to

171

them. The bloody politicians. They let him down. His old-age pension and hers don't keep them. It's my money makes the difference. They can pay the rent, and rates, and live because I'm working. But I'm not saving. What am *I* working for? What did *they* work for? What about *my* children I haven't got? If I get married, what would my mum and him do? Starve? Half-rations? What's happened? We can't pay the mortgage. If we sell, it's a dead loss. So we bash to keep a roof over us? What about medical, and all that? You think the Government helps? You'd better find out. It's a lot worse than you think."

"All right, Jo," I said. "Let's look at wages. For everybody. We've got a cost-of-living clause."

"Don't do any good," Jo said. "I don't think you've had a good look at things. Cost of living? Buying things in the shops? Better look at the rates."

"What's wrong with the rates?"

"You don't feel it at the Daemon. We do. Electric light. Gas. Post. Everything everybody's supposed to do for everybody else, I mean, it costs more. Who pays? *Us*. With what? What we take home in the pay packet? Is it enough? Who gives a goddam? It's got to be paid. That's all. *Pay*."

"Ah."

"On top of that, income tax."

The telephone rang, and Jo put the receiver under her ear and in her shoulder so that she could take a cup of coffee and spoon sugar.

"Yes," she said. "Right. It'll be ready at five sharp. Better send an extra man for loading. Thank you."

She looked at me.

"How long's it going to work?" she said, and put the receiver down.

"What?"

"*This*. What's going on. Put the prices up? All right. Put the wages up. So the prices go up. All right. So the wages go up. So everything goes up. Why?"

"Just drink your coffee, and calm down. Lots of people are thinking the same way, and they've got the same answer."

"Well, what is it?"

172

"Use your brains. Look at Mr. Waygoes' posters."

She shook her head.

"Don't understand them," she said. "I don't think he's too near it. He's got a lovely place here. But the trouble's out *there*. It's in Europe. Common Market. We got sucked in. Where's he say anything about it?"

"He's *not* saying anything about it. He's telling you how the banking system began."

"So what's the good? We've got it. Haven't we?"

"Of course. Now we have to find out how *we* use it, instead of them."

"We, who?"

"Us. You and me."

She covered her mouth with her hand and sat back, balancing the cup on her knee.

"Don't see it," she said. "A bank's a bank. What have I got to do with it?"

"Without you and me, and the rest of us, they don't exist."

"I don't understand."

"If we didn't use banks, they wouldn't be there. They'd have to shut shop."

"But what about paying bills? Wages. All that. You've got to have a bank, haven't you?"

"All right. Yes. But not to make a profit out of you and me. All of us."

"They can't work for nothing."

"Have you got a bank? Do you use one?"

She laughed, putting the cup and saucer on the desk.

"Never had the cash," she said. "Nobody in my family."

"So how many people like you need a bank?"

"Well. To cash cheques we get for wages."

"Jo. You're a lot more intelligent than that. You're an accountant as well."

She took our cups and saucers, and stood in the doorway.

"I've seen it, and heard it, all my life," she said, in a faraway voice. "Every time there's an election. They're all trotting out the same old nonsense. A different wrapper. Everybody's got the answer. Heaven's round the corner. Just vote for me. *No.* I've only voted once. I'll never vote again. *Never*. Waste of time. Let them get on with it."

"But you're giving it to the enemy. Aren't you?"

She shook her head, in a shine from sunlight, a bright mop.

"We've only got one enemy," she said. "That's *us*. We don't know enough."

I signed letters, looked at accounts and at forward orders. I had no worries. I took a poster, and three of the pamphlets in a cylinder, and put my jacket on, and Arnie Daye knocked on the open door, a big man in a red-and-white check shirt.

"Listen, guv'nor," he said, almost in a whisper. "Why've you got to be so *bloody* determined to make people miserable?"

"Hell you talking about?" I said.

"Jo's just been in here. She's out there now. At her desk. She's crying. This is the third time I've seen it. She comes in here bright's a bloody lark. She comes out, she's crying. Breaking her heart she is. What do you *do* to her? What do you *say*? I got a right to know. I want to marry her. But she won't tell me. What *is* it?"

"What you want to do is your business. Fact that Jo's crying has nothing to do with me. It has nothing to do with this company. Get back to your job. You're sticking your nose where it doesn't belong."

"I can call industrial action. I can close this place. Easy."

"Well," I said. "By all means. Close it. It'll stay closed for three months. I'll take a holiday. And when I get back, I won't take on any of you. You strike, and you can look for another job. In fact, I'm giving you a week's notice. Shove off. I can do without you."

He held up his hands.

"That's not what I wanted to say," he said, edging back to the corridor. "I was only talking about Jo."

"While she's employed here, she's nothing to do with you. If she's crying, it's nothing to do with me. If she has a complaint, she knows where to come. And she knows I'll deal with it. Anything else?"

He wagged his head at the floor.

"You've got a week's notice," I said. "Sorry to lose you. But

174

you're like a lot of others. You think you can bulldoze because of the unions? You won't bulldoze me."

"I'll close this place up," he said. "You won't print. You won't shift a piece of paper."

"Do your best," I said. "Jo and the others wanting to work will draw full wages. The rest of you can go to hell. That's all."

He looked back at me from out in the corridor.

"You can get took care of," he said. "And this place don't need much more'n a couple of cans of petrol."

I went up to him, eye to eye.

"You mean to say the man I've respected all this time as master printer has got that sort of mind? A petrol bomber?"

He looked away.

"Times you got to protect yourself," he said. "Any way you can."

"All right," I said. "After tonight, you've got three months to do as you please. We shan't be working. To hell with you, and everybody like you. You won't be coming back. Clear off. I'll come back here to lock up."

I walked out to the quiet street, not even a cat, and I remembered Bhula and the drums, and walked on, across the road to the Daemon, and his smile, and so gladly, happily, up the stairs to the set. I was absolutely not worried about closing down the plant. Nobody can be threatened for *any* reason about any*thing*. To submit is treason to the human spirit. My old headmaster had taught us that, and if that was all he taught, it was well done.

I had the poster and three of the pamphlets, and in the moments I called a cab to go to Paddington Station, there were knocks on the door.

I wondered. No bell?

But I went over, and opened.

Teucer? Well, well.

Why well, well? What else do you say?

"Ah, hullo, A.G.," he said, genial as all that. "A couple of things. May I come in?"

"Of course. Drink?"

"Splendid idea. Look. Uh. My father and I aren't so far apart

175

as it might have seemed. D'you know? We're best of friends, really. But sometimes that damned gout makes him awfully—uh—sort of—pernickety. After all, it hurts like hell. So it's told. And I try to—um—let's say—ameliorate. You *do* see, don't you?"

I simply did not like Teucer, but I poured him a drink.

"As a very great favour, could I see the letter he gave you?" he asked, taking the tumbler, and putting it on the table.

"No."

"Why not?"

"I haven't looked at it yet."

"Not?"

He stared at me, no move toward the drink on the table. I was pouring mine, and listening for the call for the cab.

"Not," I said. "It won't interest me until I return from the weekend. Then I'll take it to the solicitors."

"Why won't you let me see it?"

"I've told you. I haven't looked at it. Neither has my solicitor. Why should *you* see it?"

"I think it might be taking away part of my patrimony," he said. "It's been done with my half sister. He'll try doing it with me. But I won't let him. He's a sick-minded, mouldy-bodied cadaver. I've been trying to tell him. Times are different. He wants to build round here. He's got lovely designs. Drawings. Models. Be surprised what a marvellous job he's got in mind. But after all. You've got to get permits."

He reached for the drink, lifted, toasted me, and drank.

"So I found out, and I got the figure," he said. "All nail jobs."

"*Nail* jobs?"

"That's dead right, *nail* jobs," he said. "Jobs paid on the nail. That is, cash down, everything else after. Anything wrong with that?"

"You can *get* permits?"

"Cash on the nail? Yes."

"Did you tell Mr. Waygoes?"

"Certainly. Of course. But he wouldn't go."

"Why not?"

"He won't bribe."

"That's a nice change."

"Gets nothing done."

"Honesty's important."

"Why?"

Where he sat, light was brighter than in his father's place, and I saw traces of the beating in stretched skin about the eyes and nose, and small discolours, enough to tell he must have gone through a nasty hoop, and I noticed the slight twist of his body on the right side, not a limp, but weight bearing on one side of the hip. Boots make terrible weapons.

"I don't think I have to answer you," I said. "The real answer comes in front of a judge, with a few years in prison to think it over."

"Won't happen if you use your brains. Pick your people. Listen, I've got all the permits lined up to build a housing estate this side of Leman Street, from Wapping High up to Whitechapel Road. Worth thirty-eight million quid. Twice that by the time it's finished. Money's ready. All I need is fifteen thousand. To nail it. You on?"

"I'd have to know a lot more before I took that amount out of equities. Who *are* the builders? Architects? Who's the Council? Which councilmen are you nailing? Who's taking the nail?"

He shook his head.

"Asking the wrong questions," he said. "All I want to know is, can they deliver? That's all. If they can, I've got the money. Or, let's say, I know where to ask for it."

"But doesn't Mr. Waygoes own a lot of the land here?"

"Yes, he does. But not the area I'm talking about. That's why I wanted to see that letter. Come in with me, and you can make a bit."

The bell rang. I opened the door.

"Your cab, sir," Almond said. "Got some luggage?"

I nodded at the cylinder and suitcase, and he took them down.

Teucer finished the drink.

"You'll be sorry," he said.

"Doubtless. But I want nothing to do with elected representatives taking money. It's a prison job. If you're found out."

"That's all you're afraid of? Listen. If you got caught on a run, where would *you* be?"

"You'd better mind what you're saying. I'm not on any run. Get to know it. I've got to go."

"Let me see that lettter."

"No."

"I warn you."

I grasped him by the tie and shirt front, and pulled him to crack my forehead against his, and I saw from his eyes that he was hurt.

"You must learn never to threaten," I said. "It gets people's backs up. Now get out. Don't bother me again."

I saw him out, took the envelope from my desk and put it in my jacket pocket, had another look round, regretting I had to go away, locked the door, and went downstairs, and ran into Ol' Mabbs coming up.

"Oh, hullo," he said. "Listen. Ella Broome's gone spare, did you know? We can't find her. She went out to the dig that night, bright as sixpence. Never seen since."

"Who was with her?"

"We can't seem to find out. She generally went by the launch. But not that night. The truck never went out. How she got there, who with, we don't know. But the girls at the dig never see her, and she ain't been seen since. Bloody fine how-d'ye-do, ain't it?"

I had crawls in the gut. I could "see" the police station, and I knew that a visit from Sergeant Kemp was more than a possibility.

"Our girls don't seem to be doing too well, do they?" I said. "What's this, the third or fourth?"

"Don't know. Just that each one hurts. I knew them. They was our girls. I see 'em naked out there. In the Rotunda. Lovely. Only privilege I ever had. Cost me nothing. They was there. They ain't, now. I tell you what? If they *was* done in, I'd like to get in spit-reach of the bloke. That's all. No jury'd ever be bothered. *I'd* do him. Save a lot of trouble."

"I'll be away till Sunday night. Would you keep an eye?"

"All Sir Garnet, chum. I lay me hand on 'em? Be their *lot*. I'm on remand till Monday."

Paddington to Reading was a drink and gulp long, the car waited, and I got to Little Burley just in time for an hour or so of business, and then lunch under the trees, and a snooze, and then another couple of hours of figures and prices. I was surprised at the size of the contract, the largest I ever handled.

"Look," I said, passing him the order book to sign. "Why did you pick me for this?"

"First, you keep your mouth shut," he said. "Second, you deliver on time. Third, you're with Bayard Waygoes. So am I."

"I didn't know that."

"Lots of things you don't know, do you?"

"Always a disappointment."

"Matter of people keeping their mouths shut."

"Like the Cockneys? They don't grass?"

He smiled, and went on signing.

"They're like anybody else with intelligence," he said. "They talk when it suits them. That's never."

"Has Waygoes anything to do with this contract?"

"If he hadn't, you wouldn't be here."

"Question? What's he got to do with oil in the Middle East?"

"He started with barges. Went on to tankers. Answer your question?"

"I don't want to be nosy."

"You can't be. Just take the order. Come in and have a drink. Your car'll be here in ten minutes. Who's doing Waygoes' buying? The office work?"

"No idea. I've never dealt with that side."

"Another one doesn't grass?"

"Call it that."

"Help yourself."

"Thanks."

But there was a certain feeling in the room, in the air, in his attitude, and I pretended not to notice it, which is just as stupid as stubbing a toe and trying to ignore it.

"I'd like to ask you an important question—that is—to me," he said. "Is Waygoes all right? I'm worried. I've heard he's not too well."

"He's had gout. Apart from that, there's nothing wrong with him. That I could see. He's sharp. Works hard."

"Always did. I'm happy to hear it. This contract's going to

mean a lot to me. My wife and I've always been afraid that horrible little ape'd give him a dose of the hammer. His so-called son. We had him here a couple of times when he was up at Oxford. He interfered with the girls. I warned him. But you see, you can't do anything with somebody who thinks he's a talking millionaire. My wife was very kind to him, and she loves a joke. But there's a line. I found him near our bedroom. No need to say any more. I kicked him out, and phoned his father, and that was that. He left a bill down at the pub, here, for just over two thousand pounds. He had a rock band, and all that. The village was up all night. He was pinched for assaulting a couple of girls. Cost poor old Waygoes nearly five thousand, all told. Terrible job. He's a real psycho. Call it what you like. He's a danger anywhere he happens to be."

"Why are you worried about this contract?"

"I won't be happy till it's signed and in the bank."

"Is Teucer his son? Or adopted?"

"I don't know. He could be a by-blow. Like the daughter. What a bag. But I'm not interested. Waygoes himself I like. His word's as good as a signed contract."

"Then why are you worried about the signing of it?"

He turned to me while a girl at the door knocked, and said whatever, I didn't hear. His eyes were deep grey, baggy as if he had missed sleep, and a brown-to-grey cowlick fell over his forehead.

"Because if anything happened to him, his word's not much good. Is it? Your car's here. I'll walk you down."

"May I ask a question?"

"Certainly."

"I understood this was going to be a weekend."

He half-turned, stopped, and held his jaw.

"Christ," he said. "My wife had a call to her mother. It's no excuse. But I forgot. And I'm flying to Copenhagen at seven tonight. I'm sorry. Really very sorry. We'll have to do it again."

It sounded empty. But there had to be a reason for it. I was unable to guess.

"It's all right," I said. "The job won't suffer."

But I was worried. I was being bundled off, never mind about his wife being away. I told the driver to go to Reading Station, and when we got there, I paid him, and took a cab to Marlow, and stopped at an hotel, and got a room, and had a lovely dinner of roast lamb and crêpe suzette, and went to bed. I was up at seven, and took a train to Birmingham—I don't know why—and had a drink before going back to London with a horrible lunch on the train, and I was at the Daemon somewhere near seven, because I was in no hurry, just in case.

Nobody had anything to say, and I went up to the set so happily, and put all the lights on, and there it was, as Bhula had left it, shining, quiet, lovely.

I poured a drink, and took Waygoes' letter out of my jacket over the chair, and sat down, in the quiet, to read.

So far as I could see, I was left as property, my plant, with all the backyards on Wapping High, and five streets more, the length of Brittle Candy Lane, and up to Pickled Gherkin Street, all in rack and ruin, except for my houses, rebuilt, and a couple down the road. And my houses, put to order, were not much. The rest was a brick-and-stone stretch of thick weeds, but still a long way from my father's place. That was what I wanted. I could never get near. Danger of falling rubble? Unexploded bombs? Live? Years afterwards? But they could still blow up and kill. It took the Bomb Squad, and that cost money, but first, the building permits.

Nail jobs?

On the surface, very respectable, prim as the rest, and so proper, and rotten. Pay, and do as you like. Don't pay? Status quo. And what's that? Rubble. Miles of it. And skeletons. Once, when they had the life in them, they stank. The stink told of life going. No stink meant life gone. The heaps covered them, and the weeds grew.

Poor old London. Somewhere, I seemed to hear a Salvation Army band, the drums, the brass and silver, and "Onward, Christian Soldiers," with the tambourines clashing, lovely, cleansing the streets, blessing the people, sending up the prayer.

I saw a flicker to the right.

The three-legged chair in the alcove.

Jayb smiled. Metal glinted to the right of his head.

"Hullo," he said. "Wondered how long before you see me."

"How did you get in here?"

He put up a little finger, and took a large ring from off his ear, and swung the key in light.

"That's how."

"What do you want?"

"Now, don't get shirty. Just hold it a minute. You know you're due a visit? From the coppers? They don't like what's going on? Eh?"

"What?"

"Girls."

"Girls?"

"Them you've took out."

"I don't know what you're talking about."

"You will. When you're in the box. And the judge has a go."

"I *still* don't know what you're talking about."

"Yes, you do. Else what's making you shake?"

"I'm not."

"No? You've slopped half your drink."

"What d'you want? Quick. And get out before I call Security."

He laughed, sitting back in the chair. I wished I had never bought it.

"I shall have to kill you," I said.

He laughed, not very loudly, sitting all the way back, mouth open.

"Oh Christ," he said. "Look who's talking. Listen. There's a dozen blokes waiting to *do* you. Same way you done Teucer. Think you could slide with it?"

"I had nothing to do with it."

"The blokes are knowed. How much they got. You paid 'em. Down the Lomax. Eh?"

"You're talking so much, you must need a drink. Help yourself."

"Ta."

He went to the sideboard, and I sat down at my desk, half-turning away, so that with the left hand I could press the slide that opened the recess hiding the miniature Walther .22, barely larger than a cigaret pack, at short range, lethal.

"You've always been too clever, mate," he said, pouring scotch. "You must have knowed everybody in the house was part of the business, one way or the other? You must have knew everybody? Knew what *they* knew? And they knew all about *you*."

"What was there *to* know?"

He swirled the drink, looking down at it.

"Who you went out with," he said. "Who come up here. They all *went*. Nothink seen of 'em. Where they go?"

"Nothing to do with me."

"The coppers don't think so. Nobody else does. Listen. There's people in this house'd shop you quicker'n look at you. *If* they had the evidence. But you're a bit too smart. For the moment. Ain't you? Eh? Why'd you do it? One after the other?"

"I don't know what you're talking about."

"The coppers do. Once they've opened a file on you, they never let go. Did you know? They've got a file *that thick* on you. And pre'n'ly, they'll pounce. You'll be in the slammer, chum. You'll never get out of it."

"They can't convict without evidence. They need witnesses."

He turned to me and opened his mouth wide to laugh the whisper.

The tumbler shattered and the splinters drew blood from his face, and the second shot opened a hole in his neck. While he fell, I ran to the bathroom for a big towel, and ran back to cover him and sop blood. I went to the kitchen for a big black plastic rubbish bag, and pushed it over his head, pulled it down, got his legs in, and picked it up, spun it round, and tugged it to the west window because there was only a blank wall down to the ground. I put all the lights out, opened the sash and looked out. Nothing moving anywhere. The bag lifted easily, and I dropped it, listened to a soft fall, shut the window, and poured a drink.

There were two letters to be posted. I put my jacket on, and went downstairs. Soult was on duty, and I asked him for a couple of stamps. He had just finished cleaning the foyer and everything smelled of wax polish. I got the stamps, gave him something for his trouble, and he put on the lights and opened the door for me, and I trotted in the cold night, out to the left, to the pillar box, dropped the letters in, and on the way back, took the small stairway down to the marina. The bag lay under the window. I picked it up and quietly, carefully, paced the few yards to the stone wall. Shook the bag off him, took what was in his pockets, had a good look around, no movement, no sound except the river, and no trouble, put him back in the bag, and rolled him over the wall, heard the splash, and walked away, to the side stair, along to the main stair and the Daemon's slyly vicious smile as if he agreed with me, and I went in, thankfully, to the warmth of the foyer, said good night to Soult, and took the stairs two at a time.

I got into the set and sat down, limp. Blood spotted my trousers and jacket. I got out of them, and threw them in a suitcase with everything I was wearing, and the shoes. I picked up the Walther, and put the lights out, and went over to the window to lean out. No sound except the river. I pulled the sash shut, and went across to the south window, almost directly over the water, and opened it, and listened.

Only the river's marvellous whisper, that said anything you wanted it to, and nothing, like a girl pulling a face.

I held the Walther by the barrel, and swung once, twice, and let it go. I heard no splash, saw nothing, but I knew it was deep in the river, and that was that. I went over to the pile out of Jayb's pockets. There was a bundle of notes, probably over a couple of hundred pounds, five keys, a notebook, a switchblade knife I was glad he had been kind enough not to use on me, a pack of Kleenex, a pack of raisins, a couple of pawn tickets—pawn tickets with that clutch of notes?—a couple of football coupons filled in, and three well-taped detonators, very dangerous to carry about, because the warmth of the body could have set them off. It interested me. What was Jayb doing with detonators? Was he part of a bomb squad? I had to get rid of them. I put aside the money, the knife, the notebook, the pawn tickets, the keys and the coupons, and put the rest in the kitchen machine that chewed everything and sent it down the chute.

I had a hot shower, and I woke to the telephone and Jo Hibbs, saying I had a heap of mail and a lot of papers to sign, and two people waited to see me, nothing very important.

I got across there, and Jo brought in the papers and I signed.

But I was seeing the place with new eyes. It had always been a cover for what I did. Never had it been a business of any real interest.

"Jo," I said, putting the last letter in the filing tray. "Why do you work here?"

"Why?" she said, head up. "Well. It's a job, isn't it?"

"A job?"

She nodded.

"Or you're on the dole. So you make sure to go to work. For me, that's here."

I looked at her. She was a lovely girl, bright, sharp, nice. I wondered how she could marry someone like Arnie, but that was her affair.

"What bothers you about 'here'?" I asked her. "Anything wrong?"

"You're going to close down for three months, and we've got at least a year's work waiting out there?" she said. "I don't think we ought to be shoved out of a job just because you have an argument with somebody. Who is he? He's a good printer. All right. It's a good plant. But there's a lot more men that's better. Why *should* we be out for three months?"

"That's where you're wrong. You're all on full salary while we reorganize. I've let this business go to hell. Now, I'll start building it. And I know I can."

She put her hands to her face and cried, deep, sounds that hurt.

"I'm so glad," she got out, in breaths. "We can do a lot more work. So much more than we do now."

"Why haven't you said so?"

"You were never here. We had to refuse all sorts of offers."

"Won't happen again. Tell everybody. Full wages. Other thing. Cost of living?"

She wiped her face, under the eyes, down the cheeks, swallowed.

"I believe we could all do with a rise," she said, cold. "I'd be wrong if I didn't say so. I think we want the job. We want the wages. But I think we ought to have what we're worth. What we're getting isn't."

"Why not?"

"It doesn't buy what it used to."

I looked through the window, at rubble and weeds, and thought of who might be unburied and unprayed for beneath. They had been there for so many years.

"All right, Jo," I said. "You make out a list. How much for everybody. Taking into consideration cost of living. From now on, that will be by the month."

She laughed at the portrait of the Queen on the far wall.

"Oh, it's wonderful," she said. "Believe me, we're all so happy to work here. All of us. Now we know we have a safe job. The Indis and Pakis were so afraid we'd close down. Now I can tell them. I can take a horrible weight from them."

"A horrible *weight?*"

"*Not* to have a job? *Nothing* more horrible."

I began to wonder if we were all born just to get a job. By the Sweat of Thy Brow seemed to have another meaning, one that predicted what was to happen, with the dole queues, welfare, social security, and the rest of it. What, exactly, *were* we born for, anyway? What was the idea? It seemed so entirely stupid, that a couple should climb into bed—or not, as the time and place might be—and bang their heads off—or not, depending how they felt—and a little time later on, luckily and happily, or disastrously, as the event turned out—one of their own kind was born to do the same old thing. What for? To support moneylenders? Was Bayard Waygoes right about—as he called them—the cowrie-carrion, the wampum-wallahs, the loansharks, the usurers? What might start people thinking differently? I was starting to but I had no idea what about, or how. It sounded stupid, and I knew it was, but there was little I could do about it. It needed knowledge I had never been taught. All I knew about banks and money was confined to cheques I put in, and those I drew out, and my Stock Exchange experience came from Breese, Cliff, and Iremonger, my brokers, and their advice about the portfolio of equities and gilt-edged bought with profits from the company, though the bulk of all I had was in Switzerland, and I was thankful for the sanity of the Swiss and their way of dealing, giving me hope of security for the future.

Signs of Christmas, in piles of paper chains ready to be hung in the foyer, and big puffs of cotton wool, and rolls of tinsel and dozens of little fir trees brought back the homesick loneliness of those first years as an evacuee. I wanted nothing to do with Santa Claus or parties or even with presents, but simply to crawl off in a corner and be by myself. All these years had never cured that feeling of wanting to go away, get off, and leave the lunatics to their games and Christmas pudding and the noisy rest of it. I was almost in a state of panic, wondering where I could go. Certainly nowhere in Europe, to be chased by bells and carols, as in so many other years. Then where?

I had an idea that John Tyler might know, and I walked up Leman Street to the post office, dropped in the mail, took a bus to Aldgate, and strolled along to his agency, just this side of St. Paul's. Some of the new buildings looked like upended egg crates in metal and glass, though how they could have been passed as suitable to stand near the Cathedral, like a lot of other matters, beat me. Where property and money talk, hymns die and market howls smother the Psalms. A couple of miles down the road, bricks, stones and weeds, ramshackle miles fit for Asians, Africans, Chinese, and whatnot, with nothing except a bare roof and facilities, perhaps, in company with whites of their threadbare kind, and nobody interested. Grandiose plans, and all that. And nothing. Let them get on with it. The miracle was that they did, and nobody complained. They were too anxious to get their heads down and keep quiet in case somebody, yes, Bhula said, some racist or other patriot, full of zeal and beer, wanted to throw them out. A fine reason for keeping people in conditions little better than the bombed-out kraal. I could hear Bayard Waygoes. His posters, I saw, were all over the place. But nobody stood to read them. I must have passed twenty or more. Not a soul took any notice, even to look up, and I wondered if words and pictures were taken to be merely a form of street decoration.

We were in a bad way.

I turned into John's busy agency and took a ticket in the waiting line, but luckily he saw me and waved me into his office.

"Better than messing about out there," he said. "How about a cuppa? How've you been? I was going to ring you. I've got a lovely job for you. Right up the old alley. It's a dozen travel posters, four colours, but in print. No pictures. It's a nice idea. Ten thousand each, first print. How's it sound?"

"Where's the order?"

"Like I told you. I'll send it on. What can I do for you?"

"John, I want to get out of this Christmas lark. Where can I go? Nowhere in Europe or America or the Caribbean. All this Christ-is-born business, I tell you, I hated it since I was sent out as an evacuee. Bloody fine thing to call a child. Poor little buggers. That's all we were. Know what I mean?"

A girl came in with two cups of tea on a tray.

"Ah, ta," he said. "I can do with this. What d'you say to a drop of scotch? Salt it up a bit?"

"I've got to go back to work. I'm tee-tee for the moment."

"Please yourself. Won't stop me. Now, then. No carols, no Christmas. I don't blame you. I can't bear any of it. I'd say, nice warm sun, not too hot, comfortable hotel, not too ruddy expensive, good food and wine, lovely beaches, couple or three weeks suit you? And no Christians. None of that. How's it sound?"

"Great. Where?"

"Tunisia. Fly via Paris, start in the morning, there in the afternoon. I'll give you a letter. Owner's a pal of mine. His wife's French. No lingo trouble. Marvellous beaches. Sea's like light blue gin. Not many girls, though."

"Not interested."

"Just give us the date, that's all. What's this about Waygoes selling up?"

I looked at him, but he poured scotch in the tea.

"Don't know," I said. "Who told you?"

"We get the word down this end, y'know," he said, and held out the bottle. "Changed y'mind?"

"All right. What's the story?"

"Oh, something about he's got tired of holding on. Lots of people after him. Developers. There's millions there, y'know. He could live like a Byz. Any Arab sheikh. Nothing to worry about. Funny bloke. You see his posters?"

"I had them printed. My job."

He nodded, and swivelled the chair to look through the window, at a whitewashed wall and a coal bin. Lovely view. Modern art.

"If he's right, and I reckon he is, there'll be trouble," he said. "We've got enough already, but that'd be *real* trouble. I mean, a lot of them bloody banking lot, they'd swing. Anyway, there's plenty of lamp posts and lots of rope. Why not? I'd help. I don't like to think I've been cheated all my life. Do you?"

"No," I said, and got up. "Send me the tickets, I'll send the cheque. December twenty-two to January ten. That's a nice, quiet three weeks."

"Haven't you got a girl to take with you?"

"Wish I had."

"Hard luck. Anyway, tomorrow, all fixed up. Let me know what you think about the copy. And how long for delivery. Thanks for calling in. If I don't see you, enjoy yourself. Oh. Half a tick. What happened to Waygoes' Paris branch?"

"Didn't know he had one."

"'Course. Travel, *bureau de change*. Everything. Can't get them on the phone. Don't answer letters, telegrams. Wrong time of year for holidays. They're a funny lot. Waygoes might be funnier'n anybody."

"Wouldn't surprise me."

"Yes. Well. We did a lot of business there. Come to a dead stop. If you hear anything, let's know, will you?"

"Of course. Thanks for the tea. Come down our way. Look me up."

"Bet. So long."

I took a bus on the corner, and got my favourite seat, on top, in front, where I could see everything, and I watched the tall buildings of commerce straggle down to a couple of patched-up storeys, new windows, gaps here and there, and bricks, stones and weeds. Poor old East London. Where the Hebrews lived. Bashed night after night, for weeks, till there was nothing left except the rubble and all the people underneath, or blotted into places elsewhere.

Daemon Wente Waye looked as ever, even with a bare garden, all in order, and Valentine Harry Edwardes glowed gold letters at the sky, and lovely little bushes of red berries were all round him, and a holly tree, clipped by Amy into a ball of red with green and yellow leaves, seeming to keep him warm. Nice to have friends like that looking after you when you push off. What else is death except pushing off, painfully or not, from everything known or felt or seen, with the oarsman's blade cutting into the moss on the quay wall, the hanging moss you grew yourself, that dangles in slimy wisps, reminding of lost time, opportunities, deceits, idiocies, no second chance, all gone now in the blade's one powerful shove.

Gold letters glow at the sky, and only living minds hold memory. I had never known Valentine Harry Whasname, but he was as real to me as anybody else. At least, his monniker glowed gold at the night. I wondered if mine ever would. That was the best of having a friend with money.

Money. That was the game. I knew nothing about it. A lifetime of using it and not knowing what I was doing. Babes in Bretton Woods. Another of Waygoes' yaps. Everybody got done there, except the bankers, the cowrie-carrion, the wampum-wallahs, the loan sharks and panhandlers.

Who had any answer?

"Message from Miss Hibbs, sir," Almond said, at the door. "It's important."

I groaned and turned, and went across the garden and Wapping High, and all I could see in eyeline, left or right, in the terms of Waygoes' bequest, if that was the word, belonged to me. It was quite a property, about three hundred yards long and five streets the same size in depth, with the backyards. I had no idea what it was worth. Without permits to build or develop, very little. But with a permit, and a good architect, I could see what might be. As it was, most of the houses were only ruins, or repaired just enough to keep them standing, except for those I used for the plant and a couple down at the end. Apart from that, most had no roofs, no facilities of any kind, and sheets of corrugated iron covered doors and windows to stop squatters getting in, poor devils. I was always sorry for the lads and the girls traipsing about with their few bits in a backpack. Downriver they had miles to go to find a place to sleep. Open ground may be all very well, but you need firewood to cook meals, and shelter if only from heavy dew. There was not even a twig, and nobody thought of putting up a couple of marquees, with a firepit, and a standpipe of water every so many miles. It was little enough to ask. The youngsters were only doing what we older fatheads would have given eyeteeth to do. Just put a pack on our backs, and walk the world to find out what we might have missed. I had a constant, bitter feeling I had missed half the world.

Then why did I feel that stab—almost of hate—when Edwina came in while I was getting into my overcoat to see the solicitors, and saying with big eyes and a shaky voice that squatters had moved in next door to her and more were going in, men, women and children, whole families, with furniture.

I was in too much of a hurry to do anything about it, and I asked Jo to call the police to shift them. Those houses were going to be part of my property, and I could see other houses being taken over until the entire place was a squatter's paradise.

I took the Tube in Whitechapel Road, bought a paper, and tried to read about earthquakes and sterling in a mess and all the other pap, but my mind was on the squatters, and I was forced to admit I hated the thought of them, living on social benefit, paying no rent, doing no work, simply the other end of the system, bankers up there, squatters down here, both sucking humanity's arsehole to live, at no expense except to us, the in-betweens, the mugs.

I got out at the Temple and walked up to Essex Street, found the number, and looked at the board, and my people, God love them were on the third floor in gold letters. I went in to a small room, and gave my letter to some old dear in a black dress with a woollen scarf round her neck, and a dirty cold. She went in the other door, and came out to sneeze, blow a red nose, and nod at an open door down the corridor. She should have been in bed, poor old girl.

"Br. Jodes, a partder, will see you, sir," she said. "Just to witdess a si'dature, that's all. Wod't be loig."

It certainly was not. Mr. Jones, bald, bearded to hide collar

191

and tie, ripped the envelope, slapped the papers flat, pushed hornrims to the top of his nose, and looked at me—I thought—accusingly.

"Everything here's in order," he said, as if I had denied it. "Simply sign those copies, and I'll witness and stamp. Take them back to Mr. Waygoes, he'll sign, and that's that. You own the property. Any enquiry of any sort, please come and see me."

"Why did I have to come all this way if I could have signed at the Daemon?" I said, a bit peevish.

"Because it required a representative of his firm of solicitors to witness the signature, sign, and append the requisite stamps," Mr. Jones said, as if the business tired him out. "The documents will be ready in a few moments. If you'd be good enough to wait outside?"

Out I went, and sat on a creaky chair till the old dear came out rustling the papers into an envelope.

"There you are, sir," she said. "All id order. Ady more edquiries, call Br. Jodes, this duiber."

She gave me a card, I put the papers in my pocket, said thanks, and went out feeling less like a property owner than a lag just out of gaol.

Fresh air seemed good, and I went in a pub along the Strand for a bracer, and ran right into Ol' Mabbs and an arms-up hail.

"Same lovely idea, eh?" he bellowed. "What's it going to be? My round, no arguments. Been down the solicitors, have you? Me, too. Ol' Waygoes, I mean, he's like a fairy bloody godfather, eh? He's give me a couple of houses on the corners' Cinnamon Lane and Big Smith. Do me lovely. Rest of me life, no rent. A few quid for a carpenter to put in shelves, and a coat of paint, and bob's your uncle. Eh?"

"I wonder *why* he's done it. It's valuable property. Or it will be."

"You read it, have you?"

"Yes."

"Anythink strike you strange?"

A tone in his voice made me look at him. I had always thought of Ol' Mabbs as an artisan, sound as stone, comical at times, with all the Cockney virtues, able to laugh at himself, ignore any hardship, at all times ready to help those needing it. I might have been right about that, but there was another dimension, and I saw it in a hard, oddly lit eye, lightish grey, no nonsense.

"No," I said. "I've read it a few times, front to back."

"Your good health, and long may we prosper," he said, and looked at me over the glass. "Did you notice the bit about his trustees? Subject to their approval? That's a bolthole. The Indian bloke, round the back, there, he says you could drive half-a-dozen coaches and horses through it. The trustees can sling you out at any time they like. 'Course, they'd have a bit of a barney with our solicitors. They might have to pay. But it's a bit bloody funny, i'n't it? Making a gift, and same hand, almost taking it away?"

"I wonder why?"

"See who's boss of the Board?"

"Don't remember."

"Worst bastard he could have picked. Young whasname, Teucer. Bloody little crab. Thinks he's everybody. I told the boss, and I says, he messes about with any girl near me, I says, I'll do him, and he says, You do that, and I'll pay for your defence. That's what he said."

"Seems a lot of hate between those two."

"The youngster made a balls of his go at Oxford. Started chucking his weight about. The big scholard, y'know? Messing about with the girls. *That's* what gets me. They can't help theirselfs. He says he'll lose 'em their jobs. The old man's told him to find hisself a job. That's a dead lark, that is. Who'll have him outside the drivel coop?"

"I've heard he's a nuisance."

"Ah. A bloke like that's more'n a nuisance. He's a dirty lice. A bloke'd tell him to come outside. A girl can't. See what I mean? He can go to Mrs. Rafaele or Mrs. Hine and say, all right, that bint's out. They don't argue. It's the boss's son. They can get a dozen girls for any job. Afros, Indos, Pakis, any time you like. Why argue? So a bloody good girl loses her job because she won't drop her drawers? I tell you, I get in a proper state."

193

"I'm with you. Anything we can do?"

He laughed—huh!—and slopped his drink and sprinkled his fingers, and wiped them on his trousers.

"Listen, the girls was going to give a Christmas party in the Rotunda. Nake', of course. No better-lookin' lot than what we got. Plenty of everything. Then they was going have kiss-in-a-ring. They'd have got him in there, and they'd a' bloody tore him to bits. But I think the Boss got to know. He flanked 'em. He's off on a cruise for two or three weeks. Doctor's orders. He's had a rotten time with gout and one thing and another. He's takin' that pisshole with him. So the girls won't have the chance. I think that's a shame. They'd have corpsed him. You staying on for Christmas?"

"I'm getting to hell out. I can't stand Christmas."

"I'm with you, chum. I'll be at a farm in Arbroath. Been there the past ten years or more. Peaceful? Christ. Y'd never know there was trouble in the world. It's all snow, and y'go out in the morning to pull sheep out of the drifts. You can tell by the brown mark. Their breath. And you watch those dogs working. I tell you, it gives you another idea of life. At night, we sit round the fire, and I carve sheep horns. Dozens of them come in. They all bring their own drink. And they sing, and play the pipes. It's another life. More wonderful than anything here. I'm thinking of moving up there. They want me to. But I don't think I could leave the Daemon, and the girls. I've never bedded a single one. But there's nothing takes the place of a dream. Live in a dream. That's what it is. For me, any rate."

I wondered if we all dreamed at the Daemon.

I'm certain I did.

But back at the plant I had to face facts. More money for everybody meant that prices had to go up. Present contracts were a loss. I had to write to a lot of people and explain that I had a problem, in that the contract price took no account of the rise in wages, and costs in paper and ink and other side expenses, and wondered, in the matter of loss, if they would allow a fifteen per cent plus on what they had agreed to pay, which would bring me level, without profit or loss, and that all future contracts would contain a clause allowing prices to rise or fall according to the current rate of the pound sterling.

194

But while I wrote, I thought what a parcel of chumps we were, and Bayard Waygoes came more clearly into mind. Certainly he had an idea, and I could see it, miserably perhaps, a long way away, but because I was ignorant of the nature of economics or of banking, or the business of money, I was a victim, with all of us, and I had to take what I was allowed to get and regard the rest as a mystery. What a fatheaded lot. All of us, all the Oxford and Cambridge twats, and the rest at Harvard and Yale, and everywhere else, a lot of horses' arses, and that was an insult to any horse.

The fact was that we were all helpless. We all had simply to go on doing the job we were doing, that we knew how to do, and play it as the cowrei-carrion, the wampum-wallahs, the pay-in grille bastards dictated.

Raijathi, the new night editor, came in after knocks, with a long piece of copy. He had the largest brown eyes I ever saw in any head, and they were sad.

"Sir," he said. "I may speak?"

"Of course?"

"You have read this?"

He offered the copy. I read the first few lines.

"What is it?"

"It is in the worst degree racialist," he said. "I think we have no excuse to accept this."

I got up and took him by the shoulders, and turned him for the door.

"This plant works in print," I said. "Because of print, we live. If there are complaints, we'll take care of them. Otherwise we work. If you don't like it, you may leave at this moment. Is that understood?"

"It is unfair. It is improper."

"Many things are unfair and improper. We still have to live. Turn out the job and take your money at the end of the week. Well?"

He shrugged, and his eyes were sadder, and I felt so sorry for him.

"We turn out poison against ourselves?" he said. "Only to be sure to pay rent and feed our children? To make them a later target? Why are we so criminal in our attitude?"

195

"A business can't afford sentimentality. It has to show a profit or close down. Is that what you want?"

"I feel I am a traitor," he said, and bent his head to make his hair fall about his face. "I should refuse."

"Then? The job goes to someone else. Money out of our pockets into someone else's. Whose benefit?"

He nodded.

"It is so," he said. "Plenty of pi-dogs to take the scraps. It is a horrible world. Especially here. Where you pretend to have democracy, and ideals of Christians. You have not one or the other. We have to work between the two. They are chimeras. How can a man be honest?"

"He can do a good week's work for a good week's money. And that's that. Enough? Let's see that job finished, there's a good chap."

He went out, and I felt ashamed. But what the hell, if you refuse a job because of this, that, or the other, then soon you feed off ideals, and though there may be riches of self-righteousness, that plate stays empty of food, and without it, what happens? A business without work is bankrupt. I was sermonising to myself, but God damn it, I was far from being converted. I wished to God I had the money to turn down business not to my liking. But how long would I last? I had a responsibility to Jo and the rest for their wages. It was the worst excuse, but it would have to do. I had no wish to take funds from Switzerland to support brave notions and quixotic ideas.

Business was quite different. Morals cost money. Amen. Christ.

Bhula surprised me by turning down the Tunisian holiday with a flat *No* in a shaken head and a whispered *Impossible*.

"My father would find out in two split seconds," she said, folding a blanket, staring through the window. "He would pulp me into the ground. With kicks. My people would find out. They would point at him. There would be no peace. Here, yes, I can enjoy myself. Outside, impossible. Take with you a white. I know she cannot be what I am. So? I am not jealous. But thank you for asking. You are a gentleman."

"You mean he wouldn't let you have a holiday?"

196

"In this manner, no. The other girls would know I had gone. He would know because I would not be at home. It would be enough. I would be pulp. Pulp, you call it? Smashed. What would be the use? I am married. When I was four. My father is trying to get my husband here. He is an electrician. Perhaps in four or five years he will take his place to come here. Then we are together. It is why I don't want a baby. My father would kill us both. You understand?"

"And sympathise. You haven't any need to worry. Call on me for any help you need. Anytime. Anything."

That sari's unwinding in many-coloured rounds always reminded me of a beautiful lyrebird or phoenix whispering into the air, and then I was in Eden, and Eve sang strange words.

That was why, I suppose, I felt unutterably sorry, and irremediably robbed, when I got the sunchair, the umbrella and towels, and the icebox of drinks, and the books on the beach a little farther along than Hammamet, and sat down in hot sun for the first cold beer.

I was exactly what I had never wanted to be.

Alone.

There are people who like to be free jacks. That's up to them. I like somebody near me, or else I get the feeling of still being an evacuee. I wonder if the people in charge knew what they were doing when they made a generation or two of evacuees. Children without parents. Parents without children. Of course, there were lots of kind people ready to help. But there were too many of us. At the end of those years we had finished hating. We were simply ourselves, feeling nothing for anybody. How we managed to settle in a civilised state, I shall never be sure. But we did. The backlash came in revolt, in the slop nature of long hair, beards, bangles, necklaces, and the thin, castrati wailing of rock, pop, and the rest. I sympathised, empathised, but I had a job, and responsibilities.

I swam when heat became too much, and sat under the sunbrella to let the cool air play, and put on shirt and shorts to go up to the hotel for lunch of all sorts of tastes, and good wine from local vineyards, and I wondered why the devil I bothered about living in London, when I could spend the rest of my life in a place like this and enjoy every moment of every day. Why go back?

It was a question.

Go back to what?

Well, first of all, it was not the Daemon. Then, I must obviously be letting down Jo and the rest of my staff. And where was I to put my books and all the other items? I looked at the houses for rental, brick boxes, whitewashed. A bath up on the roof served with buckets from a wood-fire boiler in the yard, and a woman from the *soukh* to cook and clean. Very simple. But there was cess only, no sewage system, and a modern bathroom and kitchen would serve nothing. Electric light was still a little while away unless the generator was yours. But if it failed, you had a long time to wait.

I talked it all over with Jean-Luc Dourrier and his wife, Anne-France. They had a comfortable little bar, hand polished every morning by Kif'r, a big black from the interior, one enormous smile, and a desire to do anything on this earth to make me happy.

Why are such people born so far away?

"I would not buy," Jean-Luc said. "Rent, yes. Responsibility is with the landlord. Aliens? We don't like. They may be buying for others. We have suffered that sort of criminality. But the Government here is very strict. President Bourguiba is very strict. Everybody is worried what will happen when he dies. Nothing will happen. Everybody is trained. Tunisia is a special country. Special people. If they want peace, well, we have peace. If they want to fight, very well, we fight. And we win. No doubt. No. Don't buy. Rent. Or better? Stay *here*."

That was how it was, and that was how it was left. But I was more than tempted. I did sums to see how much it would cost to bring all my stuff here, and rental yearlong for three big rooms on the top floor, with bath, all in. It was far less than I paid in London. But then I would have to sell the business, and Jo and her colleagues might not be wanted. That was first mental hurdle. The second, as important, I would be too far from my father's place to take a hand in rescue work, whenever that happened. I had waited too many years for it. I still hoped. But leaving the Daemon would kill it. I had to stay.

Jean-Luc understood in a nod, and Anne-France raised brows, leaned her head to the left and raised the shoulder. But I told them that if they ever needed a partner, I was ready. In fact, I already saw myself going there at least half a dozen times a year and wondered why it had never occurred before. We have a lovely world to play in, and we never think about it except in terms of travel posters, and tours, and guided parties, that I abominate. The moment I hear a guide start his spiel, I run.

Wednesday morning was like any other and we got up in a truck with baskets and children, and went along the coast road toward Tripoli, and turned off to Kairouan, and went in the rug and carpet *soukhs,* and I bought some beautiful patches of colour for the set, and watched those Arab knuckles use age-old knowledge to bring lovely bands of sand and black, red and old yellow, and rich brown chaos of fibre into strict order on the looms, wondering how it was done, but I was there to see it.

Black coffee, and brandy from local presses, and on, to an enormous Roman amphitheatre, not a single movement, not a bird, nothing, only pillars and seats, tier on tier, white under hot sun and a plain blue sky, and I had a feeling that the Romans were a far more magnificent people than we had been taught, if, that is, we had been taught anything. I thought of Ella Broome, and tried to remember when I had last seen her, and decided I would have a real try when I got back.

We picnic'd in the arena where doubtless many a ten thousand died, but we heard nothing except crusty bread being chewed, and steaks grilling, and crisp salads in eager hands, but then the vultures saw us, and flew down, and sat, raw-necked, waiting, and I tried to think how some poor soul bleeding to death might see them coming closer ready to pick out his eyes.

"Sometimes I think the Romans of this era had decided to leave Rome altogether and come here," Jean-Luc said, cutting a fine strip of steak for Anne-France. "They had problems over there in Europe. They couldn't pay their armies. They couldn't even provide them with salt. They had so many different people against them. Uncivilised people. What did they do? They came out of Britain. Out of Gaul, and out of everywhere. Obviously, they had decided to make this the new Rome. They commanded this coast west to east. What made them build this enormous stadium? And then what happened? Why is it suddenly left? There is a beautiful town, further in the interior, well-built, streets, sewage, everything in marvellous Roman style. Why did they leave it? Why did nobody come into it? There are other Roman towns and cities in Europe. People still live there. Why not here? It is a conundrum, my friend. Plague? We have no record. Defeat? But the contrary. A natural disaster? Sand covers everything? As it covered the Pyramids and the Sphinx? All Egypt and Arabia? We have the evidence this once was a garden. Look about. Only the vultures have remained loyal. Who else is here? But which race of giants built this glory? How many hundreds of thousands died to lay stone on stone? Who was the architect? We know the names of the Caesars from coins, and what remains of writing. But the men themselves, the real *genie?* The builders, planners, the brains, in a word, of the people? Who? Here, take a nut of steak. And more wine. I love to come here. In some ways, I think I am still a Roman."

"What's the difference? You, now, an hotelier, and being a Roman?"

Jean-Luc threw a bone to the vultures.

"Here, you learn how to live," he said. "Do your job, help others, respect beliefs, support honesty, maintain the Law. I have found nothing difficult."

"But how about honest Arabs?"

He went on piling debris from the picnic into a carton, and Anne-France watched the coffeepot for a cup en route.

"There are no dishonest Arabs," he said. "Except if you are dishonest with *them.* If you are, the locality will know, and you will suffer. Wherever you go in this country will not matter. You will be found out and there is nothing you can do to stop them making your life, commercially or otherwise, a complete misery. Until you leave. Then, they will help you. An Arab's honesty is not in question until you prove, as a foreigner, that you are *dishonest.* Then they close in and finish you. Fair?"

He took the carton over to the vultures and they flew in sandy ruffles and blunderous flap, and he walked away and they settled, and the beaky tussle began.

"Everybody to the truck," Anne-France called. "We have coffee out at the Point. I *hate* vultures. But without them, what do we do? Who cleans the debris?"

We went up on the Point, with a view of fifty miles each side, of white beach and palms and cork trees, and not a speck to tell of people walking or living, a small part of the peace of Africa that so few know or care about.

"It is what I say," Jean-Luc said. "As we defend a virgin, as I will defend my daughters, so we must defend this land. It is ready to be raped. Except that we have a paternal Government. What is to come, we don't know. We can only hope to have other Bourguibas. Therefore? I have reason to feel confident."

In that air and sea breeze and that sunshine, on the way back, I wondered. If that corpus of rapists had prevented the rebuilding of East London, then how could anyone protect the virgin lands of North Africa? Was it going the way of Ibiza, Marbella, Mallorca, and the rest? What was to stop it? The money lads were always with us. Their eyes squinted around every tree trunk. Those bastards of the cowrie-shells. Waygoes, I hear you.

An evening swim was an event. I always went down for a good thirty minutes splash-about, and came out just as the air got chilly, wrapped up in a couple of towels, and went to the bar for an apéritif, generally the Jean-Luc Special, poured from a jug out of the icebox, of red wine, peach juice, lemon, orange, brandy, honey, and the liqueur of the province, a type of Cordial Médoc, with a plume of frozen mint. Two of them, and you were someone else.

Someone else huddled in pale-blue towels further along, and Jean-Luc waved a hand.

"'Selle Ghilbert, 'Sieur Bessell," he said. "According to the rules of the house, you have a second of the same *on* the house. You agree?"

She looked at me round the corner of pale-blue fluff, and smiled, and I bent waist and head.

"All right with me," I said, and put down the lees, wiping a hand where the ice had fallen, melted and cold.

But for the Jean-Luc Special, I simply could never have gone down the stools and sat beside her. But there are other worlds.

Talking is another matter. Whatever I blathered about seemed to paralyse the pair of them, and the others in the bar. I seem to remember that I was a Roman emperor giving orders for the construction of a five-floor circus of living quarters with a central market, and theatre, and a special section for comedians, because without comedy our lives are a dismal squalor.

My life was. I could find no comedy in it. As an evacuee humour was beaten out of me.

I remembered when I woke up next morning. Some of the rantings came back. In shame. I looked out at loveliest dawn, and sun coming up to the left, and all the blues were part of the sea, and black toward the nets, and the fishermen sang high with the pipes, and drums and tambourines beat, and the wind blew low.

The long black shadow walking down to the seafroth blazed from the gold-black flame of Ghilbert, in black bikini and top, hair bound in black, Eve in gold one side, part of shadow the other, and a fishing boat made a wide turn and she ran to be pulled aboard, and the boat turned out for the long line dragging nets for the catch. I had a shower and went down for Kif'r's coffee and hot croissants, a wonderful honey from the orange groves, and *Le Monde*—ironed of creases, warm on the wooden frame—of the day before. I sat in the rising sun, and read what the world was doing, that parcel of idiots, and the women began crowding on the beach, and the boats turned to sell the catch. Ghilbert came off with an enormous red fish, holding it as if a favourite son, and trotted toward the hotel, really a quite exceptional beauty, and Jean-Luc ran from behind me to meet her, and take the fish, and toss it in the air, and shout to the fishermen, and give me the biggest grin going by. Ghilbert came behind, silvered in scales, a thousand sequins of all colours in that light, and took off the head-scarf, and shook out a marvel of chestnut hair with a lot of gold in a wide circle about her head, and saw me and stood still.

She reminded me of Andromeda, on the corner of my desk.

Obviously women had never changed. They were always beautiful, in any age, under any condition.

Men? I certainly recognised myself as masculine, without much—or any—change from those shapes of a couple of thousand years ago now in long lines down on the wine racks below the Daemon's floor level.

Ghilbert came toward me, took my towel, put it down, and lay on it, and held up her arms, calling for Kif'r, and coffee before she died of—of—

"All right," I said. "Of what?"

"Too much of too much," she said. "I didn't know this world had something hidden. That we didn't know. But it has. It is here. I am so sorry to go back."

"Where?"

"To Le Havre. I have a nice boutique. I have bought many things here. But I would like to live here. Without money, how? A boutique here? Not enough custom. We can wish, we can dream. But there is a question of bread. So? I must go back. Save. Come back in a few months. But here I dream. Here I live. There, I work to live the dream."

Dreams, dreams, dreams. Everybody seemed to be living a dream, to do this, that, or the other, none of it real, all of it a nonsense of poisoned imagination, a disc of raucous bawls and howls, pretending to be what it was not, that is to say, living, part of life, contending, trying, creating, or being decently human.

"We've all got the same problem," I said. "I don't want to go back. I'd rather stay here. But I have to earn. I have to support a lot of people. Why does the conscience trouble us? What *is* the conscience?"

"It is such a fool."

"Fool?"

"Of course. A complete fool. It tells you to do what you know is ridiculous. Giving money to nuns you know you should be using yourself. Nuns? They look after children and the sick and old because they know you are fool enough to fill their boxes. We are stupid. Idiots. But?"

"If you know, why do you complain?"

She moved her long legs and sat, pulling the towel about her in puffs of sand.

"It is nice to complain," she said. "Here, in the warm sand and the salt on the lips, it is simple to complain. But the sick and the lonely? They find it nice to complain? The nuns? Have they a place to complain? I have, and it is here, and I can complain. So easy. So simple. So? I pay."

"How much?"

She threw up a hand with a snatch of sand.

"What I have in my box."

"Do the nuns know when the box is full?"

"I don't know."

"Better find out. Why don't we ask Kif'r for some more coffee, and fillets of fish from the charcoal grill? It tastes better out here."

We had those fillets every morning, with rolls hot from the grill, and salt butter from the farm behind the cork trees, and the honey, and the marvellous jams of greengage, damson, plum, pumpkin, and ginger, a glory of taste, but then, I always was *the* nut for any sort of pure taste, and so, glory be, was Ghil'.

We strolled the beach, we fished with a line on shore, or from the little cockle-pan belonging to the hotel, or we walked through the olive groves to find the flower beds grown by the women for the hotel tables, and came back with armfuls for Anne-France, and Jean gave us the Special on the terrace as reward.

Day after day, never the same, and yet always the same, because there was only the hotel, and Kif'r, and sand, sea, groves, a swim, skin-diving, fishing, lying in the sand, or strolling, little-finger-in-little-finger while the sun went down, and running back for a hot bath, a drink, and dinner.

All must end, and the morning came when I took Ghil' in the darkness to the airport, and watched her go with the driest of dry kisses, across the tarmac, a wave at the door, and looking at her become a speck, and gone. I strolled about the streets of Tunis, and had a so-so luncheon—nothing would have tasted good—and got back to the hotel just after sundown, and took the magazines and newspapers upstairs, throwing them on the bed for a good read. But I thought only of Ghil'. I was five days over my stay. Why, I asked myself, had I let her go without me? No question in my life had bothered me more. But there seemed some feeling between us that this was one place, absolutely special, that must be unlike any other place, and so there was no notion of bed, or other vulgarity, and we were two on a different plane, virgin and celibate, sealed by the interlocked little fingers.

That evening I booked a flight to Marseilles for two days later, and went on the beach, missing her with a half of me bleeding, and only just staying inside my skin by the thought that train or coach or hired car I would be in Le Havre sometime in the evening of the next day. Silly, but I could feel myself bleeding until I got there. No dry kisses, either. The plain grab, and to hell with the rest, and if she said yes, marriage. I could think of nothing better.

I read myself to sleep over a thought of her, and woke late and went downstairs. The hotel was curiously quiet, I thought. Jean-Luc behind the reception desk smiled and wished me good morning but his eyes reached only to my chest, and he went into the office. Kif'r brought the tray of fruit, and juice, and coffee and the basket of croissants and brioches, and *Le Monde*, and flourished it as a banner, but without looking at me, and no smile.

Strange.

But when I drank the juice, buttered and honeyed a croissant and drank a little coffee, and slapped the paper to read, I knew why.

Ghil's aircraft had crashed. She was named among the victims.

What is there to feel, or think, or say?

I left the paper over the chair, and went upstairs, and fell on the bed, and cried like a fool.

Kif'r came in when it was dark, and left a glass of brandy beside the bed. But brandy did nothing. It established dreams, but little more. I could see Ghil', her beauty, walking against white sand, glowing. I drank the glass, and I was drunk until I was packed in the car, and Jean-Luc came with me to the airport, and I was drunk in the aircraft, and drunker at wherever it was, and I awoke stone-cold and shivering at De Gaulle airport though how I got there nobody can tell me.

I went to the hotel in the Rue Balzac, and went into another drunk. I have never been a drunk. I always had a contempt for the drunk. But for those days, I was a drunk, knowing I was a drunk, and drunk because I had no wish to think of myself apart from Ghil'.

But the morning comes.

Blinding.

I could see Ghil's gold-black flame walking toward the sea-froth. I could feel her warmth against me. All right, get drunk. But the glass never touched. Enough is more, and then sickness.

Revulsion.

I had a few days wandering in Paris. There is no better place to wander in. What I saw or who I spoke to, God knows. I had an omelette here, and an entrecote there, a glass of wine, a bottle of beer, a coffee, and a brandy that made me sick in the gutter, and that marked the end of my stay. Clear-headed, weak as a day-old pup—my knees were paper—I felt rather than walked back to the hotel, up to my room, and fell on the bed still in overcoat with umbrella, and woke to noon bells, completely, if shamefully, myself.

And quite numb.

Numb is a funny word. Funnier still is how it feels. I was certainly myself. I rang down for coffee and the papers, and put in a call to Jo, and went in the bathroom to shower and change, and the maid brought in coffee and newspapers, and while I was towelling, Jo came through.

Everything was wonderful, no probs', there was a pile-up of work, and everybody was happy.

"So I could stay away for the next twelve months and nothing would happen?"

"Well, I wouldn't say that. Lots of cheques here need signing. People get impatient. Only you can put that right. When shall I tell them?"

"I'll be back tomorrow sometime. Everything's fine, this end. Anything you'd like from Paris?"

"Ohhh, *yes*. Perfume."

"Which?"

"You know me. Pick it out. Cheeky?"

"I'll find a cheeky one, never fear."

The Place Vendôme has always been a favourite of mine, whether for the grace of its space, or for an atmosphere created when Frenchmen led their kind in the exacting pursuit of an appreciation of what they meant by civilization.

I found the little shop, and I asked the brightie for something cheeky. What the hell is cheeky in French? Brightie, in black with a belt that did nothing to disturb what was evident, thought for a moment, and went back to the boss, and he ripped out a couple of titles, and she got them and put them on the counter, chose the test bottles and smudged a little on the inside of each elbow, and held them up for me to sniff. She knew her business. I bought one of each for Jo and Bhula, and one for Kari, a round bottle with a frosted glass stopper like a flower, that I knew she would love, and a big cut-glass bottle of toilet water for Mrs. Rapajan. When it was empty I could see her using it for the rosewater she made—"I put it on myself for my husband only"—that I found a lovely thought, having seen Mr. Rapajan, one of the least attractive Dravidians I ever saw, almost a mandrill, and Mrs. Rapajan laughed all her beautiful teeth and said. "Yes, I know he is a monkey. But he is *my* monkey, and *very* good," and cleared the air.

I declared the bottles and a fine magnum of brandy at Customs, and paid a small amount, had a usual train dinner—by comparison with the French, a disaster—and got to Daemon Wente Waye at about eight o'clock, put my luggage in Almond's care, crossed Wapping High and heard my presses almost a street away from Brittle Candy Lane, a fine, reassuring sound and yet empty, because I had promised to show Ghil' the plant, and the Daemon, and now there was something not there.

I saw the gold-black flame of her walking those beautiful legs down to the seafroth. I had to put a hand flat against the wall and shut my eyes tight, and I still saw her. Nothing eased.

Jo still tapped at her desk and the plant seemed working all-out.

I put the perfume box in her hands, and went out to the other rooms, surprised that even the packing section was at full staff with a few new faces.

"I took on a couple of printers," Jo said. "After your call I took the chance. We could use a couple more. Three new lads in packing. We're doing very nicely. There's the accounts, and there's the cheques. You've got a lovely tan. Have a nice time, did you?"

"Wonderful," I said. "I'll sign all these and leave them on the desk. Time you went home, isn't it?"

"No," she said, flat, and surprised me. "We've been waiting for this. A rise in wages and lots of work. We bought a couple of bottles of plonk."

"Right you are," I said. "Trot 'em out."

Edwina came in with a flagon under each arm that I knew came from the Bosun's Bar, and I took Jo on one side, and in the noise asked if she would give me her perfume for Edwina, because I had forgotten, and promised I would buy her the same next day, without fail. She went in the office, and came out with the parcel, and went through the crowd, and Edwina's smile lit the place. I should have stayed there and enjoyed the do, but could think only of Ghil', and I wrote cheques, and started on the letters, and Jo came in with a glass of wine, and the others crowded the doorway, and toasted me, and I toasted them and swallowed, but I felt like crying, hot in eyes, tight of throat, a nobody, nothing.

The presses started, and everybody was back at work, and I signed the last letter, and went out in fine rain, down the Lane and over Wapping High to the Daemon, and waved at his smile, and wished, *wished*, that Ghil' were with me, and sad as any man ever was, went up to my set, and the smells and warmth I knew, that Bhula and Mrs. Rapajan helped to distil, and fell in the big chair, and cried like a bloody great booby.

Mrs. Rapajan made coffee next morning, and when she brought it in, I gave her the package, wrapped with wide pale-blue ribbon, and her face changed, and she ran, and shut the door quietly.

It was Sunday, about eleven o'clock. Thick mist lay over the river. I could just see the other side. I put on oilskins and seaboots, and went down to the marina, and took the club boat, with a 10 h.p. engine, and wandered down the river toward Canvey, along the flats, and the rushes, and the birds, barely disturbed by the motor, flying over and around, perky, curious, never quite hitting me with wing-flap, but coming close enough to make me move my head, though that was my mistake. They always knew where they were going. I put out a line, and I had a rod trolling over my shoulder, and I lit a cigar, which was surely a luxury on that reach, and the smoke stayed in the air, bluish, fragrant. Cuba travels in the magic of the nose.

I heard an engine behind me, and looked round to see the hull of a river police boat prowing out of the mist. It came within five yards and held course, slowing to keep alongside.

"Ah, good morning to you," a voice said, and I looked toward the bridge, aft, and Sergeant Kemp, in black oilskins, leaned over the side. "Caught anything?"

"Not yet."

"Right day for it. Been away, have you?"

"Yes."

"I envy you people going away. Nice to be able to say, right, I'll go here, go there. Very nice. I hope you had a good time?"

"Very good, thanks."

"Nice to know. All we do is go up and down the river, pulling out the bodies. Trying to put the puzzle together. Girls, for example, throats cut. Men for example, shot. 'Course, you could say it was suicide. But trying to explain how a bloke shoots himself and slings himself in the river, well, it don't make much of a case, do it?"

"Doesn't seem to."

"Funny enough, that's what I think. 'Specially when the bag we found came from the Daemon Wente Waye. They've got their own. Marked. You still live there, don't you?"

"Yes."

"Well, have a good day. Bring home lots of fish. But be careful."

The police boat went ahead, and Sergeant Kemp waved.

"I'm always here, y'know?" he shouted. "The old firm's still in business."

I reeled in the line, and put the rod away, and turned for the marina. I was simply not sure how I felt. Even a thought of Ghil' did nothing to push aside the fear rumbling in my gut.

Rumbling. Tormenting.

I steered with the rushes, got back to the buildings and found dockside, thankfully enough, anchored the craft, and went down to the Bosun's for a needed drink. The place smelled the same, looked the same, except I knew nobody there. Even the barmen were new.

"Where's the Bosun?" I asked one of them.

"Taking a couple of weeks off," he said. "Christmas and New Year proper done him in. Don't expect he'll be back 'fore ol' Waygoes gets here. And he's been held up. That lad of his, he put his shirt on something wasn't there. First place, he never had no shirt. So the bookies come on ol' Waygoes, and he tells 'em what they can do. So they waited on young Teucer, and they done him right. Razors. They *say*. 'Course, you can't believe half you hear, can you?"

"He's having a bad year."

"Up to him, ain't it? You have a few big bets with the bookies, and you play the tables, and you got no green to start with, people get dead annoyed. And let me tell you, Jamaica's as rough as the next place. I had a couple of years there. Glad to get out."

I felt sorry for Teucer. He should have been given a decent allowance. But then, I realized Waygoes knew that all money, any money, would be thrown away, and it was not what he taught or practiced. I wondered what effect the hospital stay might have, and I was certain it would make him even more of a rebel. Perhaps giving away pieces of property was one way of bringing down the cash value of the estate when Waygoes died. But it was useless trying to gauge that mind, where it went, or how. Yet I was sorry for Teucer. Though I disliked him personally, I had a feeling he had always been treated as a crown prince, turned into a horribly spoiled toadie, screaming when denied, and in the first cold dash of adulthood, finding himself to be no more, despite his name, than anyone else, and that must have hurt. It explained, so far as I was concerned, the nonsense with the girls. They were unable to hit back, and he took his sense of powerlessness out on them. At least somewhere, he was boss. Poor devil.

I called at Celli's set and got lovely welcome of arms and lips, and the two other girls were introduced as Jac—with a C—and Loris.

"They're staying with me," Celli said, wearing a shortie I saw through and briefs, so no harm done. "We've been having a terrible time here. People trying to get in, and all that. So we're staying together."

"But surely, Teucer's not here?"

She brought over the drink.

"You ask me, he got blamed for a lot he didn't do. He might have been a bit—er—you know. But any bloke'll try his hand if he thinks it's on. Teucer might have been a bad boy, yes. But this latest lot's been while he's out of the country."

"Any ideas?"

"We've given up. There's two security guards downstairs. All the doors are locked. You can't get in at night unless you've got your key and the guard knows you. What's the answer?"

"Someone in the house?"

She raised her glass.

"That's what we think," she said. "Who, is what we'd like to know."

"Lot of places here where somebody could hide."

Celli held her elbows and crouched. She was plainly more than frightened.

"Look," she said. "Poor Bott's never been seen or heard of since the morning she left here. I thought she'd gone with Thel'. She didn't. Ella Broome's never been seen or heard of since she went off. For what? We've been to the police. Nothing. We've advertised. Not a sound. Listen, if it wasn't for my job, I wouldn't stay here. Even now, I'm looking for another place. The police have been here, asking me to identify bodies. I can't bear the thought. I went home for a few days till they got tired of calling. What are we going to *do*?"

It was no use thinking about Jayb.

With Teucer absent, then who?

"It's a real poser, isn't it?" I said, and knew inanity.

211

"I have a feeling I'll be next," Celli said. "I've got to get out. I've *got* to. I've got a feeling somebody's got his eye on me."

Loris, in a caftan split to the hip, and Jac in a long voile nightdress and nothing underneath, knelt with her, and held the shoulders and crying head.

"Don't upset yourself," I said. "No need for the moment. I'll have a couple of extra guards and guard dogs about the place from tomorrow. They'll patrol the building at night. No more worries."

"I don't want my throat cut," Celli screamed. "I can't bear it. I'm going mad."

I stood.

"Try not to take it too hard," I said. "Any sign of anything, ring me. Matter of fact, you can stay in my set. There's plenty of room. Come on up."

"Turn into a lovely booze, and I've got to be at work at seven tomorrow morning," Jac said. "We'll be all right here tonight. See what happens tomorrow, eh?"

I kissed Celli on the cheek, and Jac and Loris kissed me, and I went upstairs to the calm, shining quiet of my set, the flowers, and the scent of Bhula and Mrs. Rapajan in polish and laundered cleanliness. I heaped the papers on the table, poured a drink, and settled to a late Sunday read.

The world seemed to be in a hell of a mess, but that was nothing unusual, and I passed from page to page, and paper to paper, and stuck them in the wastebasket. It seemed to me that Waygoes was right. The lads up top were on the wrong tack. Nobody seemed to have looked at the start of the banking system, to begin with, and if not for the Bank of England, what economic system would there be? All the other banks were copies of the Bank of England. Economics was merely jargon. Banks delivered the money to keep things going. Economics yapped, and failed.

I got tired of it, and wondered how Waygoes could put his case so that ordinary people would understand. I was certainly not a bit sure.

The telly, the pools, the disco, the pub, and of course, the car, that ultimate toy, held them blind and they lived in their cocoons, drugged, helpless.

I had another drink, and went to bed, and to the devil with it.

But that Monday morning was a hellion's delight. Electric power broke down and the presses stopped. The night men went off before the day shift came on. Jo called the electrical people and they said power would be on by about ten o'clock. Bad weather, local fault. Riannes called from Paris and said there was a printers' strike and deliveries would be late. Edwina came in with the coffee and hot buns, and said the squatters were still there, and more were coming in to houses further along the road. They were all white, and they treated her like a mongrel. I asked Jo to call the police, and she came back to say they could do nothing without a magistrate's warrant, and I told her to talk to Mr. Motilal.

The Daemon barely got his smile through the mist, and I went down below, to the cubicles, to watch Colin Slenn set the Riannes job.

"It's going to be a real beauty," he said, in the Doric. "If we get a chance of finishing."

"Why 'if'?" I asked.

"The union," he said. "Either we join, that's all of us, or noth-ing'll leave the plant. And nothing'll come in."

"Finish the job first," I said. "Then we'll see."

Mrs. Osornis came in with a pot of coffee and three plastic mugs.

"Thought you might like a drop of this," she said. "Heard the news? Ol' Waygoes is back. Everybody's got to go to his of-fice Thursday and get their papers signed. Then their bit of prop-erty's safe 'n' sound. M'self, I can't believe it. For once in m' life I've been give something. Three houses up Wicker Basket Lane. Yes, they're ruins. But I get a mason and carpenter in there, buy a few things, I've got a lovely place the rest of my life. Anything wrong with that?"

"Wish it was my luck," Colin said. "Lovely coffee."

"What's the idea of going to his place on Thursday?" I asked her, and spooned sugar. "Why not here?"

"Well," she said. "I suppose he can get it all done in one go, and then we can go to his solicitors and get them filed legal. There's a lot of messing about, y'know, if you're going to get it right. 'Specially with young Teucer hanging about."

"What's he got to do with it?" I asked.

"He's offering a thousand pounds cash for anybody's papers. Like he did me. Just now."

"Any takers?"

"I don't know. I said no."

"Rudely, I hope?"

She lifted the coffeepot and went to the door.

"Can't be rude with *him*," she said. "It's bad luck. *He's* had some. He's all bandaged. And I'm glad. Hope he has a lot more. He can do with it."

She went out, and Colin looked at me.

"Funny sort of bloke, that Teucer," he said. "All the time I've been here, I never heard a good word in his grace. I've often wondered why."

"You bully the girls, you won't get grace."

"True enough. I never knew he did."

"Too few did."

I went over the road to Mr. Motilal, and found him putting his coat on to go to the Court.

"Ah yes," he said. "Your secretary called. I asked this, and I told her to ask you. Is it necessary at this time to evict those people? It is still horrible winter. The accommodation is not the best. They are your own people. Except that they go into property not theirs, and for the moment, until papers are legalised, not yours, why seek legal means to deprive them of what little warmth and shelter there is?"

"Question of principle," I said, ashamed, and not.

He polished his glasses, and squeezed his eyes at me.

"Christ was born in the manger," he said. "I like the story. The Christian tradition is always of poverty. The hermits, and St. Francis of Assisi, and the monks and nuns, and so forth. It is all wonderful. To listen to. But let us think, my friend. Let us suppose that the miracle happens again. What if another Christ *is* born in the East End of London? A great city is made the greater? The stable and a bed of straw was all his parents could afford. And yet, He changed the world. Is it impossible to think that perhaps you are landlord to holy people? How do you know?"

I nodded, and went out, down the stairs, past the dark eyes, waiting, always waiting.

My set seemed like a mother's arms, but I felt undeserving.

Mrs. Parran came in bright focus. "Poor little bastards, they won't get too far on this," and I could taste the salt of her stews, and I still spat the bones of her fish.

Christ could be born again in the East End of London.

It upset me. God knows why.

I could hear carols from St. George in the East.

Hark, the herald angels sing,

Glory to the new-born King.

Jesus Christ is born today.

Hallelujah.

Jo called and said what Motilal had told her, and I asked her to call Mrs. Rafaele or Mrs. Hine, whichever was on duty, and find out if they had any old mattresses, blankets, pillows, and whatever would be useful in cold weather, and send a van down to pick them up, and charge me. Second, to go up the road and buy a few oil stoves, and get the women together and take them to the supermarket and buy enough to see them over the weekend, and find out what else they wanted.

"Right, sir," she said. "I'll come back when I've finished. Could I ask? Where's my perfume?"

"Jo," I said. "I'll level with you. I forgot. But I'm on my way, never fear."

Up Thomas More Street, up Dock street, and Leman Street, thinking then of Penna—she never left me—and into the White-chapel Road to catch a bus to Gracechurch Street for a chemist I knew, but the assistant was no help. She thought somebody down in King William Street or Poultry might have it.

"We don't do too much with that French stuff," she said. "Comes in useful if you don't bath."

For Christ's sake.

I got what I wanted in St. Martin's Le Grand, nearly footsore, and took a cab back to the plant.

Jo danced when I came in, pretty to see.

"Burley's order's in," she almost sang. "Biggest we ever had.

And the union wants to talk to you. Either we all join, or you'll be out of business this day next week."

"We'll see about that."

"Nobody here wants to join. And Bijrath Shankar wants to leave. He's got an offer to edit a newspaper somewhere up there in Birmingham, or somewhere. I bet you never got my perfume?"

"How much?"

"Take you on a Wilson?"

I gave her the package.

"Give me the fiftypence," I said. "And ask Mr. Shankar to come in."

She played with the ribbons for a moment, looked at me, really an Eve.

"Always keep your promises, don't you? But you never even tried to touch me, did you? Wasn't I nice enough?"

"Too nice. But you were working for me."

"Make any difference?"

"I was paying you. One thing doesn't mean the other."

"Even if I wanted it?"

"That's different. Am I to know? Ask Mr. Shankar to come in, will you?"

She went out with the package, bow'd in blue ribbon, pressed to her nose, and the phone rang, and Mrs. Hine said that all the stuff in store had been packed on the van, and she was glad to get rid of it, and there was a lot of crockery and kitchenware that had been going to the Salvation Army, but if I wanted it, lovely. I said I would send the van, and Mr. Shankar came in, and I asked him to sit down.

"I understand you wish to leave to edit a newspaper," I said. "When?"

Those enormous eyes looked at me, so black, so warm with knowledge, and regret.

"I am sorry I must go," he said. "I have been very happy here. I have enjoyed every moment. But I have my duty. To myself. To my profession."

"What *is* your profession?"

"I am a journalist. I have the duty to inform my people, day to day."

"They aren't being informed now?"

He smiled.

"Of course not," he said. "They are being told lies. The papers are the property of a few people. They hope to gain with advertisements. I will write what concerns my people."

"How can you be so confident?"

"Let us see what happens in three months. The readers will decide. Or we go bust."

"If you have a hard time, but you look like getting through, let me know. A few quid at the right time can sometimes do the trick."

He put hands together and bowed his head.

"I shall save my words," he said. "May I ask a further great favour? The once editor of one of our greatest newspapers is a cleaner at Heathrow Airport. Could he take my place? Or occupy the vacancy when others move up?"

"Ask him to come and see me. What I need isn't an editor, but a master printer."

"He is the best. He taught me."

"But surely, he had a position in India?"

"A high position, sir. In prison. He is a man of pronounced views. The present regime didn't like him. He now cleans floors."

"Send him to see me. Yes, Jo?"

"The men from the union, sir. Mr. Linnett and Mr. Robinson, and a few others."

"Tell them to write a letter. I'm seeing nobody."

She went out, and I shook hands with Mr. Shankar.

"All the very best," I said. "As you see, we have problems, too."

"Far worse than ours, sir. I shall let you know how we succeed. Our first edition will appear next Friday. You will be boxed, front page, as a friend of our Community. It may help."

"In what way?"

"If you have trouble, let me know. We don't want to join a union. If there is pressure, we are ready to help. In any way."

The others came in a group, standing in the doorway, not much to tell them from any on the street.

"My name's Dilke," one of them said. "We're from the union. You've heard about us?"

"Send me a letter," I said. "I don't deal with mobs."

"You'll find out what sort of mob this is," he said. "Let me tell you, next Thursday, there's no agreement signed, you'll have the pickets here day and night, *and* at the places you deal with, and you'll stop work. Right?"

"Go to hell," I said. "Get off my premises."

"You asked for it," Dilke said. "You'll get it. Right, lads. Out of it."

They pushed out, and I was left with memory of a reddish face, an asthmatic sort of speech, and threat.

How have the mighty fallen.

That you can be browbeaten in your own place by a parcel of scuts.

Jo stood in the doorway.

"That's what Mr. Shankar meant, sir," she said, brows up. "You'll get a lot of that. But just say the word, and they won't be there, or anywhere else."

"I don't want it to come to that," I said. "People could get hurt."

"It's when they get hurt, they get some sense," she said. "There's a small deputation of the squatters. Won't take long. To say thank you."

Five—two men, three women—came in, washed and combed, but still scruffs, torn, patched clothing, thready trouser ends, shoes shredding leather, and so plainly, all of them, not so much ill at ease as defensive.

"Umm," a man began. "If you got us that stuff down there, we come up here to say thanks. It's the only time anybody's put theirself out. That's in a couple of years. Gen'ly we get chased out."

"Only thing they never done was put the dogs on us," a woman said. "Them mattresses and blankets, and the stoves and all that stuff from the supermarket, well, it's like Christmas. Only we never had one. Least my kid's going to be warm and proper fed. Can't thank you enough."

The others murmured and nodded.

"What makes you live like this?" I asked her.

"Can't find a job," the man said. "We come down from Hull. Tried everywhere. I'm a carpenter. Fred's a mason. Bob's a plumber. We can all work. Can't find a job. We've kids to feed. What's to do?"

I had a thought.

"Supposing I offered you a job?" I said. "Putting the houses where you are now in order. Masonry, carpentry, plumbing? What about it? I supply tools and the rest."

"I'll take it," he said, and the others nodded. "What's the money?"

"Going rates."

"On," he said. "Start tomorrow? Who's paying us?"

I nodded at Jo.

"Miss Hibbs will find out the rates. You apply to her. If you want it by the day or the week, let her know. When you're finished in your own places, there are a lot more to come."

"That suits us, guv," the man said, among nods from the others. "Go to work tomorrow, eh?"

"Go to work."

"Thank Christ," a woman said. "At last. Oh, Jesus. Work, and money."

"Thanks, guv," the man said. "Y'won't suffer."

"He'd better not, by Christ," one of the other women said, going out. "I'd be the first. Anybody tries anything with him, I'd have the bastard's eyes out."

"Said it," the tall other girl whispered. "Why didn't you ask him about the water?"

"What about the water?"

She turned, pale, dignified in pathos.

"They got it next door," she said. "We ain't."

"Who's the plumber among you?"

A man raised a finger.

"Get the water on," I said. "Need any tools?"

"I've me bag," he said. "I can manage."

The women screamed laughter and beat their hands, and the men put their arms round them, and the first man looked at me.

"Y'll never suffer, so help me Christ," he said, and they all went out laughing into the road.

God knows why, but I had a carol running through my head, and I could hear us, Mrs. Parran's charges—"poor little bastards"

219

—singing Awa-a-a-ay in the manger la-la-la-la-la-laaa, and not being able to remember the words, and wondering what happened to those, with me, in bastardy.

While all the others were being heroes.

What a funny lot we are.

I got tired of paper and the smell of print, and went across the road to the Daemon, and waved at him, and that wickedly merry smile encouraged, and I went in, and ran into Ol' Mabbs coming up.

"Very fella I was looking for," he said, or shouted. "Let's have one down the Skipper's Cabin. You don't know what I been going through. Listen."

Those children's voices were still singing through the bone of my skull. I had no wish to listen to anybody's nonsense, far less Ol' Mabbs's, but I needed a drink.

"Listen," he said, when we sat down. "They've found Ella Broome. In a bag. Throat cut."

"Who could do it?"

He raised the glass.

"Money's the job," he said. "The stuff she found? Worth thousands. Think there's no buyers?"

"Why kill her?"

"Way's clear. She's out. You can do as you like."

"Who is it?"

"'S what we're trying to find out. Who sold it? There's a lot in the Rotunda and down below. Who'd stick a knife in that girl?"

"Who found out?"

"Dunno. Y'know what the coppers are. They give out's much as they want. Anyway. There it is. Poor girl. I did, I liked her. Who's next?"

The carol ran in my head.

"We live in a rotten time," I said.

"Well, can you wonder at it?"

"Wonder at what?"

Ol' Mabbs turned to look at me, and put down the drink.

"Wonder at *what*?" he said, in a squeak. "Listen, we went down the road tonight. The cine, and fish 'n' chips. 'Cept we couldn't get no fish 'n' chips. Alf Clark's gone off. Had enough.

So we went down that other caff up the road, here. Hamburger. Eh? Chewed rat, you ask me. Listen, you know the trouble, don't you? Eh? You look at them films. Like we had to look at. Before the nineteen-fourteen war. All them blokes, feathers in their hats, oo, doing it proper proud. Eh? And all the rest jiggin' about. Proper jiggin', they was. No doubt about it. Oxford Street. You could see the buildings. Piccadilly. It was all there. Paris. Anywhere you bloody like. And what was they doing? Jigging about. You couldn't call it walking. And listen. The wheels was all going round the wrong way. The wrong *way*. A fine bloody lot."

"But that's the camera," I said.

"Camera, me arse," he said. "I got a camera. Listen, you're only making excuses. You can't blame a camera for what I see? With me own eyes? There they was. The lot of 'em. Streets. Everywhere. What was they doing? Jigging about. And the bloody wheels was going backwards. What d'you expect from a lot like that?"

"Look, that's an optical error."

"Ah, Christ," Ol' Mabbs said, and looked at the ceiling. "Here's another of 'em. Excuses. Any excuse'll do. Kill all the millions. Not only us. Them. Murder the women and kids. You can see it all outside here. Don't you *know*? Who was in charge at the time? Shall I tell you? Go and have a look at the films. That's a witness. Tell you everythink you want to know. They was all jigging about. And the wheels was going backwards. Any wonder? What a parcel."

No use arguing.

I went up to the set, and got into a gown and slippers, poured a drink, and read the papers, a lot of tripe, and picked out Gibbon's *Decline and Fall*, the third volume, and woke up at something past two, and lounged off to bed. I always found that if I opened Gibbon, I never needed a sleeping pill.

That morning I was late at the plant, but nothing seemed to have happened. In fact, the more I stayed away the better the job. I got there as Edwina came in with the coffee and hot muffins, as nice a welcome as any.

"The squatters' working fine," she said, in a big smile. "They got my chimley working, and the water's got real pressure. I believe I'm going to have electric light tonight. I didn't like 'em first off, but they turned out real right."

"New brooms?"

"Long's the bristles hold out."

Jo came in, took a mug of coffee off the tray as Edwina passed, and stole a muffin.

"Mr. Prakash, sent by Mr. Shankar," she said, in a mouthful.

"Get Edwina to bring in another coffee and a couple of muffins. Show him in."

Mr. Prakash seemed fiftyish, hair greying, a finely featured face, large and dark eyes, delicately boned hands, a steel bangle on the left wrist, and a thick lower lip. We shook hands, a dry touch, and he sat.

"Well, Mr. Prakash, have you had experience as a printer?"

"Thirty-four years, sir."

"I'm not talking about the newsroom. The printing side."

"We had a different system in India. You had to go through the piece. From the beginning. Oh yes. I know the printing side."

"Very well. I don't like a lot of talk. You go out there and ask Miss Hibbs for the new Burley copy. Set it up, and come back here, and let's go over it."

He smiled and straightened his tie and went out, and came back for the coffee and muffin.

"Too good to miss," he said, and I was on his side from that moment.

I went across to the Skipper's Cabin for steak-and-kidney pudding and a flask of wine, and upstairs for a liedown until Mrs. Rapajan came in when it was getting dark, to make a cup of tea and clear up for the night.

"Sir," she said hesitatingly. "Have you heard Mr. Waygoes is selling up?"

"No," I said. "And if I did, I wouldn't believe it."

"They say he is giving little bits and ruins here and there, but he will sell the bulk."

"Where did you hear it?"

"Well. About the place."

"Pin it down. Give me a name. *One* name."

She clasped her hands and turned away.

"Oh, sir," she whispered. "It is more than my life to say. I would lose my job. How could I do that?"

"All right. Let me say for you. There's no need for you to say a word. Simply nod. Teucer?"

She nodded, the barest turn of her forehead.

"Why would he do that? We know he's no good, but after all, he's his father's son."

"Some say not. An adoptive. Taken in pity."

"He *is* pitiable. Perhaps that's where the trouble is. He resents and hates. It causes serious problems. Has he tried anything with you?"

"Oh, many times. So many. But I carry razor blades."

"You never told me?"

"Why should you be bothered? When it was awful, day after day. Pinching and pulling. I told my husband. He spoke to him very angry. Nothing since."

"I'm glad. How's this nonsense being put about?"

"Chatting. Words here. Words there. The kitchen is going to be closed down. Room service will stop. The garden will finish next month. All chat. But people believe. And we are frightened. Where shall we have a job? Who will pay us?"

"Put your mind at rest. That's not Mr. Waygoes' idea. Bank on it."

She turned to me with a lovely smile. She was good.

"It is nice to talk to you, sir. Always so—so fruitful."

But that was not how I felt. Something was on the move, and Teucer would be first to know.

Waygoes was not the healthiest man. The property he owned was worth an enormous sum. The bits given away were merest snippets of very little. Any developer could come in and offer those of us with rights to a couple of houses a considerable sum to clear out. In that, Waygoes could salve any conscience he had.

But the Daemon, as we knew it, would go.

It was a sickener. What would I do?

I looked at my books, and statuary, and at Andromeda on the corner of my desk, and wondered where I might go, and I had no answer, or any hope of thinking of one, or any energy to start. Any thought of leaving left me limp. I knew what the others felt.

We had a common disease. We were frightened. There was nowhere to go.

Where *could* I go?

To one of my houses up at the plant? A fine statement. But imagining the difference made me feel sick. I went over to the window, and looked out at the Thames. There were few nobler views. Even the House of Commons panorama out on the terrace was nothing to my sweep of the river's bend, and the last of seventeenth-century London, when men built for beauty and not for rent.

I had that feeling in the gut. I think I had known it since Aunt Helen picked me up that night and ran to the fireman. The last time I remember. White hair waving, tears in glitter, the small voice under the bombs and guns.

"Off you go, son."

Hear it now.

I went up to the plant, and Mr. Prakash waited for me, in shirtsleeves, linen covers to the elbow, and a green eye-shade, the true pro of another time. It took very few moments to see that he was top of his class. It was a splendid job, and he knew from my attitude.

"Take charge," I said. "Miss Hibbs will give you details of salary and that sort of thing. Keep an eye on this job, and look at the orders coming in. If you know of other men needing a job, send them along. Up to half a dozen."

"There should be so many more like you, sir," he said.

"Many more like you, and there would be no trouble."

"It is true. We are rotten with ignorance. Your school system is no good. You pamper infants and neglect adolescents. There lies the rot. Spare the rod and spoil the child."

"You believe in corporal punishment?"

"Of course. Animals must be trained. To the whip."

"The goody-goods don't think so."

"You have the answer in the streets."

"I suppose you'd like to edit a newspaper?"

He laughed, open mouth, no sound.

"In the present and foreseeable climate, how long would I last?" he said. "I am content as I am. I am deeply grateful, I may say. For the moment. But of course I feel for our people. They are on the downward way. They are mixed with West Indians. Volatile. And nothing to do. No jobs. One thing has surprised me since I came to this country. When I was a boy, well, till the time I went to Delhi University, there was always a rigorous discipline. Really, a British discipline. Victorian, if you will? Who would think of interrupting a meeting? Or smashing a window? Or even being rude? Who? Did you want six across the backside? No? Then behave yourself. In Gandhi's day, it was a little different. You misbehaved, you went to prison, you were a hero, you had your pleasant meals, you sat there, and then you were released, not a mark on you. How very good. For us. We were not ready for what followed after you left. That discipline had gone. In the Army, yes, it was there. But as with you, the Army was completely apart. The rest fell into rot. A complete rot."

"You think Mrs. Gandhi is correct?"

"Completely. She is not responsible for the zealots acting in her name. But she has pushed and pulled until there is less corruption and less rotten politicians. Less black market. Less of the worst. But what are you to do with six hundred million people? *Six hundred million?* Most of them completely ignorant of all letters. So many starving. What do you do? Agonise? Is it enough? Let us say, she tries. As a mother with a starving family. She tries. Shall it be held against her?"

"Why don't you go back to India?"

He rolled up the copy, and smiled at me, white teeth.

"And drop into the hands of the zealots?" he said. "Sir, I prefer here. Thank you, sir."

That seemed to be that.

Late that afternoon, while I was looking at accounts for the month, Jo came in with a slip of paper. It listed amounts for purchase of cement, timber, piping, electric odds in wire and wall fixtures, a few tools, and another sum, larger.

"What's this?" I asked, pointing.

"Well, the rest of it's accounts they've made with a few of the people up the road. They phoned in, and I said you'd pay. That last one's their wages."

"But aren't they on social security?"

"Oh yes. But that doesn't make any difference. If they work they want their wages. That's the going rate. By the hour."

"But they still draw the dole?"

"Yes."

"But I thought the dole—"

"Oh no. I asked. I says, don't you get paid so much for being out of work, and so much per child, and they said yes. But that's not work. We've got our rights, same as everybody else. But a job's a job. Let's see y'money."

"You tell them to come and see me."

"Well, they've knocked off for the day. They'll be here in the morning."

Needs must where the Devil thrives.

I went down the road to Edwina's place, and found her in the kitchen making pastry, singing.

"How about these squatters next door?" I asked her.

"They did a good job in here," she said. "Look. Electric light. The chimley works, water's on, and all the rat holes got plugged. I don't know myself. They all gone out. That caff down there. They got credit."

"How?"

"They workin' for you. I told 'em, I says, you promise to pay, you pay. O.K.?"

"Edwina. They're drawing the dole, they're living rent-free, and they want regular rates of pay? What the hell kind of nonsense is that?"

She shook her head.

"I don't know, sir. It's what goes on here. There's a lot of people drawing the dole and working for regular wages, too. Seem they allowed."

"Seems to me they're breaking the law."

"You ask me, they all got their own. Don't give a good goddam for anybody. Long's they get the money, that's *it*."

I walked out in the street to cool.

And yet, why?

Poor bastards, what were they getting out of living? How were their children being brought up? In a slumhole. No bath. Lavatory outside. So was Edwina's. But she had no dole.

I walked down the road to that café, and heard singing halfway down the stair. Warned, I put my head around the corner.

The group I recognised were at a table just before the bend of the L. Bottles were on the table. The children were all in a corner. The adults drank from the necks of the bottles. All of them seemed drunk. The others in there were Asian or Afro, but taking no notice.

What was the use?

A lecture? Righteous indignation? For what? I had a far better life. But they were cheating. But thinking of politicos I wondered who cheated the more. I gave up. To hell. Let them drink.

I buttoned my coat—none of them had one—and walked back toward the Daemon, wondering what the hell we were all living for, whether for glory in the hereafter—and I certainly had no belief in it—or to promote a fat life for bankers, politicos, and showbiz piddlers, and just get by on the swill left by them, and the heirs to fortunes?

The more I thought about it, the more I believed that Waygoes had the more truth, the more reason, the more love for humankind, and therefore, he had to be supported. But how? What use was I?

And oh, God—and if we don't believe, then why do we appeal?—the day was grey, of February, clammy, snow in the air, pinkish underglow of clouds, and even the weeds bowed in cold. And if that was how the weeds felt, then what about us? Is that what most of us were? Weeds? Lilies of the field? They toil not, neither do they spin? Yet Solomon in all his glory, and all that.

I never believed it. Solomon with or without his glory could have your head cut off, or boil you in oil. No lily could. A lot was wrong that we were taught as children. We grew as adults with so many false values. Living taught us differently, and the awful argument went on inside, and so often led to the couch, and the horror wards.

I walked down toward the plant, and passed Edwina's house again, seeing the improvements made by the squatters in her place and the others used by them, and they were considerable, in new doors and windows, drainpipes, and brushed brick. It meant work, by men knowing the job, and I was not unhappy to be footing the bill.

A wonderful smell of baking came from her open door, and I went in and found her in the kitchen, tipping out rounds of pastry.

"Come on in," she laughed, big white teeth. "I been calling you. Did you know? Let's just sit down, have a cup of tea and a cake, and go to bed. Anything wrong with that?"

"If there is, I can't think of it. But why do you want to go to bed?"

"I been thinking of it long enough. I had enough of this cold, cold weather. I just like to get warm and snuggle. And get something out of myself. Play with yourself too long, you get sort of tired. Kind of strung out. And the others around here, who wants them?"

"What did you mean, *calling* me?"

"I just put my *mind* on you. You' nice. You *heard* me. Here you are. Here *I* am. Just the way it has to be. Call me Mama Ju-Ju. Don't believe me? You' *here*. Want to argue?"

She undressed, and stood, coppery-brown, volupt, a woman.

Tea and cakes were for others, and when she o-o-o-owh'd in my neck, a tenderest noise, and went on, so did I, and she had me in a ring, stressed as a fist, and I was gentlest prisoner, and I could see one dark smiling eye, and the thighs under my hands were taut, and the muscles hardened, and oo-owh'd again, and the smiling eye an inch away, and I was thighed into sleep.

I awoke in darkness. Edwina slept soft. I got up quietly and went out to the kitchen to wash, and went back to dress. I made sure the bedclothes were wrapped about her, and kissed her cheek, and went out, certain the door was on the lock, and walked down in the cold wind, an invalid, no more.

"Mrs. Rafaele's been calling you, sir," Almond said, at the Daemon. "Says it's very important. Mr. Waygoes wants to see you."

"Just say I've come back from the office, and I'm going to have a wash and brush-up. Half an hour. All right?"

I dragged upstairs. That's it. I dragged. Edwina taught me something. You can pretend, but if you only *just* have it, you suffer. But I thought it wonderful suffering, and I was ready for more.

I went down to A 1, and knocked, and the door swung, and the inner door swung, and I went in to a long table and about a dozen men round it, all smoking cigars. It was a good smell.

"This is the most senior tenant I've been talking about," Waygoes said. "He's a bit late, but it'll do. All right. Next item."

"Question of an issue of money for women," a man said, near Waygoes. "There's a lot of opposition. Disparagement. Fact, people think it's barmy."

"Why not?" Waygoes said. "Why shouldn't they? They've been taught there's only one sort of money. Men and women share it. If the *man* wants to. He decides how much the woman can have. If he happens to be married to her. Else a woman can get a job on her own. Then it's *her* money. How many of them are there?"

"How do you alter that?" an elderly man asked, on my left.

"Create another form of money only for women," Waygoes said. "They shouldn't be dependent on a man's earnings. Money, as we know it, began with the Charter of the Bank of England in 1694. If you read the Charter, it was formed *to create money out of nothing*. Those are the words. *Nothing*. Here we have the women of *our* Country. Any other country, in fact. Are they worth *nothing?* By whose judgment? The courts often award damages for personal injury running into thousands. What is the healthy human being worth? That's what we have to find out. We have to crawl out of the medieval mire and begin living— and banking—in what's risibly called the 'modern' world. We still function and keep our books as we did three hundred years ago. It won't *do*."

"I still don't see how we're going to change it," the same man said. "We'd be a laughing stock. Banks stick together, don't they?"

"I'm relying on the women to do it for themselves," Waygoes said. "There's a liberation movement. They've come a very long way in a comparatively short time. If they prosecute their demands for their own money, with the determination of their elder sisters for the vote, they'll get it, never fear. They really *can* raise the devil. Withdraw their skills and labour from commerce and industry, and you'll have chaos. It's not a matter of *more* money but of *different* money. Their own, in fact."

"But think of the glut of money in the market."

Waygoes shook his head, and the cigar singed the hair.

"Won't happen. Think of the amount of money written in the

229

form of cheques. It doesn't glut the market. To the contrary. It provides the oil. Imagine if that amount of money had to be issued in notes. What, then, about the money supply?"

"We'd be in a hell of a mess," the man said.

"Wrong again," Waygoes said, and smiled the bluish teeth. "There's too little money about. Not enough's issued. So? High interest rates. The bankers love it. The people pay to borrow their own money. It's *their* money they're borrowing. It's because they're alive that there's *any* money. You see that?"

"Look," the man said. "I'm beginning to see what you mean. Answer me one question. What happens to the banks when this women's money starts being paid out?"

Waygoes laughed, puffed the cigar, and passed it under his nose.

"Just what happened to the moneylending goldsmiths after 1694," he said. "They'll go pretty nearly broke. Not altogether. But they'll never be what they were. There are more women than men. Shift that weight to Europe and the United States, to begin with, and in a couple of years you won't recognise the world. It *will* be, no doubt about it, a far more wonderful place."

"How about the Arabs' hold on money?"

"A case in point. We've allowed it. After all, any deal in money favours the bankers. They control. We permit it because we don't know any better. Money paid into a bank can be issued in credit at a rate of interest. Banks are allowed to issue credit up to nine times what they hold. At interest. You're worried about inflation? Of course. Look at the rate of inflation, and then look at the rate of interest. The bankers, the cowrie-carrion, the wampum-wallahs are fat. They're lending you your own money. You borrow a thousand pounds. You have to pay back at—let's say—fifteen per cent. So to pay it back in a year's time, you need one thousand, one hundred and fifty pounds. Where do you get that one hundred and fifty from? Obviously from everybody and anybody else. That's the cause of inflation. And the bloody fools haven't *yet* seen it."

"I'll have to think this over," the man next to me said. "But listen. If women are paid their own money, why should they go to work?"

"No reason, or any," Waygoes said, laughing. "Women aren't born to go to work, you know? Work's only a part of the artificial environment we're living in. Men weren't born to make cars, and pollute the air, and choke the roads. It's a way of earning enough to keep their families."

"All right," the man next to me said. "What *were* we born to do?"

"Enjoy life," Waygoes said. "That's all. But they shouldn't allow cowrie-carrion to dictate the terms. Far less should women permit men to rule merely because of economic advantage. It's because women haven't been looking at what's happened—especially in the realm of banking—that they've been left behind. To such an extent that they accept the banditry that goes on as part of the common scene, not to be questioned, never to be attacked. But what nonsense. *They,* too, are a most important part of what's called economics, which means in the broadest sense, housekeeping. Why should they permit the male to dictate the terms?"

A lot of men on both sides of the table were getting restive. Opposite me, a man leaned near another, and whispered, and stood.

"Mr. Waygoes, I know you own considerable property and there's a lot you want to do," he said. "But I'm not sure I want to join your party. I don't think it'd last."

Others murmured agreement.

"I'd come under pressure from my own bank, and from others, and I know I'd have a lot of trouble in my business with the Common Market. I think, from what I've heard, your ideas'd ruin the money markets and the banking system generally. It wouldn't do any of us any good."

Waygoes nodded, tapped the cigar, and puffed, one, two, three, blue rings.

"You're absolutely correct," he said. "The cowrie-carrion would be put absolutely in their place. That is to say, in the gutter. From then on, they would be forced to use their brains, instead of mismanaging the national currency."

"That's the part I don't get," a man said, down at his end. "If it's other people's money the banks are using, lent to them, belonging to clients, then how are they mismanaging the national currency?"

"Splendid question," Waygoes said. "Thank you for it. The client's money is still part of the national currency. The bank is allowed to issue nine times that amount in loans. All at the going rate of interest. They're not only using the client's money, but the money created out of nothing. In other words, they create their own money, which is, in effect, part of the national currency."

"I'll have to think about it," the man next to me said. "I don't think I understand what he's getting at. I can see most of it. But I can't see what it's leading to."

"National bankruptcy," the man opposite said, and stood. "No. I've had enough. I can't see any sense in it. Especially that bit about the women. Their own money? I mean, Jesus."

The meeting broke, and people talked, shook hands with Waygoes, and Mrs. Rafaele was there with coats and hats, and then I was alone with Waygoes.

"That's how it is," he said, and lit another cigar. "How about a drink?"

"Good idea."

"Help yourself."

"And you?"

"I'm all right for the moment."

I went to the sideboard wondering why I was there, filled up and went back to the table nearer him.

"I asked you here to introduce you," he said. "As a trustee and testator. To the estate, of course. But I felt the resentment in them. That's why I let them go without making any effort. They were being asked to think a little beyond themselves. They've thought one way all their lives. They don't like to be told to think in a way entirely different. It's a pattern of thought that causes pain. Real pain. You saw it in their faces. Old dogs and new tricks. New ideas. That's death."

"Any way I can help?"

He smiled at the cigar.

"I think not," he said. "I'll keep on putting up posters. For what good it'll do. Perhaps a girl or two'll catch on. After all, it took the suffragettes many a long year of *real* suffering to get anywhere. But they did. This idea may take longer. But the same type of devotion and dedication will bring it into the open, and make it work. Women aren't fools. They know what's right. They want it. Need it. They've *got* to have it, if they're going to break what they always call 'male dominance.' It's got nothing to do with sex. It's a matter of money."

"But why am I here?"

He laughed again, and hobbled rather than walked to the sideboard.

"We sometimes get curious ideas," he said. "They sometimes work. I've had an idea for a long time of forming a new party. Tonight's was the second meeting. Like the first, it failed. Lack of enthusiasm. Fear of new ideas. One could feel it. Unfortunately, I'm not an orator. I haven't the *gut* appeal. So? No new party. For the moment. I'd hoped to make you secretary and treasurer. We'll put it on ice."

"How d'you know I could do the job?"

"You manage to do your own fairly well. You control a number of people. Transfer those qualities, with a talent for learning? Nothing very difficult about it. You simply absorb and use it as you go along."

He went to the desk with the glass, and picked up a long envelope, and gave it to me.

"Run your eye over this tonight, and please make it convenient to see my solicitors in the morning. They'll explain the fine points. Let's say, ten o'clock, their office?"

"How about the trustee-testator part?"

He pointed the cigar.

"Read all about it," he said. "I'm going into hospital in a couple of weeks. It'll be a fairly long jaunt, so I'm told. I want a small committee to run this place in my absence. My accountant will be chairman. My property and investments head, yourself as senior tenant, a director of my bank, and just to top it, Doctor Rahman, at the back here. He had the guts to tell me what the rest hum'd-'n-hawed about. Morever, he'll look after the Asian-Afro-Chinese and whatnot mélange here. He knows them. And they all trust him. Be a friend to him, won't you?"

233

"I have been from the first."

"Good. He has a high opinion of you, too. That's about all the back-scratching there's going to be. Why are the police still enquiring about your movements?"

A bucket of icewater.

"I have no knowledge of it," I said. "Why didn't they see me?"

"That's their business. But there must be something wrong somewhere. I've had a good look into it. I find that at all the important times, you were out of the country. I pointed that out. But they said you might have slipped back, done the job, and slid out again."

"My appointments book, passport, people I saw, order book, would destroy that idea."

"They can also be forged, can't they?"

"Why don't they come and find out?"

"They may come with a warrant."

"Then why would you want me to serve on any committee?"

"Because I don't believe any of it. If I were you, I'd put together all the evidence I had of where I've been, where I stayed, whom I saw, what was discussed, orders taken, passport particulars, and as important, bank deals, cheques cashed, when, where. All details are bits of the jigsaw. Defend yourself. You see?"

"One question. What sort of job might I have done?"

"Murder. More than once."

I got up. Those rumblings below were much worse. I drank, tipping the glass for the last drop.

"Have one for the road," Waygoes said. "Wish I could join you. Here's sand in their scrambled eggs, and may Tyburn's innocents walk again."

"Were there many innocents?"

"With drunken judges and bought soldiery, why not?"

I lifted the tumbler, and he nodded, and I drank in a gulp, and needed it.

He held out a hand.

"Don't take too much notice," he said, shaking, a strong grip. "Ten o'clock, that address, tomorrow morning? Good night."

That was a wearying journey up the stairs, and even the welcome of my set gave small pleasure. I got a drink, with a lot of

Perrier, and took out the document, five pages long, and read through, I must say, without any clear idea of the gravamen, except that I was nominated to a five-man Board of Trustees to administer Daemon Wente Waye for a fee of one thousand pounds, until Mr. Bayard Waygoes could properly perform his duties consequent upon a stay in hospital, and any further service would be recompensed at a sum to be agreed between the chairman and members.

No prob', as Jo might say, and a thousand thrown in. Not bad.

I was almost ready for the shower, and the doorbell rang.

At that hour, a shock. But I remembered Celli, and sported a towel for decency, and opened the door on the chain.

Teucer, a bandage over the forehead and plaster strips here and there.

"Could I come in?"

"No."

"Listen. I'll smash this door down."

He had one of the fire axes from the hydrant stations on the stairway. I thought of my door, a work of carpenter's art. I let the chain go, but he made the mistake of bursting through, and I thought he might take a swipe at me. I half-turned and drove an elbow into his plexus.

He went down, not a breath.

Soult had heard the noise from below and came at a run, and a security guard with two dogs on leash came up the other stairway.

"He was going to break down this door," I said. "Take him to his set and lock him in."

"He's on early call for the party going with Mr. Waygoes, sir," Soult said.

"Unlock him thirty minutes before. He's dangerous."

"Ask me, he's a proper animal," Soult said, and turned to the other guard. "Keep them dogs off. Take his legs. I'll take his collar. Right? G'night, sir."

I watched them go down, heard a door shut, and that was that.

Ol' Mabbs came out of his set a little way down, in a long overcoat and big boots with the tongues hanging out.

"What, is there something going on, is there?" he said.

"Young Teucer being a nuisance, that's all. He was taken care of."

"Ah," he said, and showed the rugose callus on the palm. "I swear the time's coming I'll fetch him one with this. Ought to been done a long time ago."

"Safe for tonight, anyway."

"You on the early do tomorrow morning?"

"No. I've got a do on my own."

He looked down at the boots, at one, and the other.

"Wish I'd had a bit of schooling," he said. "I got a lease in there. First one I've ever had. Can't make head or tail of it. Head or bloody tail. This is when you miss it. It's all words."

"The solicitors'll make it clear."

"Ah. I don't know about that. Cheating lot. All they're there for. Cheat you out of house and bloody home. I don't want to lose this place. Can't abear the thought. Why couldn't we stay with the ordinary rent? Pay in the office every Friday, what's wrong with that? No. You got to have papers. Got to go to the s'licitors. What a game, eh?"

"You go, and get it all explained. I'm certain Mr. Waygoes only has your well-being at heart. He's giving you a lease over a period of many years at a rental you couldn't match anywhere. Go and have a good sleep. I'm cold."

He boot-slopped back and the door shut. I ran a hand over my door, unmarked, and locked, chained, and felt safe, and my bath felt the better, and I thanked God for an electric blanket and the blessing of engineers whose thought had put it together. I think it a pity that we are ignorant of the names of so many of our providers of creature comforts, not even the name of the mixer of that first scotch-and-soda, or the first to put eggs and bacon together. I found it a good way to go to sleep.

But the telephone rang until I took it off the hook. Then I began worrying if Celli might be calling. The ringing tone went on. I put the receiver down, waited. It rang again, and kept on, and I answered and switched on the recorder.

"Oh, at last, eh? This is your friend. Teucer. You'll pay for what you did tonight. I'll keep every phone you've got engaged.

You'll get nothing in or out. I'll get a few of the lads round. You know what I mean, don't you? Nothing'll reach your press, and nothing'll leave. Your people'll have one warning. They'll never work for you again. Nobody will. I'm prepared to offer you the sum of five thousand pounds for your lease. On?"

"No."

"Then get ready for what you never expected. Neither Mrs. Rapajan or the other will be at your place tomorrow. You'll have no service. No light or gas or water. You'll be marooned until you clear out. If you're alive, you'll be lucky."

"Everything you've said has been recorded. Mr. Waygoes will hear it tomorrow. So will the police. If you come anywhere near me again, you'll go in the river. Understand?"

"Of course. Isn't that why the police are after you? Won't be so easy with me, I warn you."

"That's all."

I rang off and let the receiver hang. After a few moments, I heard the faint drr-drr, let it go on, and slept.

Mrs. Rapajan came in at eight o'clock with coffee, and ran the bath. I could just see the clock. The receiver was silent and I put it on the cradle.

"Good morning, sir," she said. "It is a horrible morning. Cold and rain. Mr. Waygoes and Teucer had a terrible shouting match. I am afraid of that young fellow. I think everybody is. Doctor Rahman came over and gave him a needle to keep him not shouting. I am sorry for Mr. Waygoes. He thought he had a son. He has a monster. A *thuggee*."

"If you could ask Mrs. Jaykar to let me have some of her beef curry to warm up for tonight, I think I'd prefer that. Brown rice, please."

She pushed out the trolley with a couple of boiled eggs, toast and tea, and I read *The Guardian,* and I was going to call Celli and then remembered she was with the Waygoes party.

I took my time, and got out in Wapping High at about ten to ten, and started walking up toward the Whitechapel Road. There looked like a traffic jam at the top, and I went over to a taxi and gave him the address in London Wall.

"I'll have to cut through here and go over London Bridge, up

237

Tooley Street, over Southwark Bridge, and try getting to St. Martin's Le Grand."

"That's all round the world," I said.

"I could throw in a trip to Nine Elms, guv. Everythink's stuck for a couple of miles. I don't know what it is. The streets are all blocked. Fire brigades from everywhere. They're shoving cars on the pavement to get 'em through. Must be sunnik serious. I couldn't see no signs of a fire, though. Want to try it, guv?"

"I suppose I'll have to. Can we get there in thirty minutes?"

"If there's nothink except traffic lights, dead easy."

"All right. Try."

We saw evidence in most of the side streets to the right of a traffic block, especially along London Bridge, but we got round Southwark Street, and over Southwark Bridge, but we had to go through Upper Thames Street and into New Bridge Street to Holborn Viaduct, and then it was hopeless, and I got out to walk to London Wall, and I was ten minutes late.

"Sorry about this," I said, to Mr. Whoever-he-was.

"Think absolutely nothing of it. I've only just got here myself. Must be something very serious somewhere. I've never seen the City jammed like this since the Blitz. Of course, our roadways are appalling. We simply don't seem to have the engineers. Or whatever they are. Now, then."

He gave me a calm thirty-five minutes paragraph-by-paragraph explanation, and put the pencil down, and took his glasses off.

"Absolutely no snags, and financial involvement is nil," he said. "I never saw a fairer document. D'you wish to sign?"

"Yes, and thank you."

I signed, and he signed, and put the document in a tray.

"What do you think of Mr. Waygoes' political ambitions?" he asked me, hands together on the blotter.

"Years before his time. Possibly?"

He nodded, grey-haired, clipped moustache the length of the upper lip, sharp grey eyes looking through the window to the left.

"This firm's worked for him for many years," he said. "At first, I thought he was a little cracked. I was young at the time, just

238

back from the war, not much faith in anything. Today I feel very differently. Do you belong to his party?"

"If he had one, yes. I'd have been secretary and treasurer. But he can't get people together. They think he's half-baked. His ideas won't work. That sort of thing. I think it's a shame, but people aren't educated sufficiently. I'm not. I know nothing about banking or economics generally. I can only hope, and follow on."

"Has he ever given you any ideas about income tax?"

"He certainly has. It belongs to scutage and Danegeld and all the other expropriatory systems in favour of authority, kings, barons, politicos, or bankers. It's not required. When the people find out, they'll hang the politicians. That's what he says."

He laughed.

"Splendid sight. Yes, I'd enjoy that. But I can't see how it's to be done. Can you?"

"Under present circumstances, no. But when the Arabs have finished with the national currency, then possibly we'll all start thinking. So far, we just crawl from one meal to another. When the United States is bitten hard enough, perhaps the rest of us'll yell?"

"I can't see any other method of paying them."

"He does. Not in cash, but in goods. And putting the unemployed back to work. The Arabs want goods, services. Deny them the cash, and provide what they want."

He got up, and came around the desk.

"It sounds simple enough," he said. "Why hasn't the idea been broached?"

"The banks, and the money markets, and the moneylenders don't want it, do they? They can't take the cream off the top. No rate of interest. What he calls the cowrie-carrion. But y'know, cowries are seashells. They have a value because there aren't many of them. You can't print them. But you *can* print paper."

"Ah, yes. Everyone I've talked to points out it's the weakness in his idea. We've got Weimar staring us in the face. A billion marks for a loaf of bread?"

"That was a banker's job. They murdered the Republic with a printing press."

"It could be done again. Especially here."

"Of course. And they'd try. Until they were shot, or strung up. We're a little older and a little wiser since then."

He lifted his hands.

"I wish I knew," he said. "It's been a pleasure. Any doubts of any kind, do please get in touch."

I went down to the street and found very few people, but a lot of traffic blocked both ways, a refrain of impatient horns, and even fright on some faces among the passers-by.

I stopped in at a coffee bar to take out a little of the cold.

"What's happening?" I asked the Italian barman at the machine.

"Nobody know," he said. "We must wait. Patience. Perhaps a bomb. Or gas explosion. Where? This way? That way? Nobody know. But a lot of people walk to work. It is something special. I have half my trade by this time. *Serious.*"

I went out and walked, and traffic stretched both ways as far as I could see. I turned off Aldersgate Street into Little Britain, and saw a cab coming out of St. Bartholomew's Hospital.

"Tell y'the dead truth, I was thinkin' of packin' it in," the cabman said. "It's a dead block for miles round here. Christ knows what's happened. I've never knew nothin' like it. Wappin' High you want to go? I reckon we'll have to wiggle the side streets over to Oxford Street, go down into Soho, try to cross Shaftesbury Avenue, then get down to Whitehall, go over Westminster Bridge, along Borough Road, get acrost Tower Bridge, 'long Smithfield, and we're home. But don't ask me how long, will you?"

"Do your best."

He did.

It was the damnedest in-and-out I was ever on, but with the London cabman's *nous*, he went in and out of alleys, reversed when he saw the jam, found another way, in and around, and we were in Whitehall, turning left over Westminster Bridge, and he opened the glass divide.

"I believe we done it," he shouted. "Keep your fingers crossed it's clear till Tower Bridge. We're home and dry."

There were traffic-light holdups, but he was right, and we got to Daemon Wente Waye something over an hour after leaving London Wall. I could have walked it in less. But we don't think.

Almond gave me the morning mail, and I looked at the envelopes, aware of a strangeness in his manner, usually cheerful, now almost withdrawn, cold, looking away.

"Anything wrong, Almond?"

"Sir, I don't know. Only rumours, so far."

"What?"

"I'm just waiting for the news. Being said there's been a terrible accident on the Tube."

"Yes?"

"Round about the time Mr. Waygoes—errh—took the train."

"That's not very likely, is it?"

He nodded at the clock.

"Have a look at the time, sir. He went out of here at seven-ten this morning with the rest. Take them—how long?—to get to the station? Ought to have been at his office just before eight o'clock. He was always a terror for time. But his solicitor's been ringing since about nine-thirty. There's no sign of him. And no message here?"

I turned away.

Not a notion.

Impossible. Implausible. Ridiculous. All the idiot words we use so freely, that mean what?

"I'm going up. Let me know, will you?"

He nodded, and I went up the stairs to the calm of my set.

The telephone rang. I feared to pick it up.

But I did.

Jo Hibbs, in a warm, wondrous wave of utter relief.

"Sir, Mr. Riannes in Paris just called. He's got a large order from some people there, and he wants to know when you can arrange to see him."

"What appointments have I got?"

"Three today, sir."

"Put them off. Call and tell him I'll be there sometime this afternoon. As soon as I can get to Heathrow and the shuttle. Everything else all right?"

"Well, the news says there's been a terrible crash on the Tube.

241

Lot of our people were late. There were no trains past Moor-gate."

"Moorgate?"

"That's where they say it was. Everything's shut off. Full of fire brigades."

"Do you need me over there?"

"No, sir. We're up to scratch for the next couple of days."

"Probably be back the day after tomorrow. I'll be at the usual place. Call me if you hear anything about the crash. There might be some of our people in it."

"That's what they're all saying. I'll call this evening, sir, news or no."

A fine way to leave. But I could bear no thought of staying there to hear what I feared. I could hardly believe there was anything to fear. London's Underground had always been stock-in-trade of safety. I tried to imagine how trains could have collided on single tracks, and gave it up.

A cab took me to the London Terminal, and I caught a bus to Heathrow, lined, it seemed, with newspaper placards in big black letters.

MOORGATE TUBE SMASH. HEAVY DEATH TOLL FEARED.

I thought of Waygoes, and Ol' Mabbs, and Celli, and Mrs. Osornis, and Alf Straum, and Mrs. Jaykar, and so many others over in the second house, less well known, and yet all a part of us, and the life we led, the cheerful camaraderie of the Rotunda, the warm Roman floor, and hot towels, and lovely girls, and planting a smacker on Botti's botti and she half-smiling, not even turning round, and the Bosun's chipolata sausages and ice-cold beer, and Mrs. Jaykar's curry patties, and the fish buffet, and salads on long tables, and Sunday brunch, and marvellous beef or lamb stews, or boiled chicken, roast beef and real Yorkshire Pudding, not that slab of glup, and a good espresso to go with a cognac, it was a dream, yes, but lived by so many of us.

I turned from any thought that it could end.

The armful of magazines I bought I took off the plane because I slept the entire hour, and got a cab to the hotel. Riannes had a call for me, and we met in his office at four, and we were still there at seven-thirty, with the best job I ever had, edited and ready. We dined at Fouquet's, but the sight of the newspapers wilted my appetite. The headlines seemed to howl catastrophe, and I refused the copy Riannes held out.

"You seem very distrait, my friend," he said, on the corner of the Place Madeleine. "Anything to do with this?"

"I fear a friend of mine and many colleagues are part of it. I don't wish to think of it. Or the imaginable consequence. I don't know what will happen."

"We always imagine worse than it is," he said. "We are idiots pushed by any wind. Until we are blown into the last hole. Then we are no longer idiots. Only skeletons."

"You ought to be a stand-up comic," I said. "Let's have a cognac, and go home."

"What is a stand-up comic? It sounds acrobatic?"

"Often is. He's a chap with a mike telling stories he hopes are funny. Well. Not serious. One-liners. A one-line joke. A type of acidulated nut. Popular with the half-witted."

"Half-witted? How many of us are not?"

"Agreed. I can go mad without encouragement."

"You need that cognac. In here. Now tell me. What is a one-liner? I have an acquaintance with English, but I like to learn."

We sat across a metal table top dented over the years. The waiter took the order, and I had to repossess my mind for a one-liner.

"Well," I said. "The comic says 'My wife's very down-to-earth, a stable character. She's a proper mare.' You see?"

He shook his head.

"I must learn more English," he said, and raised the tulip. "The earth combining with the mare, yes. A stable character, one that is consistent. But what is the joke?"

"I should never have tried. Tell me a French joke."

"You have not the French."

"Just as well. One more?"

"Excellent. I have always thought one cognac the same as your babes in the woods. It attracts the robins. They hide the unhappy ones."

"How do we get out of this?"

"Very simply. Drink your cognac. Take a taxi."

I looked across at trees moving in the night breeze, at the few people, and they all seemed on a different level, and lamps were doubled.

Suddenly, we were both laughing, God knows why. I thought I knew, and then it was gone, and I insisted on paying, and I got in a cab, and waved, and went up the Champs to the Rue Balzac, and managed to get through the revolving door, into the lift and onto the bed. That last cognac had done the trick.

I awoke at about midday without being curious, and undressed, and got back into bed. When I woke, the room was dark. Papers were under the door, with several messages, three from Jo, two from Riannes, and two from people I had no wish to see. I called Jo and said I had been out, and what was the news?

"I think it's terrible, sir. Ol' Mabbs is dead. In that Tube smash-up. It ran into a wall. It wasn't a collision. It just bashed into a wall."

"I didn't know there were any walls on the Tube."

"Neither did I. Who did? But that's what happened. They're still working on it. They've got to cut them out with torches. They're all stuck together. In among the steel and the seats and doors, and everything. They say the stink down there's terrible. They've been down there three days, nigh on. They won't get them all out tonight or tomorrow. They don't think Mr. Waygoes came out. No word at the hospitals. Oh, I think it's awful, awful, *awful*."

"Calm down, Jo. Crying won't do any good. I'll try to be back tomorrow. If not, certainly the following afternoon. Enough work for months, tell everybody. Just keep me posted, and take care of yourself."

Inadequate. Miserably helpless. What else was there to feel? To be down there with the firemen, what the hell use would I be? To wait at the plant? In my set? In the foyer? In the Bosun's Galley? What use?

Jo, and her tears. And how many more? I dared not think of Celli, or of the other girls.

If Waygoes had gone, a brain was expunged. I hoped he had left a lot of paper. So many questions remained to be answered, not least, the question of the women's money. I could see that becoming an issue.

I tried to think.

No use.

Paris is just as lonely a place as any other. If you want a girl, that's as simple as anywhere else. But it's not the real company you need. I had a bath, thinking of all those men in that tunnel, the work, the sweat, the stench of days-old death, and thought of our girls, and I could have cried, but I got into bed and turned out the light.

To hell.

Some of us were certainly not much further away.

The morning sounds of Paris were like music. The papers bunched under the door. I rang down for coffee, and telephoned the airline for a London flight at two o'clock, which got me to Heathrow at something after three, and I left my bag at the Daemon at a little after four.

Almond's face almost put the fear of God in me.

He had been crying.

"We've been and lost Mr. Waygoes, sir," he said, in the frailest voice. "Most of them was in them front two carriages. All gone. A few come out. They're in hospital. All my sweeties, Mrs. Jaykar, that there Celli, Mrs. Hine, Mrs. Rafaele, the lot. Gone. Poor Ol' Mabbs. The Bosun. I mean, you can't think of anythink terribler. All of 'em. One go. An' lots more besides, not ours. How d'you think about it?"

I walked up to the plant, and Jo still had a pink nose and tears began when she saw me.

"All right," I said. "I know what's going on. Just get Mr. Prakash, will you?"

"He was on the train, sir."

"God damn it, Jo. Who've we got?"

"They were all in the first two carriages with Mr. Waygoes. No chance. Mr. Slenn's here, taking charge. But he's no Mr. Prakash, is he? We haven't got an editor, that's what it boils down to."

"Except me. I've never worked hard enough, Jo. I've done the book work. Dead easy. The real work I left to somebody else. Idle. That's what's wrong with a lot of us, Jo. Idle. Indolent.

245

Don't take it seriously. Right, from now on, I'm the boss. Where's Edwina?"

"She was on the train."

I had to put a hand on those shoulders.

"Find another girl to do what she did. She'll live in the same place. Rent free, same wages. But be sure she can make tea and coffee. And bake a croissant. And make sandwiches."

"I wonder if *she'd* agree?"

"Of course not. It was her job. But this is the next day. That's different. The business goes on, and so do our jobs. Bloody awful thing to say, but what else is there?

"See what you mean. All right. Going to need more people. Mr. Prakash did two men's work. I loved him."

"Take care of Mr. Slenn. He might have trouble with union people, and lose heart. Don't let it happen. We depend on each other and he's a linchpin. See to it."

We missed Edwina and her coffee and croissants and muffins, but the new girl, Georgiana Maybloss, was certainly not far behind, and she looked a tryer, a little over six foot, thin as a rule, shyest smile, white teeth, and nervous in slopped saucers and puddled coffee.

"They need the job," Jo said. "Couple of days, she'll be right. These girls have a *go*. They don't like going down the Labour Exchange and drawing the dole. They like wages. So don't worry. She's in Edwina's place, and there'll be no trouble."

None of us talked about the missing, and the only times we had a word or so was when the notice changed on the bulletin board, with a new list of names brought out, though in those two days none of ours, and Ol' Mabbs was the only one identified by Dr. Rahman. I was called to a meeting of the Committee at three o'clock in Mr. Waygoes' set, and a more woebegone clutch would be hard to find.

"There isn't much to say," Mr. Haynes, the accountant, said. "I've been in touch with the London Fire Brigade. Apparently one coach leapfrogged the one in front. The passengers didn't stand an earthly. Most of them are unidentifiable. Crushed. It's quite possible they won't all be clear for a couple more days."

"A *couple* more?" the assessor said in a whisper. "Great God. But why so long?"

246

"They have to cut through a smash of steel. The firemen and salvage lads have been heroes. I won't go into it. Too awful. Now, to business. So far as we know, Mr. Waygoes had no surviving relatives. All those who died with him held title deeds, but those titles revert to the estate. His affairs are in perfect order. Tenants still living here with title deeds can prove his intention. There should be no trouble. When everyone's been identified, there'll be a memorial service somewhere. But no burial. Cremation is advised because of the condition of the remains. Mrs. Lina Wall's the new housekeeper, a second comes in tomorrow, and both bars will have new staff. It's all been so sudden I haven't felt any real shock yet. I'm not looking forward to it. That's all, gentlemen."

"When's the next meeting?" somebody said.

"When they're all out, and identified, and we meet to settle the memorial service date. Anything more?"

Nothing, certainly, so far as I was concerned. I had a feeling I was in the eye of a nightmare. I tried not to think of Edwina, of Mrs. Osornis, and Alf, and the rest, but they clamoured, and I had to force myself not to put hands over ears.

The call from Riannes waiting for me was at least a break, and doubly welcome because I had to think of work and imagine Paris.

Jo put him through, and we talked a little about the disaster, but I had nothing to say.

"I understand your feeling," he said. "You must know you have my sympathy. Now, I must tell you I have to go to Teheran tomorrow. It is possibly more work. The blocks for the brochures are ready. I thought it would be just as well to bring them with me to London on the two o'clock flight, and we could meet at Heathrow until my flight to Teheran at five o'clock. We have a good deal to discuss, and I may be away longer than I think."

"Great. I'll meet the three o'clock plane from Paris, and wait in the first class lounge for you."

"We shall combine business with a bottle of wine. A truly splendid emulsion."

I worked late with Slenn on editing the copy, thankful for hard thinking to take the mind off what was going on up the road. The area was cordoned, the station was shut, and trains were diverted, so that most of my people were late getting in, and I let them go earlier or they might have got home with the milk, as Jo told me.

I funked going back to the Daemon. Even his smile going in did nothing to undo that spooky feeling of being watched, spoken to by voices beyond hearing, nudged by unseen elbows. Soult nodded greeting without the smile. The place echoed. No flowers lit the stairways. The big copper bowl on the centre table was empty. Only then I remembered Amy and Joe Briggs had gone on that journey to Thanatos. I had to find somebody for the green houses and garden, because I was fairly certain nobody else would bother, and I had no intention of letting their work follow them.

But the bars were closed, and I lost heart. *Nuts.* I went up-stairs listening to a double chorus of my footsteps, and I was glad to shut my solid door. Mrs. Rapajan, at least, had been in, and the room glowed though the flower vases were empty. I poured a drink, had a hot bath, and I was almost in bed when the telephone rang.

"Hullo? This is your friend, Teucer, remember me? I said I'd give you the bother, didn't I?"

I felt like screaming, but then I grabbed control. This was plainly a recording. But who was on the other end? I put the receiver on the floor and threw a couple of cushions over it, and got into bed, and slept.

Next afternoon, Heathrow was the same dismal scuffle of all sorts pushing and shoving to get where they wanted to go, and snakes of people followed guides to Ibiza, and Marbella, and Mallorca, though why, I never found out. They were places I tended to put out of mind, except that I saw clearly why the rat-race clan would want to get into another sort of life if only for a few days rest from winter, and eat meals set for them, and stretch out in the sun, with no thought of washing up, or joining the six o'clock shift, or clocking on, or anything except luxuriat-ing in those so-few moments of freedom, savouring the fall of warm sand through lax fingers, and gulping ice-cold beer in the heat of the sun, loving the sea and miles of white beach and green rocks.

I let Riannes order the wine and we sat down to a couple of hours, going through the copy, editing, altering, replacing sections, inserting spaces for the blocks, and at the end we were both confident we had a job.

"Next time, you come with me," he said. "You will like Teheran. And there is so much work for us. I think we should consider a partnership, myself the French, and you, of course, the English. The years are ahead. Will you think about it?"

"I most certainly will. It's a matter of growth. And it's about time."

I went back to the plant knowing the meaning of hope. Jo still worked, and I let her finish what she was doing, and sent her home in a taxi.

"I shan't know myself," she said. "Wait till my mum sees me come up in a taxi. The neighbours'll think I'm on the streets. Fat lot I care. *This* is style."

Slenn and I went over the copy of the afternoon, and he put his pencil down when I suggested a drink.

"My religion as a Presbyterian forbids," he said. "But if I work among infidels, why not borrow one of their more attractive habits? What is the difference between a man able to hold his drink, and a drunkard?"

"Very simple. A man able to hold his drink knows exactly when to stop. A drunkard does not. When I feel the buzz between the eyes, or when one glass suddenly seems two, a pile of gold on the table would not tempt me to take another drink. This is my personal view. If you have the will, the rule holds good. But it's wobbly, because we're not all the same. You have to make up your mind, and be careful."

"I am very careful," he said. "I will have a double. It has more taste."

Remembering the call of the night before, I telephoned the police.

"Took you a bit of time, didn't it?" a voice said.

"I have to work. You might monitor the line and find out who's having a game."

I went across to the Daemon, waved to him, and went in to the night security guard's salute. Another list had been pinned to the board. Again, none of our names were on it. It was like being punched.

The night guard looked away. The dog sat, and lifted his nose at me.

"He won't hurt you, sir," the guard said. "I've give him the tip. You're a friend. He'd be hard luck to anyone else, though."

"Anything open?"

"No, sir. Bars and kitchen's shut today and tomorrow. Miss Waygoes'll be here tonight with new staff, but only her and Mrs. Wall and the two tenants can come in."

"*Two* tenants?"

"That's all that's left, sir. The rest's up the road, there. Proper shocking to think about, ain't it? In the paper tonight they say they got that coach off the top. Like to see it, sir?"

"No thanks. Bad enough thinking about it."

I tried not. But I did. In the set, I opened a tin of beans, and cut a slice of ham, and fried a couple of eggs, a staple meal for some days, and found the French loaf gone mouldy, almost as great a tragedy as anything else, and opened a pack of crisp-breads instead. With a piece of cheese, it helped, and I was hungry, and felt better. While I made coffee the doorbell rang, and I almost dropped the pot. I was in a twitter, and cursing, though what a curse is in those moments I still don't know. Perhaps a blur of rude words. Rude, that is, in terms of a past generation. None of them seem rude any more, perhaps because courtesy is gone, manners and politeness no longer exist except in small islands, and we are rude, all of us, on a level of the hobbledehoy of yore. What a funny lot.

I opened the door carefully.

Cecilia smiled at me.

"Come on in," I said. "Pleasant surprise. How about a strong cup of coffee and a cognac?"

"Can't think of anything nicer," she said, and looked about. "What a lovely place. Well. No need to say anything, is there?"

"Take off your coat. Sit down. I'll get the coffee."

She shook off the long fur coat, a dark ermine, and the cap, and smoothed the black dress, no jewellery, black topboots, svelte, slim. I heard the kettle sing, and came back with the pot,

250

the bottle and the tulips, and she poured coffee, and I measured the cognac. There seemed little need to say anything.

She sat in the armchair, and I put my feet up on the couch, and we listened to radio music for a few moments.

"I wish I knew what was going to happen," she said. "The estate and everything else. I haven't any claim at all. I'm happy about it. But I'm not too happy about the rest of it. Who's going to run the estate? It's worth millions. He was trying to sell when he died. The people he was dealing with won't stop trying just because he's dead. They'll put the pressure on."

"What pressure?"

She laughed, and lifted the tulip.

"There can be accidents with the water supply, gas, power, all sorts of things. They don't have to be too nice."

"They lay themselves open."

"Not them. They know too much. And too many up top."

"Nasty picture."

"Let's hold on till they're all out of that bloody place, and the oohs'n'ahhs are all over. You'll see. Unless something turns up. That's why I came here. The old lad was very fond of you in a funny sort of way. You made millions for him while you did the runs. But you never asked for more money, did you? He liked that. I expect you'll find you've got a nice present in his will."

"Much rather he were alive."

"Yes. We all do, don't we? Still. Listen. I just wanted to tell you if anything funny happens here, you can always come to the Lomax. It was the harbour master's mansion for a couple of hundred years. Then the Customs took over, and when my father bought it, you never see such a wreck. But he liked the old. He got this architect to do it over. Now it's like it was. Guests I've always put on the first floor. Sea captains and that lot. I had all the second floor. The third floor I never used. I thought of going up there but I never made up my mind. It's the best part of the house. Not servants' rooms. They're at the back. Anyway, if the worst comes to the worst, you can always come and see them."

"Hope I don't have to. But thank you. It's a kindly thought. Not many think in kindly terms these days."

"Not much of a world, is it?"

"Isn't it for you? You've got your own property. Nobody can put you out. You can go where you like. Do pretty well as you please. How many can say that?"

She went over to get the coat, and I got up to help her on.

"Does nothing for me," she said, wrapping. "I mean, I can go to bed and have a rattle when I feel like it. But when it's all over, what is it? You've got to lay there, looking at the ceiling, and you think, what was all the fuss about? Everything they told you in school. All the mystery and wonder, and that stuff. You find out it's only a bloke poking a lump of meat in you. What's that to look forward to?"

"So what's the idea of asking me to share a weekend?"

She stood, cap on, coat open, slapping the gloves into a hand, smiling.

"I thought you might be different," she said. "Well, a bit, anyway. I mean, we all feel like it now and again, don't we? I know I do. But afterwards, I get so disgusted, I can't abear meself. Wish to Christ I knew why. I tell you, I could cut me throat."

"You'll never do that."

"Won't I? We'll see. My father told me that's what my mother did. Always, always told me. It's why he got rid of me. Why I hated him. But I can't, now. She must have led him a bit of a dance, too. Got to make allowances, haven't we? Only fair."

I walked with her to the door.

"Don't forget," she said, turning. "Any trouble here, come over the Lomax. I'll see you don't get worried."

She kissed me and ran, and waved me back when I might have followed. I went to the kitchen with the glass and crocks, and washed them, stood them on the draining board, and loved every moment of going to beautiful bed, with help of the electric blanket, the greatest invention since the Apple-in-Eden, and they can call on me for a reference.

At noon next day, the bulletin board had another list of names, four of them ours. We all stood quiet, and nobody said anything —if they were like me—feeling sick, and I went back to the plant, and if anyone mentioned lunch, I might have spewed. More horrible still was thought of the six o'clock bulletin, and that whatever we did, hour by hour, those men working down there were bringing out our friends. Nobody liked to think of them as "remains" but nothing stopped us from thinking, and Georgiana cried while she poured coffee, and we knew why.

I stayed on at the plant pretending to work, and I was so glad I did, because just as I was thinking of going home, I heard knocks on the far door in the packing section. I went down, and opened, and Mr. Motilal closed his umbrella, and came in.

"I am so glad to find you," he said. "I waited at the Daemon. I wanted to talk about the leases. They will not be effective against determined opposition."

"Have a drink," I said. "Brandy?"

"It will do very well, thank you. I am chiefly worried because of the heirs. Those leases, if they had been signed by Mr. Waygoes, would have been valuable. They are now virtually worthless if somebody wishes to litigate. It could cost enormously to fight in court. Perhaps years. Costs mounting the whole time. Pyrrhic business at best. No guarantee of success. Your health, sir?"

"That's bad news. Health. What's to be done?"

"I would like to protect the families of the lessees. It is wrong they should suffer because of a quibble in law. I believe any judge would give a verdict in their favour. It was the manifest will of Mr. Waygoes to confer those gifts. The value should come down to the heirs. But the law can be a funny business. The other side can offer considerably less for the retraction of the leases. Hundreds instead of thousands. What are impoverished people to do? Hundreds is an impressive sum."

"Agreed. What do you want me to do?"

"Carry the fight. You stand to gain or lose most. Permit me to represent you. I will strive for the highest price, and on that, the rest will have a yardstick. I am Indian-Kenyan. Therefore I am suspect among many. The people I am trying to protect are also Kenyan-Indian, Pakistani, Sudanese, or from Mauritius and the Seychelles, and Bangladesh, of course. They are all struggling to maintain themselves, and a sum of money could set up many in a small business. Out of reach of social security, and other scars of poverty."

"You take charge and act for me. Get the best price for all of us. That was Mr. Waygoes' intention, in any case."

He got up, drank the last drop, shook the umbrella, and smiled.

"I feel as a god refreshed," he said. "It is the difference between hundreds and thousands, of course. I may say that you will find us not ungrateful. We are so often the recipients of deliberate unkindness and vilification, that when people are kind we tend to overdo things emotionally. Sir, I shall take my leave, and wish you a very good night, with heartfelt thanks."

I went back to the desk as the phone rang.

"Been trying to get you all day. This is Detective-Inspector Kemp."

"Congratulations on the promotion."

"Thanks. About that call. You were right. It was a recording to be sent out three times a night for the next three months. An office in the Strand. It won't go out again. I think we frightened them off. Any more of it, let me know."

"I will. Any other news?"

"Nothing nowhere. Got anything to tell me?"

"Nothing, except thank you, and good night."

Tone and manner were warning. I was still in that file.

The page I worked on seemed to slide away. I tried to concentrate on copy singing praise of Persepolis, Isfahan, but it clogged, and I was thinking of Penna Cately, and Ella Broome, and then I had enough of silence, and swung the coat over my shoulders, locked up, and trotted through fine rain over to the Daemon.

The list was up, framed black, in the middle of a green baize square. I turned at the steps. A short woman in black half-smiled, holding out a hand.

"I'm Mrs. Wall, sir. I'm one of the new housekeepers. Just introducing myself. Everything's going to be open tomorrow. I'll try to keep things as they were. Won't be easy. I had this message from the police, they said, for general information. There won't be any need for an identity check. Everybody was identified by papers on the person. They'll be cremated tonight. And I was to notify you of a committee meeting tomorrow, at four, in A 1, to decide the future running of the house, and the date of the memorial service. I think that's all, sir."

"Thank you, Mrs. Wall."

Thinking of all those people cremated gave me no appetite except for sleep. I poured a drink, and took down Gibbon's Volume IV, and I needed no pill.

The committee was woebegone as ever. We had a thistle of sherry to cheer things up, as the chairman said, and sat down to a sheet of paper.

"You'll see I've confirmed payment of wages and tradesmen," he said. "We'll have a balance sheet and bank statements next time we meet. New tenants will be found, using the Waygoes standard, bank and civic references, including a report from their last landlord. Now, the question of a memorial service. Mr. Mackesson represents Mr. Waygoes' firm of solicitors. Sir?"

Mr. Mackesson, craggy face, deep grey eyes, silvery hair, thin clipped moustache, looked the part. He put on hornrims and unfolded the papers, turning the first two, looking up from the third.

"This is an excerpt from the will," he said. "I shall read. 'On no account will any funeral service of any kind or any sort of ritual be indulged in, never mind the goodness of heart that any friends of mine may have, that is to say, after my death. I do not look forward to it, and that others may try to make it an occasion for pagan dirges offends me. To the contrary, my estate will defray all expenses for a champagne party in the Rotunda for all those caring to hoist a glass in memory of a misspent life, and if there happens to be an R in the month, then oysters as well.'"

He looked at us one by one.

"I think that takes good care of that," he said, smiling. "He was an extremely self-willed type. All we have to decide is the date. I hope I'm invited?"

"He was your client," Dawson said. "Why not? Anything else?"

"Question of gardeners," I said. "The greenhouses must be looked after, and there's a lot of work in the garden. It won't wait."

"I agree," Dawson said. "I'll see Mrs. Wall. That the lot?"

I thought it might be another night with Gibbon, but the

255

phone rang as I got inside, and first I looked at it, and then picked it up.

" 'Lo, A.G.? Cecilia here. You must be feeling right dumpish. Why not come over and have some dinner with me? I've got a lovely pheasant."

"What time?"

"Ah, that's more like it. Say, eight o'clock?"

"I'll be there. And thank you more than you know."

I tucked Gibbon back in his niche, patted him on the back, and poured a straightener. At least part of the night was saved. I took off the bow tie and put on the long blue, and decided I needed a couple of new suits and a few other things, but I had always been careless. If I needed something I bought it wherever I was, and so I had not a wardrobe but a bits-and-pieces motley, yet I made do, and at least it fitted. Shoes were something else. I had mine made for me because I had funny feet. Possibly that was why I got into the habit of looking at other men's shoes, first. If they were cheapish or shapeless, then that's how I judged them, and I was generally right. Shoddy is as shoddy does, and that applies everywhere, certainly to character.

I had to wait for a cab, and on the way I asked the cabby if the Moorgate business had been much of an upset.

"Much?" he shouted, through the divide. "Christ, if you look where the station is, all the roads blocked off, how d'you get anywhere? You had to go all round bloody Cairo. We can get through here, now. We couldn't yesterday. Much? You never see such a mess. I'm glad it's over. I'm sorry for the poor bastards down there, though. They should have took a cab."

The place looked the same, the smells were the same, beery, kitcheny, and the bars were crowded with dockers or anyway, men in working clothes. I ordered a scotch, and Cecilia, in black, though not the same dress, but soignée, certainly, came behind the long bar.

"You're not paying for that," she said. "This is my party. I've got champagne cocktails in the Mess. Drink up, and let's go. I'm thirsty, and I love champagne. You heard they got them all out? I'm glad, in a way. 'Least, it's all over. We can breathe. But they can't. Neck that, and follow me."

Exactly like a sergeant-major. But I liked it, and necked, and followed through a pretty rough crowd, though Cecilia seemed in a smiling float, and the men made way in an extraordinarily gentle obeisance.

"They treat you like the lady of the manor," I said, catching up. "What's the secret?"

"Easy," she said. "A penny off the beer and cigarettes. I lose it, but I get a bigger profit in over-all sales. The pubs round here're all up for sale. I've busted them. Then I'll buy, and I'll do the same. I don't see why a bloke should get clouted for liking a drop of beer and a smoke. They're getting penalised for living."

We had a corner table in the Mess, a place from another age of elegance, with a long refectory slab down the middle, set with linen and silver candlesticks, flowers, glassware, a rare wonder to look at. The waiters wore short blue pea-jackets and white aprons, all of them, obviously, seamen. Why does the sea mark a man, even a steward? Even? A steward's job can be among the hardest to learn, and very few survive. Those who do put out a certain aura of extreme competence. Nothing disturbs them. An explosion in the boiler room might earn a small smile. All those men looked rough as oak. The girls helping them, in blue dresses and little aprons, seemed very like sylphs.

"Where did you get these people?" I asked her, while we flipped napkins. "This must be unique in London."

"My intention," she said. "This room's more than two hundred years old. It's always been run like this. While I'm alive, it always will be, or better. And when the old lads're pensioned off, the girls'll take the job on. About time they got a look-in."

"Are you wom's lib?"

"Not particularly. They haven't got the right idea. No use bellyaching about what they've got and what they haven't. My father was right on. Till they get their own money, they'll just be a pack of cats meowing on the back fence. Nowhere. Nothing."

"How're they going to get it?"

"Same as anything else. Fight for it. They can tip the men on their flat heads. If they want to try. All they're doing is writing in magazines, trying to be clever. Well, it's a living."

She ran her necklace—of very good pearls—through her

257

fingers and rolled pellets of bread. I watched her while we ate a delicious pheasant, saw the pellets pile, heard the rattle of rippled pearls, signs of unease, but we spoke of tiny little nothings, or we listened to the accordion player.

"Right," she said. "You can see I'm in a state. I just had news there's a claim from Australia and somewhere else. The solicitors say they're relations. I don't see how this place can be in danger. But you never know, do you? Everybody with a lease can be in danger of losing the lot, depending how the will's drawn. The solicitors on my side are both dead. It's years ago. If the deeds weren't filed, how can I prove anything?"

"How long ago?"

"About, I suppose, six years."

"Nobody's contested your authority in that time?"

She shook her head.

"Then don't worry. Anything to prove you've been regarded as the proprietor?"

"Books, accounts, and all the taxes."

"If you were regarded as the boss by Inland Revenue, that's good enough. Or else they were taxing the wrong one. Wouldn't sound too good, would it?"

She sat back all smiles.

"I knew I picked the right one," she said. "Been a terrible worry this past couple of days. I've been chucked out of places since I was born. Well, that was my mother's fault. When she died, I told my dad. Cut a long story, he gave me this place. He said you'll never get chucked out of anywhere else. It's yours. Take care of it. And I have. I went to church today. I put flowers on the altar. But you know something? I couldn't pray. I hadn't got a word. I reckon that's terrible."

"If you're not used to it, you get out of the habit. The words fly off."

"But it's nice to get something out of yourself. I couldn't. I felt like a cripple."

"Don't worry about it. Think long enough, it'll come back."

She leaned across and took my hand.

"Tell you what," she said. "Let's go up and look at the third floor."

"You've got something up your sleeve. What is it?"

She turned, facing me.

"I told you I had a bit of time in that office. I happen to know a few things nobody else does. I don't believe your bits of paper mean very much. The leases, *I'm* talking about. It's why I'm worried about mine. My father was a great thinker. But he wasn't too worried about detail. I don't think anything ever worried him except this money-for-women lark. Let's go up the back stairs."

The stairway curved in a lovely walnut banister, and we were back in the eighteenth century, with some fine prints on the walls, and a series of mirrors, ornately gold of the period, almost making it a museum, with chandeliers, silver candlesticks on the tables, silver tankards hung in rows, pewter pots shining on shelves, blue and white china in racks, and a padded sedan chair in red leather and polished oaken handles, and doors with a crystal window, and a silver chamber pot under the seat.

"They thought of everything," she said. "This is the main room. I don't know if it was the top o' the shop, or some sort of office. What d'you think?"

The room stretched a magnificent forty feet at least, and about thirty broad, white-panelled walls, a glim of parquet, a marble fireplace, with three oils, one a Titian undeniably, and two Canalettos, of Venice. A trove. I wondered if she knew.

"There's a bedroom nearly as big, with a dressing room and bath next door. The kitchen's never been used. It's down here, and there's a bit of a breakfast room with a terrace. Nice for the summer. You can think about it, anyway."

"What's the rental?"

"What you're paying now."

"Can you afford that?"

"Why not? The place is freehold. All I pay is rates. If things go up, all right, I put up the rent. Fair?"

"I certainly think so."

"But you hope it doesn't have to be."

"You get fond of a place."

"I know. And your place is lovely, I give you that. But I've got a feeling."

"You know more than you're telling."

"You'll know soon enough. If it happens."

"You can't tell me?"

"It might not happen. So I look a fool? Let's see what goes on in the next few days."

Somebody ran up to say there was a call for her in the office, and she raised a hand to me and went downstairs.

"Come on down to the bar," she called in echoes. "Have a brandy. Put the lights out, will you?"

I went down to the kitchen, a new ice box, stove, and everything else, and the terrace was the rooftop, a space calling for a garden, and I could see across the dock basins to the Thames, the tips of Tower Bridge on the right, and all the lights along the reach to Wapping Stairs.

A gift, except that any thought of leaving the Daemon stuck me as a butcher's knife, and I turned from it, and switched off all the lights, and took the stairs two at a time, down to the bar.

A steward put a crusted bottle and a couple of tulips on the table, and said that Miss Cecilia was on the phone and wouldn't be long.

She came, pinker in the cheeks, and a great deal more cheerful, twirling the pearls in small circles.

"That was the solicitor," she said. "I'm all right, he says. Everything's in the clear. Can't tell you how I feel. If I was the type, I'd get drunk. But I can't. I don't like booze. Only a nice glass or two of champagne, and I've had my ration. And it's the wrong time of the month else I'd invite you for the weekend. So we'll wait for the party, eh?"

We drank one, and I got a cab to the Daemon, and we had a smile for each other, and the security guard let me in, and his dog chased me halfway up a flight.

"It's all right, sir," he called. "It's only the bad meat he's after."

I let myself in with such a feeling of relief and gratitude that I suppose it formed in a sort of prayer never to have to leave, although I knew it, then, to be childish, maudlin, mawkish, whatever. But it was the fact. Any thought of having to leave made me feel ill, stupid though it seemed even to me.

I threw it off, and took Gibbon to bed, grateful he spent the time and trouble to write such a wonderful sleeping pill, if only for me, and who the hell was I? That's right. Who *was* I? Somebody standing up thinking nonsense, when all those people I had known, and some I had loved, were ashes going cold in a pot somewhere?

A wonderful thought to take to bed. But Gibbon helped. I have probably read more Roman history than most non-professionals, and I still know nothing about it. I never saw a word, or if I did, then quite by accident. I looked for sleep in decades of human triumph and much more suffering, though I think I can say that none of it made any impression. I wonder why reading, or thinking, of suffering in past time makes so little impact? Perhaps the suffering of the day makes everything else irrelevant, or uninteresting. The agony of those people trapped in the coaches certainly came back to me as words, and made me cringe. But they were only words and pretty feelings. They had little enough to do with hurt, and cremation. I turned my mind from it. Easy enough.

Georgiana poured coffee and Jo came in, looking worried.

"There's pickets outside, sir," she whispered. "They won't let nothing in or out. It's a union black. Arnie Daye and his lot."

"Have a cup of coffee and a bun. Let them look after their fatheaded selves."

"We won't get nothing done, sir. Nothing in or out. And our lads are saying they'll get bashed for coming to work."

"Two can play that game. Just carry on."

All very well, but I had an appointment in the City, and when I went out, about a dozen carrying picket signs came toward me, and I thought I was for the jump, but then a couple of dozen men ran in from Lumm's Lane, on the other side, all Asians, some darker, with pick helves, and slashed at shoulders, arms, necks, and jabbed at the crotch, and the pickets ran, and some fell headlong, among them Arnie Daye.

I shouted to Jo to call the police and ambulance, and went back to find Georgiana and a cup of coffee, and poured in a shot of brandy, and offered one to Slenn, in his Prakash sleeve covers and green visor, calm as all that.

"You had a hand in this," I said.

261

"Of course," he said, in his gentle—suburban?—way. "I am Anglo-Indian. We are your friends, you know that? Why should these people make themselves a nuisance? There are many jobs here. People need their money. Who are these ruffians to demand we do as they say? We say no. Most of the men you saw were ex-Indian Army. As my father was. As I was. They are trained to fight. If you have more trouble, they will be here."

"That could lead to a great deal more."

He shook his head.

"I think not, if you permit, sir. Those people are bullies. They try to get what *they* want. By threats. We must prove to them that there is also what *we* want. We do not threaten. We simply defend."

I kept my appointment, and went back to the plant with one of the largest orders I ever had, that meant at least four months work-in-hand. I had to enlarge, and take on more men. I also had to find more room, and I called Mr. Mackesson.

"No," he said, and that was a shock. "You can't think of further expansion where you are now. In fact, it looks as though you'll have to move. We're in touch with the heirs, and apparently they've made up their minds to liquidate. I'm dealing with their solicitors now. But there's no question of taking over other houses as matters stand at the moment. I'm sorry."

I said nothing to anybody, but it seemed to me I ought to start looking for premises elsewhere, larger, and capable of further enlargement in view of a possible partnership with Riannes. Question was, where? I asked Jo to call estate agents, not only in London but outside, where rents were cheaper.

"They going to sling us out, sir? They've been talking about it."

"Who?"

"Lots of people. Been gossip for months."

"We'll hang on. But get some addresses. Might be short notice."

A call for a committee meeting came at four o'clock, and I went over to the Daemon with an acute feeling of defeat. Mr. Dawson's face underlined all I felt, if a face can underline. We poured sherry, and sat down.

262

"I won't shilly-shally," he said. "The entire estate is under the hammer. Nothing will be saved. The entire Daemon property is to be sold to an international hotel complex. Six more buildings will be added, Wapping High will be diverted behind, and the property will become an island for the international set. All the other properties will be rebuilt in terms of new housing, and that sort of thing. Matter of millions. The new company is disposed to be generous to those holding the unsigned leases. The figures are being negotiated at the moment. All removals will be paid for, together with a severance payment. Those details will come later. For the moment, there's notice that the estate will have new owners, and they'll want vacant possession."

"Very hard luck on the tenants," the assessor, Mr. Roe, said. "They've got a case in law, y'know?"

"We're all anxious to avoid trouble," Mr. Dawson said. "*Ex gratia* payments will be purposely generous. Other allowances will be made."

"But where the devil are we supposed to go?" I asked. "I've been here since it opened. I've got a business here."

"All been taken into consideration. I'm sure you'll find your agreement to terminate more than generous."

"That's not what we're discussing. I want to know, where am *I* going? Where's my business going?"

"We'll certainly see if we can help, there. I'm certain we can. I'll keep in touch."

"This memorial party," Mr. Roe said. "There doesn't seem the devil of a lot of enthusiasm for it."

"True," Mr. Dawson said. "Strange, but most people set a lot of store by a memorial service in a church. It implies and confers the respect they feel due the man they wish to honour. A drunken party is the reverse of their sentiment. I've found very few wishing to go. From what I know, I'd say cancel, and pay the projected amount to church funds."

"Hold tight," the architect, Mr. Barry, said. "You've got Methodists, Presbyterians, Lutherans, Baptists, and all the perishing rest. They'd all want their piece of the corpse. I don't think it should go anywhere except to a children's hospital."

"Right," Mr. Dawson said. "Which one?"

263

"Let's forget it till we know more about the amount of cash," Mr. Roe said. "I'm sorry about the party. After all, it *was* Mr. Waygoes' wish."

"That's what I think," I said. "If you don't want to give it, I *will*. He was a friend of mine."

"I respect that," Mr. Dawson said. "The party will be held on Sunday next, with champagne and oysters, and in order to have some notion of how many will attend, I'll have a list put up on the bulletin board. No need to waste money. If it turns out not many, I'll have a small bar in the Skipper's Cabin for those who want to drink Mr. Waygoes' health. How's that?"

"I'll be there," Mr. Barry said. "He was a good man. I'll drink to him. Hope you have enough oysters. Make it Colchesters."

"It's strange, y'know," Mr. Roe said, pulling his nose between thumb and fingers. "There isn't supposed to be any religion these days. But if you offend people's susceptibilities, you find out there's still quite a lot. They wanted to go to church to express themselves, a sort of pilgrimage. They'd have made the effort. But a party, just to drink? No. The majority don't give a damn. I'm not sure I don't agree with them."

"It was Mr. Waygoes' wish," Mr. Dawson said. "It will be adhered to. Anyone against?"

Silence.

"Meeting adjourned," Mr. Dawson said. "Bosun's Bar, on Sunday next, at seven-thirty. That's all."

Living between heaven and earth is one thing, but having to live between hope and desperation is quite another, and although I had full days at the plant, with Gibbon for nightly partner, so many times I wished myself someone else, *somewhere* else, never more than when Georgiana poured coffee, and stood.

"Sir, I believe everybody's going to leave?" she said, in not more than a whisper, a small girl. "I hope I di'n do nothing wrong? I been looking for a job for eight months, and my Daddy wouldn' let me go to the Labour for the dole. I like it here. I clean the offices and that, and I make the tea and coffee, and I can't bear I got to go."

She put her head down, and cried into a hand across her eyes.

"Georgiana, you'll go when I go," I said. "And I have no intention of going except where I want. You, and the rest, will come with me. Happier?"

She smiled through her fingers, and flipped wet light, walking out with the tray as if she carried Ophir's jewels. Jo came in with the day's typing, and watched her go.

"She looks happy enough," she said. "Been moaning her luck all morning."

"Jo, tell everybody not to worry about their jobs. Where I go, they'll go. We've got too much work to close up. In or out of London, all the same. Even if we've got to get lodgings."

"What, and all bunk in together? Ooh, what a capurtle, eh? I tell me mum, she' go barmy. Proper barmy. How soon'll it be, sir?"

"Too soon for me, Jo. Our days are numbered. And that's *it*. Get ready to move. Packing cases, all that. But tell everybody there's no need to worry about their jobs. *At all*."

"Them squatters up there, they're terribly worried. They like where they are. They've fixed things up lovely. Got their kids going to school. They got to move?"

"Everybody. All out."

"How can they *do* that?"

"Simple. When Mr. Waygoes was here, he was responsible for rates, water, light and all the rest. He isn't here, so *who's* responsible? The estate. They won't accept it. Therefore? All the services are cut off as from midnight when the bills don't get paid. Simple?"

"But *you* could pay."

"I'd be happy to. But the estate is the landlord. I'm not, and I've never paid rates. I always paid the Waygoes estate. It was rental, and the rates were part of the payment. In other words, I'm not responsible as owner. I'm only a tenant, and they don't want me or anybody else. They want their property."

"I don't see it's fair."

"Nothing's fair, Jo. Mr. Waygoes had a heart. An estate is only that. Solicitors, accountants and assessors, and good night."

"No heart."

"No."

The list on the bulletin board wanting to go to the party held two names on the first day, mine and Soult's. On the second day, seven, and on Friday before the party eleven, and a notice appeared to announce a party in the Bosun's Bar at seven o'clock on Sunday to drink the health of Mr. Bayard Waygoes, and his friends.

That list seemed to tell me, more than anything else, what a desert lay in front of us. Free champagne and oysters apparently were not worth a Sunday journey for some, or a walk down the steps of the Daemon for others, even to drink the health of a man at once friend and patron, landlord and foster-father. I thought of Valentine Harry Edwardes glowing his name at the night, and wondered if he, too, would have to shift, and where? Would there ever be another Amy and Joe Briggs? I could see Ol' Mabbs putting his teeth into his right-hand upper waistcoat pocket, and Mrs. Osornis stitching the buckram flowers, and Bhula unwinding her sari, and I was hit in the throat, and I had no need of Gibbon. I got into bed, and lay there, an eternal evacuee, crying itself to sleep.

It had been done so many times before.

On that horribly rainy day, it was no surprise to find Mr. Motilal shaking his umbrella outside the office door just after Jo had shut down.

"I hope I don't disturb, sir?" he said, in a smile between a laugh and an open-throat howl. "I have such very good news, I felt I must tell you immediately. I have just returned from the law offices. Everything is wonderfully settled in our favour. Of course they knew they were vulnerable, but I must say they were extremely forthcoming. No effort was made to evade any issue, or to fish in legal argument for some remote excuse not to meet my terms. Nothing like that. In fact, they were eager to accept any terms which might facilitate removal with vacant possession. The accountant's report you gave me of your business activities was a great help, and a firm basis for a just demand. I succeeded in their acquiescence of this figure."

He opened a folio and turned it to me.

The total amazed me.

"You seem pleased?" he said, with a shake of worry.

"Pleased? I'm knocked out. I never thought you'd get a quarter of that."

"There is only one obstacle. They will pay all expenses for removal and the reinstalment of machinery. To the last penny everything will be paid without quibble. But they insist on vacant possession within ten days."

"Ten days? *Ten?* What do they mean, ten days? I haven't even found premises. Where the hell do they think I'm going?"

"As you see, I stipulated, and they have agreed to pay, a daily rate, including wages, for all losses sustained during the period of removal, until you are settled to your satisfaction, and mine. You will not lose a penny piece anywhere. Are we agreed?"

"Agreed."

The expression "a heavy heart" I had known without realising what it meant. Now, I did. I could feel it, the heaviness, the weight. To leave Brittle Candy Lane made me empty in the gut. I had never truly appreciated how I felt about the place, the street, the neighbourhood. My parents' home was still under the rubble not four hundred yards away. I had roots of a sort.

And now?

Where?

Outside London?

But I had the responsibility of keeping almost forty people in a job. How were they to get to wherever it might be? Anyway, I was protected against loss, and I intended that all of them would benefit.

It hit me only when I got back to the set that I had at most ten days to enjoy tenure in the company of friends of so many years. Yet, I was alive by a fluke. I could have been a name in the disaster, at this moment part of a handful of ashes.

Plus ça change. I don't know why I thought of it. I could see our French master's mouth making funny shapes when he said it, and us imitating him, until he got into the joke and really did exaggerate, and we rolled about laughing, and the day also came when he had to leave because of family matters, and he began to speak in French and broke, and Andrew Simms stood and wished him good-bye from all of us, and started crying, and M. Resanger corrected him on a pronoun, and turned to the door, taking off his mortarboard, and looked at us, with silvery eyes, and said I love you all, and *bonne chance*, never getting it out.

I remembered that, and that was exactly how I felt.

Broken, and yet alive, myself, with a duty.

But why did I have a duty? What was the feeling? Where did it come from? Why did Mr. Motilal feel he had a duty? Why did Dr. Rahman? Why did anybody *feel* a duty? What *was* duty? Why should anyone feel any sense of responsibility for others? Where was the answer? Which philosopher told us? How was it explained?

I came to feel that wide swathes of the human estate had never been explored, far less examined. It seemed to me that we were molluscs at mercy of any tide. We lived, we died, and that was that. A handful of ashes held more than twenty people, all of them happy, hopeful, expectant of a gift.

Until.

I was reminded at the party—those pathetically few down in the Skipper's Cabin because it was smaller than the Bosun's Bar —of the extent of our loss. Less than a tenth of us had lived to drink a toast. Why expect more people?

"A dead sad night," Ari Papadopoulos, the newsagent, said. "I never had a shock like it. It was two days before I knew what happened. The newspapers were still there where I left them. You know how I felt?"

"Like me," Bill Apsley, the dustman, said. "When them dust-bins wasn't there, I thought, hullo, something's dead wrong here. It wasn't half, by Christ."

"Like me," Zach Grew, the bookmaker, said. "The old man, and I don't speak disrespectful, he always had a couple of bets every day. It was, like, a nice habit. He generally come out evens, or better. He knew his stuff. Then there was three days, nothing. So I called. It was somebody new on the phone. He wasn't there. I tell you, I got the proper collywobbles."

"All right, everybody," a voice called over, and everyone was silent. "My name's Cecilia. I was the daughter of Bayard Way-goes, as fine a man as ever I'll meet in *my* life. We're here to eat and drink his health in oysters and champagne, his greatest love in food and drink. One thing we have to remember. About a week's time, we're all out. Everything he stood for, it's gone. Money talks. He never wanted it to. He had enough. He'd have won in the end. He didn't get long enough. Raise 'em up. Fill 'em up. Here's to him, and all them with him. Let's always love their memory. Down 'em."

We downed, and she came over to my table.

"Ol' Moti' had a word with me," she said, with a hand on my leg. "You know, he's Indian, and they don't think too much of them as lawyers, so I said, you help him, see? This is Wein and Trachman, my solicitors. Well, they was horrified what he was asking, and they got on to me, young Trachman did, and I says you get in there both feet, and get every penny. So they did. You satisfied?"

"All of it, except having to leave."

She nodded. With a touch of make-up, she was beautiful in a lit sort of way because she brightened where she sat.

"I know," she said. "I know what I'd feel. Listen, Moti' told me —he's a darling of a man—you had to look for a place for your work. Is that right?"

"I haven't the faintest idea where I'm going."

"Listen, we don't have to gulp any more, or guzzle, do we? Look, the Lomax was a Customs headquarters for more than a couple of hundred years. They had their sheds behind there. Stone-built. Slate roofs. Eight of them. For spices, tobacco, all that. They're still there. What about a couple of them for your job?"

"When could I see them?"

"Now."

"Let's."

They were clean, dry, with a wonderful smell of the spices of a couple or more centuries, and the address—One, Allspice—took me.

"Right," I said. "Done. I'll start moving tomorrow. What would I have done without you?"

"Probably got by," she said. "Let's have a drink. You going to live here?"

"It's the only place. And it's beautiful. I'm grateful."

"Think about *him*, not me."

She walked away, and I got back to the cab a bit empty, but she turned.

"What about this drink?" she called. "You always forget things so easy? Let's have a quiet bottle. I've got something to tell you. Did you think them accountants could look into my father's business, and not come across the record of payments made to you for all those years? To a Swiss account?"

Frozen is the word.

I had never even thought of it. No mention of tax returns.

She smiled, and laughed at the lamps.

"I know what you're thinking," she said. "But don't worry. I'll be coming into a lot. Teucer's out of the running. So I step in as heiress, except I signed an agreement to make no further claim on the estate when I got this place. Wein says he can beat that, and I've said good luck. That's the property side. But the rest is all mine, and that includes money. So I went to the office to have a look round. It paid. I got your files and a couple of his, and I burned them. Anything else they find, they're welcome to."

I was almost too relieved to speak.

"I owe you a lot," I said.

"Well, thinking of you made me think of other things, and that's how I found the files. All of them. He was stupid to keep them. But he was that sort. Hold onto everything. Get a receipt. When're you moving?"

"Tomorrow. Have it all crated."

"And the Daemon?"

"Start tomorrow."

She lifted the tulip.

"New life. Your health, and everything nice. How about this weekend?"

"Sounds right. The best."

"Let's make it that, eh?"

The cab took me back in some sort of golden froth, and I waved at the Daemon's smile, and the new security guard let me in, and I hauled on the banister to get up to my set, had a little trouble with the key, and flattened against the door inside, sniffing the familiar, suddenly wrenched to think I must leave. I dropped in a chair and slept, cold, till after five o'clock, and woke shivering, miserable, and undressed, and slept and woke again at past eleven, and felt my way to the shower, and a dressing gown. No papers under the door, and no coffee. I phoned down. No reply. I got into a morning rage. I went downstairs. Nobody on the door. The office was shut. The kitchen locked. The foyer was still.

I stood in silence, tasting the bleak of what was to come. The place was a mausoleum. Even if the floors had opened again, I could never have lived there. It was like a tooth reached by tongue tip, pulled, and then not. It was gone.

That was the Daemon, and he still smiled outside, and I wondered if that was what the smile meant.

Dying is what you do best.

Keep smiling.

I went back to the set. Water still came from the taps and I made coffee, and current was on for the shaver. But I had a feeling it would not be for long. I went downstairs and a man met me coming from the Bosun's.

"My name's Ames, sir," he said. "I'm the day watchman. There'll be a man at night. The other tenant's gone. Any idea when you go?"

"Not for the moment. But as soon as possible."

I called the Sikh with the dark blue turban, and asked him to move me from the set to the Lomax, remembering the statuary down in the cubicles, and to look at the plant and find out what mechanics and cranes he would need to shift the lot to the sheds at One, Allspice. He took it in stride, no doubts or worries, and I had none.

I went to the plant, and told Jo to let everybody know they were on full pay during the move, and to get a telephone installed at the Customs sheds, and oversee the removal of office paper.

I think I know how a flower feels when jerked bloodily from the ground. I had no wish to think. I finished the jobs on my desk, and told Jo I would be away for a week, and went over to the set for my bag, and called a cab for Heathrow. Air France got me to Tunis that evening, and I took a car to Anne-France and Jean-Luc to a happy arms-around meeting, and I drank wine and lay in the sand for five days of nothing except sun, not even newspapers or radio, and sobered over the weekend, and got back to London on Tuesday midday. I saw the Daemon's smile at about three, and took my time and walked across to the plant.

Empty.

I went back to the Daemon, and walked up the stairs to the set, and opened the door.

Empty.

Even the smell had gone.

I was myself, me, and nobody.

I wanted coffee. There was no water from any tap. There was no coffee, or a pot or cup. I seemed not to be myself. The white spaces on the walls were where the books and pictures had been. I felt like any space. Where something had been. Whitish. Nothing. Sunshine flashed on polished boards and patchy walls. Emptiness. Bhula and Mrs. Rapajan had worked for what? What do most of us work for?

I called a cab, handed my key to Mr. Ames, and went to the Lomax, around the corner to One, Allspice, eight sheds, two and two in lines, and my property in the space, unmistakeably mine, crates, boxes, most of it weighted under tarpaulins, in puddles, but raised on piles of bricks.

I sat on a bollard in the gateway, looking.

A man put his head out of the back door of the hotel, and shut it, quietly.

Two Indian youths trotted in, and stood near me.

The back door slammed open.

"Oh, *there* you are," Cecilia shouted, or shrieked or screamed. "Where you been? Listen. I don't want you here. The coppers have been here the last few days and they want to know a bit more about you. I don't want nothing to do with coppers. *Nothing*. And I don't want nothing to do with *you*. Get your stuff out of here and shove off. You're proper poison. Get out of it, else I'll have that stuff slung in the road. Understand? That's *it*."

The door slammed.

Rain came down in slaps and pats.

"Sir," one of the youths said. "Please will you telephone Mr. Motilal? We have been waiting for you."

"Would you please telephone him? I haven't the energy."

I sat in the rain, thinking of God knows what.

A woman in a mackintosh, and under a plastic umbrella, splashed through the puddles, and smiled.

"I am Mr. Motilal's assistant," she said. "We have a very good place for you. Everything is ready. May I give the order?"

I took her hand, and we went to a car, not a cab, and turned out, away from Wapping High, but without going into Whitechapel Road, and went down the side streets north of the Daemon and stopped on a corner. I remembered it without really remembering, and followed her to, of course, the café.

It was closed, empty, and far more spacious than I had imagined, and, because of access to a wide backyard, perfect for the plant. We went upstairs, through three rooms that could be knocked into one, with space that could make a kitchen, and up to the top floor, that overlapped both ends, in itself a fine room when knocked into one, and on top, a flat roof that faced the loop in the river, with a wonderful view for miles.

"This will do," I said. "Please tell Mr. Motilal I'm very grateful. When do the workmen come in?"

"First thing tomorrow morning. Where will you stay tonight?

"At the Daemon."

"I don't think so."

"Very well. Any hotel."

"Mr. Motilal booked you at the Savoy. In the Strand. It is the best."

"He takes a lot of trouble."

"You have always been a friend of ours. We all take trouble. Come back in three or four days, and see how good."

"What's your name?"

"Names don't matter. It's what we do. The car will take you to the Savoy. Your bag is in the back. Call my father if you wish anything."

"You are Miss Motilal?"

"Yes."

"I have a lot to learn. God bless you."

"But which God? There are so many."

A hook nose, black eyes, not beautiful, but she had an extraordinary loveliness all her own, purely feminine, as a knife with an edge.

I went to the Savoy, bought flowers in the foyer, and all the magazines, and went up to a most comfortable room, and stayed there for three days, sleeping, reading, eating, listening to radio, not going near TV, and that Thursday, I thought, to the devil, what's going on? and I got a cab without knowing the address, but I knew where it was, and we got there.

My sign was over the door.

Hammers thudded everywhere. A concrete mixer churned on the pavement. But going downstairs I could smell newsprint, ink, all the warm smells of the healthy life, and halfway down I could hear our machines.

At work.

At last I was in my own place, owning what I saw and could feel, and beholden to none, except perhaps Mr. Motilal and his brethren, countrymen, or who else. Certainly I had little need to show gratitude for my own people, except that some were being generous to me for a far greater benefit to themselves. Vacant possession was a financial advantage. But I, too, had an advantage. I had my own place, freehold, with an apartment and all amenities paid for, and no further risk of dislodgement.

A good feeling, made better when I went down to the office and found Jo taking the gold cap off a bottle of champagne.

"Got into bad habits," she said. "Number Four's going on power in about a minute's time. That'll be the lot working except for Number Five, and that won't be working for a couple of days. But you're back, so we'll drink now. Don't worry. We all clubbed together, and they've got their own bottles out there. We're happy to be back on the job. We thought we were finished. We're not. So we'll drink."

The telephone rang, and Jo gave me the bottle, and I used a cloth to wheedle the cork out.

"Sir," she said, without turning. "It's the Inland Revenue."

"What do they want?"

"They'd like to see you. Or if you'd prefer, you can go and see them."

"Tell them to come here and have a glass of this."

"Oh no they don't."

She turned to the telephone and I poured.

"Drink while it bubbles, and wish," I said.

"Something's dead wrong," she said, and drank, and I poured more. "Why're they coming so soon? We're up to date. I don't like it."

"It's their job. You know what they are. A half-degree up from the underworld."

I went to the press door. The machines were on power but not running, and all the operators had a glass. I lifted to them and drank, and as the glass came down, the presses started, and Number Four flipped out the Waygoes posters. WOMEN! YOU ARE THE BETTER HALF OF THE NATION. INSIST ON YOUR OWN MONEY. PROTECT YOUR CHILDREN AND THE FUTURE. CAMPAIGN AS YOUR FORGOTTEN SISTERS DID FOR THE VOTE. DON'T BE IDIOTS. BE WOMEN AND FIGHT FOR WHAT IS YOURS. IT IS YOUR DUTY.

"Have you got the accounts ready to show them?" I asked her.

She nodded at the cases.

"They're all in there," she said. "I've only had time to unpack the last couple of weeks' correspondence, and the order files."

"Whatever they want to know, we'll tell them. That's all we can do. We're not in arrears."

"Well, I don't like it, so soon," Jo said. "We haven't been here even ten days? It might be the fizzy-poo, but I don't like it. I got a funny feeling."

I sat at the desk and opened the evening paper. Everything seemed to be happening everywhere else, though nothing alarming.

A couple came in with press pulls, and Jo checked and initialled, and the street bell rang. She reached over to press the door buzzer, and three men came down, raincoats, tweed hats, desk-baggy trousers, long hair, two beards, one mutton-chop, three umbrellas.

"Ah, Mr. Bessell?" one said. "My name's Gorringe. This is my authority. We're from Inland Revenue."

He unfolded a sheet taken from a long envelope that I disregarded.

"Please sit down," I said. "What's this about?"

"I'll come to the point," Gorringe said. "Our information is that you have a Swiss account, which you've never reported. Is that so?"

"Yes. Any work I did on the Continent was paid in Swiss francs. The pound was going up and down and so was everything else. Francs were solid."

"You didn't report it in your tax returns?"

"I think I did."

"We have no record. The late Mr. Bayard Waygoes regularly paid sums into the account. Why?"

"I did a great deal of work for him."

"Without a record?"

"Of course there is. Most of the work outside at the moment is for him. Or his company."

"Mr. Bessell, prevarication—"

"I do not permit the word."

"I beg your pardon. Procrastination, shall we say, can only lead to a confrontation situation we all seek to avoid. I suggest you see your solicitor and accountant, and prepare a statement with relevant documents over the past ten years, and submit them to me at this address."

He put the letter on the desk, and stood, and so did the other two. Jo pressed the button to open the door, and I sat there, looking at a poster of cherry trees in blossom.

"This way out," Jo said.

I said nothing, and the three went up the stairway, and the door shut.

"I knew there was something wrong," Jo said.

"Ask Mr. Motilal if he can see me. It's urgent. Soon as possible."

Cecilia had informed. What a sweetie. What a tri-pronged bitch.

To defend was another matter. I had no defence. Luckily I had left everything to do with the account in the Zurich bank. Whether or not, I could see a great deal of trouble by staying in the country. Waygoes might not have been so careful. Cecilia might not have burned those files. Knowing her a little more, I was certain she had not. But if she had not, she would have a great deal to pay. But that helped me not at all.

I looked at the files on the desk. There was nothing to prevent my going.

"Jo," I said, "You're capable of looking after this business without me, aren't you? I mean, without supervision?"

"Well, if I'm not, I didn't ought to be here, did I?"

"Right. Ask Mr. Slenn to come in. And get me Mr. Riannes."

Slenn came in with a glass, still in borrowed green visor and elbow sleeves, and looked at me over the rim.

"I saved a drop to drink your abounding health, sir," he said. "We have all already done so. We hope for many, many years of happy work."

"I've got a drop left. I reciprocate. Look, you could run the editorial side with Miss Jo, couldn't you?"

He lifted his hands.

"We have already done so with utter mutual satisfaction, I think, sir? There is nothing we could not do, I assure you. She in the office, myself in the press room? I cannot conceive of any clash."

"Good. Both of your salaries are doubled as from Friday last, and you will inform all staff that they earn a third more as from that date. Jo, will you make the announcement? Further, there will be a cost-of-living bonus each month according to the index. Run the place as if I were here every day."

The street bell rang.

"I know his ring," Jo said. "That's Mr. Motilal."

He came down shaking his eternal umbrella. Slenn bowed and smiled, and went out, and Jo shut the door.

The telephone rang.

Jo put her head in.

"That's Teheran, sir."

"Hullo?"

Riannes came down the line as if bodily to grab me.

"The very man," he shouted. "Have you thought more of my suggestion? I have so much work here. Most in English. Some French, German, Spanish, Portuguese. But so much. I *need* you, my friend. We shall be on our skates for a couple of years. When shall I see you?"

"Depending on flights, how about the day after tomorrow?"

"But it is not possible? I cannot believe. A prayer so quickly answered? I shall be waiting. Only give me line, flight, time, I am there. You will be so happy. It is a wonderful city. We have good offices. An apartment. Everything is ready. All we want is experience. Supervision. Delivery. You are ready?"

"I'll let you know when I'm arriving. I'm looking forward to it."

"One suggestion. Fly via Copenhagen. Buy good furniture for five offices. Desks. Leather chairs. Four rooms in the apartment. Two big beds. *Big.* Kitchenware. We can buy here, but you can fly it from there and we have it. Ah, yes. Icebox, you call it? Freezer. Kitchen equipment. Everything, buy. Yes?"

"I'll be there."

"It is a wonderful night. So many stars. I am blind. *Mon cher,* I shall be so happy to see you."

I sat back, and looked at Motilal.

He looked at the handle of his umbrella.

"I'm leaving the country," I said.

He nodded.

"I think it wise. The dust will come down, and a feather brush will make it settle somewhere else."

"You've heard?"

"About the Swiss business? Yes. From her solicitors. They think little of it."

"Bluff?"

"Bluff is always dangerous when you have Inland Revenue at your heels. If they sniff money, it is always a threat. When are you leaving?"

"Tonight."

He nodded again, and stood.

"I wish to know nothing about it," he said. "I shall simply represent and defend your interests. I wish you a pleasant journey, and all success. We shall often think of you. I make it plain. I mean, the coloured community at large. You have been always a good friend. I am at all times here, at your service. And I shall not say good-bye."

First tug at the roots. The evacuee-feeling came back full strength, plus a mature pain almost felt in the flesh, and I could taste the salt of Mrs. Parran's soups, a little thinner than blood.

"Book me on the next flight to Copenhagen, Jo, please. I'll send you further instructions from there. And call a cab for Heathrow, will you? And ask Georgiana to bring me a brandy and coffee. That wine's made my throat dry."

"Wine? Oh, you mean the champagne? Is that all it is, *only* wine?"

"Only? It's the best."

"I'd only hoped so often I could have a glass at your place," she said. "It's funny, you waste a lot of time dreaming, but it never comes off, do it? I'd like to come for my holiday wherever you are. If it's Teheran? It sounds lovely. The desert, and sheiks an' all that. I'd do the dance of the seven veils. Only there wouldn't be no veils."

"I'll send air tickets, and your holiday's free. Bargain?"

We shook hands and she kissed my cheek, a clinger.

The bell rang.

"The cab," she said. "Blast. Always the same, i'n'it?"

"Say *au 'voir* to all of them. Cancel the coffee. Take care, Jo."

She nodded, hand to mouth, and turned away, walking to the press room and out.

I could see Auntie Helen's face, and the blowy white hair, and the fireman taking me, and saying, "All right, son. Here we go," and I picked up the bag, climbing the stairs, shutting the door, walking to the kerb, standing. The street shone under three lamps, and rain made a muslin screen, barely allowing the cab's headlights turning in to show more than two amber circles.

"You Heathrow, guv?" the cabman shouted.

"Yes. Go down here, past the Daemon, and wait a moment or two. I want to look at it."

We turned into Wapping High, and he slowed and braked above the garden steps. I got out in a fast pelt of rain.

But the Daemon's smile had gone.

A ragged ring of concrete and plaster made a greyish hole. The tomb of Harry Valentine Edwardes no longer glowed his name, though sweet Thames still sang soft on the other side of the wall. The front doors were boarded, with all the windows on the ground floor, and barbed wire coiled across the garage gate.

A sign glared red through the rain.

RESIDENTIAL PROPERTY UNDER DEVELOPMENT. BEWARE OF GUARD DOGS.

I thought of Mrs. Rapajan polishing the rosewood table, and holding her braids to stop them thumping when she bent to look along its length for dull patches, and Ol' Mabbs showing that palm, and the Bosun pouring a drink with bar lights in his beard, and Ghil's gold-black flame walking into seafroth, and Mrs. Osornis hanging garlands of cambric flowers, and Amy and Joe filling the copper bowls with white lilac.

Had it been a dream? A few moments' sleep? Was I *who* I was? Had I been thinking and seeing and talking through that time? I wanted someone to tell me. I prayed for someone to tell me. Did I dream? Was the Daemon's smile only a part? Tell me.

Tell me now.

And again.

Where was the Daemon smiling?

Awa-a-ay in a manger, tra-la-la-la-la-leeee.

No sound so final as the slam of a cab door.